Fireflies

Fireflies

BEN BYRNE

This edition published in 2013 by
House of Anansi Press Inc.
110 Spadina Avenue, Suite 801
Toronto, ON, M5V 2K4
Tel. 416-363-4343
Fax 416-363-1017
www.houseofanansi.com

Distributed in Canada by
HarperCollins Canada Ltd.
1995 Markham Road
Scarborough, ON, M1B 5M8
Toll free tel. 1-800-387-0117

House of Anansi Press is committed to protecting our natural environment. As part of our efforts, the interior of this book is printed on paper that contains 100% post-consumer recycled fibres, is acid-free, and is processed chlorine-free.

17 16 15 14 13 1 2 3 4 5

Library and Archives Canada Cataloguing in Publication

Byrne, Ben, 1977–, author
Fireflies / Ben Byrne.

Issued in print and electronic formats.
ISBN 978-1-77089-391-7 (pbk.). — ISBN 978-1-77089-392-4 (html)

I. Title.

PR6102.Y74F57 2013 823'.92 C2013-903750-0
C2013-903751-9

Cover design: Alysia Shewchuk
Typesetting: Marijke Friesen

Canada Council for the Arts Conseil des Arts du Canada

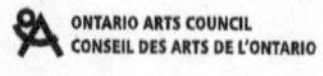

We acknowledge for their financial support of our publishing program the Canada Council for the Arts, the Ontario Arts Council, and the Government of Canada through the Canada Book Fund.

Printed and bound in Canada

MIX
Paper from responsible sources
FSC® C004071

To my mother and father

AUTHOR'S NOTE

In early 1945, the United States Army Air Forces began a campaign of low-altitude incendiary bombing against Japan. The raid on Tokyo, on the night of March 9, destroyed sixteen square miles of the city. An estimated one hundred thousand citizens perished in the firestorm.

On August 6, a single uranium bomb was dropped over the city of Hiroshima. Approximately seventy thousand people were killed, with at least as many dying of their injuries and from acute radiation syndrome by the end of the year.

On August 8, the Soviet Union declared war upon the Empire of Japan. Russian forces invaded Japan's colony in Manchuria later on that night.

On August 9, a plutonium bomb was dropped over the city of Nagasaki, killing at least forty thousand people. Associated deaths reached an estimated eighty thousand by the end of 1945.

On August 14, a radio broadcast was made in which the Emperor Showa (Hirohito) announced Japan's capitulation to the Allied powers. It was the first time the Japanese people had heard his voice.

Not quite dark yet
and the stars shining
above the withered fields
— Yosa Buson

PART ONE

SURRENDER

AUGUST 1945

1
THE SON OF HEAVEN
(SATSUKO TAKARA)

The sun must have just passed its zenith when I looked up and saw that everyone had left the factory except for me and Michiko, who was holding a shell casing, smiling at her warped reflection in the polished brass. I realized that His Imperial Majesty was about to make his speech, so I called to Michiko, and we hurried outside into the bright sunshine of the yard.

The other workers were already kneeling in the dust, facing a splintered table, where Mr. Ogura, our foreman, stood fiddling with the dial of a radio, which was making piercing whistles and strange whooshing noises. He scowled and waved us furiously to the ground, but just then a loud blast came from the speaker, and he dropped to his hands and knees, pressing his forehead into the gravel with a little whimper.

The stones stung the soft scars on my palms as I squinted around at the others. Mr. Yamada, the student, his hair as wild as ever, was staring at the ground. His fingers were twitching, and I could tell that he desperately wanted to light a cigarette but didn't dare. Behind him knelt Mr. Kawatake, the janitor, his lips moving as if he was praying. He looked just like a monk, I thought, in his shabby blue *yukata*, the sweat glistening on his bald head.

The crackling sound stopped and the signal became clear. A high, reedy voice echoed from the speaker and I heard Michiko snigger behind me. In fact, I had to hide a smile myself, because it was true — it sounded like a girl speaking, not the voice that anyone would have expected from the Son of Heaven.

I closed my eyes and tried to concentrate on what the emperor was saying. But it was difficult to understand. His language was complicated and ornate, and his words floated in and out of the radio, drowned out every so often by roaring clouds of static. At one point, I understood him to say that "the trends of the world did not blow in Japan's favour," and I thought that this must certainly be true, as I glanced up at the broken-down factory walls, the handcarts piled up with rubbish in the yard. Then, His Majesty said that he had "accepted the declaration," and my heart gave a leap. But Mr. Ogura gave a hideous groan, like a dying actor at the kabuki; he sank to the ground, shaking with sobs, and it was then that I understood that Japan must have lost the war after all.

Mr. Kawatake really did look like a monk now: he was rocking back and forth, muttering the name of the Buddha under his breath. Old Miss Miyasaki was bent over in front of me, and I saw from the little shake of her hips that she was weeping. I noticed how frayed her belt was, the blue threads unravelling from the hem.

The emperor was speaking now about our soldiers "far away on the field of battle," and I pictured Osamu, sunburned and hot on some island far off in the South Seas. In his last letter, he had written that his unit had all been gorging themselves on the bananas and other tropical fruits that grew down there. I'd imagined him lying in a hammock underneath the palm trees, stroking the thousand-stitch belt I'd sewn with ten-sen coins to protect him from the bullets and bring him good luck.

The sun was burning my forehead, and I wondered if His Majesty would carry on talking for much longer. He was mumbling now about a cruel weapon the Americans had used, a terrible new weapon that might "annihilate the entire world." He told us that we would face many hardships, that we must endure the unendurable, and that he hoped we would understand. There was a crackle of static, then silence.

We carried on kneeling there for some time, without saying a word. The old ones were quietly weeping, while the rest of us stared into space. Finally, Mr. Yamada stood up, strode over to the radio, and turned it off with a loud click. He took out his cigarettes and lit one up, then offered them around to everyone else. For some reason even I took a cigarette, though I had never smoked before in my entire life.

There was the strain and whir of a cicada somewhere nearby and the scuffle of a rat amongst the rubble. I thought that we should all be getting back to our work fairly soon, but then realized that, in all likelihood, it would no longer be necessary.

2
SHATTERED JEWELS (OSAMU MARUKI)

Dried victory chestnuts! Lieutenant Koizumi had pressed them into my hand that morning, the mad bastard, out of sight of the burly blond American guard, as if we'd been samurai, preparing our weapons and armour on the eve of battle. I rubbed my thumb over their hard shells, like the skulls of mice, as we stood in a ragged line within our barbed wire enclosure before a field radio our captors had brought out. Half a dozen of us; all that was left of our unit. Heads bowed and necks burning in the livid sun, straining to listen to the wooden oracle, whirling now with our fates.

The emperor's voice was barely audible above the hiss of insects in the malignant jungle beyond, the crash of surf and the screech of the emerald parrots that the American captain kept. As His Majesty spoke, a fragment of poetry echoed in my mind. *Je me crois en enfer, donc j'y suis* . . . I believe I am in hell, therefore I am.

The voice slowly dwindled into faint static. The volume of the jungle seemed to increase sharply. Loud, sudden cheering burst from the guardhouse bunkroom; there was the sound of thudding fists upon wooden planks and the unearthly caterwauling of victory.

From behind me there came an odd gurgle. Wetness touched my neck and I spun around to see Koizumi stagger forward, a sharp glitter in his fist. His gashed neck squirted crimson blood onto the yellow sand. With bulging eyes, he raised his hand to his neck as if to staunch the flow. Then he toppled like a drunken, sacrificial horse, as the blood leaked through his fingers. A cry came from the guard; there was the click of a rifle. A horror seeped along my spine.

Je me crois en enfer, donc j'y suis.

I believe I am in hell, therefore I am.

3
ASAKUSA BOY
(HIROSHI TAKARA)

The plane twinkled like the morning star above Fuji-*san* and I stopped walking and stared. *A B-29*, I thought, shielding my eyes from the sun. *No. Hold on . . .* The plane sailed toward me, and I clapped my hands to my ears as the deafening engines roared right over my head.

No machine gun turrets under the rear fuselage. A black F mark on the tip of the silver tail. *An F-13!* Reconnaissance. I grinned triumphantly as the plane disappeared over the charred remains of the city. They'd never flown low enough to spot before.

So Japan really has lost the war, then, I thought. *America and Britain have thrashed us.* I shrugged and carried on trudging along the road.

It was annoying to think that the planes wouldn't be coming anymore. Whenever the sirens had started blaring across the city, the red light flashing on the telegraph pole outside our window, I'd jumped out of bed to watch, while Satsuko yelled at me to pull on my air defence helmet and rush down to the shelter to join our mother. It was as exciting as being at the cinema, I thought, as wave after wave of silver Hellcats and

B-29s thundered past, their bombs drifting down through the night like blossoms.

They were both gone now, though, after the big fire raid back in March. Since then, I'd been sleeping in ruins, scavenging for tins of food in old houses. Now, the burns on my face had turned to thick rubbery welts, squishy with pus when I touched them, and my ribs were sticking out from my chest. I'd decided to head for the countryside in the hope of finding something to eat.

The countryside was enemy territory for a fourteen-year-old boy. I was an Asakusa kid, fiercely loyal to my noisy neighbourhood and the Senso Temple, no matter how dull and lifeless the place had become, according to my father, since the Pacific War had begun. As for those country bumpkins, with their sunburned faces and wooden lunch boxes, well, I'd come to hate their guts during the six months when my school had been evacuated from Tokyo to the rural villages two years before.

I spent the evening crouched in a ditch, watching a farmer patrolling back and forth across his field. As soon as night fell, I wriggled out on my belly into the mud, rooting about in the crop until my hand came finally across a withered bunch of leaves. I tugged at it, and a spindly shoot emerged from the soil. A clammy hand fell upon my own.

I leaped up, petrified. A pale silhouette stood in front of me in the darkness. *A ghost child*, I thought, *a gruesome kappa troll!*

I screamed. The thing screamed back. For a second, we stood there, howling together. Then, as my eyes adjusted, I saw that it was another boy like me, around twelve years old and sickly thin. He smiled and mumbled something, then reached out his hand toward me.

I jumped forward and smashed my fist into his face. He fell down with a whimper and I leaped on top of him, shoving his face into the mud. I stuffed the daikon into my mouth, biting off chunks as I ran away into the night. I told myself later that I hadn't had a choice. He wouldn't have lasted much longer in any case.

I hid in the ditches during the day and slunk out at night like a fox to steal whatever I could from the fields. It wasn't much fun. Rats twitched in the stubble and ran over my bare feet. Horseflies bit my sweaty skin. One afternoon, as I lay soaking wet in a half-drained paddy field, a hissing sound came from the sprouting stalks nearby. I froze. A moment later, I saw it. *A Green General.* It looped toward me in sickly coils. Then it slithered over my bare back and slipped down into the water. I splashed out of the paddy, moaning. My belly and legs were thick with leeches. I ran into the wood and rolled about on the ground, tearing away their bodies until I was covered in slime.

The countryside was fraught with terrors I could have never imagined from my old Tokyo bedroom. As darkness fell, the supernatural creatures I knew only from the kabuki plays I had watched with my father became suddenly, terrifyingly conceivable: luminous families of fox spirits roaming abroad to bewitch me; kappa trolls lurking in the river, intent upon dragging me to their watery lair . . . All were now eerily palpable in the murmur of the wind across the fields, in every whimper and shriek of the night animals in the forest.

I could feel myself growing fainter, and finally, I began to hallucinate. My mother would run out from the trees at sunset, her arms outstretched, her hair on fire. Scarecrows would wave at me from the fields, and I'd see my burly father in his *happi* coat and chef's apron, grinning and beckoning to me. One night, as I was crossing a wooden bridge over a narrow river, I heard a faint voice calling my name.

Hiroshi! Hiroshi-kun!

I leaned over the rail. There, in the flowing river, was my sister Satsuko. Pleading with me to come back to her, just as she had on the night of the fire raid, when I'd run away and left her to die in the Yoshiwara canal.

I collapsed into a shed at the edge of an orchard as the moon shone down through the broken roof slats. I awoke suddenly in the night to see a huge, broad-shouldered farmer looming over me, bellowing a curse as he lifted up his thick wooden staff. Somehow, I managed to scramble out between his legs. I sprang through the moonlight and hid amongst the crooked, ghostly trees.

The sky was glowing orange and pink the next morning as I found myself walking alongside a train track. Before long, a battered locomotive came creaking along the rails. I leaped up onto a coupling and gripped onto the side of the carriage as it trundled on through the countryside.

Before long, the fields gave way to a patchwork plain of ruin. A river grew wide beside us and I realized that I was being dragged inescapably back to Tokyo. The train finally shuddered to a halt at Ueno Station, and I slid down and made my way into the cavern of the ticket hall. Throngs of men and women in torn and buttonless shirts lay on rush mats, their mouths opening and closing like dying fish. I climbed down the steps to the subway, and curled up on a patch of damp ground by the wall of a cistern. Finally, I fell asleep, alone amongst the clammy crowd that now filled the tunnels and passageways like an army of hungry ghosts.

4
TOKYO BAY
(HAL LYNCH)

The long white chimneys of the Mark 7 guns were still pointed up at the sky. Seamen and airmen thronged the decks of the *Missouri*, spilling over the rails, straining to see the action. I was perched on the ledge behind the rear three-gun turret, holding my Leica camera, my legs dangling over the white caps of Third Fleet captains who flocked the deck below. Before them was a triangular space set with a single table, fountain pens, and the documents of surrender.

On the far side of the deck, on a platform behind a rail, the official photographers hunched over their Arriflexes, squinted through Speed Graphics, and held up their light meters to check exposure one last time. I was wedged between an Associated Press correspondent and a petty warrant officer from Alabama who kept muttering, "Oh boy, oh boy" like it was a prayer.

A sudden swell of excitement rippled across the ship, and we all leaned forward to see. Japanese launches were coming alongside the *Missouri*, desperately puny next to our gargantuan hull. Our admirals and generals swiftly stiffened into order below. The solitary table, with its two neatly arranged chairs, looked suddenly as simple and as menacing as a gallows.

I had arrived at Sagami Bay the week before, shortly after my discharge from the 3rd Reconnaissance Squadron. Before I left, my fellow crewmen had left a booklet on my bunk, entitled *Going Back to Civilian Life*, which I assumed was ironical, alongside a pamphlet entitled, *Sex, Hygiene, & VD*, which I opened to read a terrifying warning:

"Japanese women have been taught to hate you!" it read. "Sex is one of the oldest weapons in history. The Geisha girl knows how to wield it charmingly. She may entice you only to poison you. She may slit your throat. Stay away from the women of Japan, all of them."

Scrawled below, in our navigator Lazard's clumsy handwriting: *That means you, Hal!!!*

Half the nation was here now, it seemed, in the spirit form of Third Fleet battleships — the *South Dakota*, the *New Mexico*, the *West Virginia*, the *Boston*. They had an awesome look of brute magnitude as they lay anchored together upon the deep indigo water. I spent two days photographing the destroyers and carriers as they steamed along the Japanese coast. An infinite number of cruisers and transports shuttled between them, with everyone out on deck scrubbing and painting and polishing in preparation for our triumphant entry into Tokyo Bay. Beyond the fleet lay the low green coastline of Japan, the ghostly shape of Mount Fuji sloping up in the distance, tiny white clouds balled beside it.

It was close enough to swim to if you'd been so inclined. Through telescopes and binoculars we watched old men and women immerse themselves in the water, children splashing in the surf, all unhurried and apparently uninterested in the armada that lay before them, the greatest fleet ever assembled.

In the evening we watched the sun set over Japan; the mountain cast into silhouette, the ocean glittering with gold.

I'd seen it so many times, from the air. Coming in at dawn at 30,000 feet, my palm automatic on the worn shutter crank of my K-22 camera. Japanese cruisers floating out at sea; the white line of surf crashing upon the shore. The black highways and silver railways, the glistening web of canals and rivers; the dense formations of huddled houses, temples, barracks, and factories. I knew the whole country, I thought, from above. I'd processed it all inch by inch, shrunk it down to frozen impressions in the silver nitrate crystals of nine-by-nine film. Lugged the camera cylinders over to General LeMay's Quonset hut for the daily photo briefing at thirteen hundred hours. Glanced at the big prints up on the walls, labelled with arrows and statistics. The circled primary targets. The shaded inflammable zones. Photographs I'd shot over the past six months. Japanese cities. Before and after.

By the night of the Tokyo raid back in March, the city was as familiar as a framed map. We floated up above the Superforts, their fuselages tapering like artists' brushes, the guide fires already blazing below. Then, the world was a maelstrom of noise — flurries of bombs screaming down, glimmering pinpricks of light erupting, merging, and melding as the fires took hold. An endless blast of heat and a deep glow as the smoke billowed up. The next day, when we flew back to photograph the damage, it was all just burned ruin and collapsed buildings. Scarred swathes of rubble, still shimmering with heat waves.

My last photo run: to a city by the coast, to map out a bombing approach. Down below, I'd seen a bustling metropolis, busy streets and market buildings. A harbour full of fishing boats delivering their silvery catch at the docks.

When we had returned a week later, Lazard thought we were lost. He simply couldn't recognize the place. The valley was ravaged, eerie and desolate. The buildings swept clear, the estuarial rivers glistening down to the sea through the char, like tear tracks across a blackened face.

The nights since my discharge, my mind seemed to be trying to process those thousands of images. As if in my dreams, I could develop them, arrange them into some kind of sequence. I still felt myself flying in my sleep, acutely aware of the vast distance between me and the earth.

I needed to make landfall soon, I thought. I needed to see the world from ground level again.

The launches banged alongside the ship and we squinted to see who would make up the Imperial delegation. An old Japanese man with a cane swung himself forward, followed by his cronies — delegates in absurd silk top hats and frock coats. Then came the generals, drab and squat. They made a grim, surly bunch as they stood huddled on the swaying deck, surrounded on all sides by Allied men in blinding white uniform. A silence hovered over the ship, threaded through with the whir of movie cameras, punctuated by the click of lenses and the puff of flashbulbs.

The door to the bridge cabin swung open.

General Douglas MacArthur. Emerging from the doorway, collar open, shoulders square. He loomed in front of the Japanese men, hands on hips, and I was put in mind of my father, the stern headmaster, drawing his belt from around his waist.

After his sonorous opening remarks, he gestured to the Japanese to come forward. One by one, in profound silence, they bent over to sign the documents. In a few short moments,

Japan had surrendered unconditionally to the supreme commander of the Allied powers.

The general made a fine speech, full of noble sentiment and good intention. Next to me, the Associated Press man was doodling an obscene picture in his notebook. I looked out toward Japan as the seagulls cawed above us in the sky. The sun had burned through the cloud. It was a fine day.

All of a sudden, a horde of Superforts and Hellcats and Mustangs filled the air. I lurched forward, almost tumbling from the turret. They swarmed toward the coast in echelon after echelon, wings glinting in the morning sun. The crew on the upper decks were all hollering now, grinning, slapping each other on the back. Down below, the Allied generals and admirals shook hands and congratulated each other. I took a deep breath as the planes roared toward Tokyo like a flock of furious birds.

The war is over, I told myself, dumbly. *It's all over.*

And we are alive.

PART TWO

THE WITHERED FIELDS

SEPTEMBER 1945

5
NEW WOMEN OF JAPAN (SATSUKO TAKARA)

Michiko had gone off to the countryside along with everyone else to try and barter with those stingy peasants for some food, and I was sitting outside Tokyo Station beneath a sign I had written for my little brother, Hiroshi. The station was like an old, broken-down temple now, covered in handwritten signs and banners addressed to lost friends and relatives, all flapping in the wind like prayer flags. Crowds milled about, searching for their own names, or sat meekly against the walls in the hope that one of their loved ones might magically reappear. I had hung my own sign here a few days after the fire raid, telling my brother that I was now living with Michiko, my friend from the war work dormitory, in her eight-mat hovel in Shinagawa. I promised to wait for him here at Tokyo Station every day at noon. But it had been six months since then already, and still he hadn't appeared.

The ground had been baking hot beneath my bare feet, the morning after the raid, and my hands were dreadfully painful from being burned the night before. I'd crawled out of the irrigation ditch by the Yoshiwara canal and stumbled across the smoking ruins of Asakusa. The whole city had been burned, it seemed; the wooden tenements and teahouses had all gone up in smoke, and the theatres and picture palaces on the Rokku were burned-out shells. Shrivelled bodies were scattered along the roads and sticking out of the shelters. Coal-black people went by with charred bedding on their backs, pushing bicycles piled with their remaining possessions.

Our alley ran parallel to Kototoi Avenue, between the Senso Temple and the Sumida River Park. But the whole area east of the river was in ruins now, with only the odd brick building still standing. After flailing across the cinders for some time, I finally found the cracked, square concrete cistern near Umamichi Street that had once stood in front of Mrs. Oka's pickle shop. A half-naked man was slumped dead inside. My family's restaurant, with its sliding wooden doors and creaking sign, was gone. The whole alley had been incinerated, leaving nothing now but two heaped ridges of ash.

There was no sign of Hiroshi. I thought of him the night before, surrounded by fire on the bank of the canal, calling to me. Not far away, I found a charred piece of blue cloth. I pictured my mother in her cotton kimono, stumbling toward us along the blazing street.

Unfamiliar people, distant relatives, I supposed, were arriving now with handcarts. They picked out fragments of bone from the corpses and piled up any household goods that remained. I dug about in the char for a while, but found nothing but my mother's battered old copper teakettle. Then the pain in my hands became agonizing, and I had to go off to find a relief station, where a doctor gave me Mercurochrome and bandages.

I searched for Hiroshi for hours after that, at the Kasakata police station and up at Fuji high school, where the injured lay on mats lined up in the playground. But my brother had vanished. Finally, in the evening, I returned to the Yoshiwara canal, where he had left me the night before. I started to shake. Troops were fishing out bodies on a big hook suspended from a truck, piling them up in a heap on the bank. I knew I should look for Hiroshi amongst them, but the truth was that I couldn't bring myself to search amongst those slippery mounds of flesh, all pink and boiled.

A train wheezed into the station, its windows boarded over with planks. Passengers clambered down from the roofs of the carriages, and a crowd spilled out of the station carrying knapsacks and bundles of whatever they'd managed to scrounge from the farmers. Policemen with bamboo nightsticks walked up and down outside the station, eyeing the crowd.

Soon enough, Michiko appeared. Her dress was wrinkled, her shoes were covered in mud, and she looked exhausted. I asked her quietly if she'd been able to find anything in the countryside. She wrenched open her bag and gestured inside: three tiny, shrivelled potatoes, wrapped in a handkerchief.

"Three potatoes. Michiko, really," I said.

We'd had practically nothing to eat all week and I knew there was nothing left in the house now, nothing at all.

"It's not my fault," she said. "Those farmers are worse than thieves!"

She'd bartered away her favourite summer kimono, she said, and this was all she had received in return. It was extortion, pure and simple.

I wracked my brain, wondering if there was even any rice bran we might make into gruel. But I knew it was useless. I'd swept between the floorboards two days ago, and we'd already eaten whatever it was that was down there.

There were a few stalls set up by the station now, but they didn't seem to be selling anything useful except for some kind of rough booze. A couple of old men were already reeling and one of them shouted something vulgar to Michiko. But she just shouted back, saying that she was surprised he could even think of anything like that at a time like this, that they should be ashamed of themselves, sitting there swilling rotgut while the rest of the city was starving to death.

A little further along the street, she stopped quite suddenly and put her hand on my arm.

"Look," she said, pointing.

There was a large sign nailed to the charred stump of a telegraph pole. "To the New Women of Japan," it said, grandly. Michiko started bobbing up and down and tugging at my sleeve, the way she always did when she was excited.

"Satsuko," she said, "it's jobs for office ladies. We could do that!"

I read the sign with an uneasy feeling. The advertisement certainly was for secretaries, but it also mentioned "the Contingency of the Occupation" and I felt sure that this was something to do with the Americans. They'd be here soon, large and boisterous, swaggering through the streets and shouting. The thought of working right up close to them made me shudder.

But Michiko had that dreamy, faraway look on her face, which I recognized from whenever she emerged, star-struck, from the cinema.

"New Women of Japan," she said, in a breathy voice. "Just think, Satsuko. That could be us!"

I groaned in protest and tried to pull her away. But she just stood right where she was.

"Michiko," I said, "Please. I'm hot and I'm tired. Let's please go home."

The star-struck look vanished. "And what are you going to sell tomorrow, then, Satsuko? The teakettle?"

A hard lump formed in my throat. This was unkind, and she knew it, as the copper teakettle was now the only thing I had to remember my mother by.

"I don't know," I said.

She laid a hand on my arm, and her face softened.

"Satsuko," she said, "we only have three potatoes to eat today."

She could be surprisingly grown up sometimes. I knew in my heart that she was right, that we really should answer the advertisement. But when I read it again, another shiver passed through me. Michiko just gripped my arm, though, and the dramatic look came back into her eyes.

"Just think, Satsuko," she whispered. "New Women of Japan!"

We dressed up as best we could for our interview, in neat skirts and white blouses that I'd pressed beneath our futon the night before. We never seemed able to get the ash and dirt out of our clothes anymore, but these outfits were better, in any case, than the baggy *monpe* trousers we normally wore, and which made us look so hopelessly unattractive. The address was for an elegant building up on the Ginza, which seemed like a hopeful sign, but when we got there, I saw that the roof of the building had fallen down. Inside, cracked paint was peeling from the walls.

We followed an arrow pointing up the shabby staircase to a lobby, where a large crowd of women were already gathered.

"Do you think we're too late?" I said, noticing, to my unease, that some of the other women wore bright makeup. They looked like quite vulgar types.

"Are you sure this is the right place?" I whispered.

"Well," murmured Michiko, "it can't be easy for anyone to find work right now, not with things the way they are."

Just then, the door at the end of the corridor burst open and a very young girl rushed out. Tears were streaming down her face and she ran headlong into me. I held out my arms to steady her, but she pushed me aside and clattered down the staircase, sobs drifting up behind her.

"Michiko!" I hissed. "What on earth could they have said to make her so upset?"

"Perhaps she wasn't experienced enough," Michiko said. "Don't worry, Satsuko, we'll be alright."

"Michiko," I said, feeling suddenly nervous. "I think perhaps it might be best if we were to try to find some other kind of position elsewhere."

She narrowed her eyes and growled: if I had any idea of where we could go, then I should go ahead and tell her right there and then.

So we carried on waiting and before long, a secretary came out and gestured at me. Michiko gave my hand a little squeeze and I walked along to the door. Inside, behind a heavy desk, sat two men, as unlike each other as they could have possibly been. One was thin and very handsome, his hair slicked back like an American film star, while the other was as fat as a pig and had little cherry stone eyes that looked me up and down.

"Miss Takara," said the handsome man, glancing at his list. "Please come in."

I smiled sweetly.

He started by asking where I'd grown up and what my father's profession had been. When I told him that I'd been a serving girl in my father's eel restaurant, he seemed very pleased; he even said he might remember the place — after all, it had been quite famous if you knew Asakusa at all.

The pig-man's eyes narrowed. "And what do you know of our country's noble history, Miss Takara?" he demanded.

I hesitated, worried that this might be a trap. Before we'd been sent off for war work with the Student Attack Force, our class been taught that the emperor had descended from the sun goddess Amaterasu, and that the Japanese people had been uniquely blessed with a special responsibility to preserve harmony across the Greater East Asia Co-Prosperity Sphere. But I wasn't sure if this was still the case, and so I stayed silent.

The handsome man smiled. "Don't worry, Miss Takara," he said. "It's not a test."

He moved his chair aside, and pointed up at a large painting mounted on the wall. It showed a very beautiful girl from the Edo period, dressed in a pink and white kimono. She was kneeling at the feet of a fierce-looking Westerner with a big white moustache and a red waistcoat. The sea lay a little way beyond them, black-flagged ships sailing back and forth upon the waves.

"I wonder," he said, "if you are familiar with this famous lady?"

As I looked up at the painting, I had a distant memory of an operetta that my father had once told me about. The fat man stared at me. I had the sudden feeling that my interview wasn't going very well.

"This is Okichi-*sama*," the man said. He explained that Okichi had once lived in Shimoda, on the Izu peninsula. When the foreign barbarians had first forced Japan to open up to the outside world, she had been presented to the American ambassador as a "consort."

I looked at them uncertainly.

"A kind of peace offering," explained the handsome man, "and a clever way to keep an eye on the foreigners."

The fat man leaned forward. "Do you know what a consort might be, Miss Takara?"

My cheeks coloured. I gave a faint nod.

"Okichi," he went on, his voice swelling now, like the radio bulletins of victorious battles during the war, "sacrificed her body for the Japanese nation. Just as our soldiers sacrificed theirs. Now the barbarians are about to land again, Miss Takara." He raised a thick finger in the air. "Japan will need a new generation of Okichis, Miss Takara. Honourable women who will act as a breakwater, a seawall, to protect the flower of our womanhood from their rapacious lust."

An image came into my mind of the vulgar women cackling in the hallway. I swallowed.

"Your advertisement," I murmured. "It mentioned office ladies —"

The handsome man grinned. "Regrettably, Miss Takara, all of the back office positions have now been filled. But there are other positions remaining. Fine positions. For noble, patriotic women, who would be prepared to act as 'consorts' for our foreign guests, once they arrive."

My cheeks were burning as I stood up to leave.

"You would be paid, Miss Takara," the fat man called behind me. "With an allowance for clothing. And for food. Think of your duty to Japan."

I felt suddenly faint and clutched at the desk to steady myself. The handsome man hurried to help me back into the chair.

"Please don't upset yourself, Miss Takara," he said. "But please do consider our offer."

The men were staring at me. I tried to picture myself, sitting in a café with a burly American. There came an image of one, lying naked on my bed. What would it be like, I wondered, to be intimate with a foreigner? The bristly body, the smell of sweat and cigarettes . . .

The truth was that I wasn't completely innocent. The night before Osamu had been sent away to the South Seas, after his farewell party, we'd gone off to a hotel for a short time together. I wasn't ashamed. After his horrible mother had told me what had happened to him, I was glad that I had given him at least that comfort in his brief life.

I thought of the three wrinkled potatoes in Michiko's handkerchief, how we'd devoured the last one that morning.

"Well, Miss Takara?" said the handsome man. His words seemed to come from a very long way away. "We're counting on you. Will you help us?"

6
STARS & STRIPES
(HAL LYNCH)

I hitched a ride from Yokohama to Tokyo in a jeep with two lieutenants from the 5th Cavalry. Eyes front, they chewed gum rhythmically as they drove. They'd been first into Tokyo, they said, and things were already improving.

Through the rangefinder of my camera, the city seemed utterly obliterated. Fields of rubble sprouted with tall weeds; ruined factories held from collapse by mangled girders; abandoned trucks on bricks, lichened with orange rust. All the way to Tokyo, along the dirt road, men and women in rags heaved handcarts piled with refuse, swallowing our dust.

The road grew wider as we entered the centre of the city and we veered around deep potholes as edifices rose on each side. Grand once, now licked black, their windows were boarded up, great chunks of masonry torn from their structures. Crowds swarmed the avenue: Japanese women in baggy pants with bundles on their back; men in battered fedoras and grubby summer shirts. Tall GIs strolled along like stately giants; others laughed as Japanese men in split-toe shoes tugged them along in rickshaws. At an intersection of curving streetcar lines, an old man haltered an ox, his cart laden with steaming churns, surrounded by fat flies.

I hopped down beneath the cobweb of overhead electrics and unfolded my map. This, then, was the Ginza — once the grandest avenue in the Orient, its Fifth Avenue, its Champs-Élysées. I drew in a great breath of Tokyo air: smoke and fish guts and sewerage. I wiped the filthy perspiration from my brow.

The *Stars and Stripes* office was housed in a grand old embassy building. Wide concrete steps led up to the doorway, and inside, acres of wooden panelling covered the walls of a high-ceilinged newsroom. Desks were laid out in neat rows, each with a telephone and a gleaming Smith-Corona or Remington. Young men in uniform were typing away and glanced up at me as I entered. They grinned, as if welcoming me to some private member's club.

At the back of the room I spotted a familiar face: Eugene, my old college roommate, the myopic show-off who'd encouraged me to apply to the newspaper in the first place. Skinny as a rake, his curly hair now officially out of control, Eugene leaned back on his chair, an affected green visor shielding his eyes as he spiked stories from a big pile. He whooped when he saw me, leaped up, and proceeded to perform some kind of Indian war dance before bounding over and seizing my arm.

"This — is — it, Hal!" he hollered, hopping back and forth. "The place where we will make our names!"

Oh, boy. He still wore the same round wire spectacles I remembered from Columbia, six years ago, when this "making our names" business had been his obsession. He'd drawn up strategies for us — writing for the *Spectator*, acting in amateur theatricals. Finally, under the spell of the French photographer Henri Cartier-Bresson, whose portrait he'd plastered above the desk in our dorm room, he had decided that we would become photographers. For weeks we'd roamed the docks at Red Hook and the tenements of the Lower East Side with our Box Brownies in dogged pursuit of the "decisive moment." Eugene had even gone as far as setting up a darkroom in a storage cupboard beneath the faculty buildings, before he'd become distracted by a book on how to draw for the funny papers. He'd ditched his camera soon after that. I'd kept hold of mine.

"Hello, Gene. Looks like you're all settled in."

"Sure I am," he said, leading me to a door affixed with a scrawled card. "John Van Buren," it read. "Editor-in-Chief."

"Okay, let's take you to meet Dutch. He's going to give you your press pass. That's your golden ticket, see. Your get-out-of-jail-free card. It's signed by MacArthur himself. It means you can go anywhere you want and talk to anyone you want."

He knocked briefly on the door and we bustled into an office, disturbing the balding NCO who was rubbing his head as he frowned over a typed article. His desk was cluttered with sheets of copy and framed photographs of plump, corn-fed children.

"Hal. This is Dutch Van Buren, Editor-in-Chief of *Pacific Stars and Stripes*. Dutch, this is Harold Lynch. Hal's the best photographer in the Third Army. And he can write too — you just wait until you read what he can write ..."

"Okay, enough," Van Buren said, holding up his hands. "I've got things to deal with. Lynch, you're very welcome. Sit down. Eugene, why don't you give me a break and get out of here?"

"He's thrilled to be here, Dutch!" sang Eugene in falsetto, skipping out the door. "The crucible of change!"

Van Buren rolled his eyes as he shook my hand. "Oh, my aching back. You know that guy? You've got my sympathies. Well, I guess you're here now anyway. You know much about *Stars and Stripes*?"

"I read the sheet on Guam. We all did."

"Sure you did. Well, as you know, the *Stars and Stripes* has been in circulation all the way back to the Civil War. We're here to inform — just as any of the big papers are." His voice took on the tone of a prepared speech. "But in contrast to them, Lynch, we have a very specific audience — the average GI. Doesn't mean we don't go after the big stories. He's interested in the big stories. He understands the political angles. But he also wants to be entertained. He likes to see how the big stories affect the little man."

"Human interest, you might say?"

"Exactly," Dutch said, pointing at me. "You've got it right there."

"Fine. That suits me fine."

"But in addition to that," he said, picking up his pen, and waving it at me, "we've got to produce stories that the Japs'll understand. So that they'll see what we're doing here. What we're trying to build. We've got a duty to do that too."

I had a mental image of the devastation I'd seen on the long ride in from Yokohama that morning. Dutch noticed my expression and gave a sheepish smile.

"Well, heck, of course, we had to take a wrecking ball to the place first. Only stands to reason. But the next trick is to build something up. A peace-loving, democratic country."

"'The Switzerland of Asia'?" I suggested, quoting MacArthur.

"That's right," he said, pointing at me again. He stood up, gesticulating in the manner of a Roman senator. "Elected representatives. Votes for women. A free press. Yes, it's a fine experiment we've got going here, Lynch."

He turned to a filing cabinet against the wall. I glanced down at the typed article on his desk. A bureaucratic report, I saw, something about land reform. Big swathes of blue pencil had been drawn through it, initials and letters circled in the margin. Further down, blocks of text had been struck through with black ink.

"The crucible of change, Lynch," Dutch was saying, as he rummaged about in a file. "It's our privilege to have front-row seats." He turned, smiling, and handed me a small square of paper: "Don't lose it."

My press pass. The scrawled signature of the supreme commander himself graced the back. I was impressed.

Dutch held out his hand. "Welcome to *Stars and Stripes*, Lynch. I think you're going to fit right in with this bunch of nuts. A man like you could really make a name for himself here."

"Thanks, Dutch," I said, shaking his hand. "I'll see what I can do."

I'd been billeted to the old Continental Hotel, not far from the red brick ruins of Tokyo Station. When I arrived I was astonished and delighted to find that I'd been given a small room of my own. For the first time in years, I wouldn't be bunking down with a dozen other men, surrounded by unceasing locker-room jaw about pin-ups and football and the Brass. The carpet was worn down almost to the board, and an ancient black ribbon of flypaper hung from the ceiling. I unpacked my kit and set up my handful of books on the chipped table by the window.

The view outside was uninspiring. A gravel road bisected by a streetcar line; a row of ruined buildings on the other side. I poured myself a drink, and as the alcohol began to glow in my stomach, I sat on my cot and picked away the epaulettes from my jackets, along with the insignia of 3rd Recon Squadron. I patiently sewed my woven *Stars and Stripes* badge in its place.

A clang came from the road and I glanced out. A streetcar was crawling valiantly along the track, so dilapidated that I felt like applauding in sympathy. The windows were cracked, the sides all dented. Expressionless passengers squeezed up against each other on the deck, spilling precariously over the guardrails.

⁂

It didn't take me long to find a "human interest" piece. The following week, while out exploring the neighbourhood down by the banks of the river, I discovered an old man living under a jerry-rigged tarpaulin strung between two poles. He was naked but for shorts and an old raincoat, and he held a bamboo fishing rod, the float bobbing out in the river. I took Eugene and a Japanese-American translator named Roy down there one afternoon. We tapped on the tarpaulin, and after a moment the man emerged from his shelter. He stared at us, his old face lined like a boxer's, his beard as coarse as a brush.

He squinted as Roy explained that we'd like him to tell us his tale. After stroking his beard and looking up the river for a while, he gestured at his scatter of belongings on the ground. We sat down cross-legged as he filled a bent jerry can with river water and put it on a little hibachi grill to boil for tea.

I'd expected him to be half crazy, but, in fact, he was the model of eloquence. He'd been a bargeman once, he said, waving at the water, but over the years he'd managed to save enough money to buy a boat of his own. After that, he and his two sons made a living ferrying coal and timber from the factories and yards out to the big ships in Tokyo Bay.

I remembered the picture postcards I'd seen of old Tokyo: the waterways bristling with skiffs and wherries, ferrymen carrying drunken revellers up and down the lantern-lit canals as fireworks burst in the summer sky. The river was almost silent now, with long strands of weed floating around the mooring posts.

After the fire raids had begun, the man said, he and his sons had taken to sleeping on the boat, thinking they'd be safer out on the water. One night, as he had been sleeping on deck, his sons in the cabin, the sirens had sounded and the planes had started to float in.

I had a sudden premonition of what he was about to describe. I saw the flash of spinning propellers as our F-13 lurched into the sky. Eugene was scribbling away in his notebook, smiling encouragingly.

Mis-tah B — this was what the man called the B-29s, waggling his flat palm toward the horizon in demonstration — drifted in very low that night. In wave after wave they came, clouds of bombs tumbling from their bellies. From the river, it soon seemed that the whole city was ablaze, red and orange flames dancing across the sky. From somewhere, what he called a "firework" landed on the boat. To his amazement, it squirted fire all over the deck, fire that stuck to the water and blazed away in the blackness. He shook his head at the memory. *Napalm*, I thought, picturing the dewy blue flame I'd once seen spurting from a cylinder that had gone crazy after falling loose from a bomb bay.

The deck of his boat, piled high with coal, quickly caught on fire. The old man leaped into the water, shouting for his sons to come out of the cabin. But just then another white incendiary whistled down and squirted fire all over him, and he swam desperately to the bank, struggling to escape the flames.

Like an accusing ghost, he opened his coat to show us his torso — a marbled mass of pink welts and sinewy grey tissue.

From the bank, the man had stared out at the blazing hulk of his boat, its glowing heart of coal, pleading for his sons to emerge.

He closed his eyes. He shook his head. The barge had swiftly disintegrated into a mass of ash and cinder. By the next day it had dissolved away entirely.

The smoke from the brazier fluttered in the wind, the water in the can still tepid. A sheen of perspiration covered my forehead. A vein pulsed in my temple. The old man looked upstream, as if he expected to see his boat come floating down the river at any moment.

I took off the lens cap of my camera and asked him if I could take some photographs. With a noble bow, he agreed.

While I was taking the pictures, Eugene asked how he was now surviving. The man pointed at the river and made a hurling gesture as if casting a line, then an eating motion with his hands.

"He catches fish?" Eugene said. "Well, how about that."

I could see the story typing itself out in his head — "The Lonely Fisherman," perhaps — accompanied by a photograph of the old man proudly holding up his day's catch.

But the old man was running his fingers through the air with a repetitive gesture and Roy was frowning. He shook his head: "No, he means rats."

"Rats?" Eugene said. "Don't tell me he eats rats."

The old man ducked his head into his chest, clearly embarrassed.

Roy explained that rats — big bloated ones — often came floating down the river. The old man fished them out and barbecued them on his hibachi.

So there it was. Our first story. We thanked the man and presented him with a packet of cigarettes, which he tucked into his raincoat pocket before touching pressed palms to his forehead.

"Is there anything else he needs?" I asked.

The old man cocked his blunt head for a second. He knelt down, hands on his knees. Would it be possible to bring him a package of soy sauce? I promised that it most certainly would. The old man touched his forehead to the ground.

We clambered up the slippery bank to the main road. When I looked back, the old man had already disappeared back into his shelter.

~

That afternoon I processed the prints in the darkroom in the basement while Eugene typed the story in the newsroom upstairs. I knew the picture I wanted as soon as it emerged in the developing tray. The old man, cross-legged like a ragged Buddha, looking out at the lonely river, his carved face and wild fisherman's beard silhouetted against a sky piled with grey cloud. A certain "enigmatical quality," as Eugene later put it.

The piece he wrote was too sensational for my taste. It lingered on the peculiarities of the man's diet and spent little time on his account of the fire raid. But Dutch ran it on the third page later that week, and I felt a glow of pride to see my byline beneath the photograph. I'd been published for the first time.

Later on that day though, Dutch called us into his office. He looked shaken.

"I've just had a call, gentlemen," Dutch said, "from Brigadier General Diller of the Public Relations office."

I'd heard the name already, generally accompanied by blasphemy. Brigadier General LeGrand Diller — "Killer Diller" — was part of General MacArthur's inner circle, now his head of Public Relations. A surly, stony bastard by all accounts, he dictated the official line, and took any criticism of the Occupation as a direct slur against the general.

"He demanded to know what I was doing running stories about old men eating rats. What exactly was I implying? That the Japanese population is starving?"

Warily, I pointed out that the population was, in fact, starving.

"Not according to Supreme Command it isn't!" he hollered, slapping a hand on the table. He rubbed his head and accused us of being morbid, of wanting to land him in a whole heap of trouble.

I had a flash of inspiration. I told him we'd planned the story as the first in a series, to show how much life in Japan would improve as the country became accustomed to the Occupation. We'd necessarily started with some poor fellow living in the pits.

Dutch scrutinized me. "Well. You'd better just run anything like this past me in the future," he said.

I told him that we would.

"No stunts!"

I assured him we were not here to play stunts.

As we were leaving, he called out: "I liked your picture in any case, Hal!"

The rest of the staff certainly found it all amusing. They'd gathered outside Dutch's office, listening in to our dressing down. For weeks, we couldn't go anywhere without them holding up their hands like little paws and twitching their noses. One day a spoof story appeared on the notice board, claiming that rat meat was going to be brought onto the ration.

But the publicity didn't do the old bargeman any good. The Tokyo police got wind of the story and they trooped down the next week to clear him out. Half the city was sleeping in holes and ditches, but the authorities apparently considered it a violation of Japanese dignity for the old man to have so publicly shamed himself by talking to us about it. When I went down later that week with a flagon of soy sauce and some saké, he was gone. All that was left of the random clutter of his shelter were some charred sticks and a bent jerry can.

7
THE TICKET-HALL GANG
(HIROSHI TAKARA)

Two *yankii* sailors — enormous black men with flapping white trousers and tiny hats perched on the tops of their heads — were strolling amongst the clapboard stalls and counters of the Ueno Sunshine Market. I was stalking them — *Captain Takara, 1st Ghost Army* — and I'd collected half a dozen long cigarette butts already, when I saw that one of them was about to fling another to the ground.

As soon as the war had ended, the markets had sprung up like mushrooms at all the main train stations around the Yamanote Line: Shimbashi, Shinjuku, and here at Ueno. At first, scruffy men and women had just laid out whatever they had to sell on bare patches of earth — cups, pens, any old rubbish. One morning, I'd even seen a soldier sell off all his clothes, piece by piece. First his greatcoat, then his boots, then his shirt and trousers, until finally he was down to just shivering in his underwear, and I thought for a moment he was even going to try and sell that, and go off with the money wedged between his cheeks.

Soon enough, though, the yakuza gangs had decided to move in, and now the wasteground beneath the overhead train tracks was just like a real market, with electric lights and speakers playing gramophone records and peddlers who sold everything from saucepans to kimonos. There were noodle shops and counter bars selling tumblers of rough booze, and the place was patrolled day and night by the flashy toughs who worked for Mr. Suzuki, the market boss with a head like a bullet, who could sometimes be seen making his rounds, wearing his pale grey silk suit and felt fedora.

We called it the American Sweet Shop. The GIs came along on Friday nights to swap their B-rations for whisky and fake antiques. We shined their shoes and scrounged chocolate and chewing gum; kids stole things from their pockets and some of the older girls took them off into the shadows under the railway arches.

I was a cigarette boy. The yankiis all smoked like crazy — American cigarettes at that — and if you followed them for long enough, you could easily collect up enough butts to wrinkle out the tobacco into new two-sen smokes. You could then palm these off on some poor Japanese, who'd smoke them right down to the last cardboard embers.

The sailor lifted his massive hand and flung his smouldering cigarette into the air. I pounced, but suddenly, he moved, and I slammed into his leg, as thick as a tree trunk. I sprawled there, stunned, for a moment. From nowhere, another cocky boy jumped in.

"Get off!" I shouted. "This is my patch!" I twisted around and grabbed the boy, and we grappled and thrashed on the ground as the laughing sailors goaded us on, ducking and weaving behind their giant fists.

My hand was around the boy's throat and I pinned him

to the ground. But then, as I slapped his terrified face, I had a sudden shock. It was Koji, the grandson of Mrs. Oka, the pickle seller who'd lived next door to us in Asakusa.

"Koji?" I said, letting go of his neck. "Is that you?"

The boy nodded and wiped away his snot and tears with dirty little fists.

"Do you remember me?" I asked, brushing him down.

He grimaced. "What happened to your face?"

The thick welts on my cheeks had gone hard now, like the rubber on bicycle tires.

"I got burned."

His eyes grew wider. "You look creepy!"

I nodded. "What happened to your granny?"

He thrust out his bottom lip.

"Oh. Sorry. Did I hurt you?"

He shrugged.

"You hungry?"

"Starving!" he said.

He started to grin as we went over to one of the busy wooden stalls in the market. I counted out a few copper coins from my pocket, and, as we shared a bowl of cold noodles, he told me about some of the other kids he'd come across since the war had ended. There were quite a few of us Asakusa lot, it seemed, all in the same boat.

"Nobu's here," he said, and I nodded. This was a nine-year-old boy I knew from the Senso school. His dad had once owned the fishmonger, on the corner of Umamichi Street, where my own father had bought the eels for our shop there, before the shortages.

"Little Aiko, too." This was Nobu's younger sister, I remembered, a funny little thing who'd gone to the elementary school next to ours.

Koji glanced around and lowered his voice.

"That boy Shin's here, too," he whispered. "You know, the one from Fuji High School?"

I groaned. "Trust him to be here!"

I knew Shin alright. A local bully with a big square jaw, he'd been part of the tenement gang up near Sengen Shrine. His father had been a fireman, covered in tattoos, who'd lived on a barge on the Okawa. He'd sold Shin's sister Midori, one of the neighbourhood beauties, to the Willow Tree teahouse to become a trainee geisha when she was just eleven years old. Shin had taken after his father though, always fighting dirty in the battles we held in the back streets, throwing chunks of glass on the sly and striding about in a pair of rolled up khaki trousers that he swore he'd taken off the body of a crash-landed American pilot.

By the Ueno Plaza steps, the children were shrieking like monkeys as a pair of GIs revved the engine of their jeep, tossing packets of caramels into their grabbing hands. I spotted Shin straight away. He was nearly as tall as me now, wearing a torn pair of shorts. As the jeep spun off along the avenue, he sprinted after it in bare feet. He leaped up onto the bumper and rode along for a second before toppling off and tumbling into the dirt. He picked himself up with an idiotic grin and hobbled back toward us, his elbows streaked with blood. When he saw me, the grin vanished.

"Don't tell me you're here!" he said, squinting at my face. I recognized his thick lips and hooded eyes. "You're even uglier than before."

"Look who's talking."

There were scabs on his knees and his front teeth were broken. I remembered how, after our schools had been evacuated to the countryside, us Asakusa lot had been given the heavy jobs, digging octopus holes and cutting fodder for the local garrison's horses. Shin, meanwhile, had made alliances with the straw-sandalled village boys, pilfering our barley rations to trade for their silver rice.

"I suppose you want to join my gang now, don't you?" Shin sneered. "Not so high and mighty now, are you? Well, it just so happens that you can't. Not unless I say so."

"And how long have you been in charge?"

He frowned as he counted on his fingers. "Ever since —"

Everyone went quiet. Ever since March, he meant. The night when Tokyo had burned.

"You must be making pots of money, I suppose?"

He waved blithely at the departing jeep.

"We can always scrounge from the yankiis!"

The other children giggled. They were filthy. Their shirts were torn and their hair was matted. They wouldn't last another month with Shin in charge, I thought. I stepped closer.

"Do you really think they'll always be this generous?" I said. "What about when winter comes? It's October already. Chewing gum won't be much use to you then!"

Shin shrugged and gave another idiotic grin. The other children looked up at me nervously.

"Look," I said. "Here's what we can do."

Later that night, Shin and Nobu and I loitered for a few hours outside the Continental Hotel, where the American officers were billeted, and collected a pile of butts from the ash cans. Back at the station, Koji ground them up in his prize shell casing — a real beauty from a Type 89 discharger — and together, we rolled the new smokes into licked twists of newspaper. Aiko took them around the station the next morning. When she got back, I realized we had enough money to buy three whole seaweed-wrapped rice balls. We stuffed them into our mouths on the spot, grinning at each other with flecks of rice stuck to our chins.

"It's good that we're all back together, now, isn't it?" Koji remarked one evening. We were sitting up in Ueno Plaza, where some other kids had lit a refuse fire. Koji had just been showing off, a newspaper hat on his head, staggering around like a drunk GI, with Aiko pretending to be his giggling Japanese girlfriend.

It was true. It was a real relief not to be on my own any more. I missed my mother and father and sister more than I cared to let on, and I don't think that I could have survived without the company of the other children. It almost seemed like a big game sometimes, as if we'd all run off on holiday together. We played destroyer-torpedo in the broken-down houses, built forts in the bomb craters from charred planks and twisted bits of metal. We'd even made a baseball pitch in the wasteground at the back of the station, where we held tournaments with the other gangs, gambling for bullet casings and bomb fragments.

What a liberation from the war! Those days of writing comfort letters to the soldiers until your fingers cramped, marching up and down the playground, shouting songs. *Children of the Emperor!*

I never discovered exactly what had happened to Koji, Aiko, Shin and Nobu on the night of the fire raid back in March. It became a rule, early on, that we weren't ever to talk about it. I was still so ashamed of myself that I could hardly bear to think about that night. The whole city had been on fire as I'd sprinted back toward our house, leaving Satsuko alone in the dark water of the canal. I'd only made it a few dozen yards before the cotton quilt of my air defence cowl caught on fire. I screamed as I tried to pull it off, my skin smelling like roasting pork. I staggered into a pit shelter by the side of the road, where I sat all night long, the ground vibrating beneath my feet, surrounded by the sounds of sirens and planes and the stink of smoke as I sobbed in the darkness.

By the time the fires had burned out, my face was already blistering. I stumbled back up the charred street to the Yoshiwara canal, to the iron ladder where I'd left Satstuko the night before. The water below was full of floating corpses, drowned or asphyxiated, bobbing in the water amongst the blackened chunks of sodden timber.

The children sometimes cried out at night, at the station. I'd wake to see their faces glistening with tears. But it became another rule that you couldn't let anyone see you cry. If you did, the others had to sit on you, as if you were a sack of rice. I thought that if anyone were to start crying, then someone else would follow, and soon enough, we'd all be crying our eyes out and no one would be able to stop. We might go on crying forever, I thought, until we ended up like empty cicada shells, having cried ourselves away entirely.

I was playing with my metal soldiers one morning when Aiko bustled over to me. She hovered in front of me for a few minutes until, finally, I asked her what was the matter.

She frowned.

"Can people live in holes?" she asked.

"What do you mean?" I said.

Shyly, she told me that she had met a teenage girl the day before, who was living in a hole outside the station.

"You mean the slit bomb shelter?"

There were plenty of single-person earthwork shelters scattered across the city, though none of them had been much use to anyone during the fire raids. They'd been more like miniature stoves then. You still had to be wary of going inside, just in case there was a baked, rotten corpse stuck down there.

"What's she doing in there?" I asked.

"She lives in it!"

"Really?"

Aiko nodded, biting her lip

"Is she nice?"

"She's my friend."

"I see."

The girl had been sent to Tokyo from Hiroshima, Aiko said, in the Chugoko region, out on the Seto Inland Sea. Her mother had packed her off to stay with relatives a month or so earlier, but when the girl had disembarked at Tokyo Station, there'd been no one there to meet her. So she'd just wandered off on her own until she finally found herself here at Ueno.

I didn't know much about Hiroshima people, only that their city had been very badly bombed, just days before the end of the war. It had gone up with just one blast, people said.

I remembered thinking how unlucky they'd been, not to have made it through.

Aiko's face was crumpled up in sympathy, and I could tell that she'd taken a shine to the girl. It was hardly surprising. It couldn't have been much fun hanging around with us boys all the time.

"Can she come and join us, big brother?" she asked, with a pleading look on her face. "Please?"

I felt a tingle of pride. No one had ever called me big brother before. Maybe it wouldn't be such a bad thing to have another girl in the gang, I thought. She could always help out with the selling work.

"Why don't you bring her over to meet us later on today?" I said.

Aiko's face lit up and she clapped her hands together.

"Thank you big brother!" she said. "Thank you, thank you!"

Tomoko. The name itself was enough to send a delicious shiver down my spine. She wore a blue canvas jacket, a battered metal water canteen hung over her shoulder. Her hair was cut very short, almost like a boy's, and fell just beneath her eyes, so that she blew it out of the way whenever you spoke to her. Her face was quite round, but she was terribly thin from her journey from Hiroshima to Tokyo. She was thirteen years old and as shy as a borrowed cat.

That night, she slept on the floor next to us in our corner of the ticket hall. Just as I was drifting off, someone flicked my ear. I looked up to see Shin leering over me.

"What do you want?" I said.

"I was thinking," he said, as he scratched the side of his nose.

"That makes a change."

His thick lip trembled. "Listen," he said. "Don't you be so proud. You might have learned all the big words at your fancy school but I'm still Shin from Sengen Alley."

I sat up, ashamed of myself for having been rude. Perhaps he had been a bully in the old days. But all sorts of things had happened since then.

"What's your big idea, then?" I asked.

He jerked his thumb toward Tomoko.

"There's another way a girl like that could make us some money, you know."

I leaped to my feet and stared him down with white eyes, furious that I'd ever felt sorry for such a bastard. I held my fist under his chin until he shrank backward.

"What does it matter?" he whined. "We wouldn't be the only ones!"

"Don't you touch a hair on her head," I whispered. "Don't you even dare."

"What?" he said. "Want to save her for yourself, monster?"

My clenched fist stopped a hair's breadth away from his eye socket. Finally he shrugged and rolled away.

"Suit yourself."

Tomoko didn't say much, at first. In fact, I sometimes wondered whether she'd actually forgotten how to talk on her long journey across the Kansai plain. But then, one afternoon, she came over to us through the ticket hall, holding up a tattered magazine.

"I've found something," she said in a faint voice.

She was holding a torn copy of *Women's Club,* a magazine that my mother used to read. I wrinkled up my nose, but she opened it anyway to show us an article. I squinted at the title: "Let's Eat Grasshoppers!" it said.

"Well. Let's hear it then," I said, nodding in encouragement.

Tomoko blew her hair out of her eyes. Shyly, she began to read.

"Not only is the countryside full of grasshoppers, but despite what some might think, they are in fact quite delicious to eat and are very nutritious, being packed full of vitamins."

Koji made a sour face and Shin, not to be outdone, retched loudly.

But the idea didn't seem like such a bad one to me. We were all just skin and bones, after all. Even if we didn't eat the grasshoppers ourselves, we could always try selling them back here at the market. I'd seen people selling buckets of frogs before; some even sold snakes.

"Well. Maybe we'll go on a grasshopper hunt tomorrow then," I said. "First thing."

The other children started to make excited noises, but I quickly dashed their hopes.

"Just us older ones, of course. Me — and Tomoko. Shin, you can stay here and look after the little ones. You're in charge."

My heart was in my mouth as the children grumbled away. I snatched a glance up at Tomoko. Her cheeks were glowing. She was smiling at me.

~

It was a cold morning, beautifully clear and bright, as we jumped down from the Tobu Main Line train, just past Shiraoka up in Saitama prefecture. The fields were all crunchy with frost and mottled leaves were floating down from the trees, slowly, as if they couldn't bear to land. We'd borrowed some little bamboo cages from an old man at the market to make homes for our grasshoppers, but though we hunted about in the fields for hours on end, as the magazine suggested, it finally became clear that we wouldn't be needing them. There were no grasshoppers to be found.

"I wonder where they all could have gone," Tomoko sniffed.

"Perhaps it's because it's autumn now," I said. "Or perhaps other people have already taken them."

We wandered along a winding path that led through the fields, as the dew melted and a warbler called out from the trees. It must have its nest nearby, I thought, and I wondered if I should try to search for its eggs. I looked up. Tomoko was standing by a little shrine set with offerings just off the path, her eyes closed as if she were saying a prayer.

The stories I'd heard about her city swirled through my head. As we carried on walking, I finally plucked up the courage to ask her the question that had been puzzling me.

"Tomoko," I said. "I was wondering. Why was it that your mother sent you to Tokyo in the first place? Do you really have relatives here?"

She stopped suddenly, and gave me a strange look.

"She was sick," she murmured.

"Sick?"

She nodded. A wrinkle appeared on her forehead. "Not straight away," she said. "After."

I frowned. "What do you mean?" I asked. "What was wrong with her?"

She opened her mouth as if to speak, then shook her head. "I don't know," she said. "Something to do with her blood."

"Couldn't your father help?" I asked. "What did he do?"

"He was a doctor," she said. "At the naval hospital."

"So why couldn't he help, then?"

She stared blankly at the ground.

"What was it like?" I blurted. "Is it true what they say? That it all went up with just one blast?"

Tomoko held her hands tightly against her sides. She suddenly looked as if she was about to cry. *Idiot!* I thought, cursing myself. This kind of talk was against the rules.

I strode on down the path, squirming with embarrassment. After a while, I heard Tomoko's footsteps. I hardly dared look at her as she fell into step beside me.

"So what about you, Hiroshi-kun?" she asked. "What about Asakusa? Was it really as exciting as all the songs used to say?"

I glanced at her in relief, thankful to be changing the subject. "Haven't you ever heard of the Sanja Matsuri?" I asked. "It used to be the best festival of them all!"

A smile appeared on her face. "Is that so?"

"What?" I said. "You country bumpkin. Everyone knows that!"

She laughed as I told her about the rowdy celebrations that took place in our neighbourhood every year in honour of the founders of Senso Temple: the swollen crowds; the bulging-eyed men who carried the three enormous portable shrines up to the temple, swaying and crashing into the narrow buildings on each side of the alley as they passed.

"Did you ever carry a shrine, Hiroshi?" Tomoko asked.

I hesitated. "Well, yes, of course I did. One of the smaller ones, a little *mikoshi*. But you should have seen it! It was covered with real gold . . ."

I blustered on, hoping to thrill Tomoko with tales of Asakusa. But the truth was, I couldn't really remember much about the time before the Pacific War, the days that my parents had always talked about — the golden wooden horses in Hanayashiki Park and the jugglers at Asakusa Pond.

"It all sounds wonderful," Tomoko said.

I noticed her small white hand by her side. For some reason, I had a mysterious urge to pick it up and hold it.

"Maybe we could go there one day," I said. "They're showing American films again now. I could show you Senso Temple if you like."

Tomoko stopped walking. She looked at me quizzically.

"Hiroshi-kun, would you really?" she asked.

"Well," I stuttered. "Not that there's much left of it, of course."

She tilted her head ever so slightly. Her cheeks were glowing.

The shadows were stretched in the copses by the time we got back to the tracks and sat down to wait for a train to come along. After a while, Tomoko murmured that she was hungry. As I looked at her pale face, I realized that in fact, she was starving, and was trying to hide the fact by sheer willpower.

I cursed myself, thinking that I should have brought some food with us. I wondered whether I should try rummaging about in the nearest farmer's field. But just then, a blue-green four-car train came creaking toward us along the track, and I jumped up.

"Come on," I said, "Hurry!"

"Hiroshi —" Tomoko was struggling to stand. "I'm so dizzy."

I grabbed her hand and pulled her along as the train shuttled closer. A coupling came alongside us, and I leaped up, gripping onto the rail. But Tomoko stumbled, and for a second, I was dragging her along the ground, my arm being wrenched out of its socket. With a great heave, I hoisted her up and she fell into my arms. Her body was a dead weight. She had fainted.

I struggled to pull her up, grasping her under the armpits to stop her from falling from the accelerating train. Somehow I managed to shove her between me and the carriage, steadying her with an arm around her waist as the train rattled on. She let out a moan and buried her head against my chest. A scent came from her hair, and her breath fell in hot, delicate waves against my neck.

She made a small sound. As she looked up, the colour slowly came back into her cheeks. I realized my hand was sitting on the bump of her chest and I quickly wriggled around so that I was standing behind her.

"Thank you, Hiroshi-kun," she mumbled. She turned to face the locomotive, clutching onto the carriage for balance. She looked into the distance as the engine gave a long bellow and the train sped up, its wheels clattering faster and faster along the track. The last light of sunset was bleeding over the trees and bright gold glinted from the windows and the rails.

As we raced back toward Tokyo, I felt a quiver in my belly, as the smoke from the locomotive puffed around us, and the wind whipped her hair back into my face.

It was dark by the time we clambered down from the train at Ueno Station, and the children were bitterly disappointed that our bamboo cages were empty. Tomoko took the kids off to try to scrounge something to eat while I wandered away on my own, filled with the urge to lose myself in the uneasy magic of my sensations.

Not far from the railway arches was a wide bomb crater with tumbledown houses leaning over it. It was flooded with dark water, and the bubbles that rose to the surface every now and then burst with such a revolting smell that I normally steered clear of the place. But that evening, as I passed, a glint caught my eye and I froze. Over on the far bank, there was a tiny pulse in the air, a bright, thrilling glow, like a green star. I clambered around the rim of the crater to the far side and squatted down to get a closer look. It was just as I'd thought, though I could hardly believe it was possible so late in the year. Fireflies were floating up and down by the muddy bank, like ghostly little lanterns.

I took a matchbox from my pocket and shook it empty of tobacco strands. I held it open, and caught one of the creatures at the top of its ascent. Then I slid the drawer shut with my thumb, slipped the matchbox into my pocket, and hurried back to the station.

Koji gave a whimper when he saw me coming through the slumped crowds of the ticket hall. He rushed over and grabbed my arm.

"Big brother, you've come back!"

"Of course I have."

"Shin said you were gone!"

Beneath the concrete stairwell, Shin was sitting cross-legged on the floor. The children looked tearful. When Aiko saw me, she gave a squeal of relief.

"What's been going on here?" I said.

Shin gave a moon faced grin and stared up at the ceiling.

"He said you were leaving us!" Aiko said. "That you don't like us anymore."

"It was a joke," said Shin. "You damned cry babies!"

I put my hand in my pocket. There was a tiny flicker inside the matchbox.

"Shut up. I'll deal with this in the morning. Let's all just get some sleep."

The children curled up on their mats under the stairs. An old woman with a black shawl around her neck lay beside us, rasping. The station lights were extinguished, and the hall grew heavy with sleep.

I lay there in the darkness, wide awake, listening to the snores and night murmurs around me. I held the matchbox in my palm, imagining the creature trapped there in its miniature chamber of darkness, its body welling with light.

The children were dead to the world now, breathing quietly with their mouths open. Koji frowned and snorted in his sleep. Beside him, Tomoko lay very still, her lips slightly parted, the thin blanket over her shallow ribcage gently rising and falling. I reached over and tugged her leg. She moaned in her sleep, then shifted. I pulled her leg again, and this time she jerked awake with a gasp and sat bolt upright. When she saw me, she rubbed her eyes. I beckoned to her. Frowning, she edged forward. I held out the matchbox in my palm, and then pushed the drawer open. She gasped as the light pulsed in the box, and a faint green glow lit up her eyes.

She took the box from my palm and pushed the drawer open all the way. Suddenly, the creature flew up and out of the box, and hung, suspended in the air between us. We looked at each other in silent delight. She gestured to the ground beside her. I carefully clambered over Koji's body, and we both lay down and watched the firefly spiral slowly up and down. I could feel the warmth of her cheek next to mine as she fumbled for my hand. She picked it up and placed it upon her chest. She held it there beneath her fingers, and I could feel her delicate heart beat, as we lay there together on the cold, hard floor of the station, gazing up at the light as it pulsed softly in and out of existence.

8
THE COMFORT STATION
(SATSUKO TAKARA)

The comfort station was called the International Palace, and it was housed in an old watch factory, just off the highway out toward Chiba. The name might have been grand, but the building walls were crumbling and the partition rooms had no doors of their own, just sheets of cloth hanging from nails. The Americans had found their way there somehow. There was a long line of them waiting outside. They all clapped and cheered as our buses pulled up.

There'd been a celebration ceremony that morning in the Imperial Plaza. Lines of us modern-day Okichis throwing up our hands and cheering *Banzai!* as if we'd been schoolgirls off on a pleasant outing to the countryside.

The president of the Recreation and Amusement Association — the fat pig from my interview — was already inside the building, dressed like a cheap stage comic. There was an older lady too, named Mrs. Abe, who was to be our "manager." She led me to a cubicle at the end of the corridor and gave me a crayon and a piece of card and told me to think of an English name for myself. I didn't know any, and so she stared at me for a moment, then wrote "Primrose" in jagged orange letters and tacked the card up above the entrance to the room. She told me it was the name of a flower.

"Get yourself ready now, Primrose," she instructed. "The foreign gentlemen will be arriving soon."

The cubicle was tiny, hardly big enough for the straw-filled futon that lay on the floor. There was a grubby window high up in the wall and a bare electric bulb hung from the ceiling. I sat down on the edge of the mattress and drew my arms around my legs.

There was a sound from down the corridor, the heavy thud of boots and the jangling of uniforms. My stomach quivered. The Americans were shouting and laughing as they came in, bursting with excitement.

My eyes focused on a patch of bubbly mould on the partition in front of me. My heart started to pound. I remembered Osamu on the night before he'd gone away: his pale, thin body; his spectacles lying on the table.

I could hear the sounds of the girls in the other cubicles, moaning as the men grunted and hollered. Then the curtain of my room was tugged away, and the first one was standing in the doorway.

I sat on the floor of our cramped, silent house, staring at the teakettle. I told myself that I should try to sleep, but the thought of lying down on a bed made me retch. I could still smell the reek of tobacco and sweat and almond hair oil. They'd kept on arriving all day, in their uniforms and boots.

Most hadn't even bothered to undress. They just pulled down their pants and turned me around, and then buttoned themselves up as they left.

After the first one finished, I was stunned. I couldn't quite believe what had happened. But then, the curtain twitched and there was another one standing there, again, and again, and again. After a while, I just lay dumbly on the mattress and let them pull my kimono aside.

Most of them were no older than boys and only a few had any idea what they were doing. They only lasted a moment, which was a relief. One was rough. He pulled my hair and twisted me around, but when I screamed, he leaped up, clutching his trousers as he ran out of the room.

In the late afternoon, I started to get raw and jittery. The room was filthy and stinking and hot and I felt as if I was suffocating. The curtain opened again, and I let out a sob and rolled up into a tight ball.

But it wasn't an American this time. It was Mrs. Abe, who told me that my shift was over, that I should go home. I fumbled into my clothes, but when I got outside into the hallway, I very nearly started crying because I saw that most of the rooms didn't even have curtains anymore — the Americans had taken them all away for souvenirs.

I ran down the corridor. Buses were waiting outside to take us to the train station. I remembered staring at the tracks from the platform edge, glittery and endless in the darkness.

The door slid open and Michiko came in.

"Satsuko," Michiko said. "Satsuko-chan!" She rushed over and put her arms around me. "Was it really that bad?"

I stifled a sob. She had been working in a different part of the building and I hadn't seen her since she'd squeezed my hand goodbye that morning.

"Did you have to go with an awful many?" she asked, stroking my arm as my lip trembled. "Poor Satsuko!"

She unrolled my futon and made up the bed, then gently helped me put on my night clothes, tucking me in beneath the covers. I rolled over to face the wall.

I heard her yawn as she bustled about in the kitchen. I realized that she was actually humming to herself as she rummaged through the cupboards. It was amazing, I thought. She didn't seem the slightest bit concerned.

"Satsuko," Michiko said. "Satsuko! Look what I've got."

I couldn't bear to look.

"Satsuko!"

With a great effort, I twisted round and saw that she was waggling a small square bottle full of dark liquid.

"American whisky. One of the yankiis gave it to me."

She unscrewed the cap.

"Yankiis," she confided. "That's what all the other girls call them."

She sniffed the bottle, and wrinkled up her face. "Mmm!" she murmured. "Not bad."

She put the bottle to her lips and took a long swallow. Her throat moved once, and she sat there, eyes wide, waving her hand over her mouth.

"Oh," she said. "Oh, oh, oh."

She recovered her breath and poured out some more of the drink into two teacups. She handed one to me, and I sat up and gave it a cautious sniff.

"Who would have thought it?" Michiko said. "An American, giving me whisky."

I took a tiny sip, and then retched. The taste was disgusting and it stung my throat.

"And cigarettes," she said, taking out a packet from her purse and waving it at me. "Have a cigarette!"

She slid one out and lit it carefully, frowning at the glowing end and sucking in the smoke as if she had been doing it her whole life. I took another little sip of the whisky. It was very strong, but also quite sweet. When it reached my belly, I felt a warm, relaxing sensation that was really quite pleasant. My eyes grew heavy and I wondered if I was already drunk. I quickly tipped the rest of the liquid down my throat.

Then I really did feel dizzy. I rolled over on the bed, staring up at Michiko's swaying shape in front of me.

"He was the nicest one, anyway," she said, puffing away on her cigarette. "The one who gave me the whisky. Even if he was a black one."

I sat bolt upright.

"Michiko!" I shrieked. "You didn't go with a black one?"

"So what?" she demanded. "What do I care?"

She poured more whisky into our cups and I forced myself to drink it. I closed my eyes and lay back, hoping I would fall asleep straight away. The thought of the next day loomed in my mind. A throbbing pain began to pulse in my forehead and I felt a tightness in my chest. Finally, Michiko blew out the lamp and slid into bed beside me.

My mind was thick, but sleep wouldn't come. Shapes were moving about in the darkness in front of me; I could see the faces of men flickering and blurring into each other. The floor was moving back and forth, men heaving up and down on top of me; I was suffocating, and there was a filthy, cold wetness inside me…

I woke with a shriek and seized hold of Michiko.

"Michiko!" I cried. "Michiko, help me!"

She raised herself onto one arm. "Satsuko?" she murmured. "What is it?"

I didn't know what to say. Didn't she understand? She was looking at me in the darkness and I could smell the whisky on her breath.

"Is there nothing we can do, Michiko?" I whispered. "Nothing at all?"

Her answer came sharply. "No Satsuko. There's nothing we can do. So the sooner you get used to it the better. Now go to sleep."

With that, she rolled over, pulling the covers across herself. I drew my arms around my body, shivering. A few moments later, I heard a rasping sound. She was snoring.

Every time I looked up, there was another American standing in the doorway. The building was hot and airless, and my room was like a wretched, stinking cave. I spent as long as I could in the murky bathroom where we were told to wash and disinfect ourselves after each visitor, but the smell in there was sickening too, and no matter how much I scrubbed myself I couldn't get rid of the stink of chlorine and men. On the train home at night, I was sure that the other people in the carriage could smell it too, and that they were looking at me in disgust, as if they knew exactly the kind of woman I had become.

At the end of the first week, one of the girls killed herself. I remembered her from the bus on the first day. She'd worn a yellow dress with a bow in her hair. Mrs. Abe had forgotten to tell her to go home and the Americans had kept on coming for hours on end. She was only seventeen. Later on that night she threw herself under a train at Omori.

Michiko was already home when I got back that evening. She had an excited look on her face as she knelt down and took my hands in hers.

"Satsuko," she said. "You'll never guess, but I've fixed it."

"What do you mean?" I stammered.

She clutched my hands. "I've fixed it so that we don't ever have to go back to the Palace."

I stared at her in disbelief. "Please say it's true, Michiko," I moaned. "Please don't say it's one of your jokes."

"Listen," she said. "I spoke with that fat pig of a boss and he's agreed to transfer us to another comfort station. A high-class place, up on the Ginza. It's reserved for American officers."

My heart sank. *Another comfort station.*

"Will that really make such a difference, Michiko?"

She stared at me. "Are you mad? Of course it will. We won't have to go with those common types any more. We'll be just like real consorts now, Satsuko," she said. She squeezed my hand, and I saw the old star-struck look in her eyes.

"Modern-day Okichis!" she whispered.

Jeeps were driving up and down the Ginza and taxis went past with acrid smoke pouring out from their charcoal-run engines.

American soldiers and sailors strode along the street in groups, and I flinched as one raised his cap to me. He said something to his friends, and they all guffawed.

We hunted about for the address near the tall, sooty shop-front of the Matsuzakaya department store. As I looked at its shuttered windows and barred doors, I felt a stab of guilt. My mother had brought me there four years ago, on my sixteenth birthday, to buy my first real kimono. It was woven from beautiful green silk and embroidered with golden peonies. I'd had to sell it to buy rice back in June.

Next door to the Matsuzakaya was a low, white building that had clearly been used a communal bomb shelter. A large sign in English hung outside, freshly painted in pink and white.

"There it is, Satsuko!" Michiko said, tracing the letters in the air with her finger. *"Oasis — of — Ginza,"* she pronounced. "We're here!"

We walked down a flight of dingy steps. The underground shelter had been transformed into a cheap cabaret, with a small dance floor and a little wooden stage with chairs and tables set up. Red streamers and paper lanterns decorated the cracked earthen walls, and American and British flags were tacked up at jaunty angles.

"Very nice," said Michiko, nodding approvingly. A scratchy jazz record was playing on the gramophone, and a very tall and solemn-looking American man was turning slowly around in the middle of the room. A tiny girl appeared, clinging onto him — she could barely clasp her arms around his back.

Mr. Shiga's office was in an old storage cupboard piled high with buckets for water relays. He looked at us haughtily over the rims of his spectacles, and told us how lucky we both were.

"Only the best kind of girls get to work here," he said. "This place has got class." He coughed heavily and spat into his handkerchief. "So you'd better keep our guests happy. And you're not just here to spread your legs either."

He explained that, aside from the usual services, we were to encourage the Americans to spend their dollars on drinks and dances and snacks.

"And don't let them palm you off with yen!" he said.

Dabbing at his lips, he quickly went through the financial arrangements, which didn't seem very fair to me. The Oasis would take practically half of everything we earned, though we were still expected to pay for our own makeup and clothing and any medical treatment that might be necessary. But it was a sign of how desperate I had become that I just knelt meekly before him. Anything seemed better than the International Palace.

We took great care making ourselves up that night, in the cramped dressing room filled with perfume and perspiring flesh. The girls were fanning each other, slumped on the floor in their underclothes. Michiko sprinkled powder on the back of my neck and brushed it until my skin was as smooth and white as china.

"Why, Satsuko," she said, pulling my obi tight around my waist, "you look just like a real geisha!"

I laughed at the thought. But when we looked at ourselves in the mirror, I saw that I really did look quite pretty, even next to Michiko, who was so stunning.

Years before, I recalled, my mother and I had dressed up together before going to watch the summer fireworks over the river. We'd painted our faces and glued silk petals to our combs. After things had started to go badly for Japan, though, there'd been no makeup or jewellery anymore. Skirts had been banned, and the busybodies from the National Defence Women's Association went around spying, scolding you in public for any hint of rouge. *Abolish desire until victory!*

I remembered how, soon after I'd reported for war work, Mr. Ogura had ordered all the girls out into the yard one morning. He told us we were to unpick every colourful thread from our clothes, one by one. After that, it was nothing but shapeless khaki trousers for us. *No colour but National Defence Colour!*

"Whatever would Mr. Ogura say if he could see us now, Michiko?" I said.

She applied a last dusting of powder to her nose. "I think he'd keel over, Satsuko, just like he did when the emperor made his speech."

We slid open the door to the cabaret. It was already filled with American officers from the army and navy, with girls perched on their knees, pouring their beers and lighting their cigarettes.

As we walked out into the damp, smoky room, a thought struck me. "Michiko," I asked. "How was it that you persuaded the boss to move us here in any case?"

She gave a low laugh. For a moment, she had sounded just like one of the vulgar types we'd been working with until so very recently. It was a nasty laugh, of the kind that asks: isn't the answer obvious?

9
ERO GURO NANSENSU
(OSAMU MARUKI)

Japan appeared, like an emerald set in glittering blue, as our troop ship sailed at last along the winding shore, the peaceful coastline. But the soldiers sensed something amiss as soon as we clambered down the gangplank to the damaged harbour: the shops were empty, the populace unwilling to meet our eyes. From the dock, I watched as three old warhorses, their ribs showing through wan hides, were led stumbling from the dark hold of the ship, unused to the bright light of day. A young man in a grubby vest approached the stableman immediately to haggle for their withered flesh.

We were shunted toward Tokyo in a cramped train full of poisonous smells and sour faces. The city had clearly taken a smashing. Its ribs were showing too; its carcass was open to the sky. Tokyo Station swarmed with fellow returnees wrapped in thick greatcoats, lying in clumps, or drinking, red faced and angry in the squalid stalls around the plaza. The eyes avoided us here too, I noticed, and I longed to shed my woollen winter uniform, writhing now with lice. But the evening was bitterly cold, and so I buttoned my drab overcoat to the collar, pulled my fighting cap down, and, overcome with an almost exquisite weariness, began to trudge, disorientated by the burned-out streets and unfamiliar vistas, toward Asakusa, town of rainbow lanterns and sleepless sparrows: my spiritual home.

My letters to my honourable mother had gone unanswered for several months. Finally, I had received a curt note from her fellow harridans at the National Defence Women's Association, informing me that Madame had died of tuberculosis three weeks before, despite an almost complete excision of her lung. It seemed of little use, then, to return home now. With my mother gone, the main house would revert to the distant Osaka branch of her family, and I held out little hope of much assistance from them. They had long ago let me know how much they disapproved of my dissolute lifestyle, even after I had received my red call-up papers.

"Across the sea, corpses soaking in water!" the radio had sung. "Across the mountains, corpses heaped upon the grass!"

"Congratulations on being called to the front, honourable son," my mother had wept. "Your family is so proud of you."

I wandered up the shabby remains of the Ginza. The stores were mostly shuttered and those that were not lay empty and bare. As I passed the ravaged edifice of the Matsuzakaya, an Occupation bus stencilled with the name of an American city roared up on the other side of the road. It expelled a group of boisterous soldiers, who raced over to a low cabaret that had been set up next door. Painted girls in cheap kimonos advanced upon them. They squealed and clutched at their arms, tugging them through the door of the club like kappa imps dragging wayfarers down into the marsh.

I stopped suddenly and screwed up my eyes. One of them seemed very familiar. The short hair, the white oval face, dark eyes that I once knew intimately —

Satsuko Takara. The girl who had once appeared to me the embodiment of a beautiful Asakusa Park sparrow. My brief affair with whom had so scandalized my mother. The girl whose lovely face had hovered in my mind during all those nights of malarial horror in New Guinea.

Look at her now. In her prancing colours, hovering on the dimly lit street. How had she ever fallen so low? Never had she been a *zubu*, a bad girl, like the crop-haired nymphs who hung stockingless around the Asakusa theatres. She had been a delight, a sweetheart. No more, no less.

I writhed with embarrassment as I recalled my mother's coldness to her on the day of my leaving ceremony, when Takara-san had visited our house, only to be turned away, weeping, at the side door. I had listened from upstairs to my mother scolding her for her impudence — intent upon packing my cases, too cowardly to descend.

A sharp feeling of guilt flared inside me as I studied her from the darkness. Lice crawled beneath my cap, and I felt a hopeless sense of destitution. How would I appear to her now, I thought, even if I were to approach her? A frail ghost with hollow cheeks, returning so broken by war?

I smiled grimly as I watched. At last she claimed her prey: a boyish American with spectacles and a thatch of wiry hair. As she dragged him down the steps, I turned and strode quickly northward. If a girl as proper as Satsuko Takara had fallen to such depths, I thought, then things must truly be bad.

~

To comfort myself, I took a detour via Kanda, intending to then follow the river to Asakusa-bashi and walk up the Sumida from there. Most of the booksellers were gone, their volumes apparently incinerated in the conflagrations of March. But Ota Books was still standing, and I browsed inside in a forlorn attempt to get warm. To my surprise, I found a copy of *Crime and Punishment* on the shelf, the first I'd seen in years. I flipped open the frontispiece and saw the *ex libris* stamp of the Sorbonne University. A pit opened in my stomach. Another one of my dreams the war had put paid to.

Mr. Ota shuffled out, armed with a feather duster. I greeted him hopefully. He stared at me as if I were a stranger. I asked if any of the old haunts or bars were still open — the Café d'Asakusa perhaps, the Dragon, or the Montmartre — but he told me that all but the Montmartre had been destroyed in the air raids. As he hobbled outside to bring in the boxes, I quickly slid the novel into my overcoat — the pocket flaps at least were conveniently large. I followed him outside.

What a relief it was, when I finally turned down a ruined alley and saw a red lantern glowing in front of Mrs. Shimamura's shop. I paused in the street and stared, a lump swelling in my throat. The light was like a glowing beacon, a forlorn torch to welcome me home. I pulled aside the curtain at the entrance, and there it was, almost unchanged since the old days. The big map of the Paris arrondissements was still up on the wall, and there, polishing glasses behind the counter, was Mrs. Shimamura herself, wearing her famous white dress; though, as I came closer, I saw with dismay that her old rolls of fat had shrunken now to wrinkled folds of skin.

She didn't know me either, at first. As I took my old stool up at the bar, I wondered if I could truly have appeared so altered.

"*Obasan*," I said. "Forgive my presumption. But might you extend a note of credit to a returning soldier — and to a lifelong, loyal patron?"

She stared at me with a dim flicker of amused recognition in her eyes.

"Regrettably, sensei," she replied, "since the war ended, there have been so many hundreds of hungry and thirsty patrons, crawling about the city seeking notes. Perhaps sensei would better off talking to his friend Nakamura-san, whom he must surely recognize sitting at the end of the bar?"

I turned and saw him, hunched over the counter with a drink and a sketchpad. It was him all right, though he seemed almost a skeleton now. Nakamura and I had been in the same French literature class at Keio; we had even once thought about producing a Sensationalist pamphlet together. But while my stories had withered on the vine, his drawings had won so much acclaim that he had been hired by the noted magazine, *Manga*, at the outbreak of the Pacific War. I remembered his cartoons well. They grew more and more barbarous as the war progressed. Allied soldiers being bayoneted to death by loyal children of the emperor; aircraft carriers being destroyed by whizzing Zero fighters; not to mention his celebrated masterpiece, *The Annihilation of Britain and America* . . .

Naturally, I was overjoyed to see him sitting there, just as in the old days. As I slid over to him, he gave a sickly smile and quickly turned over his pad to hide whatever it was he was drawing. I asked him what there was to drink nowadays, and he told me that the only thing available was a rotten blend of distilled shochu dregs mixed with aviation fuel to give it a kick. I mulled this over for a few moments.

"Well," I remarked, philosophically. "The emperor himself has told us that we must endure the unendurable, after all."

I politely inquired whether Nakamura was still producing illustrations for *Manga*. He gave a ghastly grin, showing many broken teeth, and called to Mrs. Shimamura to pour us two glasses of the house spirit, in order to welcome me home. I thanked him politely and poured the drink into my mouth.

For a moment, I thought my throat was going to explode. I somehow managed to swallow the poisonous stuff, and promptly felt as if my eyes were bleeding. I tugged at Nakamura's sleeve to see what he was drawing. He tried to hide the pad, but I gripped hold of it until the paper tore.

My, my. What an evolution. No foreign barbarians here: instead, a Japanese soldier (who bore a remarkable likeness to Nakamura himself) bowing down in thanks to a titanic American with a colossal pair of scissors, who was triumphantly snipping the man free of the chains that tied him to a pile of tanks and bombs. I laughed long and hard at this, and told Mrs. Shimamura that we'd better have two more glasses of her awful liquor to celebrate Nakamura-san's new career. I banged my glass against his.

"Well, Nakamura," I said, "'*À l'oeuvre on reconnaît l'artisan.*" I poured the horrid stuff into my throat, and instantly slid from the chair.

Painful waves beat relentlessly against the quick of my brain. A sensation of helplessness — paralysis.

Someone was pounding on the door. I was no longer in a stockade cell on a poisonous island, I realized, nor in the dark bowels of an oceangoing ship. I was somewhere I knew well, somewhere as intimately familiar as the womb. Slowly, it dawned on me, with exquisite relief. The room above Mrs. Shimamura's shop, reserved for customers to sleep off their night's excesses. The banging came again, and my panic rose as the door opened.

Mrs. Shimamura poked her head through the door.

"Time to go, sensei. I've laid out your breakfast."

The thought of the crowds swelling around Tokyo Station stabbed my heart with fear.

"Obasan, perhaps I could ask you . . ."

"Don't be a pain, sensei —"

"Please, obasan —"

Disgusted with myself, I broke into sobs. "For just a few days, obasan. Please. I beg you."

Mrs. Shimamura's face crinkled as I knelt before her. She hesitated for a moment. I sensed victory.

Kind and noble obasan. She would let me stay — for just a few days. I was expected to carry out several duties in the bar. I was not expected to sit around the place pickling myself in saké lees.

I carried on kneeling in gratitude as she strode from the room, then sunk back into the soft blankets and closed my eyes.

I thought of the crowds at the station, the waves of refugees casting about and crashing against each other. They were far away now. Here, I was safe, hidden upon my lifeboat, bobbing about on a quiet inland sea. The sky was flowing with the stars of the Milky Way.

The artists who had survived the war were emerging now from the cracks, crawling like valiant cockroaches to the refuge of Mrs. Shimamura's saloon. Every night, around the hour of the dog, the bar filled up with the various writers, journalists, and assorted poets I had known before the war, as well as the usual students and hangers-on.

My greatest need now was for money. I was one of the few of them who had no private income of my own. I discussed the matter with Nakamura and Mrs. Shimamura one afternoon. What was the role of a writer in a world that had collapsed so entirely? How should he respond to such devastation? And how, I thought gloomily, was he ever to scratch a living? Every crevice had been swept already, it seemed, the dust rolled out into dough.

The following morning in Kanda, I was browsing Mr. Ota's bookshop again, wondering if I dare steal a bound copy of Zola's *L'Assommoir*. Two painters were working at the building next door, and I overheard the drifting words of their conversation. To my surprise, they were discussing the meals they had once enjoyed most at this time of year. Toasted *mochi* filled with chestnut jam! The crispness of the shell, the wonderfully sweet paste within . . . The other waxed lyrical about the pressed mackerel sushi he had eaten as a young man in Osaka — the vinegar tang of the silver-blue fish! The rice plump and sweet on the tongue! My mouth began to water. I recalled a strange pining that I'd had for persimmons as we had sailed on our long voyage back to Japan, a craving that had seemed, at times, almost overwhelmingly intense, the memory of the fragrant juice, the soft, mottled flesh transporting me back almost beyond childhood...

I strolled over to the men and studied them as they worked. Their faces did not seem bitter or weathered, I thought, despite the cold. Rather, they were radiant, transported, transcendent even. They were dreamily happy, lost in the innocence of their memories. A thought struck me. I had a sudden inkling of what I might write.

Nakamura and Mrs. Shimamura agreed straight away that the plan was a good one. We would sell fantasies.

Mrs. Shimamura summarised things very cogently. She poured a glass of her clear spirit and pointed at it.

"Look," she said, "if you can't afford saké, you have to settle for this."

I agreed, reaching for the glass, but she snatched it up and tipped it against her lips, swallowing with a grimace.

"What I mean is, if you can't have the real thing, you have to settle for its substitute. If you can't find food, you'll have to settle for stories about it. That's what you'll sell in your magazine. But you're missing a trick, sensei — the most important fantasy of all."

"Please enlighten us, obasan."

"Sex."

I asked her what she meant.

"Well. It used to be the only thing that was free, wasn't it? But not any more. Think of those trollops in the back alleys. They hoard it up like stingy peasants do with rice, and only dole it out to those who can afford it."

I wistfully thought of Takara-san and the gaudy girls on the Ginza, rushing over to grasp the arms of the American GIs.

"Where's the average man to find comfort nowadays? His wife's most likely dead, and the only girls around are sluts. If he's only got two yen, and a girl costs twenty, whatever is he to do?"

I took Mrs. Shimamura at her word, and jam-packed our new magazine with every possible fantasy — epicurean, erotic, or otherwise — that might appeal to the ordinary Japanese man, so lately oppressed by frustrated desires. I wrote three stories interspersed with Nakamura's drawings and cartoons — the usual erotic, grotesque nonsense we had grown up with.

The first dealt with a soldier who, on returning home, finds that his wife has taken up with his neighbour. Soon enough, he is incapable of arousing himself in any other way than by spying on them from behind a screen.

The second was a more monstrous variation on the theme. A man is forced by circumstance to take work in a brothel, mopping the stained floors and laundering the sheets. He learns that a new girl, a real beauty, is to start work the next day. An uncanny thought comes into his mind, and he hides himself under her bed that night. The next day, the presumed beauty comes in with an American soldier. They throw themselves onto the bed and start heaving and cavorting. Aroused, the man's fingers creep into his pants, and, as the bed rattles and shakes, and the girl approaches the heights of her ecstasy, he cannot help but participate in her delerium. "With the roar of a mountain lion," the American completes, and leaves the room.

The man hears the girl dressing. He sidles out from underneath the bed, intent upon presenting her with a diabolical proposition. As he emerges, she shrieks. He gasps, clutching at his chest. The girl is his own daughter.

The cover was a master stroke, lovingly drawn and coloured by Nakamura. A woman suns herself on a beach, wide hips, jutting breasts, *plus ça change.* But, this is no Japanese bathing beauty. She is a Westerner. An American lady, with just a wisp of hair emerging beneath her navel — for the first time, I was sure, on the cover of a Japanese magazine. The wife of one of the generals, perhaps? Of MacArthur himself? All of this, and more, now available to anyone for just three yen. This, I sensed instinctively, was the true essence of democracy.

The second half of the magazine was more considered. Inspired by the house painters, "The Dish I Most Lament" was based upon a series of interviews I conducted at various stations along the Yamanote Line, in which I asked ordinary citizens to describe the meal for which they felt most nostalgic. The reactions were astonishing. Some shook their heads furiously and marched away; one man even punched me on the nose. Others simply froze, then began to reel off a list of dishes as if they were reading from a long menu unfurling in their minds — sea bream cooked in chestnut rice; bubbling stews of chicken and burdock; hot fried tempura and fat slivers of bonito . . . Others smiled with that faraway look I had seen on the faces of the painters, and talked of cold buckwheat soba from a temple in Kyoto; *itawasa* fish cakes from a famous shop in Nihonbashi . . . They talked of tofu and *oden*, horsemeat and clams, but, most of all, they talked of miso. Miso, miso, always miso soup, prepared each morning by the hands of once beloved, now departed mothers and wives.

Sometimes I had to stop them talking, as my eyes would be blurry with tears. Then their smiles would falter and the wind would gust past us in the street. The interviewees would look at me bitterly then, as if I had robbed them of something precious. More than anything, I realized, it was our lost past that was the most captivating daydream. In these days of dried cod, of the rotten sweet potato, it was the most painful fantasy of all.

ERO, as we named the magazine, was an instant hit. Convinced of its appeal, Mrs. Shimamura funded the first printing. By the end of the day, all of the copies we had placed with the booksellers and newsstands had sold out. With the profits, we printed another issue, which itself sold out by the end of the week. It seemed we had struck a peculiar vein.

My financial issues then were temporarily solved. But I was troubled by the fact that in just five days, my erotic stories had sold a hundred times more than all my literary scribblings had in a decade. Even more disturbingly, while in the past I had agonized over every word and punctuation point, these stories had flowed from my pen like water. I had written them all in one night, in fact, one after the other, sitting up in my room with an inkstone and a bottle of liquor. I wondered if something had fractured in my mind during those long, malarial months of horror in the jungles of New Guinea.

What irony that I, who fancied myself the Japanese Tolstoy, an Oriental Zola, should find my métier in pornography. That the first thing I should write on my return from the inferno of war should be sensual and erotic!

10
THE TOURISTIC GI
(HAL LYNCH)

My compatriots glanced at me curiously across the basement dining room of the Continental Hotel as I attempted to lever chunks of rice into my mouth with my chopsticks. A small bowl of anonymous, gelatinous fish swamped in brown paste lay on my table, alongside a slippery white cuboid of tofu and a pot of green tea. The boy had been delighted when I'd asked him for a "Japanese-style" breakfast, but I was now envying the morning toast and powdered eggs being devoured by the staff and officers around me.

I had thrown myself into my Japanese life with vigour, keen to get under the skin of the place. I scoured the markets for books in translation and studied whatever I could find — children's folk tales, samurai dramas, medieval literature. I undertook a dozen Japanese lessons with an old man in his chrysanthemum garden in Shibuya. I even sat cross-legged through six long, baffling hours of a Noh play in a dusty, empty hall, the pain in my thighs growing more excruciating by the second.

Dutch was still sore at me for landing him in hot water.

"Give this one to Lynch," he would simper at editorial meetings. "He's swell at human interest."

My assignments so far had included a horticultural show by the Allied Women's Flower Arranging Society and a boxing tournament between the 5th Cavalry and a team of British marines.

In the meantime, I tramped the Tokyo streets, photographing the city and its inhabitants. A bald man washing glasses from a bucket in a shanty. The watchman of the metal mountain up past the Ginza, standing amidst piles of radiators, bicycles, and temple bells.

One day I was up at Ueno, exploring the stalls of the black market. Men chopped slivers of meat, squatted beside standpipes, unloaded wooden crates of fish from hand-carts. Behind the station, I came across a team of tattered children playing baseball on a patch of wasteground. A grubby boy, his face disfigured by burns, was standing against a broken-down section of wall, holding up a charred plank. Another boy in short pants flung a ball made of rags. The scarred boy whacked it hard. A piece of wood splintered off and he raced around a diamond formed of piles of gravel. The other children hollered in encouragement, their faces as filthy as his, as I pulled up my Leica and fired off shot after shot. He tore along, making it back just in time for the home run, sliding along the gravel in a great cloud of dust. The children cheered and screamed. Then they spotted me. They instantly abandoned their game, and came galloping toward me in a herd.

I hurled candy bars, of which I now kept a provident supply in my coat pocket. They swarmed me, shrieking with delight.

To give them a treat, I decided to take their portraits, and had them scribble their ages in my notebook.

"All from Tokyo, right?" I asked, in my broken Japanese. "You — Tokyo?"

The scarred boy pushed forward. His hair was thickly matted and he wore dirty brown serge trousers rolled up at the hem.

"We — Tokyo," he said in wavering English, gesturing to himself and the others. Then he pointed. "She — no."

I noticed another little girl standing a few paces behind him, apparently too shy to come over.

"Oh? Where's she from?"

The boy nodded. "Yes. She — Hiroshima," he said.

I paused. "Is that so?"

The girl wore a blue canvas jacket and was very frail. I leaned down and beckoned to her, but she barely dared look at me. I offered her a malted milk ball from my pocket. She quickly shook her head. The other children gathered around us.

"You — Hiroshima?" I said to her.

She glanced at the scarred boy, then gave a tiny nod of assent.

"You have — mother? Father? *Okasan*? *Otosan*?"

She stared awkwardly beyond me. A faint wind ruffled her short hair.

The scarred boy broke in: "Her mother — sick. Send her — Tokyo."

"Her mother was sick?"

Tears were welling in the girl's eyes. All of a sudden, she said something in a strained voice. I turned to the boy.

"What did she say?" I asked.

He wiped his forehead with his fist, frowning. "Bomb —

fall," he said. He made an explosive noise and threw up his hands. "Every people — sick."

"Sick? You mean they died?"

He frowned, apparently at his linguistic limit. He shook his head. "No die. Sick."

"The bomb? The bomb made her mother sick?"

He nodded fervently. *"So, desu."*

A memory came to my mind. The surrender issue of *LIFE*, back in September, MacArthur's face glaring from the cover. There'd been a set of photographs of Hiroshima, shots of mangled factories. Toward the end, there'd been a brief reference to reports from local doctors, stories of failing appetites and bleeding gums amongst the surviving population.

The other children were scampering around now, hurling stones about the wasteground. The scarred boy was staring intently at my Leica. As a reward for his efforts at translation, I took the leather strap from around my neck and handed the camera to him. He examined it with a fierce and concentrated delight, then held it to his face and began to swoop gently around, like a regular Robert Capa.

I finally managed to prise it away from him, and he gave me a solemn look of thanks. With a polite bow, he ran back to his game.

Dutch grudgingly printed the picture a week later. I guessed I was now forgiven. It showed the little boy earnestly holding his makeshift bat as the ball of rags flew toward him: "The Tokyo Little Leagues," the caption read.

Eugene's interest in Japanese culture was of a different strain to my own. One evening, he asked me to join him and his new friend Bob McHardy, a cartoonist at the paper, at a bar called the Oasis, next to our new Postal Exchange by the Ginza Crossing. At the door, yum-yum girls were coaxing men inside, while laughing GIs stood in line at a booth, where the hair-raising VD posters revealed it to be an army prophylactic station. Downstairs, Eugene sat at a table with McHardy, who had a gorgeous girl perched on his knee, running her fingers through his curly blonde hair. I felt a twinge of guilty lust: she should have been kicking up her heels on the stage, I thought, or starring on a cinema screen.

Another girl, dressed in colourful kimono, was perched on the chair beside Eugene. She was young and neat, with smooth porcelain skin and jet-black eyes.

"Harold, meet Primrose," Eugene winked. "She's a swell sort."

Primrose refilled his glass every time he took a sip and laughed at practically everything he said. As I drank my luke-warm beer I couldn't help but picture the gangly boy I'd roomed with in college. He'd been the kind of kid to have sand kicked in his face on the beach. *Look at him now*, I thought. Eugene sprawled on the chair with an air of easy and wanton debauch, and I felt a stab of envy as Primrose stroked his face and patted his thighs.

McHardy went off to dance and I seized the chance to tell Eugene about an idea I'd been toying with. I wanted to see more of the country and thought we might try to write some touristic reports about places GIs might like to visit on leave.

"It would give us a chance to do some travelling ourselves, Gene. Get out of Tokyo."

"Well," he said. "I guess . . ."

Primrose had taken off his glasses and placed them upon her own nose and was generally distracting him. When she reached over to pour more beer into Eugene's glass, I noticed that her palms were damaged. They were smooth, shiny in the low light, as if they had been polished.

"Come on, Gene. It'll do you a world of good."

Eugene seemed very uncertain. As Primrose lifted the bottle, I imagined for a split-second her smooth hands touching my face, passing over my back. She saw me staring, and gazed back at me for a second.

A new song came on the gramophone and, with a delighted gasp, she hopped up and tugged at Eugene's hand.

"What do you think, Gene?" I said.

"Well, why don't you talk to Dutch about it?"

"I will." I drained my beer and stood up.

"You're not staying?"

"Uh-uh."

Primrose wiped her forehead in comical fashion. She grasped hold of Eugene's arm and tugged again. I saw now how pretty she was, and felt a stab of doubt about leaving.

Primrose dragged him over to the dance floor.

"Suit yourself," Eugene called, waving his free hand. I watched them for a while, then strode uncertainly up the steps to the bustling street outside.

Dutch was enthusiastic about my idea, just as I'd suspected he would be.

"It'll be real human interest, Dutch. Aimed square at your average GI."

He beamed. "Attaboy. What'll we call it?"

"How about 'The Touristic GI'?"

"Sure," he said. "Sounds appealing."

Two days later, at six in the morning, a protesting Eugene and I picked our way through the crowd at the station to embark upon our journey to Himeji, a castle complex out near Kobe, having stocked up on tins of spam, sandwiches and bottles of beer from the PX the night before.

Japanese people crammed into the carriages, fighting for standing room on the steps, as women shoved parcels in through the broken windows. With relief, we found the carriage reserved for Allied personnel and clambered into a compartment. It was empty, though hardly luxurious. Most of the windows were cracked and the seats were busted, springs jabbing up through the fabric. But as the locomotive gave a whistle and started to tug us out of the station, I felt a thrilling trepidation to be escaping the safe, fairy-lit toy-town of Little America and heading out into the wilds of Japan at last.

We jolted through the ruined fringes of the city and out into the countryside. Green paddies stretched along each side, figures in conical hats stooped over in the fields as they had, no doubt, for centuries. We ate our sandwiches as the huge, wide slopes of Mount Fuji came into view, ice-cream white against a cold blue sky. I examined its flanks and conical tip, recalling the view of the mountain from above — we'd used it so many times as a mustering point before the fire raids that it seemed intimately familiar.

The perspective shifted; my stomach lurched. The world took on a sudden, febrile intensity, thudding engines pulsing in my inner ear.

My head was between my legs. Eugene laid a hand on my shoulder.

"Hal? Are you alright?"

I nodded, taking deep breaths until the thudding floated away. Eugene was staring at me.

"Are you sick?"

"It's a little stuffy in here."

I stepped over to the other side of the compartment and hoisted down the cracked pane of glass, concentrating on the flat paddies and a stream that wound beneath a low, scenic ridge. I heard Eugene opening two bottles of beer behind me. I took one from him gratefully.

"Here's mud in your eye," he said.

We clinked bottles and drank. Presently, I took a private glance behind. The huge mountain was gone, smeared away into mist.

A little narcotic rivulet trickled pleasantly around my brain. Eugene told me tales of the parallel life he had been living over the past few years, since I was drafted and had joined 3rd Recon. He'd applied to the newspaper almost on a whim, it seemed. Before that, he'd been working at his father's law office in Manhattan, excused from service due to his terrible eyes. Japan was his big adventure now. I joshed him about his "girlfriends" in Tokyo and he coloured, smirking.

"Come on, Hal. Don't tell me you haven't succumbed to the delights of *baby-san*?"

The question lacked nuance. Before we'd been sent to Saipan, there'd been henna-tattooed skin and plump Indian flesh in a mud shack at Kharagpur; a dose from my favourite girl at the Phoenix House in Chengtu. Always with a vague sense of brutality, as if I were a marauding barbarian.

"And how is Primrose, Eugene?" I asked, picturing the dark, candid eyes of the girl in the club. "Still blooming, I hope?"

"You should learn to loosen up a little, Harold."

"And how often do you find yourself frequenting these establishments, Eugene?"

He adjusted his glasses, a trifle uncomfortably. "Most nights, I guess."

As the train followed the line of the coast, the air grew cold and the ocean wind blew in through the cracks in the windows. We were just starting to shiver when the porter brought a small, hot brazier of charcoal, which he set on the floor between us before folding down our bunks. Dusk fell, and we squeezed into our narrow berths and tried to fall asleep under short, thin blankets.

The clattering of the train permeated my dreams, transforming itself into the pounding of aerial bombs. I was alone in a house I somehow knew from my childhood, a place that was at once intimately familiar, yet vastly lonely. The continual whoosh and blast of explosives came from outside and I felt an inexplicable sadness, as a child might feel when he is utterly abandoned. A glass door of a rifle case hung open by the wall. A single lamp burned by the stair. A knock sounded at the door and I knew with instinctive fear who it would be. I hesitated for what felt like an endless time, then opened it. The disfigured Japanese boy was standing there, holding his baseball bat, like some strange oriental cherubim, his frail girlfriend beside him. Each took one of my hands and together they led me outside into the blazing city. Then we were flying high up above a night landscape, the villages and towns below all razed to the ground. We went still higher, miles above the earth, and then we were flying amidst some strange, ethereal hinterland, surrounded by ancient, deserted cathedrals of the night...

There was a piercing shriek, and I awoke with a shout. The train was shuddering to a halt. The door to our carriage swung open, and there was a sudden blast of cold air. People scrambled inside the compartment. The voice of the platform guard barked out. He raced to the door, barring entry, shoving people out and packing them off to the carriages reserved for Japanese. The door slammed shut, and I rolled over in my berth with guilty relief.

The rest of the journey was interminable, the train groaning frequently to a halt, or stopping at small branch line stations for endless intervals. We finally clambered out, blurry eyed, into the dim morning light of Himeji to be met by Lieutenant Hartley, a shy young officer from the 130th Infantry.

As we walked along the platform, the station master slid out the destination plates from their frames on the side of the carriages. Himeji was the junction of three major lines; the train would split here. He slotted in another plate, the name of the terminus obscured by his back. Two military policemen were treading toward the Allied carriage in white helmets and heavy boots. They paused by our compartment, hopped up onto the side, and suspended themselves by the open windowpane as they inspected the interior. Apparently satisfied, they jumped down and waved. The station master blew his whistle. As the carriages shunted forward, the plate displaying the onward route came into view. Japanese ideograms and neatly written English letters listed the new destinations:

OKA-YAMA — KURA-SHIKI — FUKU-YAMA — MI-HARA — HIRO-SHIMA.

I stared at the artless syllables as the train pulled away. Just another town.

Hartley drove us in a jeep through the town — all badly burned, though the castle at the summit of the hill was white as a wedding cake. I asked him of the significance of the police at the station.

"Well, sir, Himeji's the end of the line for Allied personnel right now," he said, struggling with the gearshift as we wound up the hill.

"Is that so?"

A pained look came over his face. "Hiroshima's kind of off limits for the time being, sir," he said.

The castle loomed before us. I remembered the sloping turrets of the medieval fortress from back in July, when our bombers had poured a few hundred tonnes of incendiaries over the town. Miraculously, the castle had survived. Out front, GIs from the local garrison snapped portraits with their Box Brownies. Inside, the rooms were gloomy and austere.

Eugene was sulking. "I'm sure glad you made me come, Harold. What a splendid view!"

From the balustrade at the top of the castle, we could see far into the distance. A burned hamlet huddled beneath us; muddy fields stretched for miles around.

"Okay, Eugene. Give me a break."

There was nothing more to detain us in Himeji, so we went back to the gymnasium where we were billeted and ate a dull dinner of fried spam. Hartley came back later on and invited us into town. I refused, intent on getting my head down, but Eugene's interest was piqued. I heard him stumble back several hours later, stinking of cheap scent and whisky.

The next day was cold, and Eugene was surly. Halfway home, the train halted outside Kyoto. After much confused lumbering, it shunted into a siding, where it stayed for over an hour. Finally, the door opened, and a large man I thought I recognized climbed aboard. Thick set, with big tortoiseshell glasses and a few strands of brown hair scraped over his head, he raised his meaty hand when he saw us. At that moment, the train began to creak backward. He heaved his kitbag up onto the rack, his face brightening as he noticed our green press patches.

"Well, now, the fine men of the *Stars and Stripes*. Always a pleasure."

His accent had a European inflection. *German*? I thought. *Yiddish*?

He extended a thick palm. "Mark Ward. *Chicago Sun-Times*."

"Hal Lynch," I said, shaking his hand.

I remembered where I'd seen him. At a press conference in the council chamber of the Diet a few weeks earlier, he'd been haranguing the incumbent prime minister with a vigour the man clearly found unfamiliar and disconcerting.

Eugene shook his hand sullenly. I suspected he was resentful of the men from the "official" papers and the agencies. The *Stars and Stripes*, Japan itself, was something of a pet project for him, one he disliked having to share with others. The train started to clang along the rails. Ward winced as he eased himself into the seats opposite.

"Lord save us," he said.

"Not quite a first-class Pullman," I ventured.

"Be grateful of small mercies, young man," he replied, jerking his thumb toward the packed Japanese carriages behind us. He twisted his head until his neck cracked; then let out a groan of satisfaction.

"Interesting assignment?"

"Himeji."

He raised his eyebrows in question.

"Set of touristic sketches. About the historic places of Japan. Kinds of places the ordinary GI might like to visit."

A polite nod.

"Castles and such. Famous beauty spots."

Ward squinted at the temple roofs and tall cedars of Kyoto as they skittered past.

"Well. I guess they may as well take a peek at what's left."

I noticed with embarrassment that Eugene was studiously ignoring the man. I speculated on the possible reasons for the train's tardiness. Ward gave a sheepish grin.

"I'm the culprit, I'm afraid," he said. "I was interviewing a major here, local head of procurement, about certain reconstruction contracts he's just awarded to a local nightclub owner."

A cigar emerged from the side pocket of his kitbag, and he flicked a silver lighter at its tip.

"Well, we just couldn't stop talking and so the interview ran over. The major's secretary was kind enough to telephone the station master, who said he'd hold the train until I got there."

Eugene snorted. "Gee, I hope it was worth it." He hoisted his boots onto the seat and buried his face in a two-month-old edition of *Popular Science*.

"Don't worry about Eugene, Mr. Ward," I said. "He likes to keep abreast of his ignorance."

Eugene yawned deliberately, and went off to lie down in another part of the carriage. As the train rolled slowly eastward, Ward puffed at his cigar in the contented manner of a commercial traveller. He seemed to have visited half of the country already, though he said he'd spent most of the war in China.

"I was based in Chengtu for a spell myself," I ventured.

He examined me, as if sizing me up. "Well, perhaps we're kindred spirits, then, Lynch."

He took a flask of whisky from his kitbag and handed it over. I swallowed a glug with relish and he nodded for me to take another.

"Well, that's my sheet. How did you find yourself here, Lynch? You must have seen action, I suppose."

"Well, sure," I shrugged. "Where should I start?"

The train gave a loud shudder as the wheels shuttled on the rails. He glanced outside, where dusk was gathering now in the paddies.

"We have plenty of time."

As I told him about my war, the sound of Eugene's snoring drifted from the next compartment. I felt vaguely resentful — I realized that Eugene hadn't once asked me about my service in all the time we'd been back together. Ward's manner was avuncular and invited confidences. As the train shunted toward Tokyo, he offered me more whisky from his flask as I recalled to him days and nights hunched over the viewfinders in the belly of *Flashing Jenny*, mapping out the country piece by piece.

"You drew up targets for the Super Fortresses?"

"Eyes of the 21st Bomber Command."

The previous September. Arriving at the Isley Field airstrip on Saipan, fresh and bright in our gleaming new photo-converted Superfort, straight off the line. Bombs out, cameras in. At our first briefing with General Curtis LeMay, then head of strategic air operations, we were informed that the best map we had of Japan was from *National Geographic*. Our job was to remedy the situation. All through fall, we flew dozens of missions, debriefing LeMay in his Quonset every day at thirteen hundred, pointing out the spillways of the naval yards; the carriers and cruisers; the munitions factories turning out aircraft engines and locomotives; the heavy guns and rolling stock.

At dawn, one by one, the silver dream-boats floated off from the runways. Dipping with the weight in their bomb bays, they ascended, their fuselages dazzling bright in the first rays of sun. After dark, the ground crewmen sweated it out on the airstrip, puffing cigarettes, gazing fretfully at their watches and up the sky, until the low drone of motors sounded faraway and finally the powerful landing lights lit up the runway and the first returning planes touched precisely down.

In January, we were relocated from Saipan to Harmon Field at Guam to be closer to LeMay. Operations staff were no longer interested in industrial targets, he informed us. Instead, we were to identify the most densely packed residential areas in each Japanese city, and to grade them according to the most inflammable areas.

"The fire raids?" Ward asked.

My scalp prickled. I pictured my map of Tokyo up on the wall, the wards marked in varying shades of grey according to their population. By then we had fire jelly and white phosphorus that would stick to skin, paper, or wood and burn like hell until everything was gone. To the west of Tokyo, the new suburbs were blank white. To the east, the old wards, Fukagawa and Asakusa, were shaded jet black.

"The night of the Tokyo Raid," I said. "Lord God. You could see the flames from two hundred miles away."

Pillars of smoke rising to 18,000 feet. A wave of heat blasting up, the sky bright outside the windows of the plane. My hand pulling hard on the camera crank, over and over again.

"Next week, Nagoya," I said. "Then Osaka. Kobe. We were going to burn the whole damn country to the ground."

Ward's face scrunched up like paper.

By July we were running out of places to bomb. The face in the mirror was twitchy, my body listless and unkempt. My CO ordered me to take a week's leave, which I spent swimming around the reef at Tuman Bay, trying to shake my throbbing headaches and chronic dysentery, convinced that a stink of soot and burning flesh had ground into my skin. Floating on my back in the water. Staring up at the planes in the sky. The day I returned to duty, I was told to prepare for a new photo mission. We were to map out a bombing approach. To identify primary targets around the naval base out in the eastern city of Hiroshima.

Ward was standing over by the window. He hurled out the remains of his cigar, and it flew into the night in a shower of embers.

The next day at thirteen hundred. Operations staff hunched over my prints. LeMay suddenly turned and demanded a primary target. His bulldog face, for a moment, was that of my father.

"That white T-shaped bridge, sir," I blurted. "See? Right in the centre of the city. Clear as day. Couldn't miss it if you tried."

Ward pushed up the window. He turned to me in the darkness as I wiped the perspiration from my forehead.

"Are you bothered by what you did up there, Lynch?"

Floating over that charred plain one week later, eerie and desolate.

"You were just an observer, Hal."

I swallowed. "That's right. I was just an observer."

The train emerged from behind a hill and, for a moment, the track curved around a stretch of coast. Black waves in the distance rippled with moonlight.

He gave a sudden, jaw-cracking yawn.

"Okay, Lynch. Maybe we should get our heads down."

I rubbed my eyes. "You're probably right."

He looked up at the miniature berths, wincing. "Oh, my aching back..."

When we woke, the ruins of Tokyo were appearing in the grey light of dawn. Naked children stood outside ramshackle hovels at the bottom of the embankments, and waved up at the train as we passed. At the station, we slung our kitbags over our shoulders and made our way through the departing crowd. Ward held out his hand to me.

"It was good talking to you, Lynch. Look me up at the press club. There's some folks you might be interested in talking to."

"Okay, Ward. Thanks."

"Well then. I'll see you."

He held up his hand as he shouldered his way through the crowd, off to write up his piece about scandals and corruption. Eugene and I wandered blearily back to the *Stars and Stripes* office to file our own story: "The Touristic GI visits Historic Himeji Castle."

11
THE RYOKAN
(HIROSHI TAKARA)

I woke up in the cavern of the ticket hall to see my breath coming out in clouds. All around me, men and women were giving off little traces of vapour, like a horde of sleeping dragons. I stood up and picked my way around their mats, dodging the pools of milky vomit that stank like rotten soybeans. By the concrete staircase, an old man was shivering and clutching his wretched fingers over his eyes to shield them from the light that filtered down from above.

Smallpox. The people in the tunnels had complained of headaches and chills at first. Then they started to shiver and moan. The rashes came next, spreading amongst them like wildfire: bubbly freckles that crusted into sores and spewed white pus all over their faces, as if they'd been stung by a swarm of wasps. The skin of the sickest ones stayed smooth as glass though. Eerie blotches of purple welled across their bodies like islands on a map. They died almost straight away, their mouths gaping, as if they'd been caught by surprise.

I ordered the children to wear rags over their mouths and to stay well away from the sick. Even so, Koji came to me one morning complaining that he felt exhausted and that his mouth stung. He held up his shirt as I examined him. I was sure I could see a faint flush on his chest.

Outside, a frost had covered the city with a sheet of white that sparkled in the dawn sunlight. It lay crinkled on the waste-ground behind the station and on the jagged mounds of scrap metal. As I wandered toward Ueno Pond, I thought about the tall American in the trench coat who'd come over to talk to us the week before, and who'd been so interested in Tomoko.

The Americans are savages and demons! That's what we'd always been taught. During the war, I'd gazed at the murderous coloured double-spreads in *Boy's Magazine* for hours on end, imagining myself in the midst of a desperate suicide charge, firing a submachine gun at those monsters on the beaches at Guam. *Chun-chun-chun!*

The man had looked stylish and rugged, as he stooped over to talk to us, his camera dangling around his neck. It was some kind of Leica, I thought, a new model I'd never seen before. When he draped it around my neck, I rubbed my thumb over the exposure control and twisted the smooth aperture dial. I felt the weight of the brushed metal in my hands. It was absolutely beautiful. I held up the camera and looked through the rangefinder at the crisp twin images of Tomoko. I didn't want to ever give it back.

My father had owned a camera once. A Rolleiflex, with a hinged back, which a fat customer had given to him at the *bonenkai* party he held to thank his regulars at the end of each year. I liked to take it out and study the embossed foreign letters. One day, my father brought home some photographic film, and for two weeks I'd waltzed around the neighbourhood, a cut-out masthead of the *Yomiuri* newspaper pinned to my jacket, taking "portraits" of the locals: wrinkly old Mrs. Oka from next door; two white-faced *maiko* girls who held their fans over their faces as they stopped in for snacks on their way to a party.

A year before the end of the war, my father received his red call-up papers. I was sent back to Tokyo from the countryside. My mother had been stunned — after all, he'd been a borderline at his age. That Sunday, my father told me to dig out the old camera. He wanted to go up to Ueno Park to see the cherry blossoms before he left to join his unit. There weren't many families stretched out on the grass that year, and no classical music played from picnic gramophones. We laid out our blanket and ate a quiet meal together beneath the trees. Before we left, my father told me to take a photograph, as a souvenir. I lined the whole family up beneath the sprays of white blossom, and waved them into position.

My mother wore her pale blue spring kimono, her hand resting lightly on my father's broad shoulder. Satsuko stood beside them in green and gold. They gazed out serenely, calm and dignified, as all around them, the falling blossom floated hesitantly in the air. After a second, I pressed the shutter to capture the scene. When I tried to wind on the film, the lever resisted. The spool was at an end.

Past the crimson walls of the Imperial University, I climbed up the hill toward the older, more elegant quarter, where the merchants and artists once had their mansions. The grand old villas were mostly still standing, though many were damaged and silent now behind their heavy wooden gates. Further along the road, around the side of the stucco wall, I saw that a tree had splintered in one of the gardens, knocking out a section of brick. I looked up at it, uncertainly. Then I swung myself up by the woolly branches and dropped down onto the other side.

The wide garden was choked with tangled grasses and gnarled ornamental trees. The walls of the main building looked solid and the slanted roof was overlapping with neat slate tiles. But the windows were boarded up, and the fishpond was empty and silted.

It must have been some kind of inn once, I thought, though it had obviously been abandoned now. By the front door, the welcoming statue of a *tanuki* in a pilgrim's hat had toppled over. One of his arms had broken off, though he carried on grinning demonically nonetheless.

The padlock on the front shutters was flimsy and when I hammered it with a rock it quickly sprung open. Beyond the vestibule, ancient pillars of twisted wood supported the low ceiling of a reception hall. Dark patches showed where the rain had seeped in. As I stepped over the threshold, an eerie feeling came over me. I hoped there were no dead bodies inside.

The air was musty and slivers of light fell from cracks in the boarded-up windows. As my eyes adjusted to the gloom, my stomach quivered. Woodblock prints of almost-naked ladies were hung up on the walls. I climbed a wooden staircase to find a hallway, with rooms and nameplates set off to one side. "Peony," "Cherry-Blossom," "Ivy," and "Chrysanthemum." I put my hand to the door of "Peony" and quickly slid it aside.

A dark shape hit my face and I crashed backward. There was a heavy flutter and I gazed up to see a huge black moth, powder thick on its wings like sparkling coal dust.

Light fell into the corridor as I tugged the rotten boards from the windows. Down below was a secret garden with a palanquin in one corner, its fabric rotted away. *It must have been a real high-class place*, I thought — *a retreat for the top brass during the war.*

The tatami was frayed in the rooms, and in "Chrysanthemum," there was a charred patch where someone had lit a fire. But as I opened the cupboards, I found futons and sheets and blankets and pillows. An amazing idea suddenly occurred to me.

Night had fallen by the time I got back to the station. A group of soldiers had penned the kids into a corner, and were snoring away with hairy overcoats pulled over their faces. I stepped over their bodies and shook the children awake.

"Get ready to leave," I said. "First light. We're breaking camp."

They didn't grasp my meaning at first.

"Where are we going?" Aiko asked, rubbing her eyes. "Isn't this where we live?"

"Not any more. I've found somewhere else. A fortress."

"Are there other children?" Koji asked hopefully.

"No. Not yet. But it's a secret. Don't whisper a word to anyone. Promise!"

Shin snorted and rolled over. Koji frowned uncertainly. But Tomoko ran her fingers through her matted hair and knelt down in front of me.

"Hiroshi-kun," she said, "thank you. Please don't trouble yourself. I'll have the children ready to leave first thing in the morning."

In the middle of the night, I woke suddenly to see white lamps bobbing across the sleeping bodies. *Spirits*, I thought, *floating above the corpses of the dead*. Then I realized that the lights were electric torches. Policemen and doctors were pulling back people's heads and inspecting their faces in the pale beams. Every so often, they tugged somebody up and dragged them away into the darkness. A rod of light needled toward us and I shook the children awake. I hustled them to their feet as the figures came toward us. We hurried outside into the freezing night as the frost prickled its way across the iron-hard ground.

The house stood silent and ghostly in the morning mist. My heart flooded with relief. I'd almost convinced myself it would have disappeared overnight, like some enchanted foxes' palace. I led the children over the gap in the wall and on through the garden. They started to rub their eyes and laugh. They couldn't quite believe it.

"It's not really ours, is it, big brother?" Koji said. He pulled off his sandals and slid across the tatami of the reception hall.

"It is now!" I shouted.

I ran inside and the others came after me, letting out loud whoops and war cries as we slid crazily along the floor, tripping and tumbling into a hysterical heap.

We got to work cleaning the place up straight away. The children took cloths and buckets from the kitchen, while I pulled away the last rotten boards from the windows. As daylight flooded the hall, I saw how run down the building actually was. The wooden walls were splintered and the paper screens were torn. But for the rest of the day, we swept the floors and pushed rags up and down the corridors with our shirts off. Clouds of dust smothered Aiko and Tomoko as they beat the futons, while Koji and Nobu splashed each other with suds and had a sword fight with their broomsticks.

Shin, though, came over to me with a sly look on his face.

"What's so funny?"

He sniggered. "I suppose you know what this place used to be, don't you?"

My cheeks throbbed. I'd taken down the pictures of the ladies the day before, and hidden them at the bottom of a cupboard upstairs.

"An inn, I would have thought," I said. "Some kind of high class place."

He gave a low laugh, then made a circle with his thumb and forefinger and thrust the index finger of his other hand through it repeatedly.

"My father told me all about it."

By the end of the afternoon, the rooms were airy and the blankets fresh and clean. Nobu found a small bathhouse beyond the kitchen with a big cedar tub, and a smaller, family bathroom set off to one side. Part of the roof was missing and most of the tiles were cracked. I heaved the handle of the pump, and there was a great gasp of pipes from deep within the building, but nothing came out of the faucet except a long, spindly insect.

There was a shout. "Hiroshi-kun! Come and look!" Nobu

had discovered a large copper boiler with dials and an oil burner. After a few experiments, we managed to get it to hold a flame. As I turned a wheel, we heard gushing and the clank of machinery, and wisps of steam began to rise from the boiler. I went to the pump and tried the handle again. With a tremble of metal, a stream of water started to emerge, lukewarm at first, but growing gradually hotter.

We marched in triumph back to the hall, where the other children were lying exhausted on the tatami.

"Thanks for all your hard work," I announced. "You're all very tired. But now as a reward, we're all going to have a real bath now, in our very own *sento*!"

We all raced to the bathhouse. Tomoko and Aiko took the smaller room, while us boys took the big one. We started to sing Koji's dirty version of the Air Raid song — *Cover your ears! Close up your bum!* — as we sat on the stools and scrubbed ourselves, the cedar tub gradually filling up.

The filth on our bodies was just incredible. It had been over a year since any of us had washed, and the tiles soon became covered in grimy suds. But then it was just bliss as we sank into the big pool of steaming water, groaning like old folk at a hot springs resort. We heard the girls shrieking with delight in the other room. They must have climbed into their bath at exactly the same moment.

As we lay there soaking, I looked up at the sky through the damaged roof. White clouds were passing overhead, and I imagined that we really were at an *onsen* up in the mountains. After our bath, we'd dress in elegant clothes and dine on floats suspended over the river . . . I heard Tomoko's soft laugh from over the wall and closed my eyes. I pictured her bobbing in the water, her hair wet and stuck to her forehead. Her taut white skin; dark peaks on the bumps of her chest . . .

"Look out!" hollered Shin. "He's lifting the tent up!"

I saw to my horror that I'd gone stiff and I was peeping out of the water. I crashed my fists into the bath.

"Damn you!" I shouted, desperately hoping that the girls hadn't heard him. I got out of the tub and wiped myself down.

Shin was still guffawing, and even Nobu had a little smile on his face.

"Thinking about little Tomoko, I bet!" Shin crowed.

"Shut up," I hissed.

"A fat chance you'd have with her anyway, monster. Your ugly face would drive anyone off."

"Shut up!"

I lifted the wooden plug. Koji wailed as the water began to slurp away down the drain. I glowered at Shin, who was still smirking to himself.

"That's enough," I said. "It's not funny anymore."

Tomoko held Aiko's hand as they emerged from their bathroom. Her hair was damp and she smelled fresh. My stomach squirmed at the thought that she might have overheard Shin's idiotic talk.

"We've found some old clothes upstairs," Tomoko told me. "We're going to dress up and pretend that we're staying at a real inn!"

Aiko was trembling with excitement. She tugged Tomoko's hand and they both laughed as they raced upstairs.

Nobu found an old pair of spectacles and sat on the stool of the office. In a wheedling voice, he pretended to greet the guests. Koji rolled up a cone of newspaper and put it on his head, then sat cross-legged on the floor with a broom in his hands and plucked the strings of an imaginary shamisen. Shin tied a blue rag around his head as if he was a chef and, on a hibachi from the kitchen, toasted the rice balls we'd brought with us from the station.

Giggling came from the staircase. Tomoko and Aiko were stepping carefully down. I stared at them in surprise. They wore old, embroidered kimonos, rolled up at the hem to stop them from tripping. They had found some powder and makeup too, and had painted their faces white and lips red, like clumsy geisha.

Shin clapped his hands and started to sing a dirty song, but I shot him a ferocious look and he trailed off.

Tomoko came over and sat down. As I looked at her, I could hardly speak. She didn't look like a child to me anymore. She seemed like a fresh, delicate bud, about to burst into bloom. We sat around the grill, and she and Aiko served us water from a teapot in saké cups. As she leaned over to fill my cup, my hand started to shake so much that I spilled water onto the floor.

Koji grabbed the teapot and swigged from it. He started reeling, shouting in a slurred voice that he was drunk. He tumbled over as the other children cackled. I glanced at Tomoko. She had her arm around Aiko and was smiling at Koji like a proud mother. She caught my gaze and held my eye.

I remembered the bump of her chest beneath my hand as we stood on the coupling on the train back to Tokyo; the warmth of her cheek as we lay together on the station floor. I felt an acute, guilty pleasure as she came over and sat next to me, a faint smile on her face. She took my hand and gently pressed it between her own.

It was a soft, wonderful pressure, warm and enclosing. It could have only lasted a few seconds, but it seemed to capture the strange, magic vividity of those past months entirely.

I leaped up with a short, braying laugh. I pulled my hand away.

"Right," I shouted. "Everybody up. It's time for bed."

The children groaned as I hopped around, kicking at their legs.

"Come on. We're not here on holiday, you know."

The children trudged sulkily upstairs to the rooms where Tomoko had laid out the blankets: "Cherry-Blossom" for the boys, "Ivy" for her and Aiko. I rubbed my eyes, my heart whirling.

"Well, goodnight," I said.

Tomoko and I bowed to each other shyly, then we went to curl up in new blankets. The mattress was deliciously soft after all those months on the cold, hard stone, but as I lay there, I hardly even noticed. My heart was pounding so hard that I was terrified the others would hear. From the other side of the sliding wall, Aiko whispered something, but Tomoko gently shushed her, and their lamp was soon extinguished. Reluctantly, I blew out our own. I closed my eyes, picturing Tomoko in my mind as I fell asleep. Her clumsily painted lips. The pale skin of her throat. The soft swell of her kimono.

12
ENGLISH-SPEAKING PEOPLE (SATSUKO TAKARA)

The sign I had tacked up for Hiroshi on the wall of Tokyo Station was tattered now, the ink terribly smeared from the rain. I stood shivering in my thin coat as a group of ex-soldiers huddled around a refuse fire nearby, playing flower cards. An old woman squatted beneath a sign of her own, and gave me a sympathetic smile.

"Don't give up hope!" she mouthed, fumbling with her prayer beads. Not many people came to look for their lost relatives anymore. In fact, we were the only two here today.

I smiled back, faintly.

What would her expression be like, I wondered, if, instead of my grey dress and sweater, I had been wearing my night time clothes, my face plastered white and my lips red? What would Hiroshi himself think, even if he did miraculously appear? To discover that his big sister was nothing now but a shameless American butterfly?

It had been weeks since my last trip here, and I felt dreadfully guilty for neglecting my duty to him. They were bringing up children's bodies from the tunnels every morning now, desperately thin and blistered with smallpox. That afternoon,

I'd taken his photograph around the main railway stations, holding it up in the faces of the filthy men and women. They squinted for a moment, then sucked their rotten gums before shaking their heads. As I looked at them all, stretched out on their mats across the ticket hall, I felt completely hopeless. Perhaps I should simply accept the fact that he was gone.

I walked back into the station to take the train back to Shinagawa. A swarm of filthy brats were clamouring around the passengers disembarking onto one of the long-distance platforms. They slipped their little hands into the travellers' coat pockets as they took down their suitcases, while others grubbed about on the floor like insects, clutching for the cigarette butts that the waiting passengers dropped.

My heart froze. There, right in the middle, I could see Hiroshi. I started to run, my heels skidding on the marble floor.

"Hiroshi!" I screamed. "Hiroshi-kun!"

I thrust my way onto the platform, barging through the crowd of passengers. When I finally reached him, he was scrabbling around someone's feet. I seized his arm, rubbing the dirt from his face with my handkerchief.

The boy shook me off, swearing horribly in a strange voice. As I looked at his face, I realized that it wasn't Hiroshi at all. The boy squinted at me as I tried to catch my breath.

"Miss?" he spat, turning. "You can wipe this if you want."

He was holding his penis in his filthy hand, a gleeful expression on his face. I gasped, spun on my heel, and hurried away as fast as I could.

When I reached our alley, I paused by the door of our tenement shack. There was a radio playing inside — a sentimental children's song that I hadn't heard for years. In fact, I could last remember hearing it with Hiroshi and my mother, at the old merry-go-round in Hanayashiki Park, one Sunday on my monthly day off from the factory.

Come, come, come and see
Furry friends beneath the tree
In the autumn moonlight
At Shojo-ji Temple!

The song brought back all sorts of memories. I stood there in the alley for a moment, lost in thought.

I slid open the door. Michiko was sitting at the table with her ear close to the speaker of an ornate radio. She had a look of intense concentration on her face.

"Michiko!" I hissed, but she waved an urgent hand to the floor beside her and gestured at me to be quiet. The song carried on. But though the tune was familiar, I realized that the words were quite different. In fact, they were in English.

Come, come everybody
"How do you do?" and "How are you?"
Won't you have some candy?
One, and two, and three four five . . .

Michiko was trying to mouth along to the words.

Let's all sing a happy song
Tra-la, la la la!

She looked up at me in glee.

"I'm learning English!" she whispered excitedly.

A man's voice began to speak from the radio and she turned back with what she clearly thought was a studious expression, which mainly involved frowning and nodding at everything the man said.

Another one of Michiko's crazes! I thought, as I sat down on the other side of the table. But, as I listened, the programme did seem quite fun. The presenter's name was "Uncle," and it was the same man who had translated the Emperor's speech into common language back in the summer. Now, it seemed, he was going to teach the Japanese people how to speak English.

Uncle was very kind. He explained that the lessons wouldn't be like school, in fact, they would be more like us playing a game together through the radio. We sat there, fascinated, and after a while, even I tried to repeat some of the English words back to him. I found myself smiling and nodding as the theme song came on at the end. The new words were already standing in for the old ones in my memory.

"Satsuko!" Michiko exclaimed, after the programme had ended. "We can listen to this and become proper English speakers. Just imagine."

We already knew some English, of course, from our dealings with the Americans, but I had a feeling that none of it was especially suitable for polite company.

"'How are you? How do you do?'" Michiko said, imitating

Uncle's manly voice. Suddenly, in a fit of laughter, she leaped up, took my hands in hers, and began to spin me around.

"'How are you? How do you do?'" she sang, over and over.

Finally she let go of my hands and sighed. "Just think, Satsuko," she mused, as she poured water into the teakettle. "Now we really will be 'New Women of Japan.'"

I suddenly remembered what I had wanted to ask her. "The radio, Michiko. Where did you get it from? Surely, you didn't buy it yourself?"

"Ah! The radio," she said. "It is handsome, isn't it?"

"Yes," I said. "It certainly is. I wonder where it could have possibly come from?"

"It was a present," she replied. "Isn't it lovely?"

"Another present, Michiko? Anyone would think you had a rich old man off somewhere!"

But she just smiled mysteriously, as if she hadn't heard, and then poured out the tea, still humming away to herself: "How are you? How do you do?"

The afternoon was gloomy as I walked through the ruins of Asakusa. I had promised myself that I would visit the site of our old home, to light some incense for my parents, and for Hiroshi, now that I'd decided that he was gone.

The white-haired American officer had taken Michiko off for the day. The night before, she'd joined the band on the stage, a red plastic rose in her hair. She'd smiled into the piano player's eyes, then sung into the silver microphone in her birdlike voice, pausing every now and then to throw out little expressions that she'd learned from Uncle English. The officer sat below her, his legs spread wide, laughing and clapping along.

Empty brick shells were all that were left of the trinket stalls along Nakamise arcade. A cat scuttled along the low, broken walls to escape the streaks of rain. At the end of the arcade, the Senso Temple had more or less vanished. All that was left was a big gravel precinct, charred stumps of the ginkgo trees and craters full of muddy water, crinkling in the drizzle. I shook my head sadly as I turned to walk toward Umamichi Street.

How dismal it all was now! I thought. Even when I'd been a girl, there'd been *kaminari-okoshi* sweets and bear paw charms. Fortune tellers, jazz dancers, and troupes of actors; the overhanging stalls painted with bright scenes from the kabuki, selling wood prints and postcards and wind-up toys. Pots billowing with fragrant steam and the mouth-watering smells from the *yakitori* sellers as they brushed their smoking skewers with delicious sauces, the serving girls running between the tables, the oil lanterns bathing the street with a soft, rosy glow.

The war had sucked all of the colour away. All that were left now were hovels of rotten planks and sagging tarpaulin, the streets all churned to mud.

I finally found the square cistern in the middle of our alley. But I couldn't make out the site of our home anymore. Eventually, I found a burned patch a little way on, which I thought must be about right, and I wedged my sticks of incense into the black mud. It took me a whole box of matches to get them lit and water dripped down my neck as I stood up to say a prayer.

The sky seemed to turn several shades darker. All of a sudden, the rain began to hurtle against my umbrella, and I had the intense feeling that I wasn't welcome there. It was if my mother and father were standing behind me, ashamed and angry, hissing at me to go away. The impression grew so vivid that I became quite frightened. I hitched up my skirt and hurried away down the alley, stopping only to glance back at the incense sticks, still smoldering in the rain.

The tram was packed on the way back home, the windows misted with grimy condensation. An ex-soldier was squashed up against me, a short man of about forty. The brim of his army cap poked into my nose. I could tell by the dirt on his neck and the sour smell that he hadn't washed for quite some time. I closed my eyes and hoped that Michiko would be there by the time I got back.

A cold hand grasped me between the legs and I froze. The man in the cap was staring at my shoulder, his lips writhing beneath his dirty moustache. His hand clasped me firmly and squeezed and I shut my eyes, burning with shame. Tears welled up in my throat as his fingers gripped harder.

I suddenly opened my eyes again. *What right did he have to do this?* I thought. *Did he think he could touch me without paying? Who did he think he was?*

I jerked my shoulder violently into his face.

"Pervert!" I shrieked, "You filthy pervert! You think you can just grab anyone you want?"

The passengers jostled around us, happy for the diversion on such a rotten day.

"Who do you think you are?" I said. "Are you such a hero? You couldn't even win the war. You should be ashamed of yourself!"

The man stared blankly at the floor. His lips fluttered and, for a moment, I didn't know whether I felt hatred or pity. The tram shuddered to a halt, and I elbowed my way through the crowd and jumped down into the wet street. As the tram clanked off, the passengers stared at me through little rubbed windows in the condensation.

I realized I had left my umbrella on the tram in all the confusion, so I was quite soaked by the time I got home. When I arrived, the house was cold. Michiko was nowhere to be seen.

I let out a sob. I took the bottle of whisky from the cupboard and poured myself a cup. The fiery liquor soothed my stomach, and I sat on the floor, stock still, listening to the rain as it thrashed against the roof.

Michiko was probably off at some expensive restaurant or inn with her rich new lover, I thought. I started to feel quite sorry for myself and I poured myself another large cup of whisky. Then, though I tried to resist, my thoughts drifted to Osamu. I remembered the time he'd taken me to a comic show at the Café D'Asakusa, how the students had howled with laughter. I remembered the look of disbelief on his face the day he had received his call-up papers. He'd trembled and stammered — his mother should have applied for exemption, he said; he was an only son after all. I remembered his thin, muscular body in the back room of the Victory Hotel, after he'd come to our house on the night of his leaving ceremony. I wished now that I had let him do what he had wanted much earlier. I'd been with so many others since then, after all. If I had given in to him sooner, I would have those times to remember now as well, not just that solitary night, when he'd shuddered with joy once before falling asleep next to me. The next day, we'd waved them all off at the station. The soldiers wearing their thousand-stitch belts, sewn with good luck tokens, wrapped tight around their bellies. His mother refusing to look at me, and the women from the Defence Association cheering as the train pulled away: *Congratulations on being called to the Front!*

I wondered if memories were like precious porcelain that should only be brought out on special occasions; whether they were like fruits that lost their lustre if they spent too long in the sun. If that was the case, I told myself, I would have to be careful how often I thought of Osamu now. Or of my parents; or Hiroshi, for that matter. I didn't want my memories of them to shrivel away like withered flowers. They were the only thing I had left of them now, after all. Except the charred scrap of my mother's kimono. And the teakettle, of course . . .

The door slid open and Michiko came crashing in. She tumbled amongst the pots and pans, making a terrible racket. Then she started to sing so loudly that I was terrified she would wake the neighbours.

"Michiko," I hissed, "be quiet!"

She stumbled toward me.

"Satsuko," she wailed. "Satsuko, help me. I'm so drunk!"

She slumped down onto the floor and clasped me around the neck, giggling.

"He's in love with me!" she shouted. "He wants me to be his only one!"

I clamped my hand over her mouth. I was sure I didn't want to hear her secrets, least of all in the middle of the night. Viciously, she bit my finger and burst into laughter. Then she slid over, waving her head from side to side.

Suddenly, she sat bolt upright and made an odd sound. She rushed over to the door and heaved it open. The she fell onto her hands and knees, and retched in the alley outside.

~

The next morning, when I awoke, Michiko was already up. She was wearing a pale green dress, standing over the stove, from which a delicious smell was rising.

When she saw me, she smiled and knelt down on the floor in front of our futon.

"Please forgive me, Satsuko, for my juvenile behaviour last night. It must have been very discomforting for you."

I admitted that she had seemed rather drunk, but said that she should think no more about it. She smiled, and bowed again.

"Now Satsuko," she said. "Please come and have your breakfast."

She opened up the pot on the stove, and I cried out when I saw what was inside. A silver fish, a herring, I thought, was bubbling away in a sauce of miso and saké. The aroma was just wonderful, and I glanced at the door to check that it was closed — the neighbours would have been madly jealous if they had smelled the food.

"Wherever did it come from, Michiko?"

She raised her eyebrows and put her hands in the air, performing a little swaying dance. Then she drew an envelope from inside her dress and handed it to me.

"Look."

I gasped. The envelope was full of money, an astonishing

amount, more than we could have possibly earned even if we'd worked at the Oasis for months.

"What are you going to do with it?" I asked. "Save it up?"

She gave a short laugh. "No, Satsuko. First we're going to have some breakfast. Then I'm going to get some sleep. And then, you and I are going shopping."

~

The Matsuzakaya department store might have been burned out, but the Mitsukoshi had reopened and I felt a thrill as we stepped through its wide doors. The shop had always been famous for its opulence and luxury, and even its wrapping paper had seemed beyond the means of a family like mine. But there wasn't much opulence or luxury left now, I thought, as we walked amongst the empty shelves and rails. An icy draft was blowing through the place and there was a crunch of rubble beneath the torn carpet underfoot. The staff stood about shivering in their uniforms. They didn't look quite so haughty anymore.

They scuttled after Michiko as if she were a noblewoman visiting from her country estate. She picked up a dress here and a shawl there, telling the attendant to wrap them and have them delivered to our house. But when she gave the address, they looked at us suspiciously. After all, Shinagawa wasn't the kind of place that anyone would have associated with nobility. From then on, I had the distinct feeling they were giving us dirty looks and muttering behind our backs, as if they knew that there was only one way girls like us could afford to shop at the Mitsukoshi.

"Please can we go now, Michiko?" I whispered. Michiko glanced at the assembled staff, and a mischievous gleam came into her eyes.

"Yes, Satsuko," she said in a loud voice. "Perhaps you're right. Let's leave all this rubbish behind and go down to the Shimbashi blue-sky market instead. After all, there's so little to buy here!"

And she flounced out the door as they bowed down low, their faces frozen. She burst into laughter as soon as we got out into the street.

"Those stuck-up prigs!" she cried. "No one looks down on me anymore, Satsuko!"

In fact, there wasn't a great deal to buy at the Shimbashi blue-sky that day either, and Michiko finally had to be content with some sheer silk stockings and a floral scarf that the old woman claimed was from Paris. Just as we were leaving, we passed another stall, piled high with old, elegant kimonos.

I froze. Right on top, was something I recognized intimately. A beautiful green kimono, embroidered with golden peonies. The kimono that my mother had bought me on my sixteenth birthday, and which I'd been forced to sell to buy rice.

I leaned over to touch the hem with my fingertips, remembering at once how fine the stitching was, how delicate the embroidery. All sorts of memories and feelings passed through me then. Michiko must have noticed my expression, because the next thing I knew she was airily asking the stallholder how much it cost.

"Don't be silly, Michiko!" I said, but she shushed me and asked the stallholder again. As I suspected, the price was many, many times more than I had been paid, but without even bargaining, Michiko snapped out four hundred-yen notes from her purse and handed them over.

"Michiko, please! Don't be ridiculous!" I begged.

But the woman was already wrapping the kimono in colourful crêpe paper and tying it with a ribbon. When she had finished, Michiko wordlessly took it from her and handed it to me.

Then, I started to cry, for the first time in many months. As I stood there, shaking with sobs, I remembered how my mother had helped me dress in the kimono with such pride in her eyes; how Osamu had noticed me wearing it at the Spring Festival, and had strolled over to compliment me, blinking with embarrassment.

I remembered the face of his horrible mother, the day I'd gone to her villa, trembling with nerves, to ask if there'd been any news of him from the South Seas. Her mouth puckered, as if she'd been sucking a sour apricot.

"Dead," she had hissed. "Shot in the stomach. Now get away, you slut."

I was sobbing so much now that the woman who owned the stall sidled round and took my arm, patting it affectionately until I had recovered.

Later on that evening, after dinner, Michiko brushed my hair and made me try on the kimono again. It was as beautiful as ever, though quite loose around my shoulders. I hadn't quite noticed how thin I'd become. Michiko insisted on painting my face and then held up a mirror so that I could see my reflection. She took out a small vial and began to scrape a bright red paste onto my fingernails. To my horror, they began to turn crimson.

"What on earth are you doing, Michiko?" I said.

"Don't be so old fashioned, Satsuko," she said. "It's just nail rouge. One of the Americans gave it to me. It's very modern."

I was suspicious at first, but finally I gave in and let her colour them all. Afterward she poured us both some whisky and we giggled together for a while before going to bed.

Michiko left me not long after that. Her white-haired officer — a General, or Admiral, it seemed — wanted to set her up in an apartment of her own in Akasaka, where he could visit her whenever he chose.

"Michiko," I murmured, after she told me. "Perhaps I could come and visit you sometimes. I could even come and stay, to help you get settled in —"

"No, Satsuko," she said quickly, shaking her head, "You can't, he's very jealous, you see. He'll expect me to be there at all hours."

A hard lump grew in my throat.

"Well then," I said. "It doesn't matter."

Michiko clung onto my arm, and rubbed her face against my shoulder.

"What do you think you will do now, Satsuko?" she finally asked.

"Well," I said with a forced smile. "I imagine I will just carry on working at the Oasis. With all the other less beautiful girls."

Michiko's face crumpled and she burst into tears. She hugged me, burying her face in my hair.

"But you *are* beautiful, Satsuko," she cried, "You are!"

But whether I was or not, at the end of that week, a swish black sedan rolled up outside, and a driver came in to help Michiko move her things. He loaded up her trunks of dresses and gowns, her boxes of creams and vials. She strapped on her new high-heeled shoes and took one last look at our leaky room, then embraced me and tottered outside. With a wave, she clambered into the back seat. The chauffeur closed the door and, with a whining engine, the car reversed back down the alley.

13
NO.1 SHIMBUN ALLEY
(HAL LYNCH)

A grizzled mongrel nosed about in the dark fluid that welled from a broken standpipe on a street of ruined buildings near Yurakucho Station. On the front of the dilapidated hotel was a hand-painted sign: *Tokyo Foreign Correspondent's Club*. A staff car ground to a halt in the dirt road outside and I followed two Allied colonels up the worn steps, through a set of glass doors to a lobby, where correspondents stood in telephone booths, dictating stories. After a creaking ascent in the iron elevator, the old operator wrenched open the guardrail to reveal a hallway, redolent with the smoke of pipes and cigarettes and cigars. Two Japanese busboys bowed, and swung open a further set of doors. A polyglot clamour emerged from within.

The ballroom was crowded. A gleaming baby grand stood in the centre, a white-haired diplomat in dinner dress at its stool, holding uproarious court to his obsequious coterie. A clump of reporters harangued a U.S. Army major who spread out his hands in defence as their pencils jabbed the air around him. A pair of British naval captains, white caps under their arms, stood with woollen socks pulled high, being cheerfully molested by two old ladies in grey chiffon and horn-rimmed glasses. To the side of the room, crumpled correspondents interviewed nervous-looking Japanese; Chinese generals slumped on sofas and Allied officers sat drinking with women too pretty to be their wives. Between the encampments went Japanese boys in red and gold uniforms carrying trays laden with square bottles of whisky, delivering glasses, squirting soda siphons, slipping their tips into their side pockets and tapping them for good luck.

"Glad you could make it," growled Mark Ward as he materialized by my side. He gave a lopsided grin when he noticed my expression.

"Where are we, Ward? Casablanca?"

An exquisite Japanese lady came down the steps, her black hair piled high to show a snow white neck, a string of silvery pearls tracing the prow of her ruffled silk dress. I knew her, I thought — the pin-up from the Oasis club, who had sat on McHardy's lap that night. She was moving up in the world. A grizzled, white-haired Third Fleet admiral barged forward to greet her, and she let out an almost genuine cry of delight as she took hold of his outstretched hands.

Ward led me into the crowd, signalling to a boy for drinks.

"This is the nerve centre, Lynch — the reliquary!"

The boy handed me a glass of raw Japanese whisky and I took a large gulp.

"Who runs the show here?" I said.

"We do."

"How's that?"

"Wherever newsmen gather in the world, Lynch, needs must that they have a bar. Without such a place, stories go untold, confidences unshared. Last September, MacArthur decided that

Japan didn't need any special correspondents, with their irritating habit of independent thought and inquiry. He stopped giving them billets. So we took over this place instead."

A grunt came from behind us and a heavy hand fell on Ward's shoulder. Two bulky, shaven-headed men glared at us. One pushed Ward contemptuously on the arm, as the other jerked a warty thumb toward his mouth and emitted a phrase in some Slavic language. Ward grinned.

"Lynch, meet Gorbatov," he said. "Boris One. The other fellow's Agapov. Boris Two. Don't ever get them confused or they'll break your arm."

"Good evening, comrades."

Boris One jerked his bare head at Ward. "We drink soon," he ordered, as they headed off together toward the bar. Ward smiled as he watched them go.

"Friends of yours?"

"If you ever want insight into the dark recesses of the Soviet mind, Lynch, they're the men you should talk to. Oh, look who's over there . . ."

As we worked our way toward the back of the ballroom, Ward recounted his mental encyclopedia of all those present. At the piano, the diplomat prodded the ivories to delighted applause. The notes of a Chopin sonata floated through the ballroom.

"Anyhow," Ward said. "We're all in the library. Something that ought to interest you."

"Oh?"

We proceeded down a corridor to an under-lit, smoke-filled room. A couple of cracked leather armchairs had been set up and dozens of foreign and Japanese newspapers were draped over wooden rails. A crowd of men, waistcoats lined with pencils, shoes scuffed, were gathered around a wide table. A man with a thick brown quiff sat, gesturing at a series of photographs laid out under a green-shaded lamp.

"A friend from Chicago," Ward murmured. "George Weller. Just got back from an unauthorized trip."

As we slid into the huddle, a couple of men nodded at Ward in greeting.

"The Mitsubishi shelters were useless, of course," Weller was saying. "They were at the epicentre of the blast. The factory makes a strange sight now, I must say — like a metal ribcage, only all the bones are bent outward."

I stiffened. I knew with instant conviction what he was talking about. We'd flown over the big Mitsubishi works at Nagasaki a month before the city was A-bombed. Torpedoes and ammunition for the Japanese navy were manufactured there, and I'd been surprised to see the place still standing. A graceful city by the seaside, just like Hiroshima, sprinkled with the spires of Christian churches.

"Most of those that died did so straight away, or within a few hours of the blast," Weller continued. "But then something else happened. Something strange."

Weller held up a photograph of a ruddy-faced Japanese girl, smiling into the camera with a knapsack on her back. I suddenly recalled the thin girl and her scarred boyfriend at the back of Ueno station.

"This young girl escaped the blast itself with no more than a burn on her leg. She left the city that day to stay with relatives. She came back two weeks later. Days after she returned, she looked like this."

Another photograph. The girl was sitting up in a hospital bed now. She had the look of a scarecrow — bald patches on her head, prickles covering her skin as if she had been dragged through a thorn bush. The garbled tale of the trembling girl came back to me in flashes.

"This is her two weeks later."

The girl once more. Withered almost to a skeleton now. Completely bald, her body covered in thick welts.

Weller paused, gauging the reaction of the men.

"But here's the thing, gentlemen. This girl didn't start to get sick until she came back to Nagasaki. And that was three weeks *after* the blast."

The men scrutinized the photographs as Weller handed them around. They muttered soft prayers and obscenities before passing them on. I studied the print of the girl. She looked up with empty eyes from a frayed hospital mat, dark blood clotted beneath her nose.

"What is this, George?" Ward asked.

Weller shook his head, lit a cigarette.

"The doctors won't make a diagnosis. Because they don't know how to diagnose it. It's sinister."

"Does it have a name?"

"No. For now, it's just Disease X."

Ward glanced at the photograph in my hand, then took it and placed it carefully back down on the table.

"What's the official take?" Ward asked.

"Headquarters don't buy it. Or they don't want to buy it. They say it's a scam. That the Japs are looking for sympathy. Easier terms."

Weller unfurled a newspaper. To my dismay, I saw it was a

copy of *Stars and Stripes* — the same copy, in fact, that had our piece on Himeji Castle printed toward the back, just before the sporting green.

"This is from one Colonel Warren, of the University of Rochester medical school."

"That august institution," Ward murmured, to snorts of amusement.

"He states, quote: 'There absolutely is not, and never was,' — note that," said Weller, his finger raised, "'any dangerous amount of radiation in that area.'"

He paused. He had the men's entire attention now.

"'The radioactivity of a luminous dial wrist watch is one thousand times greater than that found at Nagasaki.'"

He set the newspaper down on the table.

"Do any of you gentlemen wear a luminous dial wristwatch?"

A few raised forearms.

"Ever find your intestines choked with blood? Blood spots in your bone marrow?"

Furrows spread across the assembled brows.

My mouth was dry. I raised my hand. "Mr. Weller?"

He glanced up. I swallowed as the faces of the other men swivelled toward me.

"Disease X. Has it been reported in Hiroshima also?"

Weller shrugged.

"God alone knows. Both cities are now out of bounds. Under penalty of court-martial."

I pictured the MPs loping along the platform, scrutinizing the Allied carriage for passengers. Vast cogs seemed to be moving, somewhere far out beyond my vision. *The bomb made her sick*? The boy's fervent nod. "So, *desu*."

Ward stepped forward. "When's this going out, George?"

Weller stubbed out his cigarette with sudden bitterness, then slumped back into his chair. "It's not."

Incredulous noises came from the assembled men.

"How so?"

"I was fool enough to file it in Tokyo. Headquarters have killed it. Every last word. Diller told me I was lucky to still be in the country. I doubt I will be much longer."

Noises of anger and disenchantment came from all sides of the room. Ward slid behind Weller's chair and raised big, calming hands.

"Okay boys, here's what we do. We form a delegation, we go to Diller. We impress upon him that this is unacceptable censorship . . ."

I barely heard him. The photograph of the girl was propped up against the lamp, her eyes boring into my own. The newspaper had fallen open at our story, and I saw the photograph I'd taken outside Himeji Castle: Eugene holding up a samurai sword, baring buck teeth with a ferocious expression.

I pushed urgently out of the library. The noise and chatter of the ballroom washed over me again, along with the frenzied crescendo of the Chopin sonata. I signalled urgently to a boy for a drink and when it came, I threw it back, feeling the alcohol liquefy the pressure in my temple, my pulse slackening. The men began to stream out of the library as the meeting wrapped up. They lit cigars and made a beeline for the bar. Ward approached me, thick eyebrows raised.

"Everything okay, Lynch?"

"Fine. Little claustrophobic."

He nodded. "Pretty strong salts, huh?"

"Yes. Pretty strong."

"Another drink?"

"Some other time."

"Okay Lynch. Make sure you come again."

A thick cloud of blue smoke curled over the animated crowd as I weaved out and took the elevator back down to the lobby. I strode into the cold night, stumbling through the refuse and mud. Just before the junction, I glanced up at a building. The front was still there, but the back was missing, like the façade of scenery in a cheap Western. You could see right through the walls, and where the roof should have been were stars.

I bought a pint of whisky from a hood at the Ginza crossing, and swigged at it as I strode back home. At the Continental, I lay down on my bed and swilled some more. Then I switched off the light, still fully clothed, and drank in the darkness until the face of the skeletal young girl had dissolved from my mind.

Down in the dusty basement of the press club, I scoured archive boxes of newspapers for any article concerning the A-bombings of Hiroshima and Nagasaki. There was precious little to read. Access to both areas was interdicted now, and there were no official reports on the state of things in either city. The London *Express* had carried a report by a correspondent named Burchett who had raced down to Hiroshima in advance of our lines. "The Atomic Plague!" screamed the ghoulish headline — but the article itself had been suppressed and the copy in the archive was scored with thick black ink that stained my fingers. There was the set of photographs in *LIFE*, the surrender issue, which showed the familiar ruined plain of Hiroshima from above, and made the brief, tantalizing reference to the reports from local doctors of bleeding gums. But the article abruptly cut to a consideration of the future of war and the place of the atom bomb within it, and no more reference was made to its victims.

The only other piece was in the *New York Times*, by a man named Laurence. He'd flown as official observer upon the *Bockscar* to Nagasaki. His writing was lyrical, almost poetic, as he described the swollen tub being loaded into the bomb bay on Tinian.

"A thing of beauty to behold, this gadget," he wrote, as if extolling the virtues of a new refrigerator or vacuum cleaner. The pilot had taken the bomb up to 17,000 feet, and from there, in the air-conditioned cabin of a reconfigured Superfort, Laurence had pondered the fates of those on the ground below.

"Does one feel any pity or compassion for the poor devils about to die? No. Not when one thinks of Pearl Harbour and of the death march on Bataan."

I'd heard the line so many times already, it seemed almost worn smooth by repetition.

His tone became rapturous, almost sexual, as he described the blast and the mushroom cloud exploding into the sky:

"The smoke billows upward, seething and boiling in a white fury of creamy foam, sizzling upward, descending earthward..."

Floating over that desolate plain. The city swept away. *Poor devils.*

The end of the article was puzzling. As if in pre-emptive defence, Laurence emphasized the official line: there was no "mysterious sickness" caused by radiation in either of the two A-bombed cities. Any such reports were "Jap propaganda," wily attempts to wring concessions from the Allied powers, a cynical ploy to win sympathy from the American people, with their big hearts and deep pockets.

I lay the paper down, and closed my eyes.

~

Hibiya Park was located auspiciously. To the north lay the Imperial Palace, aloof and remote behind its moat and thick stone walls. At its eastern corner stood the granite fortress of the Dai-ichi Insurance Building, now General Headquarters of the Supreme Command of Allied Powers — SCAP — as contained in the body of General MacArthur, Japan's most recent and now omnipotent emperor. The country's feudal past and democratic future faced off, so to speak, across its patchy fields, and the park had become Tokyo's premier site for demonstration, a rallying point for the new political parties that had burgeoned in the wake of the war's end.

A small crowd was gathered when I arrived. Up on the bandstand, a stout man in a green jersey was striding about like a boxer, bawling through a whistling microphone. Jeeps lined the flowerbeds, military policemen observing the events. The crowd seemed very much of a type — early middle age, circular spectacles, drawn faces. Despite the bitter cold, they were rapt, cheering loudly as the speaker's hoarse voice rolled across the park. Red flags and banners were unfurled and then came the first, eerie, ululating note of a chant. It was haunting and somehow melancholic and it made the hairs on the back of my neck stand on end. The men began to sing in chorus, their voices welling up above the mud of the park, floating high into the crystalline fall air.

I saw a familiar, bulky figure, who clapped gloved hands and cheered along. I strode over and touched the arm of Mark Ward's thick black woollen overcoat.

He turned to me, his eyes bright behind thick spectacles. "Intoxicating, isn't it?"

A phalanx of men and women started to jog back and forth, waving their banners with balletic fluidity. They danced forward, halted on a dime, then went back the other way. I had a sudden impression of migrating geese, of brittle red maple leaves drifting down along the Hudson. I stood there for a moment, letting the feeling wash over me.

Ward was cheerfully nonplussed by the whole affair. He scribbled briefly into his leather notebook, then slammed it shut.

"Well, that's about enough for one day. How about we get ourselves a drink?"

"That would be grand."

The night's first hookers stood shivering against the trees at the edge of the park, scuttling over in pursuit of the GIs who sauntered along in pairs. All were very young — their breasts hardly made a bump in their sweaters — and they wore motley, mismatched woollen skirts and dowdy jackets. Not many were pretty, but there was a certain sharp eroticism in the air that sprang from their brazen approach. After brief negotiation, they pulled their man off into the melding shadows, and, as the sun went down, the edges of the park came furtively alive with the faint, mingled caterwaul of swift, preprandial copulation.

A girl in a grubby yellow dress skipped over and slid her arm through Ward's, as if we were all out for a pleasant Sunday afternoon promenade.

"Okay, Joe — very cheap!" she promised, swinging his arm from side to side.

"No, sweetheart," Ward said. "I'm not your John. Get on home."

She frowned. "Very cheap —"

He raised a thick finger in warning, and she dropped his arm, glaring at him. With a muttered curse, she peeled off along the path.

"And so the country truly surrenders," Ward said gloomily.

The note of the puritan surprised me. He had mentioned a young wife back in Chicago, whom he hoped to bring over as soon as he was settled.

"At least we pay for it. Unlike our Russian buddies."

He glanced at me sharply. "What good capitalists we are."

The windows of the Dai-ichi building were still lit, the teams of bright young men burning the midnight oil as they drew up their plans for Japan's future. In the plush bar of the Imperial Hotel, an old Japanese band played Ellington covers, while colonels in well-cut uniforms lounged in armchairs, enjoying the first drinks of the weekend. The waiter brought us whisky and I sipped at mine gratefully.

"So, Lynch," Ward said, settling back. "How goes life at the *Stars and Stripes*?"

I shrugged.

"That well, huh?"

"How should I put it, Ward? It's not quite what I visualized when I decided to become a reporter."

"What did you have in mind?"

I considered the question. I pictured the shrewd eyes of the correspondents at the press club, the slumped form of George Weller as he told his uncanny story.

"Something other than 'The Touristic GI.'"

Ward nodded as he slid a large cigar from his breast pocket. He puffed away, squinting at me through the smoke.

"Something eating you, Hal?"

As on the train, I felt encouraged to confide in him. I told him of my hunt through the archives; of the trembling girl at Ueno; of the MPs searching the train at Himeji Station.

He looked at me, then studied the glowing embers of his cigar.

"I'm afraid I'm not a psychologist, Hal."

I hesitated. "I never implied that you were, Mark."

He pointed his cigar at me. "But you must understand that what you witnessed from up there was the greatest feat of destruction in all human history."

"What's your point, Ward?"

He jabbed the air with his cigar for emphasis.

"The fall of Troy. The Sack of Rome. The Mongol Horde. Nothing compared to what happened here. The destruction we achieved in the space of, what, six months? It's no wonder you're a little ... stunned."

I was grateful for his tact. "Shell-shocked" was no longer the current expression in any case.

"What's your take on Disease X, Ward?"

He raised his heavy eyebrows. "You heard Weller. He's a strong reporter."

"You think they're still dying?"

Ward shrugged. "Who knows? You can see why SCAP would want to keep it quiet. It's embarrassing, to say the least. Especially if it turns out they knew it would happen all along."

"I read an article in the *New York Times*. A man named Laurence —"

"William Laurence?" he said, archly.

"That's him."

He shook his big head. "Man's a stooge."

"He is?"

"Sure." He screwed the remains of his cigar into the ashtray. "He's on the army payroll. He's their cheerleader for the bomb."

"Are you serious?"

"Yes I am." He nodded, then grimly swallowed the remains of his drink.

"Are you interested in chasing this, Lynch?"

In my mind's eye, I saw the sparkling inland sea, temple roofs, fishing boats unloading their catch at a silver harbour.

"Might help you sleep at night."

I laughed. "I doubt it."

The place had filled up now. Tables of military men brayed and drank, and I gestured to a passing waiter for the cheque.

"Did you ever meet Wilf Burchett?" asked Ward, as we stood for our overcoats. "The reporter who went down to Hiroshima after we landed?"

I remembered the blocked-out article in the London *Express*.

"He's still here?"

"Not for long. MacArthur's throwing him out. But I'll introduce you if you like."

A blast of cold air met us as we approached the revolving door. It spun about, expelling a group of staff muffled against the cold. A tall Japanese man in a camel coat glanced at us through round spectacles, then placed a hand on the arm of a hawk-like general in an immaculately cut uniform and with hair parted in dark waves, a monocle screwed into his eye socket. The Japanese man muttered something into his ear, and the general stared at Ward for a moment. Ward stared back, rocking on his heels. The general held out his overcoat to a boy and marched into the bar, his subalterns skittering behind him.

Ward's nostrils flared.

"Buddy of yours?" I asked, as he shoved his way through the door. The cold air outside stung my cheeks.

"Major General Charles Willoughby," he said, as he gestured to the doorman for a cab. "G2. Chief of Intelligence. Shady character."

The doorman blew a whistle, and a taxi veered toward us in the road.

"Born Karl Weidenbach in Heidelberg, Germany. 'My own dear fascist,' MacArthur calls him."

The doorman opened the cab and I buttoned up my collar in preparation for the brisk walk back to my hotel. I thought agreeably of my cozy room at the Continental, the old woman who would bring up a little brazier of charcoal whilst I poured myself another drink.

"How do you know him?" I called.

"Willoughby?" he called back as he clambered inside. He threw his cigar butt onto road and stamped on it. "He's just an old pal."

The door slammed shut. The taxi drove off along the road, smoke pouring out into the bitter night.

~

I met Burchett two days later. The room, on the second floor of the press club, was ripe with the aroma of men in close confinement, the unmade beds were draped with newspapers and damp underwear. He was packing his kitbag with stacks of notebooks and clippings. He wasn't British, I realized, but a blunt, amiable Australian with a cynical and amusing manner.

"Lucky you caught me. They're slinging me out next week. The bastards."

He was impressively cheerful. The men at SCAP had removed his press accreditation a month before, a fact which he ascribed to the article he had written, with a typewriter on his knees, in the ruins of Hiroshima, just a few days after we had landed. When I told him I was curious, he raised his eyebrows.

"Oh, you are? Well you're in the minority. I bet they're still dropping like flies. If there's any left of them, that is. We'd not hear a dicky-bird about it in any case."

"How did you get down there?"

"How? I got the bloody train like anyone else. Caused quite a stir, I don't mind telling you. Bunch of army samurai chappies didn't quite take to me."

He described how he had landed with the first parties of marines on a beach near Yokosuka. As soon as he had entered the surreal wreckage of Tokyo, he'd rushed to the station and boarded the first train toward Hiroshima. The carriage had been packed with Japanese officers, bitter and glowering — it had been the day of the surrender signing aboard the *Missouri* — and he'd been the only white man on the train but for an old German priest.

"Drank some of that saké stuff with them though. Seemed to calm things down a bit. Just goes to show, doesn't it?"

"What about Disease X, Burchett? This radiation disease?"

His face became suddenly serious. "Atomic Plague. That's what I called it. At first the locals thought it must have been caused by some kind of poisonous gas from the bomb."

He described stumbling across a makeshift hospital on the outskirts of Hiroshima, scores of people lying on rush mats, deteriorating almost before his eyes.

"Came in complaining of sore throats. Days later, their gums were bleeding. Then their noses, then their eyes." After that, he said, their hair began to fall out. The doctors, desperate, injected them with vitamins, but the flesh rotted away around the puncture points.

"Gangrene," Burchett said, his nose wrinkling with the memory. "You can smell it a mile off."

Some died soon after. Others held out for a while longer, complaining of an overwhelming inertia, a strange, heart-breaking malaise. Then they died too.

Burchett let out a long sigh. "And that, sir, is more or less the size of it."

"Who else knows about this?"

He snorted. "Brass are doing a bloody good job to make sure no one does."

"And do you have photographs?"

"Ha!" he barked. "Did have!"

My stomach tightened. "There's no photographs?"

"Therein lies a tale," he said. "After I got back to Tokyo, I was ordered to visit a military hospital. No doubt to check I wasn't glowing. Two days later, my camera disappeared from my kitbag. Along with my notes, my typewriter, and five rolls of film. 'Sorry Mr Burchett, must have been that shady chap on the other side of the ward.' All very mysterious."

My head began to swim. "There's not a single image of what you've been describing to me?"

He shook his head.

It seemed astonishing, terrifying, that an entire city and its inhabitants could disappear without a trace.

"Unless you chaps took any snaps for posterity. Or the Japs did. Even so, I doubt we'll be seeing any of those at the flicks any time soon."

Wild thoughts swirled around my head.

"Anyway. Need to pack up now, old chap. Getting shipped back to the mother country in the morning. Oh, for London in the winter."

He gave a theatrical shudder and I wished him luck.

"Good luck yourself, mate," he said, looking me straight in the eye. "Believe me, you're going to bloody well need it."

My dreams that night were relentless and harrowing. Standing on a desolate plain, the wind howling around me. An inferno swept from the horizon, fireballs pelting down from the sky. A ruined schoolhouse, a stench of rotting meat. The assembly hall piled with skeletal bodies. A little girl, her mouth agape, her body covered in welts.

Endless corridors, men in pursuit. A door to an office. Behind the desk, a chair. My father. A shotgun barrel in his mouth, still open in a ghastly smile. His brains thickly smeared on the wall behind.

Three days later, I woke early. In the pale light of dawn, I sliced off the *Stars and Stripes* blazon from my jacket and sewed on my lieutenant's epaulettes once again. My knapsack was bulging. I'd visited the PX the night before, packed my bag with chocolate, tins of Spam, a bottle of Crow, and two cartons of Old Golds, along with ten fresh rolls of 35mm Kodak film.

I travelled in the Japanese section of the train, despite the insufferable crush. People blankly made way for me and my uniform, and I squeezed myself into a cramped seat by the cracked window. Babies hoisted on women's backs swung perilously close to my head. The carriage was filled with the tang of unwashed bodies and wet wool. The windows were mostly gone and cold blustered through the carriage all the way.

The inspector looked at me in mortification after examining the ticket I'd had a Japanese boy buy for me at the station. Brow furrowed, he rubbed his hat back and forth over his bald head. I held my fingers to my lips in question, and his eyes lit up. I handed him the first of my packets of cigarettes, a five-dollar bill folded inside. After a moment of shameful deliberation, he gave a sickly grin, slid both into his pocket, and politely clipped my ticket.

The train stopped often throughout the night, halting in lonely tunnels, shunting into sidings for what seemed like an eternity. Snow whirled outside and there were clangs and shouts as men tried to restart the engines. The passengers pressed their faces to the windows to watch, their breath freezing against the broken glass. There was the lonely sound of metal being hammered in the darkness as handcarts of coal were hauled up to the locomotive.

Later on, we passed through Kyoto, where most of the passengers disembarked. A few hours later, I recognized the white alabaster of Himeji Castle up on its hill, pale in the light of a bright full moon. I fell into a troubled sleep against the comforting bulk of a large, warm woman who sat beside me, my pack drawn close against my knees.

I was awoken by the woman jabbing me in the ribs, repeating Japanese words in a loud, obstinate voice. I tried to crawl back into the drowsy shelter of my dreams, but she poked me again, hard, and I sat up, rubbing my eyes.

The carriage was almost empty, and, outside, the first light of dawn lent a rose-grey tint to the horizon. We were passing down onto an immense, bleak plain, rugged mountains looming in the distance. The wheels screamed on the rails as we slowed on our approach to a shattered station. The train shuddered to a halt. The platforms were gone, and there was a sharp drop from the train to the compacted dirt below. A solitary wooden sign was nailed to the wall of a battered brick building and I struggled to identify the ideograms as the woman, still jabbing her finger into my side, began to intone the syllables, over and over, in a strange, mellifluous voice:

"Hiroshima, desu, Yankii. Yankii — Hiroshima desu."

14
UNAGI
(HIROSHI TAKARA)

From where Koji and I sat on the stone bank of the canal, we could just about see Fuji-san, its peak sprinkled with snow, off in the distance beyond the ruins of the city. We had set off early that morning with our bamboo fishing rods, walked over the Kototoi Bridge and up to the lock with its little castle keep. Our lines were hooked with chicken gizzards, dangling now in the depths of the black water, the slick surface glistening with rainbow whirls of oil. We were fishing for eels.

My father's shop had sold eel, of course. The rich, sweet aroma had infused my childhood. The shop had always been popular with the patrons of the theatres and cabarets that once lined the streets of Asakusa, and it was a regular haunt of the stagehands, theatre managers, and actors who came in at odd times of the day between shows for some snacks and a glass of saké. They bantered with my father, who was a true fan of the kabuki himself — of the rough-and-tumble style popular in Tokyo back then. Prints of the Danjuros, the famous dynasty of actors, were plastered all over the shop walls, and he liked nothing better than to chat about famous performances of the past, cracking jokes in that gruff, smart way that Tokyo people liked, all the while steaming and grilling the strips of eel. He brushed them with thick sauce from his famous pot, an earthenware thing he'd inherited from his own father — bound with wire, sticky, and smeared from generations of service. As he stood there, surrounded by fire and smoke, he almost looked like a character from a kabuki play himself, one of the wilier, earthier types.

Ours was an old-fashioned shop in that the live eels were kept in a big glass tank at the front, by the street. My mother skinned them on a block: she pinned them through the head, and tore away the slimy skin with a swift movement; she pulled out the backbone and sliced the fillet into strips in an instant. I used to press my face up against the glass and watch the animals flap their fins and slip around each other, glistening like they'd been freshly coated with lacquer. My father had once told me that every eel in the world had been born in the same place, out in the middle of a distant ocean. I dreamed about the place sometimes, the sea cloudy, as the transparent elvers drifted away, to be tugged apart from each other by the ocean currents.

The first day my father took me to the Kabuki Theatre in Ginza was the day after the Pacific War had broken out. Our headmaster had gathered us in the assembly hall of my school, and we'd nudged each other, trying not to laugh, because Sensei had tears streaming down his cheeks.

"Children," he said, his voice wavering. "Japan has entered the great war against America and Britain at last!"

Banzai!

We were thrilled, of course — we could hardly believe that Japan had actually gone and done it. Our country was going to annihilate the enemy. In the classroom that afternoon, our teacher unrolled a huge map of the Pacific Ocean and pinned it to the wall. We spent the lesson searching for Honolulu, and stuck on a little rising sun flag when we finally found it.

The next morning, my mother washed my father with warm water from the cedar tub. She passed the cloth over his muscular back before she towelled him down and helped him dress in his yukata. Then she arranged my clothes and brushed my hair as the radio burbled away with another excited report of the glorious attack. I noticed that she and Satsuko were still dressed in their normal work coats and aprons.

"Why aren't you getting ready, mother?" I asked.

"Your mother and sister aren't coming," my father said, winking at me. "It's just us men today."

Us men! I was beside myself with excitement as we made our way into the theatre, which was blazing with lanterns and filled with smells. His big hand gripped mine as the patrons called out to him, sprawling in their boxes with *bentos* and bottles of saké laid out in preparation for a good long afternoon's entertainment ahead. When my father told them I was his son, they studied me with approval and remarked on my dark eyes, declaring that I had the ferocious glower of a Danjuro myself. My father smiled with pleasure.

We took our place in the centre of the hall and he set out some rice crackers to nibble on. They played the national anthem at a deafening volume, then there was a loud bang and the lights went out. I seized my father by the arm and he laughed uproariously as a cloud of smoke billowed on the stage. I smiled at him in bashful excitement and we settled back to watch the play.

There were flashing lights, sudden explosions, the wail of horns and voices and clouds of colourful smoke. As the actors came onto the stage, men cried out *Banzai!* and the audience all laughed. At the climax, the clappers rang out, and the audience roared their approval, pounding the sides of their boxes as the actors pulled their faces into ferocious, cross-eyed tableaux. Afterward, everyone spilled out into the light of the bustling evening to eat and drink amongst the stalls and shops, and I rubbed my eyes as if emerging from a dream.

A few years later, a tragedy occurred. Rice was being rationed, the fishmonger had gone out of business, and my father was forced to close the restaurant. The women from the neighbourhood association visited the next day, asking him to donate his grills to the military as they were made from such good iron. *Let's send just one more plane to the front!*

Then came the final blow. The fire raids began, and the theatres were shut down. His call-up papers arrived soon after that. On the evening of his purification ceremony, we ate a solemn meal of sea bream and red rice. Afterward, my father put a lid on his ancient pot of sauce and sealed it with wax. He wrapped it up in oilcloth and placed it in a cedar box, which he stood in an alcove in the corner of the room, underneath the family altar. As we stood before it, he put his hands on my shoulders and rubbed them over and over.

"Take care of that until I get back, Hiroshi-kun, do you hear me?" he said.

I nodded. He pointed his finger at the pot.

"That's our only family treasure."

My father heaved his kitbag onto the train at Ueno Station the next day. He was going to report at the Yokosuka air-naval base. He squatted down on the platform and embraced me tightly as the platform guard blew his whistle.

"Remember what I told you," he whispered.

I nodded.

"I promise, father," I said.

"I'm counting on you, Hiroshi-kun!"

The train pulled away from the platform. There was a shriek from the locomotive as the wheels began to turn. He leaned out of the carriage window for a moment and waved his fighting cap.

And then he was gone.

Koji shouted as something writhed violently at the end of his fishing line. I leaped up and quickly wound the line around my arm as it veered from side to side. The taut line angled up, and I prayed that it wouldn't snap as I staggered backward. I heaved as hard as I could. There was a sudden splash, and then, there it was! A dark, shining eel, coiling and writhing on the bank. Koji hollered in triumph as we dangled the spiralling creature over our bucket, spluttering with delight and revulsion as slimy water flicked in our faces. We dropped it into the pail, where it whumped away with a dull clanging noise.

Finally, the creature became calm, and we covered the bucket with a plank of wood. Together, we hoisted it up, and triumphantly carried it down the canal toward the river as the water sloshed back and forth.

The light was just failing as we met the other children at Ueno Station. They crowded around us excitedly when they realized that we had actually caught something. When I slid the plank away, they gasped. The eel was curled up now, like an evil black snake in the bottom of the pail. Aiko leaned over, very warily. Suddenly, the thing wriggled and flicked water into the air, and she screamed and fell onto her backside. The children cackled with laughter as Tomoko helped her up. Aiko began to whine as Tomoko brushed her down.

"Cheer up, Aiko-chan! You won't be bellyaching when Hiroshi's cooked the eel for our dinner."

Tomoko glanced at me, amused, as Aiko grumbled away. I smiled back. I remembered my father at that moment, standing over the cedar tub as my mother massaged the bunched muscles of his shoulders.

The lights of the market glowed, and spattering flecks of black on the brickwork of the railway embankment marked the start of rain. GIs went to and fro in their rain capes to haggle for stockings and trinkets for the night ahead. Shin was showing off now, dipping the tip of his finger into the water to goad the eel while Koji and Nobu watched warily over his shoulder.

Aiko's high voice piped up. She pointed over toward the far railway arches. Two GIs were walking along in the shadows. We had four last cigarettes left — should she go and ask if they would buy them?

"I'll go!" Tomoko said, brightly.

Aiko handed over the remaining cigarettes and Tomoko sprinted off. I sat down on the gritty bank. The children were daring each other to touch the eel, jerking back whenever it moved. A train rumbled up on the tracks as I closed my eyes and smiled to myself.

Some instinct made me look up. I glanced through the drizzle, and saw one of the distant soldiers looming over Tomoko, pulling her toward him. I leaped up. Tomoko resisted, but then, with a quick movement, the soldier grabbed her. There was a scuffle, and, somehow, her monpe were around her knees. The man pulled her toward iron struts of the railway bridge and I heard her cry out as he pushed her up against the column.

The world melted as I tore toward them, a sharp stone in my hand, my mind filled with a piercing roar. Tomoko stood pinioned to the wall, and the soldier had one hand beneath her chin as the other pulled at his open trousers. He suddenly turned and saw me and dropped Tomoko just as I leaped into the air and swept the stone down hard toward his forehead. His brawny arm shot up and struck me in the jaw and I crashed down into a heap of charred, wet timber. I looked around desperately for a weapon. My fingers fell upon a piece of rusted pipe and I started to swing it as the man hovered in front of me. His shirt billowed from his fly, and he was breathing heavily.

I felt a sudden wave of fear as the man approached. I swung wildly with the pipe, but to my horror, he caught it with one fist and ripped it from my hand. He took me by the scruff, and I screamed and flailed at him as he slapped me with his hand, swearing at me. His companion came up and grabbed his shoulder, but the man bellowed at him and he shrank away. I was hoisted slowly upward. The veins in his neck bulged and I could smell his breath. Sweat and blood and rain were dripping from his brow. I must have caught him, I thought, in grim satisfaction. I kicked out wildly. He slammed his left fist into my eye — there was an explosion of pain and I collapsed onto the ground. A boot stood by my head, smeared with mud, the laces looped and tangled around the ankle. I was deaf except for a far-off ringing in my ears.

I felt the tremble of iron rivets. Another train was passing along the track above and sparks flew down from the rails. Passengers hung from its side and peered down as it passed. There were shouts. The other soldier clasped his friend by the neck, pulling him away. The GI resisted for a second. Then he swung his boot straight into my belly. The boot lifted me from the ground, and I collapsed in agony, struggling to inhale. The train began to screech along the rails as the soldiers disappeared beneath the tracks, their shadows jerking along behind them.

I tried to stand. My head was still ringing. Tomoko stood a few yards away. She struggled to pull up her monpe as I crawled toward her.

"Tomoko? Tomoko-chan?"

Dread spread from my stomach to my fingertips. She clutched her arms around her body and began to shiver. I reached out to touch her but she jerked violently away with a whimper.

"Tomoko?" I whispered. She didn't respond. "Tomoko-chan!"

The rain poured down around us, saturating our thin rags. Her silhouette shook against the iron column.

I got up and walked unsteadily over toward the children. It was dark now, and the lights of the market were bright smears in the rain. The children stared at me as I approached. The zinc bucket was still there, perched unevenly on the ground. With a sudden fury, I kicked it as hard as I could with my bare foot.

It reverberated with a dull clang and the water slopped onto the ground.

There was a movement and the black shape of the eel slithered forward. It shivered up the slope and waved over the broken slabs and gravel until it reached the edge of a flooded bomb crater, frigid with dark water. It paused for a second at the edge, then slid in. The silhouette hovered at the surface, as if stunned. Then, it slipped down, writhing, and disappeared into the blackness.

15
PHILOPON
(OSAMU MARUKI)

Philopon. Drug of the day. Glint in the eye, pulse in the vein. Saviour of the downtrodden. Sacrament of the lost. Bright white light to the woe-struck, lice-ridden, starry-eyed artists: the stupefied, raving philosopher-poets of the burned-out ruins.

Mrs. Shimamura's bar swirled for hours each evening now, the intellectuals variously mournful and long faced or else frantic and electrified, circling sections of the newspapers spread out on the bar, their eyes shining with morphine and methyl.

We came together as drunks or tramps do — to hold each other up in swaying arms. The bar was a sanctuary to which we retreated to comfort ourselves with raw, amniotic liquor, to keep our minds numb and distracted with absurd toasts and peculiar drinking games. What conversation there was now was of rashes, blisters, coughs, ticks, rations, hunger, thirst, and cold. Mostly though, we just drank, night after night, holding our glasses aloft and crashing them together — *shoo shoo shoo!* — before tipping the fluid down our throats. Glass after glass, until the light compressed into pinpricks and we collapsed face down on the bar. The bright stars of Japan's literary firmament. We were nothing now but slurred aphorisms and pulmonary complaints.

Everything was so bleak and petrified in Tokyo that winter that it was no surprise that many of us began to supplement our meagre diet of rotgut and sweet potato with the small, crystalline Philopon pills we'd been fed during the last days of the war: those little tablets of courage that had steeled our nerves against the battery of Australian and American guns, and kept us feverish and alert through those long nights of grisly carnage. A glut of the drug flooded the city sometime in December, and thousands upon thousands of green ink bottles appeared in pyramids at the black markets, passing from hand to chafed hand in the cramped, leaky bars. Before long it seemed as if the whole city was munching the pills like sardines, washing them down with tears and tiger's piss in an attempt to blunt the teeth that gnawed at our bellies; to propel our battered bodies through the freezing streets, and the cluttered train compartments.

Prior to this, I had developed another, more sinister addiction. Those evenings when I had reached my alcoholic peak, as it were, my mind illuminated with stars, I boarded a tram to the Ginza, alighting near the American PX and the Oasis cabaret. There I took a place on the curb on the other side of the avenue, between the peddlers with their straw mats displaying figurines and fountain pens, watching as the Americans crammed down the staircase of the brothel. Infrequently,

I would be rewarded with a glimpse of Satsuko Takara as she performed her routine outside, pulling at sleeves and enticing the officers to enter. Sometimes, I would see her leave, hours later, buttoning herself into her coat as she strode away into the night.

I tormented myself with the thought of her, down in the secret cellar, American hands sliding over her back and along her pale thighs. I pictured the brief hours we had spent on a straw-filled mattress in the Victory Hotel, the night before I was sent to war. A victory of sorts, for me. My last. The Americans had polluted her now, as they had polluted me. One night, I stood with a grubby girl at the back of a ruined building, my eyes brimming with tears as I handled her, urgently trying to imagine her as Satsuko —

It was no use. They had taken my very manhood.

Philopon came not a moment too soon. A glimmer of life came back into my eyes, my spirits leavened. Lazarus clambered from his tomb. I still drank of course, until I collapsed, but the periods of consciousness between grew now more animated and urgent, my spirits more sprightly and vital.

I sat on my mattress, accompanied by a flask of shochu and a vial of Philopon, writing until the tiny room was littered with balled up clumps of paper, the air clotted with ink fumes. I wrote stories inspired by the strange articles that filled that day's newspapers: the grandmother, murdered by her grandson on his return from Manchukuo; the blind children found living in the sand dunes of Izu. My stories were macabre, catastrophic, stygian. They were also unreadable, I realized. Yet I thought, perhaps, they might represent a kind of literary self-immolation, a spiritual disembowelment that might somehow purify me, and set me free from the past.

One evening, I came upon a writer I was somewhat familiar with, tottering on his stool at the bar. He was breathing heavily, giving occasional tubercular rasps into his silk handkerchief. His conversation became increasingly feverish as the evening drew on, his pen scribbling faster as he yelled out choice epithets to us all. At last, he leaped up, seized the arms of his nearest companion and dragged him off into the night. After he had left, I found his notebook on the bar amidst the confusion of newspapers. I flicked through it at random, until I found a page of dislocated words, which together seemed to form a kind of occult, chemical sutra:

> Morphine. Atromol. Narcopon.
> Pantapon. Papinal. Panopin.
> Atropin. Rivanol. Philopon.

Philopon. Could Japan have survived the winter without it? Philopon was the true hero of our age, our Eucharist. In the paralysis that followed surrender, it was the rod that kept our spines stiff, the glue that kept flesh adhered to our bones.

The special attack pilots, in those last, surreal days of war, had tied emblazoned bands around their foreheads. Together with their brother officers, they had sung the national anthem and offered *banzai* to the emperor. They toasted each other with ceremonial saké, just as samurai had once sprinkled it upon their swords on the eve of battle. Then, they had ingested

Philopon, before climbing into their flying machines, and roaring off into the suicide of the setting sun. What modern men they had been.

Philopon was the symbol of our new age. Who needed the emperor when we had MacArthur? Who needed saké when we had Philopon? From the emerald paddy we had been transported to the laboratory, from the bloody field of battle to the dissection tank. We traded fireflies and lanterns for the flood lamp and the phosphorus shell, the kabuki for the cabaret, rice for amphetamine. Who needed tatami in the age of concrete? What use was steel in the age of plutonium? Goodbye, Nippon, goodbye! Farewell Amaterasu — hello America! And welcome, Japan, welcome: to the bright, white chemical age!

16
AFTERMATH OF THE ATOM
(HAL LYNCH)

I vaulted down from the train, as a dozen other people, mainly women, trudged over to the station building. They eyed me with frank hostility as I approached; I was aware of how conspicuous I was in my uniform. The train gave a piercing whistle and as it lumbered away, I lingered, watching it disappear along the tracks. An acute, heavy silence descended.

The roof at one end of the narrow ticket hall had caved in. Riveted iron beams hung down from the brickwork and rubble was heaped high on the floor. The other end of the hall was bare but for a solid desk, where a guard sat, his moustache bristly beneath his peaked cap. He gasped when he saw me, sprang to his feet, and bobbed there for a second, as if unable to decide whether to salute me or not. I extracted my crumpled train ticket from my pocket. As I tried to press it into his hand, he shrank backward.

In broken Japanese, I asked him the way "to the city." He tugged at his moustache for a second, then beckoned for me to follow him through a pair of splintered wooden doors. He pointed.

The desolate plain stretched for several miles to a heavy ridge of rugged mountains. About halfway across, hazy outlines marked an isolated outcrop of buildings. Nothing else was standing but charred spindles of telegraph poles that marked long-vanished avenues.

"Hiroshima desu," the guard said, staring at me with watery eyes.

I heard a cry and turned to see a policeman, his nightstick dangling against his leg as he hurried over from a corrugated hut, inside of which was a table and a solitary chair. A rusted bicycle was leaning against its side. I made sure he could see the epaulettes of rank on my shoulder, and he stopped and glowered for a moment, before finally twisting his hand against his forehead.

I pointed over toward the ghostly buildings in the distance.

"Hiroshima?" I asked, quite aware of how ridiculous the question sounded.

He seemed torn between his misgivings and instinctive submission to my authority. Eventually, in painfully slow English, he asked: "Why you go Hiroshima?"

I took out a folded piece of paper upon which Burchett had scribbled an address.

"Hospital?" I asked.

He studied the paper, then conferred with the train guard. Finally, he raised his hand and wriggled his fingers in the general direction of the ruined buildings.

"Thank you, gentlemen." I gave them a curt nod and slung my bag over my shoulder.

As I started to walk down the track, I heard footsteps and then felt a tap on my shoulder. The policeman held his fingers to his lips with a cringing motion. I split another pack of Old Golds from the carton in my bag and tossed it to him. He bowed, then strode as imperiously as he could back to his shack.

I surveyed the blank plateau before me. It was like a hardened, empty desert. The sky was swirling with heavy cloud that almost obscured the ridge of mountains in the distance, and snow was drifting down from the sky. I took a deep breath and started to walk, my footsteps crunching upon the earth.

Tokyo didn't come close, I thought, *even at its worst*. There, at least, the remnants were identifiable — the broken frames of buildings, the hewn chunks of masonry and cauterized brick. Here, any human vestige, any recognizable form had been ground into abstraction. The landscape was moulded from pulverized fragments as fine as sand, and thick, gravelly dust formed strange, surreal hummocks and formations, hardened now by the rain. It was a wasteland.

Every so often, a figure on a bicycle creaked toward me. The riders wore cloth masks over their mouths and turned their handlebars to steer in a wide arc as they passed.

I began to detect a vague tang in the air — a bitter, acrid smell I couldn't place. I followed the shadowy outline of what must have once been a streetcar track, the overhead lines swept clear away. Fifty yards from me, in a solitary heap, was the twisted metal frame of a destroyed trolley. I saw a narrow river up ahead and a high step to a stone bridge. As I peered over the side, I saw a trickle of pungent water at the bottom of the channel. Rotted corpses of fish and dozens of mangled bicycles cluttered the riverbed. I took out my camera, and began to take shots.

For a long stretch after the bridge, though, there was nothing to document. No broken-down houses, no graves, no signs of settlement whatsoever. Just a vast expanse of thick, reddish-brown dust, punctuated by clumps of bushy yellow grass and spiky, poisonous-looking shrubs. The light was hazy and grey, the sun a pale, far-off disk, and I had the feeling of walking on the surface of a distant planet. Time seemed somehow disjointed, as if I was floating through a dream landscape. There was no sound of birdsong or human activity; no trees or vegetable gardens. The place was poisoned, stricken, dolorous.

By the banks of another, much wider river, a shattered dome appeared, like the frame of an observatory, surrounded by a sunken wall. I recalled the umbrella roof of the central market building from my aerial photographs, and realized I was coming close to the hypocentre. Clumps of plaster still dangled from the curving struts of the dome, and plants were growing in the ruins — spiralling tendrils of dying morning glory creeping amidst the broken tiles; tangles of thorny herbs and small yellow broom-like flowers that clutched at the blackened brick. There were signs of life on the other side of the river. On an avenue parallel to the bank, a man led horses pulling a laden cart, while other men went by on bicycles.

I picked my way out of the dome and walked to the bank. Fifty feet to my left, I saw it. The big, white bridge across the river that I'd proposed as a primary target. The cement structure was askew, as if it had been shoved from its supports. The stone itself seemed ancient. As I crossed the bridge, I recalled mythical tales of rivers to the underworld, the fields of lost souls on the other side.

Shanties stood beyond the road with lines of laundry strung between them. Down by the river, women were scrubbing clothes in wooden tubs, and children splashed about in bathing caps.

I was so absorbed that I didn't notice the rumble of the army convoy until it was almost upon me. I turned and froze, gazing at the silhouettes in the back of the trucks through the cloud of dust raised by the heavy wheels. I wondered whether I should run, but some instinct told me to stay and so I stood rigid, my hand held up in stiff, formal salute. I spotted British markings on the sides of the vehicles. My panic turned to relief as the cheerful troops in the back started to wave, thumbs held up in salute as they rumbled past. The friendly sound of a horn blared out, and I watched as they disappeared in a cloud of red dust, my heartbeat slowly subsiding.

I strode along the avenue toward a tall building that looked as if it had once been a five- or six-storey office block. On entry, I found that the impression was illusory. Only the outer shell was still standing. The interior walls had collapsed. The ground was gutted and charred, full of nothing but rubble and emptiness.

Further along, another tall building seemed solid and undamaged. People came and went through its main doors. As I approached, some glanced up, stopped in their tracks, and stared at me. But most just looked through me, or turned away. I pushed through the entrance into a large, high-ceilinged hall, where desks of clerks were flipping through ledgers and stamping forms, counting out coins and notes for people lined up before them. As I glanced around at the blackened walls, I noticed a huge clock hung at the end of the room. I glanced at my own watch. The hands of the clock had been frozen in time.

I raised my Leica, the image of the clock sharpening as I focused the lens. I felt a hand pulling at my arm. For a second, I thought that I was being robbed, and I raised my fists as I spun around. Two policemen stood before me, one cowering while the other stepped gingerly forward and attempted to grasp me again.

"Come — please," he said, clutching at me with his bony fingers.

"Hands off," I said, shoving him away. He stood there for a second, apparently contemplating another attempt, before he clearly decided discretion to be the better part of valour.

"Come — please," he repeated, walking toward a wide stone staircase that led away from the lobby. He stopped at the foot of the staircase and waved his fingers at me as if beckoning to a cat. I followed him up puddle-stained stairs to the third floor, through a set of doors that bore the insignia of the police force. Inside, men sat at splintered desks laid with maps, scrolls, and jars of cloudy tea. They wore overcoats as they worked — the room was cold enough to see the vapour of their breath. They glanced up at me curiously as I was led through the room. The officer knocked softly at a door. At the sound of a bark from within, he opened it, saluted, and hustled me inside.

A man with a silver beard sat behind a desk, glaring at me with sharp eyes under a beetling brow. The room was bare except for a beige raincoat slung over a screen in the corner and a portrait of the emperor that hung askew on the cracked wall.

The man fired off a torrent of angry Japanese.

"I can't understand you, Chief," I said, "No matter how loud you shout it."

He stomped around the table to face me. He was tough and grizzled, and about a foot and a half shorter than me. He jabbed a sharp finger into my chest.

"Hold on now, Chief," I said loudly, grasping my epaulettes and thrusting them into his face. "Let's not forget who's who."

A timid knock came at the door, and a dishevelled man with a toothbrush moustache came inside.

"Excuse me," he said in English, with a hesitant bow, "I am translator."

The chief growled and retreated to his desk. He snapped at the man, who nodded meekly every now and then, pencilling words in a small notebook. The translator turned to me and cleared his throat.

"He asks, 'Why are you in Hiroshima?'"

"That's a good question."

He gave me a look of anxiety. I took pity on him.

"I'm here to visit the hospitals."

"You are doctor?"

I shook my head. "No, I'm a reporter. *Shimbun kisha desu.*"

As the man warily translated, the Chief uttered a guttural volley of Japanese that crescendoed with a slam of his hand on the table. The translator looked at me and cringed.

"He says — no reporter in Hiroshima. Forbidden."

I wondered whether I should try to bluff it out with my press pass. I thought I might do better with cigarettes and a few tins of Spam. The chief tapped his fingers against the table, apparently unable to decide what to do with me. Suddenly, he picked up the telephone, and barked into the receiver. There was a crackling voice on the other end. The chief grunted as he listened.

I went over to the window and looked outside. Flat ruins stretched for miles around. *Here I am, then,* I thought. *Ground level at last.* Millions of tiny snowflakes were falling through the air.

They stuck to the glass and melted away into tiny droplets of water.

The chief replaced the receiver. He stood up and put on his coat and hat. He flung a few words at the translator and wrenched open the door.

I looked askance at the man.

"Where are we going?"

The translator dipped his head. "He says — to visit hospital."

"We are?"

"Yes. We go now."

"Why should he take me to the hospital?" I asked, hurrying after him.

A look of painful embarrassment passed over his wrinkled face. "Excuse me."

"Yes?"

"He says — to show America what it has done."

The chief himself drove the battered sedan, the car toiling over the pits and crevasses in the road. The translator sat next to me in the back and I asked him about the state of the city now. He responded with terse, nervous answers. Yes, people were returning, though most still clustered on the outskirts, too scared of sickness to venture further in. No, there was no electricity yet. They still relied on the army generators. No, they rarely saw any Westerners. Teams had come a few weeks after the surrender, dressed in protective clothing and carrying peculiar pieces of equipment. They had drilled in certain areas and taken away samples of rocks and brick, but had not returned since.

I rolled down the window and started photographing. Men in rubber boots and helmets shovelled debris, sawed planks, and dug foundations. In an open patch of ground was a long, low building painted in crude camouflage, with piles of scrap metal set up outside — warped radiators and railings. Men in blue overalls dragged over still more, sorting and arranging it by type.

We bumped along a dirt track lined with rows of identical wooden huts, newly built. There were black squares of vegetable gardens between them, the earth dotted with tiny sprouts of green.

We drove past a long yellow brick wall and emerged into the muddy yard of what had once been the Red Cross hospital. The car slid to a halt and we clambered out. The chief snapped at the translator, gesturing toward the building.

A doctor, a bespectacled man in his mid-fifties, his beard cut in a tapering European style, emerged from a side door, stepping delicately around the muddy puddles as he approached. I thanked the police chief for his help, and he laughed mirthlessly.

Frankly, the translator said, he should have had me arrested at the station when he had been alerted to my arrival. He had orders to call the Allied commander of the area if any unfamiliar personnel arrived in the city.

"And yet he chose to ignore his orders," I said.

The chief scowled at me.

"He says — it is better for you to see for yourself."

"I agree."

The chief's eyes narrowed and his face became full of contempt. He gestured once more at the hospital. With that, he climbed into the car and slammed the door shut. It trundled away, the worn wheels splashing through the flooded potholes as it went.

Dr. Hiyashida had studied medicine at the University of Heidelberg and spoke good English. He had come to Hiroshima from Osaka to make a special study of radiation disease. Shamelessly, he told me that he hoped his thesis would glean him a position on the medical council.

"You weren't here yourself on the day of the blast?"

"No," he said, frowning. "And now there are no more than a few A-Bomb cases still in the hospital. It is most unfortunate."

The inside of the hospital was a shambles. The window frames were warped, the glass gone. An icy wind blew in from the hills, visible in the distance.

"How are conditions now?"

"Improving," he said, apparently without irony. "We have more medicine now, vitamins and plasma. But we still need more operating tables, X-Ray machines."

Patients wrapped in bandages were lying on mats on the floor, sleeping or reading miniature books.

"You see?" he said in a frustrated whisper as we passed amongst them. "Few of them have any interesting symptoms any longer. They just say they feel empty and listless. They complain of tiredness and melancholy. I find that difficult to ascribe to radiation. After all, who ever heard of a bomb causing melancholy?"

Further on, in another ward, he kept his more "interesting" cases — the more grotesquely injured victims of the bomb that I guessed he hoped would form the notable chapters of his thesis. I felt acutely awkward as he strode from one patient to another, ordering them to display their symptoms, as if they were performers in a circus freak show.

One young man raised his shirt to expose his midriff. It was covered with the same thick, rubbery colloidal scars that the victims in Weller's photographs had shown. Another man had the striped pattern of the yukata he'd been wearing burned into his skin by the flash. The doctor urged me to take photographs — "For your newspaper!" — and he poked and prodded his patients, snapping at any of them who appeared too listless or embarrassed to respond. I grew irritated. He put me in mind of a particularly difficult superior officer I had known during my service, and I felt an incipient wave of hatred for the man.

I walked ahead, noticing an old woman, her white hair pulled into a bun, sitting on the edge of her bed. I asked the translator to politely inquire whether I might talk to her. Dr. Hiyashida rushed over and took her arm, shaking it, which made me so angry that I almost struck him. I ordered him to leave us, and he slunk back to the doorway, glancing at us every now and again with a sulky look.

She had been beautiful once, that was clear. Her eyes were almost pure black, and her nose was still a soft, elegant curve. But her face seemed to have slid an inch or so around her skull, like a loose mask, and her skin was etched with a deep web of lines and whirls, as if she had been supernaturally aged by many hundreds of years.

She spoke in a low voice, almost without intonation. She had been a dance instructor, she said, though she'd had very few students left by the end of the war. She had arrived at her studio in the centre of the city at around eight o'clock on the morning of the blast. She had been walking along the corridor on the first floor, where she had paused for a moment to open a window to let in some air, glancing as she did so up at the mountains, thick with green against the blue summer sky.

There was a flash. An explosion of glass pitched her backward. She tumbled in the air with the last thought that a bomb had landed directly upon her. When she awoke, she was pinned face down in the darkness, her mouth full of plaster. The floor above her had collapsed and she lay there for several days until men dug her out of the ruins. Outside, the city was flattened. Drops of oily black rain were falling from the sky.

Barefoot and dressed in rags, she made her way along the river to the park where hundreds of women and children lay dying. Some were vomiting up their innards; others had flesh peeling off. She saw two of the women from her neighbourhood association squatting by a fire, and hurried over to them. When they saw her, they turned their faces away, aghast. The next morning, she went to a pool in the river and looked at her reflection.

She closed her eyes, and gestured with an elegant hand toward her face. Her brows looked as if they had been pushed in by the thumbs of a sculptor, and her lips were almost entirely smudged into her face. She made an almost imperceptible noise and hunched back over. As I left, I happened to glance at the chart on the edge of her bed. I felt an uncanny prickling on my scalp. The old lady was just twenty-five years old.

On the other side of the room, I saw two old men lying side by side in bed. One sat up and smiled vaguely as the translator and I came over. His scalp was bare and blotchy and his arms were as thin as twigs. As with the girl in the photographs that Weller had showed us, his withered chest was speckled with red liver spots. The other man was asleep and his breath came in rasps.

The old man spoke so softly that I could barely hear. He smiled and made tiny gesticulations to illustrate his story. Sir would never believe it, he whispered, but they'd both worked on the railroad as labourers until just six months before. They'd been brawny and tough back then, with full heads of hair — wives, mistresses! They'd both been working on the tracks that morning, when the man had noticed the far-off glint of "Mr. B" in the sky, but they'd assumed it was just the weather plane and ignored it. There'd been an air raid warning earlier that morning, and it had passed without incident.

"Hiroshima was lucky, we used to say. The Americans didn't want to touch it."

He'd never been on a plane himself, he said, but as he'd looked at the silver glint in the sky, he'd wondered what Japan must look like from above.

"How beautiful it must be to fly, sir," he murmured, "to see the whole country stretched out beneath you."

He'd watched the plane as it passed. He'd put his hand above his face to shield his eyes from the dazzling sun. That was the moment.

There was a flash. There was no sound. He felt something strong and terribly intense and there was a pulsing of colour as he was hurled forward. He lay splayed on the ground with fragments of stone like teeth in his mouth. He thought he was dead.

Great crashes came from all around and he saw train carriages tumbling across the ground like toys, as an immense cloud rose up and blotted out the sun. Then, all around, debris and dust began to rain violently down from the sky.

He fell silent, staring into space.

"How do you feel now?"

He drew in a breath, then let out a long sigh. He rubbed his hands together dreamily, as if he were washing them. Last year, he said, he'd used his hands every day. Flinging a pick, hammering rivets, laying track. His body had been all muscle. He held up his shaking hands for me to see, then laughed. He didn't even think he could lift a glass of beer now. He felt so light that he thought he might float off into the wind like a feather. I took his photograph and thanked him. He gave a trembling smile and bowed, pressing his hands against his forehead as if in prayer.

As we left the ward, Dr. Hiyashida shook his head and crossed his hands behind his back. "Awkward cases, these A-Bomb people."

~

Darkness was seeping from the hills and I needed to catch the train back to Tokyo. It was the only passage for two days and the idea of being stuck here in this strange city at night filled me with a baffling fear. Dr. Hiyashida insisted that one of the hospital ambulances drive me to the station and this at least I gratefully accepted. I told myself I should be wary of encountering army personnel, although, in all honesty, it was the thought of traipsing back across that mournful wasteland in the dark that filled me with dread. What I desired more than anything was to be back in my room in Tokyo, a brazier smouldering away on the floor, a large glass of whisky in my hand. Dr. Hiyashida waved me off at the hospital gate, the translator having now departed. He promised to send me a copy of his thesis when it was published. He urged me to be sure to mention his name "in your newspaper."

"I'll make sure I do," I called back.

The driver of the ambulance was a handsome young man of around twenty. To my surprise, he spoke English too — his parents had been Christians, and he'd been taught German and English by the monks at the church school, though the English lessons had come to an end several years earlier. He'd lost both of his parents in the blast, he said, but he himself had survived largely unharmed, a feat which he ascribed — admirably, under the circumstances, I thought — to "God's grace." All he'd suffered were some small burns that wouldn't seem to heal. Out of thanks to God, he had now dedicated his life to helping the sick and the injured.

As we drove along the dark, wide gravel road, he recounted some of the grim stories and grotesque myths that had persisted in the wake of the blast. The bomb had been the size of a matchbox, they said. The bomb had been tested on a mountain range in America, which it had destroyed entirely. Some other stories had a ghastly ring of truth. A group of soldiers had wandered lost in the park that night, holding each other's hands in a macabre line, their eye-sockets empty, their eyeballs having melted down their cheeks. A whirlwind had torn through the city a few hours after the blast, uprooting trees and sucking dead bodies up into the sky.

I pictured the old man as he lay on his hospital bed, the dreamy look in his eyes. He'd been imagining what it would be like to fly, thinking how beautiful the world must seem from up there.

Poor devil.

I asked the driver if he'd suffered any effects of radiation disease himself.

He said he didn't know. He'd lost some hair, but it had grown back. Far worse were the headaches he got at night, the inertia that sometimes pinned him down for days.

He frowned, then carried on in a low, confidential tone.

"The worst of it is that the women's menses have stopped. There are fears over whether they will ever begin again. My wife and I were only married last year, and we so want to have a child one day."

It was pitch black by the time we reached the station and I said goodbye to the boy with a fervent handshake. The snow was coming down in steady drifts now, and in the ticket hall, the shivering inspector made me understand through sign language that the train would be delayed.

I wandered around the back of the station to the railway sidings. A long chain of carriages was tipped over on its side, the wood scorched. There was a low hill nearby, and partway up, exactly one half of a *torii* arch marked the entrance to what had once been a temple. Nothing remained now but the broken stones of the votive pool, which was still bubbling with water from some mysterious spring, and the stumps of what must have once been enormous cedars. Beyond them I found a mound of rubble, and atop it, two perching Buddhas, about to topple. The face of one was sheared away. The other gazed at the ground, his hands resting in his lap, a silent, secretive smile on his face.

As I walked back down the hill, soft snowflakes brushed my face and settled between the tracks and along the rails. I stood on the lonely platform and watched the snow fall until finally, with a distant glow, a train approached the station. When it pulled in, I clambered up into an empty compartment where I took a hard wooden seat by the window. With numb fingers I slid the whisky bottle from my knapsack and took a long swig as the train jerked into motion. I craned my head out of the window as the train gathered speed, and I watched as the station passed into the distance and snow whirled silently in the black sky. For a second, there was a faint glimmer of light somewhere far out on the plain. Then came a scream of wind as we plunged into a tunnel, and it was gone.

17
THE BLOOD CHERRY GANG
(SATSUKO TAKARA)

The Ginza was crowded with American GIs wearing fur hats and thick gloves. They slid along the frosty avenue and flung little icicles at each other, bellowing with raucous laughter. I didn't even notice the plump streetwalker girl until she had almost barged into me. Wearing a violet dress and reeking of liquor, she peered at me and cursed. Then she spat full in my face.

I stood there speechless as she started screaming. Her face was twisted with rage. Who did I think I was, she shouted, with my airs and graces? Was I superior to her?

"You're just a whore like me!"

It was awful. People stopped to stare, the faces of the Japanese men twitching with spiteful glee, the Americans folding their arms and sniggering as they watched the show.

I stepped past them down the avenue, wiping my face with my handkerchief as the dreadful girl hurled insults behind me.

There seemed to be nothing but streetwalkers in Tokyo that night, lurking in the shop doorways, darting out like crabs to grab passing men. They really were a wretched mob, I thought, their makeup smeared, their bare legs puckered from the cold. Perhaps I did think I was in a class above them, like that floozy had said. Girls such as I drank Scotch in cabarets, while they swigged shochu dregs in dead-end alleys. Allied captains reserved my company in orderly private rooms, while hideous old men pummelled them in the storefronts and frozen bomb craters.

Michiko had despised them, of course. She called them harlots and tarts, filthy *pan-pan*. While she, of course, was a modern-day Okichi, a courtesan, a handmaiden of Genji.

It just went to show, I thought, as I hurried home. People always needed someone else to look down upon, no matter how far they'd fallen themselves. After all, even the dogs that roam in the streets and eat trash have hierarchies of their own.

The next morning, when I woke up, I felt very odd. Rain was dripping into the pail, and I felt as if there was a great weight pressing upon my ribcage, as if I were a butterfly pinned to a card. It was so cold that I could see my breath. When I finally dressed, I felt dizzy, and had to lie back down again.

Late in the afternoon, I was still on the futon, staring up at the stained ceiling. After a while, I began to have the uncanny sensation that someone else was there in the room with me. The feeling grew stronger and stronger, until I became convinced that my mother was sitting over on the tatami by the table, looking at me. I closed my eyes tightly and hid my face in the blanket, but the feeling grew so intense that suddenly, I spun around and looked.

And there she was. Sitting on the floor, staring at me with her lashless eyes. Her blue kimono was scorched around the edges, her hair all burned away. All of a sudden, there was a terrible smell of char in the room and I started to scream and fainted.

When I came to, she was gone. But I could still picture her, staring at me grimly, smouldering in accusation, and I knew that the reason she had returned from the other world was to punish me for having betrayed our family by becoming a prostitute.

I wondered if I should return to our alley and light more incense, but I doubted if that would help. Over the following days, I set out once more to search for Hiroshi at the schools and the railway stations, hoping that by finding some trace of him, I might somehow quiet her restless spirit. But it was useless. There were no graves I could visit, no fragments of bone that I could inter.

I grew frightened that Hiroshi's ghost, or Osamu's, might visit me now as well. Sometimes, when I left the Oasis, I thought I saw a pale figure standing on the other side of the avenue, gazing at me. I imagined that it followed me through the crowd, solemn eyes upon me as I strode through the streets. But whenever I turned to look, the figure was gone.

Mr. Shiga must have noticed that I was on edge, because one night he summoned me to his office.

"Takara-san," he said, "if you can't get a grip on yourself, then you're fired. Your gloomy face is causing our customers discomfort."

I gave a shrill laugh and bowed and apologized, asking him to forgive me. I tried to explain that I was just very tired.

He opened the drawer of his writing desk and took out a small green bottle, which he held up to the lamp.

"Take one of these each evening, Takara-san, before you come to work." He shook a small white pill into his palm, and placed it in front of me. "Our noble troops were given these at the end of the war to revive their stamina. You may find they help."

Later that night, I swallowed one of the tablets shortly before I went to sit at a table of American sailors. I realized that my mind was quite calm, that I felt pretty and sparkling. Their conversation seemed very amusing, and I began to chatter coquettishly away in broken English, an unusual confidence and excitement quivering all through my body. It was quite extraordinary. The Americans gazed at me and made jokes with their friends on the other tables. They all asked me to dance one after the other, and in a few hours I had earned more for tea dances than I normally did lying down on my back.

Some of the other girls were in the dressing room when I finished my shift. They smiled when I showed them the bottle of magical pills.

"We've all been taking them for weeks now," they laughed. "They really are amazing!"

The pills had the added benefit, they said, of stopping you from getting hungry, so you wouldn't get too fat, either. We all laughed at that one: none of us were anything but skin and bones in any case.

From then on, I swallowed a chalky pill as soon as I arrived at the Oasis. It fizzed inside me as I dressed and painted my face. The Americans gave me swigs of whisky, and I felt as if

I was on a glowing merry-go-round as they twirled me across the dance-floor. Finally, I took a yen taxi home, still wide awake, but then I just drank more whisky, and the room would spin deliciously around me as I sank down into a deep, dreamless sleep. And then, even if my mother, or my brother, or Osamu did come and visit me from beyond the grave, I was always too dead to the world to notice.

~

I dreamed that I was far out on the Pacific Ocean, on a battleship, ploughing through the waves. My father was tucking me into a bunk, but the blanket wouldn't quite stretch. He climbed into the bunk beside me, and I was ashamed, but then he turned around, and he was Osamu. There was a loud explosion, a clanging alarm, and sailors were running through the galleys — we had been struck by a torpedo, the boat was sinking, and I was deep beneath the ocean, the sea water pouring into my lungs —

Michiko was leaning over me, holding an empty glass. Water was dripping down my cheeks. She smiled. "Satchan!" she said. "I thought you'd never wake up. Really, you should be ashamed of yourself."

I glanced at her groggily as she shivered out of a thick, luxurious looking white fur coat, which she hung from the nail on the wall. *She's put on weight*, I thought. She had a nice sleek look: a pink flush in her cheeks. As she laid out tins on the table, I saw a flash of silver around her wrist.

She sat down and stretched herself out. As I clambered over to make some tea, she launched straight away into a tirade about her admiral.

"Such demands, Satsuko," she wailed. "I sometimes think I would have been better off at the Oasis."

I smiled thinly, glancing at the thick fur coat.

"He won't keep away. He treats me like I'm a prisoner!"

"That must be very unpleasant for you, Michiko," I agreed.

She gave a sad nod. "But he loves me, you see, Satsuko. He's going to tell his wife in America that he's leaving her."

I stifled a laugh. "And marry you, Michiko?" I asked. "Is that really likely?"

"He's very wealthy," she said airily, ignoring the question. She took a small, jewelled mirror from a leather purse and applied an invisible dusting of powder to her face.

"And you'll never guess, Satsuko," she said, dramatically.

"What's that, Michiko?"

She cleared her throat and stood up. With one hand against her breast, she sang the notes of an ascending scale in a pure clean voice.

"Very melodic, Michiko."

"Do you think so?" she said, with a proud smile. "I'm learning how to act as well."

She had persuaded her admiral to pay for lessons with some old stagehands from the Minato Theatre, and had even managed to cajole him into buying her a piano. In fact, she said, it was to be delivered later on that very day.

As the kettle boiled, I felt quite queasy and thought instinctively of my vial of pills in the dresser.

"It's kind of you to visit, Michiko," I said, as I poured the water into the pot, "what with all your new distractions."

My stomach suddenly heaved.

"But I've missed you so much, Satsuko!" she said.

"Do you know," I said, inhaling sharply, "I was at the cinema just last week. I saw an American film that starred an actress who resembled you. Could it be Ingrid something?"

"Ingrid Bergman?" she cried, clapping her hands. "How clever you are, Satsuko! I think so too. There's a definite resemblance."

I turned my face away, swallowing bile. I wondered if I could politely ask her to leave. But, to my relief, she waved away her tea in any case.

"Satsuko," she said, "please forgive me. I really must go. My piano is to be delivered at any moment."

"Please come again, Michiko. You're always very welcome," I said.

"As soon as I can. Oh, and before I forget..."

She picked up a package wrapped in red crêpe de Chine and placed it on the table.

"I've no need for gifts, Michiko," I stammered. "I'm doing perfectly well..."

"Please accept it, Satsuko," she begged, kneeling in front of me. "You really must."

A horn blared outside. Before I could respond, Michiko had scuttled to the door. She whipped out her mirror and applied a last, rapid puff of powder to her face. Then, with a wave of her gloved hand, she was gone.

The powder hovered in the air, a pungent flowery smell. Suddenly, I gasped, reached for the pail and heaved up the pitiful milky contents of my stomach. My eyes were blurry with tears as I held onto its cold metal rim.

After several minutes, I slid over to the table. I took the package Michiko had left me and held it on my lap. There were several silk bows and ribbons criss-crossing the package and I fumbled with them for some time, until finally I gave up and just ripped open the red tissue paper.

"Oh, Michiko," I said.

A fur stole lay in the box, taken from a white fox or some other expensive animal. I lifted it out. It was so beautiful that I felt tears spring into my eyes. The fur was the softest thing I had ever felt in my life, delicate and supple and luxurious. I stood up, and held it against my cheek for a long time. Then I went over and lay back on the futon, and drifted away, lost in its fleecy softness for the rest of the afternoon.

A Joe with a pockmarked face was fast asleep on top of me, snoring loudly in my ear. He had been celebrating his birthday that night and his cronies had strong-armed him into swallowing one bottle of beer after another. With an effort, I rolled him off onto the floor and rang for Mr. Shiga. When the man's friends came to take him away, they snorted with laughter and put his clothes on back to front, which was just the kind of childish joke the Americans seemed to continually enjoy playing upon one another.

So I wasn't in a very good mood as I waited in the cold drizzle for a tram that never came. Eventually I decided that it would be just as well to walk to Shimbashi Station and take the overground train home from there. I drew my fur stole close around my neck and walked into a slanting wind.

It was deep winter now and I wondered how they survived, the pan-pan girls. Several were sheltering under the low arches of the overground railway line. They stood on either side of the short tunnels, each with a leg bent up, cigarette smoke curling in wisps. I quickened my step, dodging the icy pools of water as I fingered the stole around my neck.

I heard a light crunch of footsteps and a shadow lengthened beside me. I glanced back. A group of women were walking about fifteen paces behind me. I sped up, focusing on the lights of the station, a hundred yards ahead. The footsteps came closer. My heart started to pound in my chest. A voice in my head screamed at me to run, and I hoisted up my skirt. A fist struck me and I collapsed onto the ground.

There was a shrill chorus of voices around me. A tooth was loose on my tongue and my knees were torn. Thin, strong hands seized my arms and pulled me up. Three women surrounded me, and in the darkness, I recognized the stout girl in the purple blouse who had spit at me the week before. My fur stole was draped around her neck. I smelled cheap tobacco and sour sweat as she stepped forward. She slapped me as hard as she could. She hawked and spat at me once again, and I felt chewing gum caught in my hair.

"Where have you been tonight, you bitch?" she demanded. She slapped me hard again and I yelped. "Still think you're better than us?"

I shook my head, but she grabbed my arm and twisted it.

"You American whore!" she screamed. "I should stab you in the heart right here and now!"

I gasped as she shoved me. She seized my bag and began to rifle through it. Another, very tall woman stepped in front of me. Dressed in a crimson frock, her eyebrows were painted high up on her forehead, giving her a permanent puzzled look. She reached for a clump of my hair and twisted it around until tears sprang into my eyes.

"What are you doing down here anyway?" the tall woman whispered. "You know this is our patch."

I tried to shake my head, gasping in pain. Her other hand moved quietly in the darkness and I felt a sudden cold, sharp point between my lip and my nose.

"We own this ward," she said, staring at me with startled eyes. "You'll pay your share like anyone else."

The point jabbed into my flesh and I screamed. She suddenly drew it away, and I fell sobbing to the ground. The girls were pulling my things from my bag now, pocketing what they wanted and flinging the rest away like foxes devouring a chicken. The stout girl was stroking my stole as if it were a cat.

The woman in the crimson frock squatted beside me. The knife blade glistened in her hand.

"I've seen you before," she said, in an empty voice. "I've seen how you look at us."

I shook my head desperately.

"Do you really think you're better than us?" she asked. She raised the knife and drew the blade around my neck. My entire skin crawled. A humiliating seepage came from between my legs. She smiled as drops spattered against the ground. "See? You're no different."

I fainted dead away.

When I came to, the women were disappearing underneath the iron struts of the railway bridge, curses and animal shrieks echoing behind them. My blouse was torn and my stockings were shredded. When I touched one side of my face, my mouth was swollen, and my fingers came away smeared with dark blood.

As I struggled to my feet, I squinted at a card that lay on the ground in front of me. It was ornate, emblazoned with a red satin peony, and inscribed with hand-brushed words. The symbols spelled out a name. *Ketsueki Sakura Gumi*, I read.

The Blood Cherry Gang.

So it seemed we really were to have equal rights in Japan now. Women would be able to vote and the men could no longer divorce us whenever they chose, and now we even had our own lady gangsters to terrorize us, just as the men had had the yakuza all this time.

The Blood Cherry girls were already infamous at the Oasis, I discovered. The rumour went that they had all made a blood pact. Their leader, Junko — the woman in the crimson frock — had once been the famous geisha "Willow Tree" and the mistress of Akamatsu, the ace fighter pilot. They were witches in human form; they were *kitsune,* fox-spirits, who could bewitch men and even shift shape when they chose to. It was all nonsense, of course, but, when I recalled my nightmarish meeting with them, it was still enough to send a shiver down my spine.

In any case, the gang was composed of the very worst kind of pan-pan who worked the area between Yurakucho and the Kachidoki Bridge, which they now claimed as their own territory. Dressed in lurid clothes, their faces garishly painted, they claimed the right to organize all the girls in the surrounding streets, which meant harassing them, bullying them, and stealing from them as much as they could. And it was the Blood Cherry girls who, for some unfortunate reason, had decided that I needed to be punished.

I was squatting in the filthy lavatory shed outside the Oasis when I felt a sharp pain, as if hot needles were passing through me. I knew straight away what it was. The other girls had talked about it often enough.

The doctor confirmed my suspicions when he made his rounds the following week. I was distraught. Mr. Shiga would be informed and I would be obliged now to take several weeks off work, in which time I wouldn't earn a sen. I'd have to find the money for medicine to treat the condition, which was only available through the black market, and which, of course, was extremely expensive.

I approached Mr. Shiga on my hands and knees, begging him to advance me a loan. To my horror, he dismissed me, right on the spot.

"You've been an embarrassment for months now," he said. "Just look at yourself, Takara-san. This is the last straw."

Stunned, I packed up my makeup and my collection of trinkets. I said goodbye to some of the other girls, and walked out of the old bomb shelter for the last time. When I got home, I filled the pail from the standpipe in the street, then went inside and sponged myself slowly down. Afterward, I studied myself for a long time in the mirror. Hollow sockets stared back at me, and my hair was lank and brittle. My belly was swollen, and my arms and legs looked like sticks. A red sore had formed at the side of my mouth and my ribs showed under my shrunken breasts. I looked like a ghost.

Wearily, I wrapped up my beautiful green kimono, and took it back down to the Shimbashi market.

"Back already, dear?" the old lady clucked. She smoothed out the fabric and counted a few notes and coins into my palm.

It was less than half of what Michiko had paid. Confused, I asked if she had made some kind of mistake.

"Take it or leave it, dear," she said, her nose wrinkling. "There's plenty more like you about."

Over by the railway arches, I saw a flash of colour. I was in the heart of Blood Cherry territory. I hid behind the old woman's table, laden with kimonos, as unfamiliar girls headed toward the market.

Somehow, in the light of day, they seemed different. They glowed with life as they scoured the stalls, cursing and biting apples and flinging the cores over their shoulders. They barged their way through the dreary crowds in their bright Western dresses, flicking banknotes under the noses of the peddlers. As I stood there watching, I felt a sudden stab of realization. They really were different from me, I thought.

They were honest. I'd let Michiko and the managers fill my head with sheer nonsense — that we were Butterflies, Foreign Specialists, modern-day Okichis! But we were all just whores. These girls admitted it. They were the lowest of the low, and they just didn't care.

Just like that, they'd washed their hands of the slogans and lies we'd been fed for so many years. The curbs and controls that had made us slaves and that had brought our country to the brink of ruin. These were the New Women of Japan, I thought. Not us. No happy endings for them, no heartbreaking affairs like Kyoto geisha. They would smoke and spit and sell themselves out for the last penny, until one day they would collapse, dead in the gutter, free at last.

The next day, I washed, dressed in my brightest clothes, and painted my eyes in vivid colours. In the afternoon, I took the Yamanote Line to Shimbashi, and walked in the direction of Tokyo Bay past the old, abandoned market of Tsukiji by the low, dull arches of the Kachidoki Bridge. I examined the card that the Blood Cherries had left. The sky was pale and blustery, and there was a reek of fish.

Their house was a big, broken-down mansion that must have belonged to a merchant once. A girl dressed in a short green skirt opened the door. She wore a sprig of clover in her hair and her eyelids were shaded with silvery-green powder, like the wings of some exotic butterfly.

I bowed meekly as she showed me through to a gutted hall. The place was like an enormous, smashed up doll's house. Landings jutted out from the walls, and splintered stairs and ladders led up through holes in the collapsed ceiling. Dozens of girls lounged about in their underclothes on the bare flagstones with cigarettes in their mouths, playing flower cards and swigging from a large bottle they passed between them. Piles of clothes and empty saké flasks were scattered all around and a large mirror stained with verdigris was ratcheted to the split wooden panelling of one wall.

Underneath the staircase, a gaudy little shrine had been set up, decorated with star-shaped scraps of silver paper and burning candles. Pictures of angels, torn from Western books, had been pasted in a circle on the crumbling plaster. In the centre, a carved statue of Jesus Christ was splayed upon a wooden cross, naked but for a loincloth, his head turned away, as if he couldn't bear to look at the world.

The stout girl was kneeling on the ground before it, hands clasped, mumbling to herself. As I stood there, Junko emerged unsteadily through a large, dark hole in the wall. Her face was smooth and white, framed by tight black curls, and she wore a pair of round sunglasses. She walked toward me, steadying herself every now and then. When she stood in front of me, I noticed little pricks along her inner arms.

"Did you know that Maria-sama was a virgin when she gave birth to Jesus Christ?" she rasped, gesturing at the stout girl. "Yotchan over there believes that if she prays hard enough, Jesus Christ will make her a virgin again!"

As she laughed, I noticed faint lines on her forehead. Her cheeks sagged beneath powder. Her fingernails were painted crimson and the skin on her hands was wrinkled.

"How old fashioned!" she spat. "Relying on a man for everything."

She gave a tight smile and took off her sunglasses. Her eyes shrank as she looked at me.

"So you've come to work for me now, is that it?"

"Yes," I said.

"They always do." She counted on her bony fingers. "We charge eight yen a time. That's the standard rate so don't forget it. Four goes to us and two more goes on food and drink. You work out the rest for yourself."

Two yen, I calculated. It really wasn't much. A packet of cigarettes alone cost twenty. But I just nodded, feeling a sudden, painful itch between my thighs and a sharp desire for one of my little pills.

Junko came very close and pressed her fingernail against the skin of my cheek.

"Holiday season for the yankiis," she mused. "Plenty of work for a pretty girl like you."

All of the other girls had abandoned their games now and crowded in front of the big mirror, painting their faces and trying on different pieces of clothing.

"Well, then," Junko said, "time to get ready."

I nervously prepared myself behind the scrum of girls. After half an hour, Junko clapped her hands and we all stood in a wide circle and turned to face each other. The girl next to me stretched out her tongue. All the other girls were doing the same, placing little tablets into their open mouths as they looked into each other's eyes. The girl beside me delivered my tablet, and I felt my heart pounding as it dissolved upon my tongue. The big bottle of shochu went around the circle and I took a deep swig, washing the pill down my throat.

The girls held each other's hands. We stepped forward and swooped them up into the air. *Banzai!*

Excited and nervous, the girls streamed toward the door. As I passed, Junko gripped my wrist.

"You see?" she hissed. "You're just like us, after all."

The night was freezing and there were patches of black ice on the ground. The girls were dressed in all the colours of the rainbow, their hair styled in rumpled permanents, their lips like dark petals. Restless from the pills they had taken, they screeched out vulgar comments to nervous passersby.

Junko walked beside me with Yotchan following. The faint smell of the sea drifted toward us from the nearby bay, and as we passed the pale green roofs of Hongwan Temple, some of the girls began to peel away down side streets. Junko prodded me in the back to indicate that I should carry on. My throat was very dry and my heart was beating fitfully as I thought about the night ahead.

The streets grew busier as we crossed the Ginza and turned north toward Yurakucho, following the brickwork of the overground train track. Delivery men rode by on bicycles, and the Americans were muffled up against the cold, grinning and shaking hands as they passed each other.

"Over there," Junko commanded, as we arrived at the back of Yurakucho Station. She pointed to a low-slung arch beneath the train tracks and I walked over and leaned against the tunnel wall, my fingertips pressing the cold, glazed tiles. Junko stood beneath a nearby streetlamp in a freezing cloud of mist.

An elderly Japanese man approached. His breath was heavy as he inspected me through his glasses.

"How much?" he asked.

"Eight yen, sir," I said. "And worth every sen."

He squeezed my arm so violently that I cried out.

"Not so rough!"

"Come on," he ordered. "Hurry up."

Junko was still standing against the streetlamp as he pushed me deeper into the low tunnel. Her arms were folded, and she had a look of triumph on her face.

Headlights blazed white all around us. Sirens blared and there was the throb and roar of engines as military trucks careened toward the tunnels, men leaping down from the cabs. The old man thrust away my hand and limped off as fast as he could, as the jeeps screeched to a halt on each side of railway track, searchlights blazing in great white beams. Women were running out like rats from their holes, screaming as American military and regular Japanese police seized hold of them. They hauled them by the waist and swung them into the open-backed trucks as if they were sacks of rice. Shadows veered wildly as a truck skidded to a halt in front of me, its tires sliding in the icy gravel. Two Japanese policemen leaped out and advanced upon me with torches in their hands. I gasped as one of them grabbed my wrists, jerking so hard that my arms nearly came out of their sockets. The other gripped the collar of my dress, and I heard the fabric tear as he dragged me toward the back of a truck like an animal.

"What are you doing?" I shrieked. "Get off me!"

"We're clearing up tonight," the policeman snapped. "You whores are giving Japan a bad name."

Us? I thought, speechless with rage, despite myself. *Us, giving Japan a bad name?*

"How dare you," I cried. "We're the only honest ones left!" I kicked at his leg, but he shoved me heavily into the back of the truck and I tumbled onto the cold, rumbling metal floor.

As I pulled myself up, I could smell cheap perfume. Girls were perched on the narrow benches that lined each side of the truck bed. All of them were pan-pan, and they had covered their faces with their hair in shame.

"Where are they taking us?" I asked.

Through the canvas flaps, I could see the lights and the bustle as herds of Americans crowded on the Ginza. We came to a juddering halt near the junction by the Continental Hotel. Staff cars were dropping off elegant men and women in dinner dress, and uniformed bellboys were rushing over to escort the guests. Just as the truck jerked forward, a sleek American sedan pulled up and a boy saluted as he opened the back door. A white-haired man in dress uniform climbed out, clasping the hand of a petite Japanese woman. She was wearing a black velvet cocktail dress, and draped over her arm was a white fox coat.

"Michiko!" I screamed. "Michiko!"

I thought for a moment that she had heard me. She cocked her head to one side, then stood on tiptoe and kissed the man on the cheek. His hand slid down her back as he guided her up the red carpet toward the foyer. The truck pulled away, their figures shrinking as we accelerated up the avenue.

We crossed the Kanda River and turned onto the Edo Road. Very soon we would pass through Asakusa. I pictured the Sumida Park to one side of the road, the charred remains of my neighbourhood on the other. As we passed the Kototoi Bridge, I had a sudden, sharp premonition of where we were being taken.

The Yoshiwara canal was dark, the water low, and as we crossed over the bridge, I had a vivid memory of Hiroshi, standing on the high bank opposite as I floundered there, the fire pelting from the sky.

Thank heaven he couldn't see me now, I thought. Thank heaven he was dead. I groaned and pulled my hair over my face.

The truck crunched to a halt. The canvas flaps were pulled aside to show a huge, solitary building with flat grey walls lit by floodlights. Women were shouting and screaming as policemen hauled them from the trucks. I climbed down, shivering in the freezing night, and blinked. American soldiers and Japanese doctors in white coats were herding women toward a gatehouse. From high above us there came eerie shrieking. I gazed up at the towering building, shielding my eyes. Women were leaning out the windows on each level, waving and howling. As we swarmed toward the building, more trucks rolled up to deliver yet more girls. The women called down in a dreadful chorus, their hair falling wild about their shoulders, their tattered white gowns swaying in the wind. It was as if they were a horde of screaming souls, welcoming us all to hell.

18
PUBLIC RELATIONS (HAL LYNCH)

The corridors of the Continental were quiet and the peace of the Sabbath reigned throughout the building. A smell of roasting chicken drifted from the basement dining room and from somewhere came the regular report of an endless game of ping-pong. I locked my door and heaved my knapsack onto the bed and retrieved my rolls of film. Jittery and exhausted, I needed to sleep, but felt a deep and anxious need to develop my photographs straight away.

I figured I could use the darkroom in the basement of the newspaper office without being disturbed, so I took a taxi without changing my clothes. As I'd hoped, the newsroom was empty, the building silent. I went downstairs and unpacked my kit.

I felt a tightening in my stomach as I drew the first spool of glistening negatives from the reel. I'd had an irrational fear on the train that something would have gone wrong with the exposure, that the radioactivity in the city would somehow have damaged the film, that all I would be left with was blank prints and the uncertainty of memory. But now I could identify the scenes in miniature, as they threaded out under the red glow of the safety lamp, mute testament to the fact that all had truly occurred.

Once the negatives were dry, I lined up the paper beneath the enlarger head, and fed the strip through. I exposed the paper to the light, ticking off the seconds until they were done. One by one, I shook the sheets in the developing fluid. Slowly, the mysterious images welled back into existence.

As the pictures hung there, dripping on the drying line, a sensation of almost unbearable loneliness washed over me. The mangled pile of bicycles in the riverbed. The curving ribs of the ruined dome. The silent Buddha smiling enigmatically as snowflakes settled upon his head. I recalled the strange story the ambulance driver told me of how people's shadows had been burned into the bridges at the moment of the flash, and as I looked into the ancient eyes of the dance instructor, at the frail smile of the withered railwayman, I had a sudden comprehension of the deep, lingering malaise the victims had complained of, the terrible void that had developed within them, as if a cancer had devoured some vital part of their souls.

While the prints dried, I went upstairs to the empty newsroom. I sat at a desk and fed a sheet of carbon paper into the drum of a Smith-Remington. I stared at the blank page for what seemed like an eternity, lost in thought. Then, almost without thinking, I began to press my fingers down on the keys and a confusion of words and letters slowly clicked out onto the page.

"The Aftermath of the Atom," I titled the piece. I described the day as clearly and as simply as I could, from the moment that I had arrived at the station to the second my train back to Tokyo had passed into the tunnel. Darkness had fallen behind the big plate windows by the time I had finished, and the pool cast by my lamp was the only light burning in the building. I rolled out the final sheet and read the last paragraph out loud.

"While most of the victims of 'radiation disease' are now dead, it seems clear now that this terrifying new weapon has a capacity to destroy even beyond that which its creators could have foretold. It has the capacity to plant the seeds of a lethal sickness in men's bodies, to scatter poison into their very souls. Whatever moral justification may be found for the nuclear bombings of Japan, any government that believes in justice surely has a duty to help those that it has exposed to this creeping death, that still lurks in their bloodstream so many months after the smoke has cleared. The first step must be to acknowledge its existence."

The door creaked and I lurched in my chair. A tuneless whistle came from the corner of the room as the big overhead lights glimmered on. Eugene. He assumed the comical expression of a boy caught with his hand in the cookie jar.

"Hal!" he exclaimed, striding toward me. "Don't tell me you're working? It's Sunday night, you chump."

Hastily, I rearranged the pages on the desk.

"How about you, Eugene? Feeling guilty about something?"

The corners of his mouth turned down.

"Let's just say I forgot something." He opened the drawer of his desk and palmed a package of prophylactics into his overcoat pocket. He parked himself down on my desk with a grin.

"Where have you been, anyway, Hal? I hardly see you anymore."

I felt a wave of hopeless sympathy for my old roommate. He'd never seen any action, like all the other fresh recruits now garrisoned in Japan. The country was just a playground for him.

Grime and dirt were ground under my fingernails; developing fluid stained my skin. As I looked up at his cheerful freckled face, the wire-rimmed glasses crooked beneath the thatch of hair, I felt a curious collision of instincts. After a moment of hesitation, I gathered the sheaf of papers on the desk and handed it to him.

"Proof this for me, Eugene."

He licked his thumb and forefinger as he flipped through the pages. Surprise, astonishment, confusion progressed across his face as he read. I slumped in my chair, aware of the sour reek of my unwashed body.

When he finally finished, he gave a low whistle.

"Boy oh boy, Hal. Do you think Dutch'll go for it?"

I laughed, despairing. "You know, I wasn't planning to file it to the *Stars and Stripes*, Eugene."

"So where are you going to file it?"

I paused. "I'm not sure yet. One of the nationals, maybe. On an overseas line."

His face crinkled with distaste.

"So you're a Fancy Dan now, Hal?"

I shrugged, shook my head. He adjusted his glasses.

"I don't get it Hal. Why are you so concerned about the Japs all of a sudden? They started it, didn't they?"

I didn't know what to say. I led him downstairs to the basement and gestured at the prints. He examined each of them in turn, pausing every now and then to take a closer look. Then he became silent for a long time.

"They're quite something, Hal."

I nodded.

"SCAP was upset enough about our rat man."

Dear Eugene. I pictured the old bargeman in his raincoat, looking out at the river. Dutch, in his office, accusing me of being morbid. I wanted to laugh and cry all at once.

"So they were, Gene. So they were."

He looked at me with doubt.

"You're sure you want to do this, Hal? You know you could get in trouble."

I nodded again.

He frowned.

"Come for a drink?" he asked, hopefully.

I shook my head, my eyes heavy.

"Okay, Hal. You get some rest, do you hear me? I'll see you tomorrow."

He patted me on the shoulder before climbing back up the stairs. There was a vague sound of whistling and the heavy office door closed with a thud. I was hopelessly fatigued. I took down the prints from the line, peeled the carbon from the typewriter, and slid the photos and the story into my drawer.

The next day at noon, freshly showered and shaved, I walked back into the newsroom. Faces glanced up at me, then dropped swiftly back down to their typewriters.

"Did the emperor die?" I asked.

No one replied. I approached my desk with a sharp pang of trepidation. A scribbled memorandum in Dutch's fine handwriting lay upon it: "ASAP."

My scalp prickled as I casually slid open my drawer.

It was empty. I looked over at Dutch's office. Figures were silhouetted against the glass, and the muffled sound of argument came from within.

Watching the door, I hurried downstairs to the darkroom. I switched on the lights. The developing tins were neatly stacked in the corner of the room. Even the drops of fluid on the floor beneath the drying line had been mopped clean. I hurried back up the stairs just in time to see Eugene arriving at his desk. He glanced at me, the sudden look of a whipped dog passing over his face.

The door to the office swung open and two military policemen stepped out, followed by an extremely anxious-looking Dutch.

"Ah, our roving reporter!" he called when he spotted me.

As the MPs loped over, Dutch stood by his door and rubbed his head.

"Mr. Lynch?" one asked, squaring up to me. He was puffy faced, his skin as soft as a boy's. I realized, absurdly, that I recognized him: the petty officer I'd sat next to on the gun turret of the *Missouri*, on the day of the surrender signing, months before. He frowned in vague recollection.

"We've been asked to fetch you, sir."

His friendly southern drawl was incongruously loud in the silent newsroom. Everyone was still staring down at their typewriters in studious concentration.

"By whom?"

"Just come along with us, would you, Mr. Lynch?" he said, placing an encouraging hand on my forearm. "There's some folks who want to talk to you."

The Public Relations office was located in a sinister-looking building that had once housed Radio Tokyo, the voice of the Japanese Empire. From here bulletins of lightning victories had rung across the Pacific, the shortwave siren song of Tokyo Rose. The concrete box was painted jet black for camouflage against night attack.

Flanked by the MPs, I walked up the stairs to the wide doorway as a man I somewhat knew emerged. George LeGrand was a photographer from *LIFE* magazine who'd approached me a few weeks earlier to ask my advice on aerial photography.

"Hello, Lynch," he said pleasantly, nodding toward the MPs. "Everything in order?"

"Hello, LeGrand," I said. "It seems the brigadier general wants to speak to me about something."

"Baker?" he asked, raising his eyebrows. "Who did you shoot?"

"Might just have been myself."

Brigadier General Frayne Baker was MacArthur's new head of Public Relations — a stony, white-haired North Dakotan, as mean and surly, by all accounts, as his predecessor.

"I wish you luck. In any case, you'll find him in good cheer."

"Is that so?"

"I've come from him just this moment. We've all been on an exciting duck hunt."

"Oh?"

"Oh, sure. The Imperial Palace invited him to the Imperial Wild Duck Preserve to try his hand. They give you these big nets, you see . . ."

The southern boy cleared his throat.

"I'd best be on my way, LeGrand."

"Okay, Lynch. See you around." He glanced at the MPs, then gave me a quick wink. In a stage whisper he said: "Don't worry too much about Baker. He's had a damn good lunch."

When I opened the door to the office, Baker was sitting behind his desk, cap askew, eyes closed, and hands clasped across his chest. A trio of ducks lay on one side of the desk, necks tied together with twine, beaks hanging disconsolately open. A musty smell came from his person, and I had a sudden recollection of my father's den when I was a boy, a bottle on his desk as he slept off a lunchtime load.

I spotted my missing piece on the desk, heavily scored with blue pencil, thick initials circled in the margins. Two photographs lay beside it. I recognized the picture of the schoolteacher. Next to it — strangely, I thought — was the photo of the Buddha statues. Both of the prints had been torn precisely in half.

Baker's eyes flickered open. He spent a second staring at me, attempting to focus on my face.

"What the hell are you doing in here?" he snapped.

"I was told to come, sir. Obliged."

He gave a sullen growl and rubbed the stubble on his chin.

"Who the hell's your editor?"

"Dutch. That is, John Van Buren, sir."

"*Stars and Stripes*?"

"That's correct."

He placed his big, liver-spotted hands down on the table.

"You do him a great disservice. As you do your paper. You call yourself a reporter?"

"With the greatest respect, sir —"

"Respect?" His eyes flashed. "Respect? What does a *Stars and Stripes* man know about respect? Do you respect military interdict? What in the hell is a *Stars and Stripes* reporter doing in a restricted area in any case?"

"With the greatest respect, sir, the *Stars and Stripes* has a tradition —"

"Damn the *Stars and Stripes*, sir!" The fist slammed down upon the table with such violence that the beaks of the ducks rattled faintly together. "Damn you. Don't you know I could have you court-martialled right here and now? Do you understand that?"

My mouth was dry. "The public has a right to know what is happening in Hiroshima —"

"The public has all the information they need about Hiroshima, son!" A vein bulged in his forehead, and I recoiled, picturing my father at the height of a fit. "Don't you worry about that. This —" He gestured at the table. "This — horseshit? You think you know better than our best medical men?

"I want to report what I saw, sir —"

"What you saw? What you were shown. And who showed it to you? The Japs."

He stood up behind his desk. As he leaned forward, I could smell the boozy cave of his mouth.

"Did it ever strike you as convenient, what you saw, sir? Gave you a guided tour, did they? Your own private freak show. Ever consider why they were so keen to show you around?"

He was panting slightly, perspiration on his forehead. I felt a faint stab of doubt. In my mind's eye, I saw the police chief as he scowled at me: *Now — show America what it has done.* Dr. Hiyashida's familiar wave, his gleeful pride as he showed me his most pathetic victims. *Take more pictures! For your newspaper!*

I swallowed. Baker's eyes twitched. "Played you for a fool, you damned idiot. Don't you see? You're a sap. A first-class sap." He picked up my article and slapped it with one hand. He snorted, as if faintly amused. "Radiation disease."

He threw the pages in the air, and they fluttered incoherently to the floor. "Horseshit. Tell me, son. Were you ever in a battle against the Japs?"

"I was a lieutenant in Third Recon —"

"Well, I was a general at Bataan, Lieutenant!" he hollered, smashing his fist upon the table again. "You ever hear of something called the Death March? Does that mean anything to you? You ever hear of a place called Pearl Harbour?"

His eyes were blazing, consumed with fury as he flung a ferocious finger toward the door.

"Get the hell out of here!" His ruddy face had ripened to a deep maroon, his tongue lolling from his mouth like an overheated dog's. "Get out!"

I rotated swiftly and marched out the door, as tiny, ruffling feathers floated up from the corpses of the ducks.

Dutch stroked the ginger-blonde hair that he grew long below his pate, looking at me with watery eyes.

"There's no chance, Hal, I'm sorry. No chance at all."

His face was grave, as if he were a doctor informing me of a terminal illness. "And there's trouble. It's gone all the way up.

They've been asking me some pretty tough questions about you."

"Such as?"

"Such as whether you're some kind of subversive. Whether you are a communist."

"Am I, Dutch? In your opinion?"

He sighed. "Times change, Hal. They say there's another war coming soon."

"What did you plead?"

He frowned. "I told them about your fine work in reconnaissance. I told them about your commendations. I told them that you may have been . . . disturbed by what you saw up there. That you may be feeling the need to make some kind of recompense."

"So I'm a bleeding heart, Dutch, is that it? Or are we pleading insanity?"

"Hal, I'm putting my neck out for you here."

"What's the verdict Dutch?"

He shook his head. "You're suspended, Hal, for the time being. Pending their decision on what to do with you."

A long moment passed.

"What about my other pieces?" I said, sullenly. "'The Touristic GI?'"

"I'm sorry, Hal," he said, with more emphasis.

"And you've agreed to all this, Dutch? What kind of newsman are you? Whatever happened to the crucible of change?"

He laughed. "What do you want me to do, Hal? They're threatening to have you court-martialled for travelling to a prohibited area. How can I publish journalistic pieces from a military prison?" He looked down at the desk, guiltily. "And I've been asked to take back your press pass, Hal. I'm sorry."

An unexpected lump rose in my throat as I slid the crumpled paper out of my wallet. I looked at the scrawl of MacArthur's signature as I placed the pass upon the desk.

"What's going to happen to me, Dutch?"

He leaned forward. *Sotto voce* he said: "Strictly between you, me, and the gatepost, Hal, I think you've been lucky. Believe it or not. I get the impression there's been some kind of falling out upstairs about what to do with you. There's a certain amount of . . . tension between Intelligence and the New Dealers."

"So they're not slinging me out?"

"Not yet."

"I can't write, but I can stay?"

He shrugged. "For now at least."

Limbo, I thought. *The realm of lost souls.*

"Okay, Dutch. I'm going to go get my head down."

A pained look came over his face. "That's something else I need to tell you, Hal. You're going to have to find another place to live. They're taking away your billeting rights."

I let out a short laugh.

"I know, I know. They're a petty, vindictive bunch when they want to be. And you won't be able to draw rations either. You've got two weeks."

"No more powdered eggs, Dutch?"

"'Fraid not."

"No more gratis Luckys?"

"No sir."

"Alright. Thanks, Dutch."

"Wait, Hal," he said as I stood to leave.

"Don't tell me. I'm not invited to the Christmas party."

His face was serious. His throat moved. He opened up his drawer and took out a slim envelope and slid it toward me.

I glanced at him in question. His brow rippled.

"It's very bad form for a photographer to leave his negatives in the enlarger head, Lynch."

I tried to recall leaving the darkroom the night before, dizzy with fatigue.

I half opened the brim of the envelope. Inside was a cut spool of maybe twenty photographs, shots I recognized from the hospital. I felt my heart leap, and I leaned over to grasp Dutch by the shoulders, kissing his bald head.

"Alright, alright," he spluttered.

"I won't forget this, Dutch. I mean it."

He wiped his head with his handkerchief. "Merry Christmas, Hal. Enjoy it while you still can."

I suddenly pictured Dutch in his paper Christmas hat, playing Santa amongst his horde of red-headed children. I couldn't help but smile.

"And your eggnog!" he called out plaintively, as I left the room.

19
CHILDREN OF THE EMPEROR (HIROSHI TAKARA)

Tomoko and I were lying on the cold floor of Ueno Station, gazing up at constellations of fireflies. A moment later, we were standing on the concrete embankment of the Yoshiwara canal, the water strewn with fire as I kissed her and stroked her black hair.

A pulse went through me. I tried to stop the dream, but it was already too late. We were standing beneath the iron tracks, a train screaming overhead as I opened the fly of my khaki uniform, twisting her hair in my fist as I pulled her toward me —

I woke with a shout, repelled and ashamed. It was freezing cold. In the darkness next to me, Koji whimpered in his sleep.

Tomoko had become almost completely silent since her attack, just as she had after her mother had sent her away from Hiroshima. No one had spoken as we walked back home that night. After we'd reached the inn, I told the children to go straight to bed. They were aware that something awful had happened.

Tomoko shuffled to the bathhouse and slid the door shut behind her. After a while, there was a clang of pipes and the sound of water. I realized that the water would be icy cold and

I told Aiko to go through and ask Tomoko if she would like us to light the boiler. After a moment, she came back and shook her head.

"Go upstairs then. Lay out her blankets," I said.

She bowed and darted up the staircase, hardly daring to look at me.

As I gazed at the paper screen of the bathroom door, it was as if I could see right through the panels to the other side. Tomoko was sitting naked on a low cedar stool, strands of wet hair clinging to her face. Her monpe were crumpled in the corner, growing darker as the water soaked into them. I imagined the white skin of her rib cage, her head in her hands as she stared into the puddles of cold water...

To my horror, I realized that I'd become stiff.

There must be a demon inside me, I thought, as I tramped along the Ginza. In the old Matsuzakaya department store, behind the steamed-up windows, crowds of GIs filled the aisles, and they streamed out carrying boxes tied with ribbon. Next door, Japanese whores stood at the entrance of a club, trying to coax them inside.

As I watched the soldiers I was filled with violent fantasies of revenge. *I'll find a pistol,* I thought, *a Nambu Type 14. I'll find that bastard, I'll track him down. I'll wait outside that club until he comes out drunk into the street: fire right into his face... Bam! Bam! Bam!*

Long after nightfall, I found myself walking past Hibiya Park toward the corner of the Imperial Plaza. Two huge pine trees stood erect and glittering in front of the Allied headquarters. As I squinted at the yellow windows of the building, I wondered about the men who worked up there. Probably all of them had slept with at least one American woman. Probably a Japanese one as well. Even the ugliest amongst them would know the great masculine secret that still lay beyond me.

I walked over to the palace moat. A full moon shone in the sky, the light rippling in the water. I remembered how my father had always told me to look for the rabbit in the moon when it was full. Something bobbed down in the darkness and I wondered if it were the swollen body of a dead rat. Another lump floated over, and then, in the moonlight, more and more came into view, bumping against the high stone wall of the bank.

A thin American in wire-rimmed spectacles stood beside me, his mouth open in a yawn. He fumbled for a second, and then pissed, a solid splash against the water. The sound slackened to a vague stream and he shivered like a dog. He gave a belch of satisfaction as he buttoned himself up and strode away. As I looked down, I slowly realized what the shapes were. Legions of abandoned prophylactics were bobbing about down in the moat.

As I crossed the avenue into the Imperial Plaza, there were faint sighs, regular grunts, and sounds of surprise. Against the wall of the gate, twisted shapes humped against each other, the moon lighting up the white buttocks of men encircled by pale coils of legs as vague moans of pleasure came softly, then sharply.

It was hopeless. A moment later, unable to stop myself, I ran over to the trees and thrust my hand into my underwear. I rubbed myself swiftly and furiously until, after just a few seconds, I felt a dark warmth rear inside my belly, overwhelming me, until I shuddered, gasping, hot and cold all at once, as if my stomach had melted out over my thighs. I stood there, breathless in the shadows, holding onto the tree, quivering with shame.

~

The eaves of the warped tenement houses were low and stank of fishguts and nightsoil. We were rummaging about in a set of garbage cans, and I was arm-deep in refuse, the sickly sweet smell of rot swamping my nostrils as the other children hunted a little distance away.

Below my fingertips, I felt a soft, smooth sphere, tender and forgiving. I clutched hold and tugged it out. My heart suddenly quivered. It was exactly what I'd thought! A whole bean jam bun, untouched except for a tiny solar system of silver-blue mould on its surface. An intense pang of hunger knotted my stomach as I held it to my face and breathed in the smell of the bean jam.

Tomoko was hunched over ten paces away, delving through a heap of old peelings. Her tunic sleeves were rolled up, her arms as brittle as sticks.

The dough of the bun was sticky in my fingers. I urged myself to go over and give it to her. Here it was, I thought. The magical token that might somehow break the awful spell upon her, that might give her back the ability to speak again...

From nowhere, an image came into my mind. Bodies writhing behind the gate of the Imperial Plaza; my hand wet and sticky in my pants.

Aiko stood beside me, her eyes wide.

"Look what you've found, Hiroshi," she cried. "Will you give it to Tomoko?"

Tomoko glanced up as she heard her name spoken. The welts on my cheeks throbbed. I gave a short laugh.

"Tomoko?" I said. "Why should I?"

"But you always save bean jam for Tomoko," insisted Aiko.

Tomoko stared at me. I felt like I was standing on the edge of a cliff, and there was an impossible drop between us. I laughed again, the sound shrill in my ears. Without knowing why, I stuffed the bun into my mouth and took a big, wolfish bite, chewing with my mouth open like a peasant as Aiko watched me in fascinated horror.

The dough was so dry that it made me gag. I almost choked, and spat out what was left. Aiko stared at the remains, as if she was about to cry. Tomoko turned and bent over, her arms by her side. My eyes filled with sudden tears. There was a shout. Koji appeared from the alleyway and held up his little fists in triumph.

"Come and look at what I've found," he hollered. "I've found a real feast!"

I paused for a second, then rushed after him down the alley. There was a gap beneath a wooden fence and we climbed through into the yard of what must have once been a teahouse. Crates of rubbish and empty bottles lay on the ground and a stench came from an old latrine shed.

"Look!" Koji crowed. He pointed at the empty bottles and crates. There were piles of obvious morsels between them: apple cores, fish bones and mouldering pumpkins. The children scrambled toward them and I was just about to follow when suddenly I saw something from the corner of my eye.

"Stop!" I shouted. "Stop right now."

As my eyes adjusted, I saw the sleek corpse of a rat, twitching between the crates. Another appeared, then another, both dead, unmoving — their mouths open, their wiry tails coiled, tiny sharp teeth bared in pain. I poked one with my foot but it didn't move. I tipped it over.

Its puffy flesh was writhing with maggots. I gagged.

"Get away!" I hollered. Don't touch anything."

Koji's face fell and his frail chest heaved up and down.

"Get away now!"

The children stood there, as if unable to believe that we would be leaving all of this food behind.

"Now!" I shouted. One by one, they slid back under the fence. As we gathered in the darkness of the alley a terrible tiredness came over me. It would be best just to go home, I thought. It really had been the most ominous night.

"Right," I muttered. "Back to camp. No dawdling."

The children whinged in frustration.

"Be quiet!" I yelled. "I can't stand it!"

Icicles hung from the eaves of the tenements as we crept through the back streets like a clan of goblins. We had just reached the wasteground at the back of Ueno station when I heard a commotion behind me. I spun around, my fists raised in fury.

My heart stopped.

Tomoko lay on the ground as the other children stood above her and tried to pull her up. She shivered uncontrollably, as if she was having a fit. Aiko started to scream as I rushed over and knelt down in the earth beside Tomoko. Her hand was gripping onto something tightly and I tried to prise open her stiff fingers. She started to choke.

I thrust my fingers into her mouth and tried to wrench out whatever it was she had eaten. But she writhed violently from side to side, vomit seeping from her mouth. She suddenly retched and half-eaten fragments of fruit emerged. There, in the moonlight, were the black teardrops of apple pips on her glistening chin.

She gave an awful bark and her back arched and her limbs thrust out. She stared straight up at me and gripped onto my hand. Her eyes were filled with tears. She seemed to shake her head, and then started to gasp. She froze, and then her whole body rose up, as if a terrible pain were passing along her spine. She shuddered and sank back down again. She stared at me as a fine, white froth leaked from her lips.

Her fingers slowly released their grip on my own. She slumped to the ground. A strange gargling sound emerged from deep within her body, and I fell backward.

Her features seemed to soften. She was gazing up at an uncertain point high above, as if toward some distant star, far away in the sky.

20
SILENT NIGHT
(HAL LYNCH)

The festive season was upon us. In celebration, SCAP hoisted two Christmas trees outside headquarters with a ten-foot banner across the façade: "Merry Christmas!"

After I got my marching orders, part of me considered leaving Japan. I'd go back to New York, I thought, get on the GI Bill and return to Columbia. Join one of the big agencies or magazines or dailies and make a living snapping mobsters and sports stars. Or I'd move to some honest-to-God small town, a Knoxville or a Jacksonville, take a job at the local paper and cover the high school football games, the petty brawls and larcenies that came to the county court each week. I'd arrive at the office bright and cheery in my gleaming new Cadillac every morning, settle down with a Southern girl and raise a litter of my own...

Then I thought of Christmas dinner with my mother and my aunts in the depths of a New England winter — the empty plate laid for my father, his sullen portrait glaring down from the wall. The snow falling silently outside, as if it were passing over the very edge of the earth.

So I decided to stay in Tokyo, to get drunk, and to see what the new year would bring. The men that still haunted the

Continental were subdued now, almost meditative, resigned to another Christmas away from home. Most of the boys who'd seen action were already back home, their feet up in front of their well-deserved hearths in Lexington and Harrisburg and Worcester and all the other countless villes and burghs that make up the vertebrae of our nation. Those left behind walked the halls in their socks, wrote letters, played rummy and whist, busying themselves with innumerable small tasks to while away the time.

On Christmas Eve, SCAP organized a party. There was to be a dinner, a movie show, and then a performance by "native musicians." I pictured the overheated hall, the red-faced officers in their paper party hats attacking their tinned turkey and eggnog. Douglas MacArthur standing up to make some flowery speech as the officers slumped over their trifles. It was all too god-awful to contemplate, and so, early in the evening, I wrapped up warm and headed out into the streets, alone.

It was bitterly cold, and everyone had their hats pulled down over their foreheads, mufflers pulled up to their eyeballs. I hitched a ride to Shinjuku on an infantry truck, but the driver got lost and took an unaccountable detour and we passed through the abandoned districts, the shantytowns of the old city. The water that flooded the bomb craters had turned to ice, and old pieces of metal and timber were frozen within, sticking out like the limbs of witches. Between the craters, clumps of people huddled around miniature braziers, burning paper, kindling, pieces of old furniture — anything that could hold a flame. Their hands cast flickering shadows over orange faces as they stared into the fires. They didn't look up as we passed.

The Infantry finally let me off outside the brightly lit, newly covered market by Shinjuku Station, where groups of fresh, excited young GIs were swapping their cigarette ration for beer and whisky. I did the same and took a couple of nips right there to warm myself up. Then I wandered the streets with no particular goal in mind. Tacked to a newly cut telegraph pole was a handbill advertising a concert. Handel's *Messiah*. This intrigued me, so I asked a man for directions to the theatre. As I strode up the street, a couple of kids ran past me, frosted white from head to toe, as if they'd been rolled in sugar. I wondered whether this might be some strange Japanese seasonal custom, but then the rumble of a truck came from around the corner with GIs hanging from both sides, pumping out a great, whirling mass of white powder like a blizzard of fine snow — DDT. Folks were hurrying along after the truck to get disinfected as the powder drifted down and settled in restless shoals on the frozen ground.

I finally found the old theatre. Elderly couples in Western dress were walking inside as I paid my entrance fee to a beaming young woman. The roof of the amphitheatre was mostly gone, the building open to the sky. From a slat seat above the stalls I looked up to see a silver needlework of stars. Down below, the orchestra and choir sat on metal chairs, their breath emerging in glistening clouds. A couple of GIs were scattered solitary in the aisles, huddled up, clutching their arms for warmth. Everyone was shivering, so I had the bright idea of passing the whisky around. I tapped the shoulder of the man beneath me, who glanced at his wife, and then took the bottle with a murmur of surprise and gratitude. After he took a sip, I gestured for him to pass it on. It went steadily around members of the audience, who directed glances of appreciation in my direction, before it finally returned to me with barely a sip remaining.

Down below, the conductor tapped his stand and counted two silent notes in the air with his baton. Then the voices began to fill the frozen night and there was an exhalation from the audience. We all sank back into our seats, watching and listening as the exquisite voices of the choir billowed up into the sky in clouds of tiny diamonds.

I pictured the notes floating up, rising high above the ruined city, above the men and women who lay shivering in their shacks and hovels far below, huddled together around their flickering fires, silently staring into the flames and wondering what the future would bring. The voices flowed out across the night, and I thought about the folks back home in America, the Christmas trees lit up and the children scampering about in the snow as their mothers stood in the doorways, calling them in for dinner. I saw men and women all across the world, reunited after all these long years of war, mothers hugging sons, girls embracing sweethearts, fathers with tears in their eyes as they welcomed their children home, home from the war, back home to where they belonged, at last, for war was over — *and they were alive.*

I saw stricken refugees trudging across the plains of Europe, frozen and weary as they settled down by their campfires, snowflakes whirling around them, holding each other's hands as they haltingly began to sing. I saw solemn glasses being raised to lost fathers and brothers and sons — to the ones who had not returned — and I heard prayers of requiem and the sob of quiet mourning float up into the sky, mingling with the precious, holy notes of the chorus. I heard the great, melancholy music float out across the world, over the shattered cities and the bombed-out ruins, the fields of carnage and the tangled remains of the living and the dead, the terrible music that floated through the darkness that shrouded our silent, injured world that Christmas night, as far below, its men and women all sat huddled together in front of their fires, staring into the flames, and wondering what the future would bring.

When the concert ended, I applauded the orchestra for a long time, my hands numb within my gloves. I climbed down the steps to congratulate the conductor, then presented another bottle of whisky to the members of the orchestra, who smiled and bobbed their heads in thanks. I bowed back, and we all laughed and took sips, trembling with cold. The rest of the audience quietly departed.

There were few people on the streets as I headed for the station, and those who were out looked grim and unhappy. I offered the bottle to people at random, but most veered away, and I realized that I was drunk. Only one fellow took it — he unscrewed the cap, took a big swig, then grinned and gave me a thumbs up: *Merii Kurisamasu!*

I finally reached the station. The chemical truck had just passed and dashes of white powder were drifting about in the air. Time for bed, I thought.

Then, from nowhere, a group of elegant old ladies in colourful kimonos were tugging at my sleeve, their eyes twinkling, their faces as wrinkled as walnuts. They must have been freezing near to death, but their hair was styled to perfection, their kimono belts exquisitely tied, and they were bowing and smiling for all they were worth.

"Please, please," they asked me in English, "can we *sing* with you?"

I couldn't quite understand. Then one of them explained — they were Christians, she said, and this was the first Christmas they had been allowed to celebrate for several years. This made me pretty emotional and so I said yes, of course they could, in fact, we would all sing together, and we took each other's arms. And then, this bold young man, and these delightful, wrinkled women whose country I'd helped raze to the ground, well, we all stood there together outside of a ruined train station as flakes of DDT floated down from the sky like snow, and then, God help me, we began to sing "Silent Night."

PART THREE

APRÈS GUERRE

JANUARY 1946

21
YEAR OF THE DOG
(OSAMU MARUKI)

Mrs. Shimamura sang along to the radio as she washed the glasses. The inane and mournful chorus of "The Apple Song" was playing for the tenth time that day. She picked up the glasses one by one from the basin, twisting them this way and that so that drops of water flicked away from the rims, then swaddled them in the dishcloth and rubbed them vigorously, as if drying a child in a towel.

Her dimples had returned, I thought, as I watched her from my seat at the bar. I had my head in the pages of a story by the master, Jiro Tanizaki, my old idol, from his erotic, grotesque period. Once again, I revelled in his description of a lurid children's game, a leg bruising blue beneath sharp slaps. Ever since the end of the war, I had felt a jolt of excitement whenever I read the story, an odd pleasure in the thought of a sudden, stinging palm striking my own numb flesh.

A cold draft gusted in from the doorway. I gulped back my drink and shuddered, feeling a kind of sordid torpidity settle upon me. I studied the cover of the book. Tanizaki would still be writing, I thought, he would still be slogging away. Wasn't it at times of just such extremity and extenuation that art truly flourished? Tokyo eviscerated, a foreign army parading the streets — what would Tolstoy have made of it? Maupassant?

And yet here I sat, my lice-ridden overcoat draped over my shoulders, scribbling fantasies for the lost and the lonely. Hunched over my foul rotgut, tormented by constipation, a cough racking my lungs, my toes dissolving into the mouldy morass of my boots. Keening around a decent woman like Mrs. Shimamura like a camp dog, whining for scraps and sympathy. A wave of disgust washed over me, and my hand instinctively reached to my pocket for the tablets I kept there for such moments of despondency. I popped one into my mouth, and bit down on it.

I felt a sharp crack and a shooting pain screwed all the way up the front of my face. I urgently probed my mouth with my tongue. There was a gap next to my front incisor, the rotten gum spongy like dank vegetation. I tasted rotten, metallic blood and spat the split remains of my tooth and the dissolving Philopon pill into my cupped hand: a swirl of blood and saliva, the amphetamine fizzing into tiny bubbles, the decayed tooth a black pearl.

Whatever next? I thought. Would my eyeballs dim with rheum, the last of my hair fall out? The dull ache in my liver seemed to pulse and flare. I felt utterly destroyed.

"It's all gone," I muttered. "Everything's gone."

Mrs. Shimamura came over to me and put her tender, matronly arms around my neck. To my disgust, I began to sob into her bosom.

"There, there," she said. "Stop being such a baby."

She turned to the bar, and poured me a glass from her private supply. Then she folded her arms and became stern.

"Now, sensei. Don't go getting yourself so upset about everything. You don't have it so bad. You're no worse off than a million others. So pull yourself together."

She turned back to her sink of dishes and started crooning again. I shrugged meekly, and went off for a lie-down upstairs.

There were many things that I pined for in those days following the war. Things that I fleetingly craved with an urgency I had never known before in my life. Persimmons were one of these, as for some reason, later on, were tangerines. I had always been partial to persimmons, of course, but tangerines I had never had any particular feelings about one way or another, until, on my return to Japan, quite suddenly, their dimpled, waxy skin, their tart sweetness, and, more than anything, their bright orange colour began to exert a powerful hold on my imagination. I could spot them from a hundred yards off, amongst the covered stalls and booths of the black market. Beyond the cups and spoons cast from melted fuselages, the muddled heaps of cast-off army garments: the tangerine vendor, his vivid fruit wrapped in newspaper at the back of a handcart. Cruelly, their price shot up almost as soon as they became more widely available; they all came via the American Postal Exchange, descending to us from the gods, as it were. And so they were to remain, perpetually hoisted just beyond my reach.

What I longed for most of all, however, was a really decent pair of shoes. Since my repatriation from the green hell of the camp on New Guinea, I had worn my hobnailed army boots day and night, as did most of the other returnees from the battlefield. After countless miles of trudging, swelling and shrinking, the cowhide had welded to my feet, so much so that it was now an effort to remove them. But they repulsed me. They were a badge of shame, a decrepit symbol of servitude to a suicidal ideal. They were uncomfortable as well: the metal heel rims had worn away, the seams had long since split, and icy water leaked in around my toes whenever I stepped in one of the freezing puddles that lurked across the city. I cursed them every time my heel scraped through the worn sole, every time the sodden laces squeezed the fragile bones of my foot. I had heard that certain black market shops sold looted officer's boots — high, elegant cavalry affairs cut from soft leather or European kid. But the thought of their buttery smoothness made me nauseous: they reeked of everything I despised. Perhaps, I thought, I could revert to wearing split-toe *tabi* and wooden clogs, as some of the other writers had done. But for all their homely charm, they seemed fundamentally feudal to me, and, after all, they were hard and uncomfortable, and so very cold in winter.

No. What I truly aspired to was a good, sturdy pair of Western shoes. Enviously, I had observed an American civilian on the tram a few weeks previously wearing precisely the style I desired. A smart pair of burnished Oxford brogues, reddish brown, aglow with heathery tints. A thick lock of coffee-coloured hair fell over the man's angular brow; he bore a striking resemblance to the Hollywood actor Gary Cooper. A neat, moulded camera case was slung over his shoulder as he sat, elbow on knee, chin perched on hand, newspaper raised by a spray of fingers. One leg casually dangled over the other, a neat Argyll sock clasping the ankle beneath. Below that was the beautiful shoe, rocking faintly back and forth to the rhythm of the tram.

I stared, racked by a sudden, violent desire. When he alighted near Yurakucho Station, I pressed my face to the window. I pictured myself casually clipping along the street, as he did now, pausing to glance in the window of the occasional bookshop. *Well*, I thought. *There at least goes a serious man.*

Perhaps, as a man with real shoes, I might feel like a human being once more, after years of being nothing but a soldier and subject. Perhaps the stopped clock of my life might start ticking once again — as a man of purpose, striding boldly into the future. Rather than just another faceless non-entity in a city of pinched, weary men, our service caps pulled over our eyes, our shoulders sparring with the wind as we trudged the disconsolate streets.

I hoarded every penny like a miser, denying myself tobacco, even shochu. I avoided the temptations of Kanda, and busied myself instead with my third edition of *ERO*. To my delight and good fortune, it met with considerable success. Struck by the popularity of the feature in our last issue, "The Dish I Most Lament," I decided this time to expand it to encompass the entire panoply of frustrated desires hidden in our citizens' souls that winter. Once more I circumnavigated the Yamanote Line, stopping passersby and asking them to describe their heart's most secret desire. They were hesitant at first, unsure of how to respond. Then, the words began to spill out like a flowing river of dreams, as tears welled up in their eyes:

"My wife."

"My son."

"A good, long Noh play."

"Pickled plums."

"The knowledge that all of us Japanese were on the same side."

"A real coat."

"A working watch."

For me, though, it was always the shoes. I had taken to leaving my boots in the street at night now, plugged with newspaper to contain their rotten smell of fermenting soybeans. The cowhide was crinkled and frosty by morning, and I had to rotate the boots over the brazier to thaw them out. But even outside, they haunted my sleep. I would dream they were calling to me, that they might somehow slip back into the building, hop up the stairs and lace themselves back onto my feet while I slept.

I was in Shinjuku one afternoon when I saw a man wearing a sandwich board. When I read it, I thought that heaven must be smiling upon me at last. A shoe shop was opening that very day, not half a mile distant. I rushed over to the place, and urgently scanned the window display.

There, in pride of place, was my heart's desire. A stout pair of russet Oxford brogues, stitched on each side with bronze thread. Barely worn, looking to be more or less my size. I darted in, demanding to try them on. The shopkeeper eyed me suspiciously while I wrestled them onto my feet. A perfect fit, snug and tight. I asked the man to tell me how much they cost.

The price was absurd. But I barely gave it a thought, and told him I would return directly. I hurried home to fetch all of my hoarded savings. Walking back to the shop, I became suddenly nervous, wracked by the thought that someone else might have purchased them in my absence. But when I arrived, they were still there. I thrust the money into the man's hands and tore my old army boots from my feet. I took the Oxfords in my hands and inhaled the cedary fragrance of the dappled leather, turning them to admire their subtle, coppery tints. Then I slipped them onto my feet, and firmly laced them up.

"Should I wrap these old boots in newspaper, sir?" asked the shopkeeper.

I glanced at them with loathing.

"Please dispose of them as you see fit, sir," I said. "I have no wish to see them again."

I turned on my heel and left the shop, feeling as if I were walking on air.

I made my way along the street, pausing every now and again to glance down. The leather pinched a little; I told myself it would take a while for my feet to become used to real shoes again. On the tram, I even crossed one leg over the other as I had seen the Westerner do, but quickly realized that it was an uncomfortable, constricting position. Several of the passengers, I was sure, took sidelong glances at me. I casually extended my legs, rotating my feet from side to side in order to impress upon them the dazzle and flash of the shoes' superb leather.

So absorbed was I that I entirely missed my stop. I was now some way from home. My feet were quite painful now; though of course, this was only to be expected at first; this was simply how it was with proper shoes. An alley led off from the main avenue, and I was surprised to see the lantern of a public bathhouse halfway along it. This was an unexpected treat. Most of the *sentos* had been badly damaged during the bombings and those that remained had little fuel available to heat the pipes.

For a people who so valued cleanliness, this was a considerable discomfort. I hadn't had a chance to bathe for several months, myself. The thought of taking off my shoes and immersing myself in a hot pool of water filled me with exquisite pleasure.

It was a rundown tenement area and two children were tormenting a cat outside the building. As I approached, they looked up. The cat went mewling away and the children slunk off, glancing, I noticed with helpless pleasure, at my bronze beauties as I ducked underneath the curtain.

The place must have been old fashioned even before the war. Against the wall of the entrance hall was a row of wooden compartments with slotted hatches in which to store one's valuables. A scrawny woman dozed away in a booth, her neck a mass of chicken skin. I unlaced my Oxfords, with some relief now, admittedly, and placed them in a compartment. I rapped a ten-sen piece on the counter and the woman yawned and waved me over to the male changing room.

The place was deserted but for the trickling sound of water. A faint mould was growing over an engraved relief of furiously bayonetting soldiers along the wall. As I peeled off my clothes, I was appalled by the odour of my body. I piled my coat, shirt, and underclothes into a basket. Covering my nether regions with a hand towel, I slid open the door to the bathroom.

The air was dank and there was a chemical smell. But steam rose appealingly from the main pool and I shivered in anticipation at the thought of climbing in. I took a wooden bucket, filled it from the tap, and then, on my low stool, began to soap and rinse myself with the deliciously hot water. The hue of the bubbles that ran off down the drain was disturbingly grey. My body was speckled with a patchwork of sores and bites from legions of ticks and fleas and the rampages of bedbugs. I was horrified. I made a solemn vow to myself that I would track down one of the American trucks that were criss-crossing the city blasting out insecticide, and subject myself to a frosting.

Eventually, I seemed more or less clean enough, and I slipped into the big, steaming pool. I moaned with pleasure — it was utterly divine. I placed my hand towel on my head, and submerged my body in the hot water. After a minute, I opened my eyes.

What a startling sight. Somehow, I hadn't noticed how pale and shrunken my body had truly become. My skin was as white as tofu and my ribcage seemed to have sunk entirely into my chest. What a transformation had occurred since I had been called to the front. What an old man the war had made of me.

I sighed and sank back into the water. I mustn't feel sorry for myself, I thought, picturing Mrs. Shimamura's face with affection. After all, didn't it seem now as if things might finally be on the up? The magazine went from strength to strength; it kept at least some flesh adhered to my bones. Perhaps I could fatten myself up a little. Cut back on my daily doses of shochu and Philopon, regain some of my prior sturdiness . . .

My thoughts drifted to Satsuko Takara, and I felt an acute sense of lonely shame. The last time I had gone to the Ginza in the hope of glimpsing her outside her cabaret, she had not appeared, though I waited, shivering, until dawn. Perhaps she was dead now, I thought. Perhaps those visions of her on the street had been heaven-sent driftwood, a lifebuoy to which I should have tightly clung. Pride again — always pride.

I thought of the night when I had taken her to the anarchic revue at the Moulin Rouge, when she had laughed along as heartily as the students, even though she was just a shop girl by trade.

A shop girl. What did it matter, in any case? The war hadn't cared much for class, had it? That careful social gradation my mother had ruthlessly applied to every facet of her universe, from the pattern of a kimono belt to the arrangement of a teacup, proved worthless. What a mockery death had made of it all. Of rank, of ancestry. As if our blood type had mattered as it poured from our veins; as if the bone fragments of a lowly private were distinguishable from a general's as they'd sluiced into the sinking mud of that tropical hell.

And if Satsuko Takara was a fallen woman, wasn't it I who was to blame? The man who had taken her virginity, as if it were a prize, the day before going to war?

I needed to find her again, I thought. I would seek her out, wherever she was in the city. I had no hope that we might rekindle our lost love, such as it had been. The war had slaughtered my romantic capacities after all. Yet, perhaps, I might apologize to her for my failings. Make some small recompense.

I emerged from the bath feeling entirely cleansed. I dressed in my clothes, overwhelmed by their tarry stench of cigarette smoke and sour sweat. I vowed that I would make a bonfire, burn them all up in a great blaze. I'd buy myself a new set entirely, before going on my search for Takara-san.

I stood in front of the mirror; combed my hair; gave my teeth a quick scrub with my finger. I might even visit a teahouse on the way home, I thought. I felt more refreshed that I had in years.

As I emerged from the changing room, a sudden panic came upon me. The scrawny old woman in the vestibule was asleep, her head tilted backward, a line of drool dangling from her mouth. The door to the compartment where I had left my shoes was open. I rushed over. The latch was up. The compartment was empty.

I seized the woman and shook her violently. She stared at me in dull incomprehension.

"Where are my shoes?" I demanded. "Why have you moved them?"

"I haven't moved them anywhere, sir," she complained, "Why should I?" She'd been right there, she said, keeping an eye on things all this time.

I had a sudden vision of the two boys outside. With choking trepidation, I darted out. The street was empty. Back inside, the woman was looking vexed, sucking at her lips and shaking her head.

"Oh sir!" she moaned. "Those two dirty children! They were playing right outside! They must have noticed sir's handsome shoes, and taken it into their heads . . ."

Oh, it was wicked, sir! Those dirty, wretched, evil little shrimps. Scampering about right by the entrance, she had told them to clear off, but she must have just dozed away for just a second. Oh sir! Whatever must the honourable gentleman think? Such evil little urchins. What a wicked place Japan had become, that two innocent little children could do such a shameful thing!

Methodically, I opened every other compartment as she ranted away, praying that I had somehow been mistaken, that I would open a wooden hatch to see amber contours glinting calmly back at me.

It was to no avail. They were all empty. I felt a hard lump in my throat, an intense sensation of loss, as if someone close to me had died. Wretchedly, I went back outside and looked up and down the street. It was no use. The area was deserted. The shoes were gone.

I shuffled from the bathhouse with bales of newspaper wrapped around my bare feet. They grew sodden and bitty as I negotiated the puddles, and soon threatened to disintegrate altogether. People went by me with smiles on their faces.

I stubbornly filed a complaint at the police box. The officer on duty rolled his eyes as he wrote out a form. He suggested that I go down to the nearby black market and search for them there — that was where most of the stolen goods in the area ended up, he said.

If he knew that, I asked myself sullenly, as I prowled up and down the aisles at the market, then why didn't he do something about it? Icy water had risen up the legs of my breeches now, and my feet were almost naked. It was dark by the time I found a stall selling shoes on the very edge of the market. It was just as the officer had suspected. My Oxfords were sitting there, in pride of place upon the trestle table.

I pointed at them. "Those are mine."

The stunted stallholder squinted up at me.

"Four hundred," he said. He glanced down at my naked feet. "Perfect for a gentleman like you."

"Four hundred? What are you talking about? I paid three for them just this afternoon."

He shrugged. "Take it or leave it."

"But they're mine!" I shouted. "They were stolen from me this afternoon."

The man came a little closer. "So I'm a thief, am I? Is that what you're saying?"

"Yes, yes, you are," I said. "They were stolen from me this afternoon by two urchins, no doubt paid by you —"

A heavy hand fell on my shoulder and twisted me around. Beneath a felt fedora, glittering little black eyes stared at me — the sharp yakuza boss who ran the place.

"What's the problem here?"

I stuttered, acutely aware of the pincer-like grip around my arm, the bulging muscles beneath the man's pale silk jacket.

"Those are my shoes," I managed to say. "This man has stolen them from me."

"Oh yeah?" he slurred, picking them up and looking at them with a bored expression. "Well, they look like a pretty common style to me. There must be thousands like them in Tokyo. Don't you think you've made a mistake?"

"I should hardly think so. I had them on my feet not two hours ago."

He rubbed his forehead with a pained expression. "Look, mister, I think you've made a mistake. There's no need to be making wild accusations in public."

"But it's true," I said, frantically. "Two children stole them from me this afternoon!"

"Look, mister," he said, squaring up. "You've made a mistake, now calm down."

"But they're mine!"

There was a piercing pain in the socket of my right eye, as his knuckle crunched against bone. I collapsed onto the ground, my vision black on one side, my head ringing.

"You've made a mistake, mister," said the tough, looming above me. "So forget about it now. Either buy something or push off."

He strolled away, wringing out his fist.

I slowly picked myself up. My glasses were dangling from my ears, smashed and useless. I could still see the dim, reflective red glow of my shoes upon the table, the man standing over them protectively.

"Alright then, damn you," I said. "I'll buy them back. But look. I can only afford a hundred."

I took out all the money I had left from my pocket, and laid it in a pile on the table. The man straightened up, as if I had offended him.

"One hundred!" he said, haughtily. "Outrageous. Don't you know these are Oxford brogues — they're made in London! I couldn't take anything less than three."

I almost started to sob as I looked helplessly down at my numb feet. The last of the newspaper clung to them in soggy strips, and my toes were raw and shrivelled.

The man grew more sympathetic.

"Look," he said. "A pair of these wouldn't suit you anyway, sir. They're far too fancy. But I'll tell you what I can do. I can sell you a good pair of boots for fifty yen."

Good heavens no, I thought, *not boots again, not after all this time.*

He reached beneath the table to pull out a hulking pair of army boots and laid them heavily down upon the table.

I recognized the smell straight away — the rancid odour of rotten soybeans. I picked one up and held it in front of my face, fingering the chafed cowhide, poking my finger through the familiar holes. Wearily, I pushed fifty yen in coins across the table to the man, who pocketed it neatly. I bent down and tugged the boots back onto my feet.

"Look!" the man said cheerily. "A perfect fit. You see, you're lucky after all."

Wordlessly, I strode away from the market as the darkness and rain fell about me. As I trudged back home along the mucky street in my old, detested army boots, I had the curious feeling that they had somehow magically engineered the whole affair, that they possessed some supernatural power. That now, reunited with me again, they were content, and were smiling in secret triumph.

22
THE YOSHIWARA
(SATSUKO TAKARA)

It was shivering cold on the ward, yet the women insisted on opening up the tall, cracked windows late in the afternoon to clamber up on the sills and look down at the street below. It was like the cinema for them, I thought, as they hung there, screeching like vultures. They saved their loudest chorus for any passing American soldiers, who waved back in salute even as the girls made vulgar gestures at them.

We were on the top floor of the crumbling, grey venereal hospital, up five worn flights of stone stairs. Large chunks of plaster were missing from the walls and you could see the brickwork and horsehair beneath. The hall was lined on each side with thin straw mattresses, patients' belongings arranged beside them: wiry military blankets, envelopes of tea, tangled strips of dried cod.

One afternoon, I came back from work, my back aching from scrubbing and polishing the floors of the dining hall all morning. A plump lady was laying out her things by the mattress next to mine. I knelt down and introduced myself, and she nodded and smiled, showing deep dimples in the slabs of her cheeks. Mrs. Ishino was her name, she said, and she ran a restaurant down in Nihonbashi. There was something familiar about her face, I thought. It was as if I'd seen her on some forgotten theatre poster, many years before. She held out an earthenware jar and beamed at me.

"Help yourself!" she said. "Pickled plums. Nothing like them to keep the doctors away."

I almost gasped as I tasted the sour juice for the first time in years. Mrs. Ishino spread a cloth between our mattresses, and laid out some rice crackers and dried seaweed, urging me to help myself. As I nibbled away, she glanced toward the doors at the end of the ward, then pulled out a small flask of clear liquid from beneath her kimono jacket.

"Have a nip of this as well, dear," she said, handing it to me quickly. "Nothing like it for the cold."

It was strong and she nodded at me to take another sip. It was warm as it reached my belly. As I handed back the bottle, I realized that I was smiling.

Mrs. Ishino told me her story as we ate. She waved her hands in the air, acting things out, imitating people's voices just as if she'd been a comic storyteller kneeling on a stage. The day before, she said, the police had banged on the door of her bar in the middle of the night. They told her that they were there to enforce new regulations, and they'd carted her off to the hospital, along with the two girls who worked for her, Masuko and Hanuko. At the hospital, the doctors performed their usual tests. Masuko and Hanuko were given the all-clear and sent home. Mrs. Ishino, however, had been diagnosed with something very unpleasant.

"And I know exactly who's to blame, Takara-san," she said, waving a thick finger at me in menace. "And he'll be in for it as soon as I get out of here, you mark my words!"

I clapped my hand over my mouth, trying desperately not to laugh. Mrs. Ishino took a long swallow from her bottle, then burst into loud peals of laughter herself.

The women wore padded kimonos of faded grey-green as they slouched on the floor. Some got on with piece work they'd been given to pay for their treatment, stitching trousers and dresses from strips of old grey uniform or painting little dolls to sell as toys and souvenirs in the hospital shop. The others sat about nattering about the same old tedious things until evening, when the generator finally gave out and we were plunged into darkness again.

Those first nights, I lay parched, desperate for just one of my pills. I tossed and shivered with feverish nightmares, and the bed was soaking wet when I woke. But before long, I started to feel almost calm again. The terrible dreams that had haunted me began to slowly fade.

One afternoon, I walked over to the big window of the ward to look out. Opposite the hospital, the first plum blossom had budded white against a row of scorched trees.

There was a glint in Mrs. Ishino's eye as she sat down on her mat. There was a frayed towel draped over her shoulder, and her hair was wet from the bathhouse.

"Good news, Takara-san," Mrs. Ishino said, as she tugged a tortoiseshell comb through her hair. "I'm finally escaping at the end of this week. I've been given the all-clear."

"Oh," I said. I glanced at the fine wrinkles around Mrs. Ishino's eyes. I realized that I'd become quite used to her matronly presence next to me when I woke up each morning. "Well, I'm certainly very pleased for you, Mrs. Ishino."

She pursed her lips in a sly smile, and then poked me in the shoulder. "And that's not all," she said.

"What do you mean?"

"I've heard a message on the wind that you'll be getting out as well, Takara-san!" she said.

I looked up at her in alarm. Despite the pungent smell of the bedpans, the back-breaking work, and the chemical soap that left my hands as scaly as snakeskin, the long ward with its high ceiling had become like a refuge, a place where I could hide from the world and all its horrors.

Mrs. Ishino twisted her hair into a knot and knelt down on the floor beside me. "Tell me, Takara-san," she said.

"Please ask me anything you like, Mrs. Ishino," I said.

"What is it that you intend to do with yourself, Takara-san?" she asked. "When you leave here, I mean?"

The main doors to the ward swung open. The doctors appeared in their white coats to begin their rounds. A sharp chemical smell swirled through the hall. I had a sudden memory of my room at the International Palace, the orange card tacked over the entrance.

"I'm not sure, Mrs. Ishino," I said. "Perhaps this, or that... Perhaps I'll go back to the Oasis, to see if they'll have me."

Mrs. Ishino looked at me sharply. "Haven't you heard, Takara-san?"

"Heard what, Mrs. Ishino?" I said.

"The comfort stations, Takara-san. The Americans have closed them all down."

"But why?"

She snorted. "I expect there were too many yankiis going home to their wives in America with unexpected conditions like mine."

I thought uneasily of the broken-down mansion in Tsukiji: the drugged girls in their vivid dresses, the colour of bruises. We'd all be wretched pan-pan now, forced to work in the alleys and craters, to go with anyone who came along, American or Japanese, decrepit or even violent...

Mrs. Ishino cocked her head to one side. "Takara-san," she said. "I wonder if I could possibly make a request?"

I nodded. "Of course," I said. "Anything at all!"

"Perhaps you might consider coming to work for me?" she said. "The shop could always do with another pretty girl. Someone who's worked in the trade before, you know."

Gratitude and relief flooded my heart. It would be just like the old days, I thought, working at a real restaurant again — I'd go to and fro amongst the tables with my skirts hitched up, a big bottle of saké on my back, serving the dishes and joining in with all the banter...

"I run it for the Americans of course," Mrs. Ishino said, holding my eye. "We're a liberal establishment."

The warm glow fluttered away.

"And there are extra services we provide. Discreetly, of course."

My heart sank.

Mrs. Ishino took my hands in hers. "Why not come and work with us, Satsuko? It's not such a bad place. You're sure to get on with the other girls. You could do much worse, you know."

She was right, of course, and I knew it. I could only do worse.

I took a deep breath, then knelt before her and bowed my head.

"Ishino-sama," I murmured. "I'm certainly not worthy of your trust and affection. Please accept my gratitude, from the bottom of my heart."

Mrs. Ishino's face lit up. She beamed at me and squeezed my hands.

"Don't you worry about that, Satsuko-chan," she said. "Don't you worry about anything at all."

23
THE HOLIDAY CAMP
(HIROSHI TAKARA)

The plum blossom's finally here, I thought, as I walked home from Ueno Plaza, past the arch of Yushima Tenjin shrine. The trees in the garden were prickly white, and bundles of wooden prayer plaques had been tied to the racks outside, so I guessed that the snobby kids from the Imperial University must be having their examinations again. A crowd of GIs in khaki uniforms were gathered in the garden with their backs to me, and I wandered over to see what they were looking at. As I got closer, I felt a wave of excitement.

They all had cameras, and they were squinting through the viewfinders, the shutters clicking and film whirring. Beneath a blossoming plum tree stood a Japanese girl, dressed like a geisha, her face hidden behind a golden fan. She wore a purple and crimson kimono and held a tasselled parasol over her shoulder. She waved the fan once, then suddenly snapped it shut.

Satsuko.

She looked so much like my sister that my heart actually stopped. Suddenly, in my head, I saw her treading water in the fiery canal; I could almost feel the flames scorching my cheeks, and I had a sudden terror that she would turn around and see me. I tried to duck out of sight, but then one of the GIs called out and the girl shifted.

There was something wrong with her nose, I thought. It was the wrong shape, though the white powder on her face made it hard to tell. Her eyes seemed small and narrow as well, not deep and black like my sister's had been. As I stood there staring, the illusion floated away. My sister was dead, after all. I was flooded with an awkward sense of guilt and relief.

The girl looked as wooden as a doll as the soldiers pushed their cameras right up in her face, pulling her about by her kimono sleeve and pushing her into position. I glanced jealously at the cameras, wondering how much they must have cost. Down by the girl's feet was a cardboard sign scribbled in clumsy English. "Genuine Japan Geisha girl," it said. "Photograph — 1 Yen." There was a tin can next to the sign, already filled up with bank notes.

She started spinning her parasol, pushing out her chest and posing in a way that no real geisha would ever have done. I almost felt like jeering at her. The idea that I'd mixed her up with my sister made me feel stupid and sheepish.

The men were all grinning and whistling now. I thought of the tall American in the trench coat who'd come over to talk to us that day behind the station, who'd taken our photographs by our old baseball pitch. We'd played almost a whole series against the other gangs that autumn afternoon, running and scrambling amongst the stones until hours after dark. I remembered the solid weight of the American's camera as I'd held it up to my face. How I'd caught Tomoko in the rangefinder for a moment, the twin images of her shy face, one sharp, one blurred, as I squinted through the lens.

She was buried not far away from there now, I thought. We'd carried her body to a shallow bomb crater in the wasteground and covered it up with a sheet of corrugated tin. Later on that night, I crept back down to say goodbye. I sat in the pit with her for a long time, her body blanched in the splinters of moonlight, withered away almost to a skeleton. I held her hand in mine, until her fingers began to thaw out just a little. Finally, it became too cold to stay. I climbed out of the pit and dragged the metal sheet back over the top.

A GI was squatting in front of me. I suddenly shoved him as hard as I could, and he stumbled forward. I darted down and grabbed hold of his camera with both hands, and for a moment, the man was choking, clutching his throat as the thin leather strap garrotted him. Suddenly, the leather snapped, and I went tumbling backward. Thrusting the camera under my shirt, I leaped up and sprinted through the garden, faster than I'd even run before, as crunching footsteps pounded behind me, the soldiers hollering.

I nearly stumbled in front of a bus as I sprinted across the main road. As I ran along by the university walls, I snatched a glance behind me. The men were standing on the other side of the street, caught by the traffic. Spinning around the corner, I slipped through the famous Red Gate of the university. Students and professors were coming out of the buildings and they yelled at me as I dodged around them. I ran out through the back gate at the other end of the quadrangle, and slid down against the wall, completely out of breath. As I pulled the camera out from beneath my shirt, my heart started to pound even harder.

A Leica. Just like the American had used!

I gazed at the elegant dials and knobs, rubbing my thumb over the finely engraved letters and embossed serial numbers. I felt a sudden, sharp stab of guilt about what I'd just done. But as I pictured the children's faces, when I'd get back and tell them my idea, I could hardly stop myself grinning.

At the entrance to the inn, through the long grass of the garden, I put up my hand to the wooden screen door. I stopped. I could hear Shin's hoarse voice bellowing away inside.

I slid the door open a crack, and peered through into the reception hall. The children were all kneeling in a circle on the tatami, engrossed in some kind of game. Nobu, Koji, and Aiko had their heads bowed low and were whimpering like little dogs. Shin had a blanket around his shoulders, and was strutting up and down in front of them, holding a broomstick like it was a sword.

"Please, sir, take me," Koji was saying. "Please!"

Nobu jerked up his head. "No, sir!" he begged. "Take me!"

"And what will you do for me," Shin demanded, "if I take you home to our mansion?"

He was pretending to be an aristocrat, I realized. The accent was just appalling. He jabbed the broomstick into Nobu's shoulder. "Well?" he asked.

"I'll do anything, sir," Nobu whimpered, as he pressed his head down to the floor. "Anything at all."

"Kiss my feet, then," Shin said.

Nobu glanced up as Shin waved his muddy straw sandal in his face. Puckering his lips, he gave his foot a quick, unhappy peck.

Shin suddenly spun around and squatted over Nobu's head, gripping onto his shoulders as he spread his bandy legs.

"Eat my shit?"

Nobu brayed like a donkey and shoved him away. "No, sir!" he shouted. "Please don't make me!"

I shoved the rattling door wide open and strode forward into the hall.

"What the hell's going on here?" I said.

Shin's face froze. He gave that stupid grin of his, showing the wide gap between his broken teeth.

"So big brother's back, is he?" he said. "Got any apples for us today, big brother?"

I almost gasped. It was as if he'd punched me in the stomach. I saw Tomoko's body, lying in the moonlight. The black apple pips glistening on her chin.

"Up on your feet. All of you," I said.

One by one, the children stood up, looking ashamed of themselves.

"Well?"

Koji stammered, "We were just playing a game."

Shin slapped his hand over Koji's mouth. "It's none of his business!" he said, angrily.

"A game? So why don't we all play?"

"Because it's none of your business!" Shin shouted. His face was red.

Koji pulled Shin's hand away and tugged at it. "Why don't you tell him?" he whined. "Just tell him!"

"Tell me what?" I asked.

"About the holiday camps!" Koji said, desperately. "The holiday camps!"

I hesitated for a second. "What are you talking about?" I said, warily.

"The holiday camps," Aiko said, nodding earnestly. "We're all going away to be adopted."

The hair prickled up at the back of my neck. I sat down cross-legged on the floor.

"Please tell me what you're talking about," I said.

Slowly, they all sat down in front of me.

"Well," Aiko started, "I don't really know —"

"The Americans," Shin said. "It was their idea, wasn't it?"

"One at a time."

Koji frowned, then drew a vague shape with his finger on the floor.

The Americans, he said, had decided to set up holiday camps in the countryside, for all the Japanese children who had lost their families during the war.

"Children like us," Aiko said, with a firm nod.

Some of the camps were by the seaside, others were up in the mountains, in the old noble mansions and monasteries. They had proper beds, and the children were fed three meals a day, hot soup and rice with them all. You could choose if you wanted to help with the farm work, digging the fields and crops or taking care of the animals, or you could just go back to school and have lessons. There were all sorts of activities and toys, board games and model airplanes for rainy days, trips out to the countryside and to the beach, swimming galas, running races, butterfly collecting . . .

Koji rubbed his eyes as his story dwindled into confusion. "At least that's what everyone's saying," he said. The other children were looking at me, as if they'd been hypnotized.

It all sounded so marvellous. Just for a second, I let myself imagine that it was true. I felt a rush of excitement as I saw us all, miles and miles away from Tokyo, racing along a shimmery beach, splashing and diving amongst the blue waves.

I imagined Tomoko standing by a rock pool. Wearing a white swimming cap, the skin brown and sunburned on her shoulders.

Aiko nudged Koji in the ribs. "Tell him about the family visits," she whispered.

Koji nodded earnestly. "They're the best thing of all."

Every Sunday, he said, mothers and fathers who had lost their sons and daughters in the war drove up to the camps. They inspected the children, asked the headmaster about their behaviour, and then chose one to take home with them.

"We're going to be adopted," Aiko interrupted, her eyes bright.

I clasped my hands around my knees. A horrible, empty feeling welled up inside me.

"Please," I said. I shook my head helplessly. I felt as if I were holding a hammer, about to smash a mirror. "I'm so sorry. But someone has been filling your heads with fairy tales."

Koji smiled doubtfully, as if he thought I was joking. Shin's eyes narrowed, and he gave me a look of pure hatred.

"I'm so sorry," I said, my voice wavering. "I wish it was true as much as you do. Really I do. But it's just not."

From somewhere in the garden came a faint sound, like a bird, or a child, crying far away.

"I'm so sorry," I whispered, waving a hopeless hand at the hall around us. "But this is all we've got."

Aiko burst into tears. Koji looked at me in confusion, as if he could see ghosts fluttering in the air.

Shin crashed his fist into his palm and clambered to his feet.

"You're so clever, aren't you, you bastard?" he snarled. "You're always right about everything, aren't you? Well, this time you're fucking wrong!"

His thick lips were trembling.

I stared back at him, appalled. This was the worst thing of all, I thought. That such a bully as Shin could get caught up in such helpless fantasies . . . It was hideous.

Shin lurched toward me and I slid backward on the floor as he rotated his shoulders.

A horrible feeling of guilt and shame came over me. I realized he missed his violent, drunken father as much as I missed my own. I'd never even imagined it was possible.

As if a boy from Sengen Alley was too stupid to feel pain, as if only a smart kid like me from Senso High School was sensitive enough to feel hurt, to feel loss.

The children stared at me tearfully as Shin edged closer, his face twisted in anger.

All those times when they'd cried out in the night, I'd ignored them. Every time they'd started to snivel, I'd told the others to sit on them, as if they were unfeeling sacks of rice. I'd made them work the streets day and night, forcing them to pick up saliva-soaked cigarette butts, to root about in the filth and night soil, grubbing about like animals, acting as if I was their big brother, their father even! What kind of dad would do this to his kids? Force them to work until they were fainting, locking them in at night in this collapsing ruin, which was nothing more than a filthy old whorehouse, and where we'd probably all die together —

"We're sick of you, you bastard," Shin hissed. He clutched his fingers into a fist, and I backed away, suddenly scared.

They'd have been better off without me, I thought.

Tears flooded my eyes as Shin raised his elbow into the air.

Tomoko would still be alive —

The fist slammed into my face and I toppled backward.

Shin loomed over me, the other children gathered behind his legs, as if for protection.

"It's all over, big brother," he said, waving a trembling finger at my face. "We're not going to be your slaves anymore. We're going away to the holiday camps. And there's nothing you can do to stop us."

My slaves! Tears ran down by cheeks and I spoke through wrenching sobs.

"Go away then. Do whatever you want. Just see if I care."

I raced outside, through the long grass to the bottom of the garden. With a howl, I sank down onto the earth. I clutched my shirt to my face, and pounded the ground with my fist, whimpering with bitter tears.

The signs for lost relations in Ueno Plaza were all peeling in soggy strips from the bronze statue of Saigo Takamori. The shoeshine boys were playing catch as I smoked a newspaper cigarette. Last year, there'd been signs everywhere, I remembered. Scrolls unfurling from every wall and notices tacked to every telegraph pole. One night in winter, a bunch of kids had gone around tearing them all down. They'd brought them up here in piles and lit a huge bonfire, dancing around the flames and whooping as the names and addresses and hopeless messages all turned black and went up in smoke.

I was so lost in thought, that I didn't notice the policemen until the very last moment. There was a flash of blue, and then they pounced. One clouted my spine with a bamboo stave and I sprawled on the ground in agony. A boot landed on my head, pressing my face into the gravel, and my arms were jerked up behind my back, making tears spring into my eyes.

A hand pulled my head up by the hair, and I saw an inspector with round glasses and a straggly loach moustache, bawling at me, spraying my face with saliva.

"You filthy shit!" he hollered, slapping my face. "How do you think you dogs make us look?"

The shoeshine boys were slinging their boxes over their shoulders now and racing off down the steep banks of the plaza. More policemen were swarming up the steps, holding out their arms and trying to corral them as if they were escaping pigs.

With a twist, I managed to suddenly break free, but the inspector's hobnailed boot swung up straight away and caught me right in the balls.

"You dog," he snarled. He started to kick me in the behind, knocking me all the way across the plaza. At the bottom of the steps, there was a military truck with a wide canvas awning, its engine already rumbling. Policemen were standing at the back, hoisting children in, counting them off on their fingers. I half rolled, half fell down the steps, my head cracking against the stone. My camera was under my shirt and I clutched it against my chest, desperately trying to protect it. I landed at the bottom, stunned senseless. The inspector hoisted me up, grabbing me between the legs, and shoved me inside. I toppled forward, and the tailgate of the truck slammed up behind me.

There were about a dozen other kids in there already, and they shouted in panic as the truck lurched forward, throwing us all to the floor. Liquid was trickling about, and I realized that some of the little ones had wet themselves. I recognized a few of them, shoeshine boys mostly, but there was an older boy too that I'd never see before, who sat on the floor with his head between his legs. His thin arms were covered in purple and yellow bruises, and the top of his forehead was gashed, crusted with dried blood.

The truck spun about and I went flying again. As it began to rumble down the road, the children spoke in terrified whispers.

"Where are we going? Where are they taking us?"

I saw a strip of sky and the flash of buildings through the gap between the tailgate and the roof.

"They're taking us to prison," someone whimpered.

Another boy shook his head. "That's not what I heard." I recognized him — he'd come back from Manchukuo the winter before, and he'd once told me about a German Shepherd dog he'd had, which the Russians had shot when they'd invaded. "They're taking us out to the Arakawa River," he said. "They're going to shoot us one by one, and shove us in. They don't want kids like us around anymore."

The older boy lifted up his head. His eyes were bloodshot, and behind a harelip his teeth were broken.

"You're all wrong," he said, quietly. Everyone stared at him. "They're taking us to an orphanage."

For some reason, the word sent a shiver down my spine.

"How do you know?"

"Because I just escaped from one. They're like hell."

Fresh blood glistened as he scratched the wound on his head. "They feed you worse than on the streets, and keep you locked up in cages. Half the time they leave you naked so you don't run off."

My scalp suddenly crawled. *The holiday camps.*

I took a running leap at the tailgate of the truck, and somehow, I just managed to get my fingertips over the lip. I scrabbled my feet against the metal, and finally got some purchase. As I hoisted myself up, I saw that we were driving down a dirt road between suburban houses. The truck was moving fast as I clambered out over the lip of the tailgate. Terrified, I looked down at the racing ground. Suddenly I leaped out.

The sky and earth was spinning, and then my bones were cracking over and over in the dirt, the strap of my camera strangling me, the metal stabbing at my chest. I heard the violent blast of a horn, and I twisted and rolled into the tall grass at the side of the road, a split second before the massive wheels of another truck crunched past my head. Other trucks went by in convoy, one after the other, dark green, anonymous, their wheel wells coated in dust.

I tried to stand up, but an agonizing bolt went through my ankle and I collapsed. For a few minutes, I lay there, trying to catch my breath, desperately squeezing the flesh and bone beneath my fingers. Then I suddenly thought of the children and I started to panic. *The holiday camps.* How had the story got so tangled up? Were we really so desperate now? That we would believe anything at all?

My ankle throbbed with pain as I tried to stand up again. Slowly, I started to hobble down the road, back in the direction we'd come.

About an hour later, I crossed a bridge, and finally came to the overground train tracks. My ankle was white and had swelled up to twice its normal size. My forehead was clammy and I felt sick. The sky was darkening to grey, and rain began to fall as I leaned against a shopfront to rest for a moment.

The children's faces flashed back into my mind. *Hurry!* Almost crying with pain, I stood up straight. The rain started to fall violently around me as I grasped the camera beneath my shirt, and started to hobble, with agonizing slowness, up the hill toward the inn.

The wooden gates to the courtyard were wide open and the broken locks were dangling in the scrubby weeds. A heavy juddering came from inside, and I heard the shouts of strange voices. A long Fuso bus was parked right outside the porch, its big, white headlights blazing in the rain. A driver in spectacles sat hunched behind the wheel, staring out through the windshield with a bored look on his face. At the back of the bus was a policeman, facing the doorway of the inn.

Nobu and Koji came out, carrying little bundles tied with string. Aiko came next, and I saw that she was carrying the little suitcase that I'd found for her one day in the rubble of an old house, made of scratched tin and painted with the smiling face of a kitten.

The driver gunned the engine, and I heard her squeal with excitement as the officer hoisted her up. Nobu and Koji clambered inside as the officer tapped them on the heads with his pencil. Finally, Shin came out, still wearing the torn shorts I'd first seen him in. He frowned, and paused for a moment, gazing back at the broken-down house, as if he wanted to freeze it in his memory.

"Get in!" the officer bawled. Shin hopped aboard. The officer slammed the back doors of the bus, then came up and clambered in to the front. As the bus lurched forward, I spun around, pressing my back up against the wall. The bus rumbled through the gateway and I could see the face of the driver as he glanced through the dirty windshield and heaved the wheel around. The heavy wheels crunched into the road and the bus drove right past me. Aiko's and Koji's faces appeared at the back window, and they heaved down the panes and leaned out, waving at the inn.

"Bye-bye!" they cried. "Bye-bye!"

Aiko suddenly saw me crouching against the wall and her jaw fell open.

"Hiroshi!" she screamed. "Hiroshi-kun!"

I started to stumble after them, but my ankle suddenly gave way and I collapsed into the road in agony. "Come back!" I shouted, waving at them desperately.

Nobu's head appeared at the window. His eyes lit up when he saw me, just as the truck began to accelerate down the road.

"Come on, Hiro, come on!"

"No!" I yelled. I struggled to my feet and somehow made it a few steps forward, a sob clutching in my throat. "No," I cried, "Please!"

"Come on Hiro! We're going away to the holiday camps!"

My ankle was burning as I hobbled forward. The children's faces were screwed up with excitement and they pounded against the doors with their fists.

"Run, Hiro! You can do it!"

I could hardly speak, I was crying so hard. "It's an orphanage!" I shouted, "An orphanage!"

My ankle gave way and I fell, the gravel slicing my knees open. As the bus reached the brow of the hill, I tore open my shirt and held out the camera, waving it desperately in the air.

"What about your portraits?" I shouted, as the tears streamed down my face. "I wanted to take your portraits!"

The bus rolled away down the hill and I saw the children waving at me from the back, through the rain. I collapsed into the dust, clutching onto the camera. As the bus disappeared, I could still hear their faint voices, calling out my name.

24
PRIMROSE (HAL LYNCH)

My new home was a room on the second floor of the press club that I shared with three other men. I had a lumpy mattress and a coarse woollen blanket that reached either my neck or my toes, depending on my preference. I'd hunted around for Mark Ward after I arrived, anxious to talk to him, to show him my negatives and ask his advice about what to do next. But he was travelling in the north now, up in the Snow Country, working on some piece about unions and sharecroppers, and wouldn't be back for weeks.

One afternoon I was walking along the riverbank, near the Nihonbashi Bridge. I realized I wasn't far from where I'd first encountered my bargeman all those months ago. It was as if some mysterious inner compass had compelled me to return to the place. I paused for a while as I looked out at the grey river. Dusk was falling, and I became seized with a powerful urge to drink a whisky — perhaps several whiskies — in the warmth and comfort of some cozy saloon. I ventured into a warren of low shops and rundown tenement houses. Halfway down the street, I saw a red lantern, glowing like the Sacred

Heart of Jesus. I hurried toward it, already feeling the drink warm and radiant inside my belly.

I ducked under the blue half-curtain. A hefty woman was polishing glasses behind the bar and called out in welcome, waving to a line of stools set up at the empty counter. The place was neat and snug — exactly what I'd had in mind — and I took my seat with a pleasurable sense of anticipation. The woman was taller than any of the others I'd seen in Japan, and deep dimples appeared in her cheeks as I requested whisky. She poured me a glass of Suntory, which I sipped with intense satisfaction.

"American?" she asked.

I tipped my glass toward her in a rueful gesture of acknowledgement.

She placed her elbows on the counter, supporting her chin with her hands. She gazed at me with a frankness that I found somewhat disconcerting.

"GI-san?" she asked. I braced myself for the inevitable offer of a girl. But then she frowned, shaking her head.

"No, you not GI type I think."

I was amused. "Oh no? What type am I then?"

She squinted. "You artist type, I think."

I grinned. "Is that so?"

She nodded, apparently sure of herself. "Yes. I think."

I liked the woman already. She was burly and maternal all at once, with a dash of sultry sexuality lurking somewhere beneath it all.

"I wish I was," I said. "But I'm just a reporter. *Shimbun kisha desu.*"

"Oh." She raised her eyebrows. "*Repootaa.* Very good Japanese."

She topped up my drink and poured one for herself also.

"*Chis-u.*" She held her glass in the air. I clinked it against my own. She knocked hers back. I did the same and an agreeable warmth hit my guts. Why hadn't I visited pleasant places like this more often, I thought?

"Where you stay now?" she demanded.

I laughed again. "Well, that's a funny thing..."

Leaning over the counter, as if I were a regular soak in a downtown speakeasy, I found myself explaining that I'd recently been obliged to leave my quarters. She looked me up and down for a second, then her eyes brightened and she hurried around the bar and took my arm.

"Come — look!" she said, pulling at me.

I was feeling pleasantly tight by now, and let her lead me away through a back door to a flight of narrow steps. At the top of the stairs, a door opened to a small room with a stained ceiling. There was a futon in the corner and a battered-looking desk pushed up beneath the window. Big raindrops were trickling down the cracked panes.

"You stay here," she said, excitedly. "Very cheap!"

Stay there? I thought. Maybe it wasn't such a bad idea. Exclusive rights to my own reading lamp, unlike at the press club. A good enough place to lie low, plot out the next steps of my life. I could rewrite my Hiroshima piece, read books, drink whisky. And what a change from the Continental, with its white-haired officers in dressing gowns, scratching at their bristles in the mouldering bathrooms.

I turned to face the lady and negotiate terms.

A mischievous gleam appeared in her eye: "One more whisky?"

~

The next day I heaved a knapsack and suitcase up the steep wooden staircase to my new home. I lined up my tattered collection of Japanese books along the window ledge and lay a typewriter case I'd requisitioned from the *Stars and Stripes* on the desk. The room was quiet, private. At one corner of the room, I prized up the floorboard with my jackknife. I placed my Hiroshima negatives beneath it, the envelope hidden inside a cigar box and wrapped up in a cotton sweater for good measure.

I lay back on the futon and lit a cigarette. The room was filled with a pale grey light, and I listened to the rain patter against the roof and the windows. The place reminded me of an old forestry hut in the woods near our home, which I'd found when I was a teenager, just after my father had died. I'd hidden out there for a week, until my uncle had finally tracked me down. He'd put his arm around my shoulder. "Come on home, Hal. He's gone. Your mother needs you now..."

Glancing, butterfly dreams. When I awoke, I was disoriented to find that it was dark outside. Night had fallen, and the crackling voice of Josephine Baker was drifting up from the bar below. As I came downstairs, I saw my new landlady, Mrs. Ishino, arranging bottles of liquor on the shelves. A portrait of a Japanese man in a flying jacket hung above them. Officers sat at the tables; a couple of girls in plain dresses were laughing away with them, their hands over their mouths. They weren't exactly beautiful, I thought, but seemed warm and friendly and were somehow the more appealing for that. As

I took a stool at the bar, Mrs. Ishino smiled indulgently and poured me a drink.

"On house," she announced, proudly. She called out in sharp command, and in the kitchen behind her, from where wisps of steam were emerging, an answering voice sang out with a long, high-pitched, *"Hai!"*

She turned to me maternally. "You like room?"

"Yes. I sure do."

"You welcome."

A girl came out from the kitchen with a steaming plate of small dumplings, which she set in front of me with an incline of her head.

"Lynch-san," Mrs. Ishino said. "This is Satsuko-chan. My new favourite girl."

The girl looked at me. She had the darkest eyes I'd ever seen. They were almost entirely black from the pupil to the iris, and her face formed a smooth oval, the wide lips parted slightly to show small, regular teeth. Her pale skin was flushed from the heat of the kitchen and there was a faint perspiration on her brow. She wore a blue cloth tied around her forehead, which gave her a vaguely boyish, piratical air.

"Well. Here's to her," I said, raising my glass.

Hands tight against the sides of her apron, she bowed. Mrs. Ishino gave another sharp command. With another obedient *"Hai!"* the girl hurried back to the kitchen.

"Satsuko-chan . . ." Mrs. Ishino began, but just then, a couple of officers wearing rain capes emerged through the curtain with Japanese dates on their arms. They held up hands in greeting, as if they knew the place well. Mrs. Ishino led them over to a table. I sat there alone at the bar for a while, sipping my drink and feeling almost absurdly content.

The girl bustled in and out from the kitchen several more times that night, bringing small plates of chipped potatoes and sandwiches for the men. Before long, I realized I was drunk. The place filled up, and, at one point, I helped Mrs. Ishino move the tables aside to make a space for dancing. There was none of the wild jitterbugging of the Ginza clubs here — the men were stately and senior, and moved their partners gracefully back and forth like ballroom dancers, hands on backs, chins on heads, swaying expertly to the music. Others played cards while the girls poured their beer, and a soft haze enveloped the place as Saturday evening toppled gently into the arms of Saturday night.

Later on, the girl came out. She'd removed her head-gear and had made up her face now, a simple brush of powder and a crimson curve of lipstick. She wore a green flower-print dress, and a red, plastic peony in her hair. She came over to me, eyes downcast, and placed a light hand upon mine.

"You sit with me?" she asked.

Her hand was cool, the impression of skin smooth upon my wrist.

"Let me tell your fortune," I said, turning her palm over. She suddenly resisted, and I dropped her hand, afraid that I'd offended her. But then, with a curious look in her eyes, she relented, and held out her hand in front of me.

There were no lines on her palm, just a smooth, shiny surface, like polished marble. I had a sudden recollection of Eugene, in the Oasis that night, the girl pouring out his beer. *Hal, meet Primrose. She's a swell sort!*

I glanced at her. It was the same girl, I was certain.

I felt a strange collision of emotions as I looked into her candid, coal-black eyes. Curiosity. Admiration. What kind of life had she lived? I wondered. What bleak adventures had she witnessed since the last time we met . . . I felt a frank, swelling attraction as I glanced at the curve of her chest, the pale skin taut across her breastbones.

There was a sudden thickness in my throat, a roaring sound in my ears.

Her smooth palm was touching my cheek, holding my head steady. She looked into my eyes with an expression of concern.

"You tired, I think?"

The roaring faded. The music from the gramophone and the sound of conversation gradually reasserted itself.

"Yes," I stammered. "Yes I am."

She patted the side of my face.

"You go sleep," she said, before walking to a table in the corner of the bar. As I sat there, brooding over my drink, I noticed her throwing me occasional darting glances. Finally, I stood up to approach her again, but just then, another Western man — a civilian — entered the bar and walked over to her table. They talked for a short while, and then she stood up and took his hand. She led him away through a low door at the back of the bar and I caught a glimpse of her bare arm as she pulled the door shut. I didn't want to see them emerge. Into my mind's eye came an unwelcome glimpse of his scratchy white legs, the red peony askew amidst stray strands of her black hair. I threw back my drink; said goodnight to no one in particular. Then I clomped up the stairs to my new abode, took a long drink of water from the jug, and passed out on my new bed.

In the lobby of the press club, correspondents hammered out copy with typewriters on their knees. The long-distance booths were jammed, urgent stories being dictated into the glossy black telephones. The *Asahi Shimbun* was dominated by stories of the unrest sweeping steadily across the country in the wake of the crop failures. The first reports of starvation were already emerging; there'd been rice riots in the north and strikes at the coal mines and here at one of the Tokyo newspapers. A leading communist had been welcomed home from China that week like a movie star. Philip Cochrane from the *Baltimore Sun* told me that mobs had greeted the man at the station, the whole place a sea of red flags.

Mark Ward had an inch of beard on his face and a glitter in his eye when we sat down for drinks in the bar later on that evening with Sally Harper of *TIME*.

"Welcome home, Ward. How was the Snow Country?"

As we drank our raw Japanese whisky, he regaled us with stories of evenings spent in sharecroppers' huts, peasants gathered around fires with padded blankets on their knees, spilling tales of despair as the oxen moved about in the mulch and the snow fell thick on the ground outside.

"This country's a tinderbox, my friends. Believe me. The place is just waiting to explode."

"You're a true believer, Ward," I said.

"I was." His eyes narrowed. "G2 pulled me in yesterday."

"G2? Are you serious?" Sally said, her eyes wide with concern. G2 was Intelligence, the most muscular and secretive of the Occupation divisions, presided over by General Charles A. Willoughby — MacArthur's chief of intelligence, and Ward's nemesis.

"How was the interview?"

"They asked why I was writing a piece on Japanese union organizers. Whether or not I sympathized with them."

"Do you?"

"I told them that people were starving to death because our land reform directive was taking so long to draft, and that you could bet your bottom dollar that I sympathized with them."

As I looked at him, I strongly recalled a painting I'd once seen in the Metropolitan Museum in New York. Chagall: an old bearded man in a thick overcoat, a sack slung over his back, floating across a dream landscape of snow and yellow baroque architecture.

"What did they say to that?" Sally asked.

His voice fell in surly imitation. "They said: 'Listen Ward. Things have changed since we arrived. We're at war with the Russkies now. Whose side are you on?'"

He shook his big head, his voice sour. "You know they just slung out two of your friends? Brown and Christopher?"

I vaguely remembered the demure, grey-haired Californian and the effeminate New Yorker, both of whom had been working at the *Stars and Stripes* when I'd arrived.

"You're kidding? For what?"

Ward waved his meaty hands in the air. "'Communistic leanings!'"

I laughed. They'd been poring over baseball statistics when I'd first met them, apparently more concerned with sports than politics.

"They're Reds?"

"Sure! They've been sprinkling the whole paper with subversion."

"What's happening to them?"

"They're sending them to Okinawa. To keep them out of trouble."

"That's real tough for them."

He glanced at me sharply.

"You don't understand, Lynch."

I noticed the wattle of skin beneath his jowls as he shook his head sullenly.

"Are you in some kind of trouble, Mark?" I asked.

He stared at me, mildly incredulous. "Don't you get it, Lynch? I'm next on their goddamned list!"

Sally left us, and Ward and I went out to get a snack at a low noodle place bustling with GIs and their dates. We drank lukewarm beer and slurped at our noodles in the Japanese fashion. Ward began to pluck at his plate of fried dumplings with his chopsticks.

"And how about you, Lynch?" he asked, absently. "The *Stars and Stripes* send you anywhere interesting?"

"They fired me," I said.

The chopsticks paused in mid air. "What happened?"

"I went to Hiroshima."

The chopsticks clattered onto the table as an incredulous expression suffused Ward's face. "You actually did it?"

"Yes. Yes, I did."

The edges of his wide lips curled up.

"How did it look?"

"More or less the same. Oh, and by the way, Disease X is real."

The jowls lowered and the inevitable cigar appeared. I told him of the long walk across the red fields, the pulverized city centre, the victims I'd met at the hospital. He clutched my hand, steam beading on his brow from the billowing stockpots.

"Did you take photographs, Hal? Please tell me you took photographs."

I nodded.

"Where are they?"

"Safe. Most of them. The prints got lost."

"How? By whom? Got a name?"

"SCAP. Public relations." I realized that I hardly knew. "They raked me over the coals when I got back, anyhow."

His eyes narrowed behind a cloud of fragrant smoke. "Who's the pigeon?"

"Does it matter?"

I'd been so tired that night. Eugene's face the next day had been grey and artless, though that could just as well have been his daily hangover. It could have been anybody in the newsroom, I thought. I couldn't even remember if I'd shut my drawer.

Ward's face was animated now, the glow of the restaurant lanterns reflecting in the wide lenses of his spectacles.

"How are you going to play it, Lynch? I can help you. We could file the story here, overseas line. But what about the pictures? They'll never make it out. And the pictures are the story."

"I know that, Ward."

He frowned, puffing at the cigar, releasing several big clouds of smoke. Finally he spoke again. "There's only one way I can see it, Hal. You've got to get back to the States. Take the negatives with you. Or have someone else go for you. Then pound on some doors until they're published."

I pictured a ship, somewhere mid-Pacific, sapphire waves crashing against the hull. An editor's office in New York, overlooking the Hudson. Snowflakes touching the glass, shivering away to nothing.

"They won't let me back in, Ward."

"Probably not."

He considered the glowing end of his cigar. "Anything special keeping you in Japan, Hal?"

I pictured my drafty room in Nihonbashi. My mess of blankets, the typewriter on the battered desk. Mrs. Ishino leaning over the bar and pouring me another glass. The serving girl, Primrose — Satsuko — at a side table, a red plastic peony in her hair.

"I guess not."

He suddenly grinned, shaking his head.

"My goodness, Hal. You really are a dark horse. You know that? A real dark horse."

He rested his big paw on my shoulder and looked me straight in the eye.

"Just remember me when you get your Pulitzer, okay?"

I took the long walk home along the river, past dark, ruined fields. As I ducked past the curtain, I saw the place was busy.

Satsuko-san wandered over as soon as I sat down, just as if she happened to be passing. She opened up a beer and poured it into two glasses.

"*Cheers*," she pronounced, smiling at me.

"Cheers," I replied.

We exchanged pleasant banalities for a while, the familiar patter about food in Japan and back in America. She gave little gasps of surprise and admiration as I regaled her with the exotic dishes I had tried in her country. There was a lull in the conversation. Her lips moved, silently, as if she were phrasing a question. She looked back up at me with a very serious expression. Slowly, she asked: "Do you have pet?"

I laughed.

"Well, yes I do. Or rather, I did once . . . " I found myself telling her about Finn, the adored, glossy red Irish setter I'd had as a boy.

"When I was young, I used to sleep with my head on his fur. Like it was a pillow. You know — pillow?"

She looked startled. "You go sleep?" she asked, mimicking slumber.

"No, no. Not yet."

Finn had gone lame as I'd gotten older. One winter morning, just after my twelfth birthday, I was awakened by a distant noise. My breath billowed in the air as I came downstairs. The glass door of my father's gun cabinet hung open, one of the rifles missing. I creaked open the door and touched the smooth metal barrel of its twin. At that moment, my father came tramping back, holding shotgun and shovel. There was sweat on his head, a frail scent of sulphur.

"You have any pets, Satsuko-san? A dog?"

She smiled.

"Cat," she pronounced with a look of satisfaction. "We feed —" She slithered her hand through the air.

"Eels?" I asked, in a moment of inspiration.

"So." She made a snapping movement with her mouth. "Eel head."

A great wave of warmth and sympathy coursed through me, a curious sense of privilege to have this fragmentary glimpse into her past, her life before all of this began.

I laughed and she looked at me in surprise. Then, slowly, to my delight, she began to laugh too. Not the tittering laugh of a whore, eager to please, but the genuine laugh of a live woman, a woman with a childhood and a past, who considers her reflection in the mirror, and nods with wistful acceptance.

Finally I stood up, fully intending to head upstairs.

"You sleep now?" she asked.

"I'm going to try."

She placed her cool hand on my wrist. Her eyes were candid.

"You want take me?"

I hesitated. I felt the delicate pressure of her fingers upon my skin.

"Maybe another time."

The corners of her lips turned down sulkily. She crossed her arms.

"Well," I said. "Goodnight."

I lay fully clothed on my bed, cursing myself as I pictured the inevitable events unfolding below. Men arriving, the gramophone playing, couples swaying back and forth. Satsuko leading another man to the back room. I pictured her smooth, slim body as she pulled her dress over her head, a glimmer of light in her jet black eyes. I almost got up and headed right back downstairs to ask her to come up after all. But before I knew it, I had fallen dead asleep.

25
MRS. ISHINO'S SPECIAL EATING & DRINKING SHOP
(SATSUKO TAKARA)

The water was just coming to a boil as I dropped the scrubbed potatoes into the pan. From the crates piled up in the narrow kitchen, I took cans of spiced meat for sandwiches, tins of dried egg to mix bowls of gluey omelette for the night ahead — those simple snacks that the Americans seemed to find so delicious. They kissed their fingers and applauded as I set bowls of chipped potatoes and greasy fried egg sandwiches in front of them. A far cry from eel liver soup and *unagi-don*!

As I was pouring the water into the sink, Mrs. Ishino sidled into the kitchen through a big cloud of steam.

"Well?" she asked, pinching my arm. "What did you think?"

I frowned, concentrating on the potatoes as they tumbled into the draining basket.

"What did I think of what, Mrs. Ishino?"

"What did you think of the Westerner, of course!"

The American who slept in the attic room upstairs had taken me to the cinema that afternoon.

I shrugged. "I'm sure I don't know, Mrs. Ishino," I replied. "Does he really seem that different to the rest of them?"

Mrs. Ishino frowned as she considered the question. "Don't you think, Satsuko? More, the 'sensitive type,' I thought."

"Really, Mrs. Ishino?" I said, pouring oil into the pan. "Do you think any of them are sensitive?"

Mrs. Ishino let out an exasperated noise.

"Why not find out, Satsuko?" she said, stamping out of the kitchen. "It might not be such a bad idea to have a foreigner looking after you these days!"

I spluttered with laughter as she marched out. As I slid the potatoes into the spattering oil, I pictured the American sitting beside me in the cinema earlier that day, gazing up, bemused, at the screen.

Men in short sleeves had been bustling around the cinemas on the Rokku as we stepped down from the tram in Asakusa that afternoon. Several of the theatres had reopened along the wide avenue now, though their brickwork was still stained by black smoke. Banners for new shops fluttered on bamboo poles in the brisk spring wind, and cinema posters were mounted on billboards above the street, showing Western men with stern jaws and cowboy hats and women with blonde hair and large bosoms.

Just past the old Paradise Picture House, I glanced up. On the side of the wall was a big painted sign advertising a new Japanese film. I froze. Then I grasped hold of the arm of my American. Up there, larger than life, was a picture of Michiko.

My jaw fell. The resemblance was unmistakable. The American misunderstood my expression, and he walked straight up to the booth to buy two tickets. Still stunned, I tried to explain that the film would be in Japanese, that he wouldn't understand a thing. But he just shrugged and smiled, took my hand and led me inside.

There was only one row of seats left at the front of the damaged theatre, and as we took our places, the audience standing behind us seemed restless and agitated. As the light flickered onto the screen, my stomach tightened. The thought of seeing Michiko again — and in such a manner! The names of the actors blazed up on the screen. My eyes widened. *Michiko Nozaki.*

The film began, and soon enough, she appeared. I almost clapped my hands in delight. She wore a white, pleated skirt and casually twirled a summer parasol. I settled back in my seat to watch the film. The American squeezed my arm and offered me a hard candy from a paper bag.

I could hardly remember the plot, afterwards; a simple love story, it was all faintly ridiculous. Michiko was the true star of the film. Her beauty simply flooded the screen. The audience jostled behind us whenever she appeared, sighing when she gave that eager, encouraging smile I knew so well.

Her leading man was very handsome, with sharp cheekbones and piercing eyes. I glanced up at the American, who was quite unaware of my emotions as he munched away on his snacks. He looked rather handsome himself, I thought. I squeezed the tiniest bit closer to him.

Toward the end of the film, there was a shock. At the height of the drama, the man accused Michiko of covering up a crime. She tore herself away from him with tears in her eyes. He rushed over and took her in his arms. She turned, half-resisting. And then, quite openly, he leaned forward and kissed her.

A gasp came from the audience. He had kissed her! Full on the lips, in public — just like that. Of course, we had never seen anything like it on the screen before. The audience started shouting and my American laughed, quite bewildered by it all.

As the crowd poured out of the cinema into the spring sunshine, he took my arm and we walked together through the streets of Asakusa. Men were going by with sandwich boards, and some of the stalls on Nakamise Arcade had reopened now, selling flimsy mirrors and trinkets to the passing soldiers.

Cherry blossom hung from the scorched trees that leaned over Asakusa Pond, though it was more like a flooded bomb crater now. We sat on a bench and gazed at the flowers for a while, and I pointed out the scorched patch that had once been Hanayashiki Park with its golden horses, and, on the other side, the mound of rubble that had once been my old high school.

"Where did you live, Satsuko?" he asked, quite suddenly.

I frowned, and waved my hand vaguely in the direction of Umamichi Street, over on the far side of the temple precinct.

He fell silent for a long time, apparently lost in thought. Perhaps he really was different from the other Westerners, I thought. Darker, more brooding. I knew so little about him. Where had he fought during the war? Had he been a pilot, up there in one of the planes?

It was the question that none of us girls ever asked. I might have seen him one night, I thought, as he flew low across Tokyo. His handsome face behind the quilted nose of the cockpit, the glass glinting with the light of the fires raging below.

A muscle tightened in his jaw. I should hate him, I thought, for what they had done. But as we sat there in silence together, he took my scarred hand and held it between his palms. For a moment, as the breeze blew the blossom onto the surface of the dark water, it felt as if the sky was exhaling, as if the earth itself were silently offering up flowers for the souls of the dead.

The potatoes hissed and sizzled in the pan as Masuko came into the bar and switched on the radio. My ears pricked up straight away.

"Who Am I?" had come on the air that month. It featured displaced persons from all over the Japanese Empire who had lost their memories during the war. Now, on their return home, they were trying to discover exactly who they were and where they had come from. The presenter interviewed them on air in the hope that someone out there might recognize their voice or recall some clue about them.

"Can you remember anything about your childhood, sir?" he was asking, as Masuko turned up the volume. "The village festivals, perhaps, or where you went to school?"

A man's voice crackled in reply. "I can't remember much of anything, sir, just that we lived in the countryside. Our teacher was Matsukawa-sensei. He was so strict! I remember he beat me once when I lost one of the buttons of my school uniform..."

Masuko laughed out loud, and I took the pan from the heat and walked through to the bar in my apron. She was a short girl, as cheery as a sparrow, and had a lovely hint of the south in her voice. We'd quickly fallen into an enjoyable routine together, visiting the market for vegetables in the morning, clearing and polishing the bar in the afternoon and gossiping about Mrs. Ishino and what we referred to as her "mysterious past."

Masuko found the show very entertaining, though for all the wrong reasons. A sly smile played on her wide lips as she listened to the next segment.

"And now for some success stories," announced the presenter. "Last week the loyal wife of Mr. Kawachi heard her husband's voice on our programme, and boarded the train straight away from Kobe to come to our studio and collect him. They are now reunited in joy in their marital home."

"What rubbish!" cawed Masuko. "I bet Mrs. Kawachi's just some old hag who can't find herself a husband. She heard his voice on the radio and thought that a man without a memory would do her nicely!"

I smiled politely. But the truth was that I listened very intently to every minute of the show, and my stomach quivered as the men began to speak. What would it be like, I wondered, if Osamu's voice suddenly emerged from the crackling radio? If he had been lost somewhere in the South Seas, falsely reported dead by his comrades? Would I have telephoned the radio studio, if I heard him, I wondered? Even now?

My memory of him was fading, I realized. The picture of us together in my mind was frozen in time now, like an old photograph.

I became nervous as well when the young boys began to speak, telling tales of lost mothers and fathers. Tears had welled in my eyes one afternoon, when as an Osaka boy described losing his family in the fire raids just nights after I lost my own. I'd been filled with hopeless guilt and despair. What would I do if Hiroshi's voice suddenly, miraculously emerged from the speaker?

"I lost my sister, Satsuko Takara, on the night of the Great Fire Raid, but can remember nothing more. My only wish is to see her again ..."

Had I given up the search too soon? Mrs. Ishino had told me I'd done more than my filial duty, that I must simply get on with my own life now. But so many of us were still lost, it seemed; so many were still struggling to find their way back home.

I sighed as Masuko switched off the radio. She began polishing ashtrays and laying them out on the tables and I went back to the kitchen to salt the fried potatoes. After a while, I heard the sound of footsteps from upstairs. As I put my head around the door, I saw the American sitting at the bar, reading his book. He glanced up in surprise. I smiled at him shyly. His face lit up and his deep blue eyes gazed directly at me. He slid a match into the pages to mark his place and placed the book down upon the counter.

26
LA BOHÈME
(OSAMU MARUKI)

I spent much of spring in a state of dissolution, my vow to seek out Satsuko Takara blurring steadily away to transparency in countless glasses of *kasutori* shochu. I relapsed into torpor, a paralysis, as if the natural cords between motivation and action had been entirely severed.

Then, I was seized with a bout of the stunning, virulent malaria that had tortured me in New Guinea, and while the cherry blossoms blushed along the canals, I spun in and out of high fever, harrowed by visions of green chasms and purple corpses.

Thus it was not until the end of April that I had the energy, or the application, to take up my pen once more. I dedicated my convalescence to writing a novella, which, I was convinced, would capture the elusive spirit of our times. It followed the transmission, in excruciating stages, of a virus from an American soldier to a young Japanese artist. I felt it was by far my most compelling work to date, and I confidently submitted it to several of the leading literary reviews of the day, entitled simply, "The Germ."

It proved too avant-garde to be published. "Obtuse," the responses noted. "Incoherent." But this was just further proof, I realized, of something I was coming increasingly to understand.

Men were starving to death in the Tokyo streets, our nation knelt grovelling before an army of occupation. This was no time for deep examinations of the human condition. What was needed now was diversion and distraction: American pin-ups and bare-knuckle wrestlers; baseball games and "The Apple Song" piped through countless speakers. It was an age for fairy tales, I thought, for the rabbit in the moon.

I received the last of my rejection notes in the morning, and was slumped drunk by midday, the manuscript of "The Germ" in cinders in the stove. When I awoke later that evening, I felt maudlin and out of sorts, and I reached in my drawer for a faithful tablet of *courage*. As it dissolved beneath my tongue, a cheery chemical abandon erupted into my bloodstream. The room seemed suddenly claustrophobic, and so I slipped downstairs to immerse myself in the comforting waters of the *demi-monde*.

The bar was busy. A haze of acrid smoke lapped the walls, the revelries already in full swing. Two editors from a leading review of the day were sitting in an advanced state of disrepair at the counter, dribbling over their glasses.

In the centre of the room was a clique I didn't recognize. They were celebrating, and I hovered nearby on the off chance they might offer me something to drink. At the centre of the party was a man with a goat beard, wearing dark, round glasses and a wine red beret. The young people at his table refilled his glass each time he took a sip, laughing uproariously at every word he said.

"Who's that?" I asked Nakamura, who had appeared by my side. He was grinning drunkenly, and seemed very pleased with himself.

"You're behind the times, sensei," he said. "That's Kano, the famous film director."

"Oh," I murmured. "Well, the cinema . . ."

I had heard of the man of course — his "kiss" film had been the talk of Tokyo for weeks. One could hardly enter a room without overhearing allusions to his genius, his "distillation of the modern spirit."

"Why don't you come and meet him?" Nakamura suggested.

"You're acquainted with him, I suppose?"

"Oh yes," he said, grinning. "He wants me to work on his next film. Just some sketches for scenery, you understand . . ."

That wily old raccoon. Taking advantage of my illness to cozy up to film directors . . . Several of Nakamura's new cartoons had been published in the *Asahi Shimbun* that month. He had even started to ramble about founding a new magazine devoted entirely to manga.

"Well," I said, "perhaps I'll drop over later. Though I haven't much time for cinema people."

"Come on, Maruki," he said, gripping my arm. "Don't be such a snob."

"Nakamura, not now, please . . ."

"Come on," he said bluntly, and I smelled the booze on his breath. "It's his birthday. And he's buying."

With a sigh, I let Nakamura draw me over to the table, sharply aware of the Philopon now off on its gleeful spirals around my bloodstream. Most of the men at the table were young, with slick hair and gaudy shirts, shrieking with laughter as theatrical types so often do. None looked up as we approached, and I found myself considering them resentfully.

To my embarrassment, Nakamura suddenly shoved me forward and I banged against the table.

"Maruki-sensei!" he announced, sniggering, "The famous, talented writer!"

The group looked up at me askance. I tried to back away, cursing Nakamura for his boorishness, but Kano held up his hand. He took off his dark glasses and turned to me with a twinkle in his eye.

"We were just discussing our traditional Japanese culture, Maruki-san. Whether it still has any place at all in a modern nation. What is your view?"

I wondered if it was a trap, as I looked around at the shining eyes, the arch smiles. Someone pushed a glass of shochu toward me and I drained it. As I looked at the smug faces, I felt a sudden wave of recklessness — inspired, no doubt by the combination of shochu and amphetamine now pulsing through me. I'd throw their superiority right back in their faces, I thought.

"I think our 'magnificent culture' has all turned to piss, sensei," I said, turning on my heel, deciding that I would march straight out to another, less condescending watering hole.

To my surprise, a peal of high laughter came from Kano. Quickly, the rest of his disciples followed suit.

I turned. Kano was smiling at me.

"Thank you, Maruki-san," he said. "You see, we've just returned from the theatre."

I felt a tinge of doubt. "Well, the kabuki, of course —"

He cut me off. "Actually, I was thoroughly bored by it all."

A smile played on his lips. The heads of the others swivelled toward him, like acolytes waiting for a sutra to drop from the mouth of the Buddha.

"Is that so?"

He smiled. "Don't misunderstand me, Maruki-san. I have always been a great fan of the theatre, ever since I was a boy. But so much else has been lost that it seemed somehow meaningless to me. Hence my boredom."

"I see," I muttered, not quite following.

"It was as if one was attending a birthday party, surrounded by all sorts of delightful guests, and treated to all manner of delicacies, only to be told that the host had just died."

The acolytes chuckled, though I knew that none of them had a clue what he was talking about either. He took a cigarette from a packet in his side pocket — French, I noticed, they must have cost a fortune — lit it, then blew out the smoke in a tangled ring.

"And just then. Just think. I visited the urinal."

There were snorts of laughter. Kano was smiling dreamily. "I thought to myself — how many thousands must have pissed here on this same spot in the past? How many generations have passed water here over the decades, the centuries, even. How many gallons of saké and shochu have drained away; how many fathers and sons have stood here, aiming, shivering with the same primordial satisfaction? That most universal, absent-minded moment of pleasure, when even the most sophisticated man approaches the divine simplicity of the Buddha . . . The smell was overwhelming, and yet I stood, inhaling the fumes, thinking to myself — how wonderful! How delightful! And then — do you know what I thought? I thought, *This is it. This is the true smell of culture.* This is where the soul of a nation truly resides."

The disciples shook their heads at such erudition. Mrs. Shimamura approached the table carrying two large bottles of saké.

Kano looked at me directly. "Culture's a pretty sorry thing if it lives in a few temples and monuments, isn't it?"

I nodded.

"But it's always still there, you see? In the habits, the manners, the customs of the people. They can't be destroyed, Maruki-san. The way people talk. They way they laugh. And yes — the way they piss. And so thank you, sensei, you are indeed correct. Our magnificent culture has indeed all been turned to piss. And that, if I may say so, is where it's always been. When everything else has been stripped away — that is where any culture finds its true essence."

Loud and enthusiastic applause burst from all sides of the table and there was a hammering of feet upon the wooden floor. I hardly knew where to look. Kano raised his glass, and proposed a toast: "To a true scholar of the modern age!" Another large glass appeared in front of me. With an unsteady grin, I raised it to the assembled company and tipped it down my throat.

Room was made for me at the table. As Mrs. Shimamura set down bottles and snacks, she glanced at me in amusement. Soon enough, I felt relaxed and cheerful. Every so often, someone would bang the table and stand up and declare that they were "off to analyze our true culture" and everyone would laugh as the man went outside to urinate in the alley.

I found myself sitting next to Kano. He pushed his cigarettes toward me in an encouraging manner. The tobacco was delicious, and he talked to me in a conspiratorial way, as if we were both men of the world.

"And how are you surviving these morbid times, Maruki?" he asked politely.

"Well," I said, hesitantly. "I print a small journal. Nothing of any great consequence, you understand."

Mrs. Shimamura was leaning over the table, wiping away a spillage.

"Oh?" Kano inquired.

"It's been a great success, sensei!" Mrs. Shimamura piped up. "Better than half the other rubbish out there at the moment."

My face flushed. Hastily, I insisted: "It's just popular entertainment of course, sensei. Nothing of any artistic merit."

He frowned. "What's it called?" he asked.

"It's called *ERO,* sensei," interjected Mrs. Shimamura, her eyes twinkling with amusement. "It's really very popular. I was just thinking, perhaps, that sensei might like to take a look at it himself. In fact, I think we have a few spare issues behind the bar."

I jumped up from my seat. "Thank you Mrs. Shimamura! That won't be necessary! Now, if you'll excuse us . . . "

But Kano was looking at her. "There's no need, obasan," he said. "I've read every copy."

I was stunned. *Kano,* I thought, *reading my rag?*

"Not so much for the erotic pieces, you understand," he went on. "But for the 'man-in-the-street' interviews. I think they are are an act of genius."

I was speechless.

"Yes, they're quite remarkable. I look to them for inspiration. You truly have the 'human touch,' Maruki-sensei. You are a true pioneer."

A lump formed in my throat. "I had always hoped..."

"There is a childlike simplicity to your work."

"You don't say?"

"Oh yes," he murmured. "And now, as never before, we must return to a state of simplicity."

I was dizzy as Kano himself poured me another large drink. I felt absurdly pleased with myself. I had started out the evening as a pornographer and a literary flop, and now looked set to end it the pioneer of a new *naïf* school. The room began to glitter around me and I felt a great warmth toward everyone there.

"I'd like you to write something for me," Kano was saying, his figure blurring in and out of my vision. "Something about the men and the women of the Tokyo streets. You're the expert, after all."

Mrs. Shimamura drew up a stool.

"How much?" she demanded.

"Mrs. Shimamura, please," I protested, "Sensei, you must ignore her."

But Kano was smiling, and he casually named a sum that made my jaw drop. Mrs. Shimamura jotted figures on a piece of paper, crossing out numbers and totting them up as she murmured to herself.

"That's five months' rent — overdue now, if you please — shochu, food, breakages... Well, sensei, I think that should do nicely to start with."

She stood up and put out her hand, Western-style. Kano shook it with a smile as the rest of his disciples gathered their things.

"He'll start on it first thing tomorrow, sensei, don't worry," promised Mrs. Shimamura. "I'll make sure he does."

"Please do," smiled Kano. "And thank you Maruki-sensei. I look forward to reading your work."

As I stood up, I felt the floor sway beneath me.

He bowed formally. "Maruki-sensei. Please write it from the heart."

The heart, I thought — the heart, of course. I started to slip toward the floor, and felt Mrs. Shimamura's hand underneath my armpit, more to soften my landing than to raise me up again. As I rested my cheek against the hard wood, I was vaguely aware of Kano and his party hovering just above me. His words came to me as if through water.

"Just look. We're all at the bottom now. Isn't it glorious!"

Metallic laughs echoed from all sides.

"After all — it's only after one collapses that one can learn to stand on one's own two feet."

The next day, I took myself to Asakusa to watch Kano's famous "kiss film," in order to gain some understanding of his style. The damaged theatre was packed to the rafters, most of the seats having been removed, and I squirmed through an excited crowd to stand behind the sole remaining row of chairs at the front of the auditorium. Before me was the glossy head of a Japanese woman who sat next to a tall, handsome Western man. As the projector rolled, the screen lit up. The woman turned to whisper something into the foreigner's ear.

A bolt of shock.

It was Satsuko Takara. Her hair cut to a bob, the light of the screen playing upon the curve of her cheek. The shape of her mouth as she smiled up at the man, the obsidian eyes with long lashes that threw into relief the glittering pupils. She turned back to the screen and rested her hand lightly upon the man's well-clothed leg. A man, I realized with growing astonishment, that I also recognized: last seen on the Yurakucho tram, reading a newspaper, wearing a glossy pair of chestnut Oxford brogues.

I felt a ridiculous sense of wounded pride, and, at the same time, a dismal, masochistic satisfaction. To be so justly punished for my hopeless vacillation, my weakness, my impotent conceit.

She was gazing at the screen as the American put his big arm around her. After a while, she rested her beautiful head upon his shoulder.

With a rueful smile, I pushed my way back through the crowd. The spring sunshine was bright as I walked slowly back to the Montmartre, my heart spinning with hopeless desires. When I got home, I marched straight upstairs. I locked the door and took out my notepad and pen.

I wrote the script entirely from the heart, as Kano had asked me to do. I poured every atom of my being into its pages, scribbling away until long in the night.

I infused the story with "childlike simplicity." I captured the spirit of the times. From the crystalline vials of Philopon pills, to the dimpled tangerines at the market, I employed every image I had seen on my long voyages around the Yamanote Line that winter, every encounter I had witnessed on my solitary peregrinations through the freezing streets. The American, with his moulded camera case and shoes. The urchins outside the bathhouse. Satsuko Takara, standing poised outside her brothel, the night I returned home, broken from war.

The script became a love story, as is so often the case. But it was one far removed from the frustration and obscenity that made up the dreary leitmotifs of *ERO*. Much of the action would take place overground, I decided. The city itself would play a starring role. As I wandered the streets of Tokyo that spring, I saw the first cherry blossom on the scorched trees, the flash of fresh-cut cedar among the houses, green shoots sprouting in the charred black soil. Could there be hope here still, I wondered, despite all the death and ruin?

I cannot pretend that the script was not sentimental, even melodramatic at times. But Kano was overwhelmed when I showed it to him. It made him weep to read, he said. We were required to submit it to the American censors, and it emerged back a few weeks later, thick with blue pencil, shaved of some limbs, but still with its heart intact.

The day after, we set out from the white warehouses of the Toho Studios with a young and excited crew to film the first scenes in the streets of the city. And it was there, in those burned-out ruins, that for the first time I saw our new star in the flesh, as she practised her lines outside a broken-down house. The actress who I knew straight away would come to define our age, who would capture the hearts of an entire generation of cinema-goers: the glorious, the exquisite, the unmistakable Michiko Nozaki.

27
FRATERNIZATION
(HAL LYNCH)

The flats beside the river park were strewn with rubble, and all that was standing were charred telegraph poles and tin shelters from which emanated wisps of smoke and the scent of charcoal. Faint outlines showed where houses had once stood. There was nothing inside now but strands of rusted iron, broken tiles, shards of crockery. Satsuko led the way through the labyrinth of soot.

I'd asked her if she would take me to see her old neighbourhood. She had seemed terrified for a moment, as if a ghost had appeared before her. But then she looked up at me, searchingly, and finally she nodded, apparently resolved.

We walked in silence through the char, negotiating mounds of earth and ditches filled with brambles and weeds. There was a quality to Satsuko that I couldn't quite define. Behind the frank warmth she exuded as she sat beside me at the bar, as she poured my beer and we talked about the little things, there was an aura of profound tragedy, and yet, endurance. She was an enigma to me, I accepted, but not fatally inscrutable, as so many of my countrymen tediously asserted the Japanese to be. However short our common frontier, however deep our hinterlands, I felt a curious bond with the dark-eyed girl, as she sat in her woollen skirt and white blouse and dealt out playing cards between us on the counter. We had established a wonderful shelter of banality, a soothing, subtle sanctuary of the trivial and the everyday within which we both seemed tacitly content to hide. I flattered myself that we were more than just another man and woman cast together by the great currents of the world. That the flashing sensation I sometimes had when I was with her was correct: that I understood her, and — even more puzzling — that she understood me. But the nights of fire that lurked on the borders of my dreams lay between us, still, and I'd decided that I needed to see the site of her home — the place of her ruin — if I were to hope to fathom her mystery; if I wished to salvage something of myself.

We reached a canal, and walked halfway over a green, iron-riveted bridge. She leaned over and looked down at the concrete bed, streaming with shallow water. She pointed upstream.

"Factory," she said. "Chemical."

I nodded, imagining the explosion. She stood there, slim-waisted and willowy as she gazed out. Along the banks of the channel were lumberyards, wet, black ash soiling their cobblestones. Frail stacks of wood stood like piles of burnt matchsticks, waiting to be blown away. Further upstream, a set of lock gates were warped and splintered. She pointed, making a swimming motion with her arms.

"Swim? You used to swim there?"

She nodded. "Children. I. My brother."

I pictured boys and girls diving into the water, ducking and playing hide-and-seek as they swam around the timber barges. From the other side of the canal came the faint sound of children chanting in unison. We walked on past a schoolyard and finally came out onto a wider avenue. A little further down, by the entrance to a furrowed alleyway, she stopped. She clasped her arms over her chest, and I saw that she was scared and was trying to summon up courage. I attempted to take her hand, but she pulled it away and shook her head. She took a deep breath and strode forward.

We walked down a row of incinerated buildings until we reached a square concrete cistern. She stopped and frowned.

"This. I think —"

She crossed an invisible threshold onto a patch of ground, littered with ash and broken glass. I hesitated at the boundary. Weeds had sprung up, as high as my thigh. She closed her eyes, held out her arms, and then gently spun about, like a little girl in a daydream. I watched as she stood there, the field of rubble stretching to the river beyond, and I imagined her that night, the air quivering, as the planes roared over in a great metallic typhoon.

She turned to face me. She sprinkled her fingers in the air to mimic falling bombs.

"My house," she said. "Burn down."

I nodded. On the map, the whole of the Asakusa ward had been shaded the darkest of blacks. *Inflammable Area — Grade 1.*

She was standing, her arms extended, palms down, as if measuring the space around her. She pointed into the air. "My mother —"

I frowned. "Your mother's room?"

"So."

She turned and pointed again. "There, my brother —"

"Your brother's room?"

"So." She frowned and touched a finger to her nose. "My room also."

"What happened to your mother, Satsuko?"

She held her hands up, waving her fingers around her head. "Fire."

I swallowed. "And your brother?"

She looked down at the ground and slowly shook her head. It was then that I stepped over the threshold. I walked to her and took her hands in mine. When she looked up, her eyes were streaming with tears.

"Satsuko —"

What could I say? Please forgive me, Satsuko? I'm sorry, Satsuko, for burning down your house? For killing your mother and your brother? I rubbed my thumbs against her smooth palms, as if, like some saint of old, I could miraculously heal the scars.

"Satsuko —"

She looked up at me, sobbing. She thrust her face into my shoulder and I held her shaking body in my arms. Then she lifted up her face to mine, tears wet upon her cheeks. I pulled her forward and clasped her frail torso. As our cheeks pressed against each other, I imagined the two of us together like this, that night, silhouetted on the blackened plain, the chemical works burning like a livid green candle behind us, as rivulets of fire streamed across the sky.

Finally, we drew apart. The wind gusted around us, ruffling the feathery fronds of the weeds. I gripped her hand in my own, and, together, we picked our way out of the rubble and walked back toward the avenue.

Our shadows cast long in the afternoon sunshine as we strolled among the bustling crowds on our way to the train station. Satsuko drew closer. Western men and Japanese girls occasionally passed us, the men briefly glancing at me with expressions of awkward complicity. I put my arm around Satsuko's waist. I imagined the two of us, walking together along Fifth Avenue, Christmas shopping in the December snow, at the Metropolitan Opera, drinking cocktails before a concert. The pompous looks of disdain from the fur-coated women; the envious eyes of the patrician men in their dinner suits. I was still smiling when a jeep pulled up beside us by the scaffolded gate of the Senso Temple. A press card was wedged behind the windshield.

Eugene took off his aviator sunglasses as he clambered out the door. Japan had filled him out — there was a mottled fleshiness to his face, a hint of gut beneath his khaki shirt.

"Hal," he exclaimed, holding out his hand. "I didn't know you were still here!"

"Hello, Gene. Where else would I be?"

He hesitated. "I figured you'd gone back to New York."

"Not yet."

He glanced at Satsuko and his eyebrows raised in lewd question. I pictured her for a moment in her cheap kimono, tugging him onto the dance floor of the Oasis. I felt a stab of panic that he might recognize her. I looked at Satsuko. *Primrose.* Her face betrayed nothing.

"Gene, this is Satsuko."

He grinned and saluted.

"Hello Satsuko."

Satsuko nodded demurely, and drew closer to me.

"Working on something, Gene?" I asked, pointing at the Speed Graphic around his neck.

He rolled his eyes. "The monks here," he said, jerking his thumb toward the temple. "Apparently they keep prize chickens."

"Huh. Sounds like Dutch. Human interest?"

"Can't all be hotshots like you, I guess, Hal."

I studied his face. Acne had erupted across his cheeks and thin hairs were growing on his upper lip, as if he'd just now entered adolescence. Satsuko excused herself, and walked over to browse a stall. Eugene watched her appraisingly, then gave a low whistle. He turned back to me with a triumphant leer.

"So you finally succumbed to yellow fever, Hal. After all your innoculations. Maybe you're human after all."

I forced a smile. "It's not like that, Gene."

"Oh no?" He squinted back at her. "What is she? An imperial princess?"

"She's just an ordinary girl."

He laughed. "She's got her claws into you, Hal. All of them try sooner or later, trust me. They all want to see New York. She ask you to marry her yet?"

"No."

"So what's the deal, then Hal? Angel with a broken wing?"

"Does it matter?"

He shrugged. "I guess. I'm glad you've found yourself a piece at last. Do you good."

My fist tightened involuntarily. "She's not a piece of anything, Eugene."

My house, she'd said, staring at me with tears in her eyes. *Fire.*

His eyes widened. "Is this what they call penance, Hal? Atonement for your sins? Or is it just good old Catholic guilt?"

I felt a sudden rage and moved forward.

He jumped back, fear in his eyes. Then suddenly his face became wreathed in a smile. Satsuko had wandered back over. She put her arm in mine and I felt her fingers squeeze my own.

"Well, it was good to see you again Hal," Eugene said. "You two look swell together. Mind if I take a snap?"

My rage slowly ebbed as he held up the camera. Satsuko combed back an invisible wisp of hair and smiled up at him. I waited for the flicker of the shutter behind the lens.

"Smile!"

When we got back home that night, we went straight upstairs. I shut the door and when I turned around, she was naked. It was cold in the room, and she stepped lightly over to me, putting her arms around my neck. I rested my chin on her head for a moment, rubbing the ridges of her spine beneath my fingertips. She looked up at me, and I kissed her gently, feeling the soft warmth of her lips on mine, her small tongue darting timidly into my mouth. I quickly undressed, and she led me over to the futon and I blew out the light and pulled the covers over us.

Moonlight was falling into the room as we lay there, very close, holding each other tenderly. Haltingly, she moved around until she was lying on top of me and pressed against my ribcage. I felt her hand move, and then her chin tilted upward and she gave a small gasp. Her pale belly was trembling in the darkness, black tresses of hair falling down over dark-tipped breasts. She placed both of her hands on my chest and, with a deep sigh, pushed down. Slowly, she arched her back, and I could see the indentations of her ribs rippling like shadows beneath her breasts. Her eyes closed and her cheeks flushed and finally, with a moan, she twisted her hips and gasped. Her breath came out slowly, in shivers. She gazed at me, and I heard her whisper my name; in the darkness, I could see her black eyes glistening with blurry stars; the smeared reflections of faraway fires.

28
AN ONLY ONE
(SATSUKO TAKARA)

America.

I couldn't remember ever having even seen a map of the United States before. But Mrs. Ishino had an old atlas of the world on her shelf, and I sat with it now at the back of the bar, spelling out the unfamiliar names of the cities and rivers and prefectures, trying to commit them to memory.

New York, where Hal-san had studied, was famous, of course, and so was Chicago, with its skyscrapers and gangsters and jazz cabarets. But what about Nebraska? Utah? Albuquerque? Half of the names were unpronounceable, even if I had been able to speak English fluently. I closed the atlas in frustration. The thought of America was becoming an obsession. I was worried that I would bore Hal silly by asking him about it. I picked up the wrinkled magazine that someone had left on the bar earlier that week. There was a long feature with a set of colour photographs of California inside. While New York and Chicago might have been exciting places to visit, I'd decided it was California that was the place for me.

San Francisco seemed almost Japan-like, I thought, as I studied the photographs in the magazine for the hundredth time. Brightly painted wooden houses stood up on the hills and fishing boats were docked at the bustling wharves. There were forests and mountains in the distance, you could see that, and Mrs. Ishino had once told me that other Japanese people lived there too, so I might still be able to buy miso and *katsuobushi* whenever I had a craving for Japanese food, or felt homesick for Toyko.

Not that there seemed much chance of that. The magazines were so glossy and the colours so startlingly rich that I wondered if the sun might somehow be brighter in America than it was in Japan. The pages were packed with pictures of healthy-looking men playing baseball and tennis and golf, lounging by swimming pools and smoking cigarettes, whilst neat, smiling housewives in bright calico dresses stood next to refrigerators laden with meat, churned yellow butter, and glass bottles of orange juice. There were advertisements for everything and anything, from syrup to stockings, spectacles to hats. Silk gloves, leather shoes, bedsheets, perfume, whisky and wedding rings. Everyone was happy, and judging from the way America looked in the magazines, that was hardly surprising.

I sighed and placed the magazine down. I walked over to the open doorway. The sky was grey and the street outside was full of churned mud. Children ran half-naked past the shanty houses, and a toothless man walked slowly past with hollow eyes, his clothes loose upon his body.

The idea that I might go to America had started as a joke. One evening, as we sat at the counter, Hal-san was telling me about his old college in New York, which sounded quite similar to the castle-like buildings of the Imperial University. Just at that moment, he caught my eye.

"Would you like to live in America someday, Satsuko?" he said.

My heart rose to my throat. For a moment, I had thought he had actually asked me to go away with him, just as casually as he might ask me to the cinema. I started to stammer. Then my cheeks flushed as it dawned on me, that, of course, he had just been asking a general kind of question.

I pretended to laugh. America certainly sounded wonderful, I said, but I couldn't speak English very well, and of course, I'd miss all of my friends. He put his hand on my wrist and stroked it gently. I wondered if he wasn't a little bit drunk.

"We could find you a teacher," he murmured.

I laughed again, more cynically this time. Teaching you English was something they all promised to do.

"Cat, sat, mat," I muttered. "How are you? How do you do?"

It was a stupid thing for him to have asked, and I felt annoyed at him for suggesting it.

But then I saw that he was looking at me quite seriously. For a moment, I let myself imagine what it might be like, living far away in a foreign country. A house beside a shady park that stretched all the way to the ocean. I could grow daikon and burdock in the garden. The days would come and go. Hal went off to work at his newspaper every morning, and I would visit the beach, and listen to the seagulls, as our children played around me in the sunshine.

Posters were appearing all over Tokyo with Michiko's beautiful face upon them. Everyone was looking forward to her new film. The cinema magazines reported that the action was to take place in the burned-out streets of the city itself, and I found myself watching out for the film crew whenever I visited the market.

For weeks, I had been convincing myself that I should write to Michiko and tell her where I was living. But as I pictured her, lounging in her glamorous apartment, surrounded by clothes and magazines, I wondered if she would even open a letter from me. She might fling it from her in terror when she saw my name, repelled by the thought of contact with this spider from her past.

But finally one afternoon, I sat down to write in any case, intending to keep the note brief and to the point. I wrote out my address, and told her that I was working in a restaurant again, that I had several warm-hearted companions and that life was full of possibilities.

"I was so thrilled to see you on the screen last month, Michiko," I wrote, "when my American and I visited the cinema together."

I stared at the words I had just written. My American? My heart started to patter, as I picked up the pen once more.

"Yes, Michiko, it's true. I too have found an 'only-one,' as you yourself did last year. I very much hope that you will have the chance to visit us soon. Please do not be too embarrassed to come. I admit that I was upset when you moved away, but I know now that it was all for the best. After all, you were simply choosing to live, Michiko, in the only way you knew how. Just as we must all try to live."

I started to feel quite emotional. It was at this point I got carried away. "I hope, in any case, you will be able to come soon, though I know how busy you must be with your cinema activities. Because very soon, Michiko, my American will be taking me away from Japan. We will be going to live in San Francisco, and I may not return for a long time. So you see, Michiko, it is not only film stars like you that can have exciting romantic adventures!"

My heart was in my mouth as I sealed the note and hurried to the post office. I quickly copied out the address of Michiko's studio from the back of a film magazine and handed the letter to the postmaster. As I did so, I felt as if the flimsy note was a votive plaque that I was hanging at a shrine, a hopeless prayer that I dreamed might somehow come true.

When Hal came back to Mrs. Ishino's that evening, he seemed worried and drew his fingers through his thick hair. My stomach tightened as I went to make him a sandwich. I poured him a drink. After a while, he seemed to relax.

Later on, casually, I took down Mrs. Ishino's atlas, and opened it up to the map of America. His eyes lit up and he laughed. Taking my hand beneath his own, he drew my finger to the eastern side of the country.

"New York," he said, pointing at himself. "The Empire State."

I smiled and shook my head. I drew his hand back to the other side of the map again.

"No empire. San Francisco," I said.

He started to laugh again, the glorious, warm laugh that poured from his chest.

"You want to live in San Francisco, Satsuko?" he said.

I smiled. "Yes. You take me."

"You want me to take you to San Francisco?" he said, sweeping his fingers through his hair. "Sure! Why not? Let's go to San Francisco. We'll take the next boat."

I couldn't quite tell if he was joking or not. He shook his head with a faraway smile. He gazed at me for a second, then looked away, rubbing my hand over and over again.

We went up to his room soon after. His body was strong and taut and I felt a great, piercing sense of relief sweep through me. In the middle of the night, I woke up and gazed at his smooth, white skin, his chest moving softly up and down. I wondered whether I should slip downstairs to my room, but the nest of blankets was so cozy, and there was such a gentle warmth emanating from his body, that I just lay beside him, clasping my hands around his broad chest, and fell away into a deep sleep.

When I woke in the morning he was already getting ready to leave. I lay there dozing for a while, taking pleasure in the sound of him washing and getting dressed. Just before he left, he leaned down over the futon and kissed me on the forehead. For a moment I could smell the musky scent of his cologne on his smooth cheeks. Then the door closed and I lay there in a shaft of spring sunlight, breathing in the scent of the sheets, watching the motes of dust dance in the air. I thought that I should probably get up and go on with my work quite soon, but then I told myself I should stay for a little while longer, that I deserved to be happy, just for this short time. And so I lay there, smiling secretly to myself, stretched out on the bed like a satisfied cat.

29
THE YAKUZA
(HIROSHI TAKARA)

From the top of the old railway bridge, I scanned the market through the sight of my sniper rifle.

Captain Takara — deep behind enemy lines.

Slowly, I swept from side to side, as the huge American flag flicked on its pole, casting a shadow over the GIs who were ambling amongst the stalls below. *Easy targets*, I thought. *One bullet left. Aim for the heart —*

There was a flash of colour over by the station as three girls flounced toward the market. I fumbled with the aperture of my Leica and urgently twisted the rangefinder. Through the lens, I focused on the stocky one in the middle, the one they called Yotchan.

I could almost make out the shadow that curved between her breasts. *Fire!*

I pressed the shutter and the flutter lens closed. *Bull's eye!*

A hand cuffed me on the back of the head and I spun around to see Mr. Suzuki, laughing at me, hands on his hips. The shoulder holster of his pistol showed beneath his grey silk jacket.

"Getting some cute pictures up here, are you, little shit?" he said. "No wonder you spend so much time up here."

My cheeks began to throb.

"Put your dick away. It's lunch time."

Mr. Suzuki wasn't a man to argue with. The market boss had almost killed me two weeks before, when I'd been at the station, trying to drum up portrait business. I'd spotted him at the mouth of the market, looking up and down the road as if he was waiting for someone. The grey felt fedora was pulled low over his forehead, and a white silk handkerchief ruffled from his breast pocket.

I ran over and held up my Leica in question.

"Sir —"

I didn't get a chance to finish.

"You want me to break that thing in your fucking face?" he snarled.

I backed off right away — I got the message all right. He glared at me, and I noticed a faint squint in his eye. Suddenly, a memory came to me, of an afternoon long ago, years before the Pacific War had even broken out.

Back in the days when our shop had been open, my mother had sometimes asked me to deliver box lunches to especially important customers in the neighbourhood. One afternoon in July, a huge order had arrived just after midday. It was the very busiest time of the year — the real dog days when the line snaked all the way down the alley, with everyone desperate to eat their fill of unagi-don to revive their flagging spirits.

My father glanced at the name card, then raised his eyebrows and wiped the sweat from his brow. Politely, he told the customers out front that there would be a short delay in serving them, and he tightened the cloth around his head. He piled up charcoal on the grill, and started brushing the sizzling strips of eel with sauce from his pot as fast he could, calling to my mother to pile them onto rice in our best lacquered boxes.

As she loaded the parcels into the carriage of my delivery bicycle, she grasped my arm and wiped my face with her sleeve. "Go as quick as you can," she said. "And keep a civil tongue in your head!"

When I reached the address on the card, up in the tenements near Sengen Shrine, I thought I was lost. There was nothing but an abandoned house with broken shutters, stray cats stretched out asleep on the roof. Then from inside, I heard faint voices shouting out numbers, rattling and slamming noises. Nervously, I tapped on the door. A moment later, a half-naked man slid it open, waving a silk fan against his upper body. He squinted down at me. The rippling torso was completely inked over with colourful tattoos.

Mr. Suzuki stepped toward me.

"Do I know you?" he said. His voice was slurred like a proper yakuza.

I bowed my head. There was no way he could remember me, I thought, not a chance.

"What the fuck happened to your face?"

I stared at him, hardly able to believe it.

"I got burned, sir," I murmured.

"You don't say."

He peered at the camera around my neck. "You know how to use that thing?"

I nodded.

"So come over here."

On the other side of the station, a huge sign was hoisted up alongside the overground train track, made of high-powered electric light bulbs that spelled out the name of the market, so that people could see it from miles around. Mr. Suzuki stood underneath it, and tipped his hat over his eye, almost daintily.

"Be sure you get the sign in the picture," he said, jerking his thumb into the air.

As I twisted the lens, his blunt face came into focus. A ribbed, crescent shaped scar dimpled one of his cheeks.

"And make it a good one, kid," he called. "I might not be here so long."

I stifled a grin. This was exactly the kind of thing that gangsters were supposed to say! I held up my hand in a professional manner, and pressed the shutter firmly. He strode back over and roughly pulled the camera from around my neck, grunting as he turned it about in his clumsy hands.

"You really know how to use this?"

"It's not so hard."

He stared at me for a moment. Then he draped the camera back around my neck.

"Hungry?"

My eyes lit up as he jerked his head toward a stall just inside the market. Clouds of fragrant steam were billowing from the pots and my mouth started to water. The spry old chef welcomed us in like royalty: he hurried out to wipe down our stools and poured a frothing bottle of beer that he set on the counter in front of Mr. Suzuki.

"Make yourselves at home, young sirs," he said as he bustled around his pots and pans. "You're very welcome!"

"What filthy soup are you using today, granddad?" Mr. Suzuki drawled.

"Dog and crow, sir." The man giggled and stirred the big metal vat on his makeshift stove with a long ladle. Mr. Suzuki grunted.

"Two of those, then, granddad. Extra chives, extra jewels, hard-boiled egg."

"Coming right up!"

As I shovelled the almost unbearably delicious noodles into my mouth, I wondered what the man could possibly want with me. I didn't want to be any part of the yakuza, I thought, even if I had stolen the camera. My father would have been ashamed of me. But even so, it was pretty exciting to be sitting next to a real live gangster. People going past glanced at me with interest, and I cocked my head casually, as if eating with Mr. Suzuki was something I did every day of the week.

"Where do I remember you from, kid?" he said, taking a sip of his beer.

"My father used to own a food shop, sir. Not far from your old office."

He grinned, as if remembering far-off, sunlit days. "Takara Eels?"

My heart almost burst with pride — my dad's shop!

"Fucking great," he said. "Shame it closed down. All dead now, I guess?"

A pit opened in my stomach. I bowed my head. "Yes, sir. I'm sorry."

"Even that cute girl? She your sister?"

I suddenly glowered at him. Mr. Suzuki raised his eyebrows and held up his hands in apology.

"Alright, little shit — don't go upsetting yourself. Where'd you get that contraption from in any case?"

He pointed at the camera, and I drew it closer to my chest, fingering the knot in the leather strap.

"Steal it?" he smirked.

I stayed silent.

"Suit yourself."

He drew a big pile of noodles onto his chopsticks and gazed at the steam that came off.

"No family left at all?" he asked, stuffing the noodles into his mouth.

I shook my head.

"That makes two of us."

He slurped down the last of the soup, then lit a cigarette.

"Want to take some pictures for me?" he asked as he squinted through the smoke.

"Photographs, sir?"

"I could use someone with sharp eyes."

There was something about him that made me nod straight away.

"Good boy," he said. "Work hard for me and I'll see you're treated right."

There were little wrinkles on his forehead. As I stared at his blunt features, I realized that he was older than he looked. He snapped his fingers in front of my face.

"See?" he said with a grin. I found myself grinning back at him. "Now you've got a friend in the world."

~

I had left the inn soon after the children had gone away. It felt too lonely after that, the paper screens torn, the tatami littered with dead moths and butterflies. The grass was waist high in the garden when I went, the cracked statue of the tanuki still lying grinning on the threshold.

Now that the weather was warmer, I slept in Ueno Park, beneath a tarpaulin stretched from a tree not far from the shogun's graveyard. The lotus plants in the pond were leafy again, and green and black ducks dabbled in the water. I hung around the clapboard bars in Yurakucho where the Americans drank at night, and held up the camera as they lurched out. They drunkenly posed for me, arm in arm with their friends, or hoisting Japanese girls up on their shoulders. They scribbled their names and their billet in my exercise book, and I circled the number showing on the exposure counter. An old chemist developed the film for me at the back of his tiny studio in Kanda, and I delivered the prints to the Americans a week later and collected my fee. I stood in the marble lobbies as they flipped through the shots, trying to smile as they patted me on the head and I waited for my money.

Mr. Suzuki gave me a ninety-millimetre screw-mount lens for my camera and a big pair of field binoculars that must have belonged to some officer during the war. At the top of the old railway bridge, he showed me a series of flags to run down a wire stretched over the market if there was ever a sign of trouble — white for American military police, red for Koreans or Formosans. I stood there watching every day from dawn until noon.

For the rest of the afternoon, I was free to roam wherever I wanted. The market turned into my personal cinema, as I squinted through the rangefinder of my camera, the cool, heavy frame a comforting weight against my face. I took pictures of the traders laying out piles of old boots, the drunken ex-students who ran the liquor stall. Then, there were the pan-pan girls, who strutted through the market as if they owned the place, shrieking like vixens and calling out insults. They grabbed any man that they fancied by the arm, or by the crotch, and dragged him away to the wasteground beneath the railway arches.

The girl in the purple dress gave me a sharp thrill whenever I saw her. She must have been about eighteen, and her hair was cut in a straight line so that it fell just above her eyes. There was something about her thick legs and giant breasts that made my stomach melt; so much so that I had to scramble up the ladder to the top of the railway tracks and helplessly relieve myself. As I watched her through my camera, day after day, a stealthy plan began to form in my mind.

Mr. Suzuki had told me that I was getting paid at the end of the week, fifty yen. Yotchan cost ten, I'd heard. Finally, I decided. It was time.

Mr. Suzuki must have noticed that I was distracted, because toward the end of the week, he called me into his office, a wooden hut on the edge of the market. He told me to sit down. A crisp pile of black-and-white photographs lay on the desk in front of him, and he grinned as he flicked through them. At the end of the stack was the blurry shot of Yotchan.

"Cute," he said. "Not my type, though."

He leaned forward. "You want to see some real pictures of girls?"

My heart began to thud as he took an envelope from his desk drawer and slid it over to me. I quickly stuffed it under my shirt as he gave me a wink.

"Don't worry, kid. I was just the same at your age. Though I'm guessing you're a man already, right?"

I swallowed, glancing down at the picture of Yotchan. He grunted. "No? Well. I'm disappointed in you. It's about time, isn't it?"

My pulse started to race.

"You've worked hard all month," he said. "You could do with a break. I'll tell you what, next weekend, we'll go to a place I know in Shinjuku. They'll show you the hills and the valleys."

I started to tremble. *This was it.* I bowed my head, clutching the envelope beneath my shirt. He called to me as I was leaving the office.

"They're all good girls," he said. "Not like real geisha. More like *Daruma* dolls."

I stared up at him, lost. He started to wheeze with laughter. "You can roll them over as much as you like!"

I kept my head down as I shuffled through the market, painfully aware of the envelope hidden beneath my shirt. I didn't see the girls until I had walked straight into them. Something soft bumped against my head and I was suddenly surrounded by a choking cloud of perfume.

"Hey, look where you're going, scorch!"

Clouds of coloured nylon and cotton swirled around me. The girl's faces were plastered with makeup and they grinned at me like jackals. Yotchan jerked her hand up in a brutal sexual motion.

"Gone blind have you?"

My cheeks pulsed. It was as if she could see right through me.

A nasty grin came over her face. "Oh well. I don't suppose you get much with that melted face of yours. How old are you anyway?"

"Fifteen," I muttered.

Her eyes narrowed as she edged closer. "Well. You're practically a man already, then, aren't you?"

My face was nearly touching the pale skin between her throat and her breasts, my nose filled with the sour animal smell of her sweat.

"Want to take me on, kid? You've got money, don't you?"

Despite my panic, I felt an almost excruciating excitement. *Please*, I thought, *don't let me lose control, not right here and now.* Yotchan was staring at me slyly, her bright red lips moving round and round as she chewed her gum.

Suddenly, her hand shot out and she gripped my privates. She squeezed as I gasped and her eyes grew wide.

"Well!" she said. "You are a man after all."

She pulled my head toward her and crushed it against the pillow of her bosom. I heard the other girls shrieking with laughter, and I struggled to free myself, spluttering. The stall-holders had all gathered round now and were cackling away, enjoying every moment.

Yotchan snorted. "Well. He knows where to find me."

I stumbled backward. Yotchan fluttered her hand in the air.

"Come back tonight. Make sure you bring enough money."

I slunk away, my cheeks throbbing.

Yotchan suddenly exploded with a splutter of laughter. "Hey! You've forgotten something."

I froze, suddenly aware of the lack of weight within my shirt.

I hardly dared glance back as I ran toward the railway embankment. Yotchan was bent double as she waved the photographs in the air, and the stallholders were all roaring with laughter, tears streaming down their faces.

30
SENTIMENTAL JOURNEY (HAL LYNCH)

Ward was subdued as he sat at the kitchen table in his fine new house in Shinjuku, freshly decorated in preparation for the arrival of his wife, Judy, from Chicago. A new set of wicker furniture graced the room and the sliding doors were wide open to disperse the lingering smell of fresh paint and pickled radish. I felt a pang of jealousy as he showed me the neat garden outside — the wisteria in bud over the doorway, a cherry tree ablaze with white blossom and filling the air with scent that mingled with a thread of incense from the temple nearby. His beard was thick now, streaked with silver, and he wore a long silk robe, as if he had just stepped out of some antique Japanese painting.

"So where are we, Ward?"

"I've talked to more people this week, Hal. Harry Welles from *LIFE*. Auberon Fox from *TIME*. They're intrigued. They want to see your pictures as soon as you arrive home."

The whir of a cicada came from the trees. I went over and stood in the doorway. Up above the slanted tiles of the temple roof, a red balloon was adrift, pitching higher and higher in the breeze.

"Are you ready?" he said.

The balloon grew smaller in the sky, and finally became a scarlet dot in the heavens.

"Almost. When's Judy arriving?"

"Friday."

"Everything fixed up?"

Ward grunted. "Almost."

He stood up to fetch a bottle of Guckenheimer from the sideboard and poured us two glasses. Birdsong trilled from the garden; there was the faint, far off drone of Buddhist prayers being recited.

"It's a beautiful home, Ward. I'm sure you'll be happy here."

He nodded steadily and sipped at his drink.

"You're going to miss Japan, Lynch. Isn't that so?"

I thought of the imprint of Satsuko on my bed that morning, the silent echo of the contours of her body. Stray strands of black hair upon the pillow. The cedarwood cigar box still waiting, hidden under the floorboard in the corner of my room.

"You won't look back from this, Lynch," Ward said. "Believe me. It'll be the making of you."

I nodded.

He draped a sandalled foot over his big thigh and blinked heavily. He rubbed his eyes and gave a lopsided grin. "You know that I'm proud of you, don't you, Hal?"

I nodded. "Thank you. Mark."

He poured more whisky into his glass and sighed again, then turned to look at the last cherry blossom in the garden. My throat tightened. In the pale sunlight, sitting in his chair, for a moment, he looked just like my father.

The first warmth of summer was hovering outside my window as I gazed over the crooked planks of the tenements below. A horse-drawn cart paused in the alley, and a ragged child stroked the animal's flank. I rolled out the carbon from the drum of my typewriter. I was in shirtsleeves, rewriting what I hoped would be the final draft of my Hiroshima piece.

There was a quiet knock at the door and Satsuko came in. She was carrying a glass of beer and some rice crackers. I sat her down upon my knee as I read over what I'd written. I ran my fingers through her hair. I kissed her. The sweeping horns of "Sentimental Journey" were drifting up through the floorboards, and streetcars clanged in the road as the dusky sunlight streamed over us.

The USS *New Mexico* was leaving the following week for San Francisco. I'd booked my passage that morning; the ticket was safe in my jacket pocket. At the Military Affairs office, I'd made inquiries about the legal procedure of Japanese emigration and entry to the United States. The captain had rolled his eyes and told me I was the third person to ask that day. The *Alien Exclusion Act* was still in place for Orientals, he said, but everyone thought it most likely would soon be rescinded, judging from the number of potential war brides strolling on the arms of American soldiers. Satsuko could join me later, I thought, after the restrictions were lifted. Five months, six at the most. After my photographs had been published. After the whole world had changed.

We undressed and lay down on my futon and I inhaled the scent of her pale skin, feeling the warmth of her body against mine. She was naked except for a narrow wristwatch that I'd bought for her two days before.

She reached over for her purse. From it, she took a small, velvet jewellery box, which she shyly presented to me. Inside was a small silver crucifix on a chain. She took it out and draped it around my neck, then fastened the clasp. She pulled me over so that we both faced the cracked mirror on the wall. She pointed at the reflection of our entwined bodies.

"Look," she said. "Adam — and Eva."

31
THE BRIGHT LIGHT FROM THE WEST (SATSUKO TAKARA)

Not long after breakfast, I felt very sick, very suddenly. I dashed to the latrine outside, where I retched up the miso soup and pickles I had just eaten. Dizzy, I looked down at the filth, swamped by the smell of rot and sewage. As I shuffled back inside, Mrs. Ishino emerged from her parlour room at the back of the bar, wearing a plain kimono. She saw straight away that something was the matter. She ushered me onto a stool at the counter and asked me what was wrong.

When I explained that I'd been sick, she fell silent. She looked at me closely.

"How long, Satsuko?" she asked. "Since your last cycle?"

I puzzled it through, doubtfully. All of our cycles had been highly erratic for some time, just like everything else, so it was very hard to keep track. But I suspected that it had been several months now, at least.

Mrs. Ishino picked up my hand and squeezed it.

"Please don't worry, Satsuko," she said. "I'm convinced that Lynch-san is a good man."

I stared at her for a moment as I grasped what she was saying. Then I burst into tears.

Sheets of type-written paper were piled up on Hal's desk next to his typewriter, and socks and shirts were draped over the back of his chair. The futon was still on the floor, the blanket crumpled where we had left it that morning. There was a faint film of dust on the windowsill, and I drew my finger through it absently. A battered pigskin suitcase stood in the corner of the room. A curious feeling came over me, and I walked over, knelt down and pushed the hasps. The locks flicked open.

A couple of vests were balled up inside, and there was a smell of mildew. Beside the vests was a stack of newspapers, and as I spelled out the title, I recognized the name of the paper that Hal had once worked for. I picked up the copy on the top, and leafed through it. Photographs of men and soldiers, as usual. I picked up another. Carefully, I began to study the names that were typed beneath the pictures. I felt a tingle of expectant pride. Wouldn't it be lovely if I found Hal's name there? I thought. Toward the end of the pile, I turned over the front page, and my finger paused. There it was. "Harold Lynch."

I studied the large, blurred photograph above it. A group of street children were playing a game of baseball on a patch of wasteground.

I screamed.

A boy with a disfigured face held up a charred plank, as another boy flung a ball of rags toward him. It was Hiroshi. Unmistakably, I thought, as I brought the page close to my face and stared at the blurred dots of the image. Despite the tangled hair, the disfigured face, it was him.

I started to feel very faint. It was my brother. He had the same earnest look of concentration on his face as when he and my father had thrown baseballs in Ueno Park, the same excited tension in his eyes as when he'd gazed up at the cinema screen of the Paradise Picture House on Sundays, when we'd gone to watch a film together.

I realized that I was softly moaning. All this time. Hiroshi.

I stood up and placed the newspaper upon the desk. I held my palm over my belly. I felt the faintest swelling beneath the cotton. Hopeless images flashed through my mind. The boiled bodies being hoisted on a hook from the Yoshiwara canal. Sitting beneath my hand-drawn sign at Tokyo station in the rain. The horrible urchin on the railway platform, exposing himself to me. I closed my eyes. What if he'd seen me, I thought, standing outside the Oasis, my face plastered white as I clutched at the arm of another passing GI? *Come in, yankii! Very cheap!*

Then, into my mind's eye, came the pictures of America in the magazine. The smiling families in their motorcars, the advertisements for soap, for lacework wedding dresses. The photographs of San Francisco; the white city rising between green hills, thousands of miles away, beyond the ocean.

Before I knew it, I was clawing at the thin, rough newspaper, tearing the picture from the page. Urgently, I ripped it into shreds. I heaved open the window, and flung the fragments of paper into the air outside. They fluttered for a moment, like falling blossom, then drifted randomly down, scattering into the muddy puddles in the alley below.

Election posters were pasted all over the city, painted with doves and slogans. The ration fell, and the Imperial Plaza grew more crowded every day with gaunt men and women waving placards and chanting. A rumour went around that the grain ship from America had sunk, that there was only enough food left for a week. Prices shot up at the market, and gunfights broke out in the streets. Men dangled out of the windows of the office buildings, using magnifying glasses to light their cigarettes with the weak rays of the spring sunshine.

At the table at the back of the bar, Mrs. Ishino was drinking a glass of clear liquor. She was in a sentimental mood. Masuko had found her the disk of a Puccini opera that morning while we'd been out shopping, and the soprano was warbling now from the gramophone.

"Madame Butterfly!" she said, pointing at me and laughing. "Do you know we used to dance to that, Satsuko, here in Tokyo?"

Her arms swayed in the air.

"So many rules, Satsuko! They shut us down because Lieutenant Pinkerton was an American."

I pictured the huge portrait of Okichi, the maid-servant presented to the Americans in the Edo period, framed on the wall of the sooty building on the Ginza, at my interview all those months ago.

"What happened to your husband, Mrs. Ishino?"

She glanced at me abruptly. I had always been too shy to ask about her mysterious past. I thought she would tell me now.

She shuffled over to the phonograph, and lifted the needle-arm from the disk. The music stopped. Then she took a stool around to the other side of the bar, climbed up, and reached for the picture on the top shelf, above the bottles. The framed photograph of a handsome man in a flying jacket. Masuko and I had long ago decided that the man must have once been Mrs. Ishino's lover. She clambered back down, brought the photograph over, and placed it on the table between us.

"Lieutenant Ishino," she said, touching her fingertip to the glass over his face. She swallowed her drink and wiped her mouth. "We were childhood sweethearts, though he was a year younger than me. Can you imagine?"

I bowed my head.

"He chose to die."

I looked up sharply. She nodded, staring at me.

"Yes, Satsuko. He did. He was stationed over at the Tsuchiura airfield. My dance school had been closed down by then. Planes used to pass over the city every day, and I'd always jump and wave, imagining that it was him up there, looking down at me."

She stared at the empty glass.

"What happened to him?" I whispered.

"He came back home one night, last April, without any warning. It was raining, I remember. I'd been asleep when I heard knocking at the door. There had been an air raid earlier, and it was still pitch black. I could only just see him on the doorstep."

"He'd come to visit?"

"He said he'd been given overnight leave. He'd been selected as group leader for a special mission. He didn't know when it would happen, only that it would be soon."

She swallowed, and I saw tears in her eyes. She looked at me. "I knew there was only one reason men were given overnight leave back then, Satsuko. He knew he was going to die. He had come back to say goodbye."

I felt a hard lump in my throat.

"We held onto each other all through the blackout that night. I begged him to try to get out of it somehow — what was the point of dying, I asked? But he refused. It was his duty, he said. He asked me to forgive him. He left at around five in the morning, without telling me where he was going. 'Look for me in the spring,' he said. Those were the last words he spoke to me."

I felt myself starting to cry. Mrs. Ishino opened up the frame and removed the glass. She slid another photograph from behind the first. It showed the same man, in his flying jacket, standing beside a Zero fighter. Around his forehead he wore a headband, emblazoned with the rising sun.

"Eiji flew the lead airplane. He took off just after six a.m. He's smiling. Look."

She pointed at his face and stared at the photograph for a long time.

"Why, Satsuko?" she said. "Why is he smiling?"

She wiped her eyes and went to the bar and poured out another glass of liquor.

"Did you know one of his friends tracked me down last winter, Satsuko?" she called. "Eiji had written me a letter. Do you know what it said? He implored me to forgive him. He asked me to live purely and honourably after his death." She laughed bitterly, gesturing around at the wooden tables and chairs. "Honourably! What chance did I have, after what he had done? After he went off to fly his plane into some American ship? After he left me here alone?"

She let out a sudden sob, and I rushed over and put my arm around her as she shook with tears.

"For what, Satsuko? Why did my husband choose to die?"

I drew her close as she spoke.

"I'll never forgive him for that, Satsuko, never. No one should ever choose to die."

She turned to me and held my hands tightly in hers, the tears trickling down her cheeks.

"You see, Satsuko?" she said. "We can choose to live, now. Don't you see? Satsuko, you must choose to live!"

~

My fingers were clumsy as I helped Hal button his shirt. Protests were slated to take place all across the city that day, and he was going along to watch them. In a quiet voice, I asked him to meet me at Asakusa Pond later on that evening.

He stroked my hair and held my scarred palms to his lips. He kissed them, then kissed me goodbye and walked out the door.

I heard his footsteps going down the stairs as I walked over to the window. I saw him emerge from the door down below; I held my hand over my belly as he strode away up the alley.

I spent most of the day preparing. Mrs. Ishino and I walked to the bathhouse, where she soaped me and scrubbed my back. Afterward, she rubbed a special almond-smelling salve onto my hands. Back at the bar, she took me into her cluttered parlour room. A spring mattress lay on a Western-style brass bedstead, with horsehair bursting from its seams. A row of ivory-coloured ballerina shoes was draped on a rail along the wall. She sat me in front of the mirror and spent several hours combing and arranging my hair, painting my neck and face before she carefully helped me on with my clothes. We decided upon the green and gold kimono that my mother had given me, and which I had finally bought back from the pawnbroker after several months of saving.

Mrs. Ishino stood behind me and pulled tight my embroidered brocade sash. As I looked in the mirror at my reflection, I saw that she really had done an expert job. My neck was pale, my cheeks were pink, and my hair was beautifully styled, pinned up with a mother-of-pearl comb.

She would come with me as far as the Asakusa tram stop, she said. Evening was darkening outside and I became suddenly nervous and started to tremble. Mrs. Ishino made me drink a glass of whisky and told me that everything was going to be all right. She stroked my wrist as I drank the fiery liquid down. Then she looked up at the clock on the wall. It was six o'clock. She pinched my cheek and said that it was time to go.

32
TOKYO GIANTS
(HIROSHI TAKARA)

Ueno station was swarming with people arriving on the packed trains from the towns and villages outside the city, all decked out in their best spring suits and kimonos, wearing sashes and aprons and holding up painted banners and placards: *Mothers for the Rice Ration! Railway Men for Reform!*

I felt suddenly nervous as I watched them. The demonstrations had better not interfere with our big night out, I thought. Beneath my shirt was an envelope of cash as thick as my finger. Mr. Suzuki had given it to me that morning. He'd told me to scrub up at the bathhouse, to get my hair cut, and to buy a collar shirt and a tie.

"Get yourself nice and relaxed, kid," he said. "Then you won't be so nervous later on."

As I boarded a tram for the Ginza, I looked down at my new watch. Five hours to go. At eight o'clock, I was to meet Mr. Suzuki at his office at the market. From there, he was going to drive us both over to Shinjuku himself, in his luxury black Daimler with the brown leather seats.

As I sat in the barber's chair, the old man fussing around me with his comb and scissors, I wondered why Mr. Suzuki liked me. Maybe it was because I was from Asakusa, I thought. Maybe he'd liked my dad's eels. Every night, after the market closed for business, I sat with him in his office as he went over the accounts in his oilskin ledger and totted up the day's profits. When he'd finished, he had me check the numbers, while he went over and took a square bottle of whisky from the iron safe in the corner of the hut and poured himself out a glass, full right up to the top. With a sigh, he'd loosen his collar, put his feet up on the desk, and shove the cigarette box toward me.

"You and me, little shit," he liked to say. "We're like two badgers from the same hole."

My real job, I sometimes thought, was to listen. As he worked his way through the bottle of whisky, he'd tell me violent stories from the market: about vendors who hadn't paid their dues, about the vicious Formosan gang who'd blasted him in the shoulder. About the American officers who double-crossed him worse than the crooks they'd kicked out, the bastards who'd taken all the reconstruction contracts by paying out bribes, the lying politicians in the Diet, General Douglas Fucking MacArthur, and all the other pigs and snakes who were making Mr. Suzuki's life a misery, keeping him from his only true pleasures in life, which were gambling and women.

Asakusa seemed like his great, lost love. "You should have seen it, little shit!" he'd roar, as the bottle got close to the end. "Nowhere else ever came close."

He told me about the Casino Folies, the Russian dancers there who'd kicked their legs right up into the air; how when he'd been a kid, there'd been two Bengal tigers in a cage at

Hanayashiki Park. But it was the games of flower cards he'd run up in the old abandoned house by Sengen Shrine that seemed to be like the pure land of paradise for him. His eyes sparkled and his hands fluttered when he remembered them, as if he was still rattling ghostly dice cups.

"Shirt off, blue and green flashing, sweat dripping down my back. Howling out the bets as the old ladies doled out the cash from their kimonos, the grocers slapping down their wages on the table. That was the real Japan, little shit, not the crap all those military bastards shoved down your throat in school."

I remembered how our heads had been shaved right after the attack on Pearl Harbour. How every Friday they'd given us a lunchbox full of rice with a pickled plum in the middle to look like the flag of the rising sun.

Mr. Suzuki would slump forward on the desk, the bottle empty, practically cross-eyed. "And look at me now, little shit," he'd slur, as he stubbed out his last cigarette. "I'm like a carp on the fucking cutting board."

After he started snoring, I'd drag him over to the futon in the corner and pull a woollen military blanket over him. He'd be rolling about, muttering and grunting, as I left to greet the crows that flapped about the market in the light of dawn.

Rain hammered against the window as my train curved around the overground tracks toward Ueno station. Up in the distance, I could see the bright spotlights of the market sign as they blazed away in the dripping night. My hair was trimmed and brushed neatly now, and I wore a grey worsted wool jacket and trousers and a white cotton shirt I'd bought at a tailor shop off the Ginza. The old man had stared at me over his spectacles when I walked through the door, but sure enough, the pile of notes I slapped down next to his sewing machine was enough to get him on his feet in a second, pulling out his measuring tape and getting on with his cutting and stitching as quickly as he could.

I stared at my reflection in the window glass. I bared my teeth. *Monster*, Shin had called me. I turned my head this way and that. I looked almost respectable now, I thought. Almost handsome. It was amazing what a collar and a tie and money in your pocket could do.

The train curved around the embankment, the wheels screeching on the rails. Down below was the wasteground where Tomoko had been attacked, the day Koji and I had caught the eel. I remembered her body pressed against mine, as I'd held her up on the carriage coupling, and the train rattling through the countryside all those months ago. It almost seemed like a dream to me now.

On the other side of the track was nothing but blackness. It stretched across Asakusa all the way to the Sumida River. Buried below it, somewhere, were my mother and my sister, charred into ash, dissolving now in the rain that fell across Tokyo, washing away into the river that flowed out to the sea.

You just had to get on with life, I thought.

~

Outside Mr. Suzuki's office, the black Daimler was streaked with gleaming rain. The door to the hut was half open. Something was wrong.

I pushed the door gingerly and walked inside. The room was lit by the single black metal lamp on the desk, and Mr. Suzuki sat on his chair, his close-cropped, bullet-shaped head tilted to one side. His mouth was stuffed with dirty, crumpled pages of newspaper.

The grey suit jacket was hanging on the chair behind him. His stubby fingers, bitten to the quick, were clutching at a dark, gaping crimson and black wound in the middle of his chest and blood was seeping like ink into the white cotton of his shirt. A haze of blue smoke hovered by the ceiling. There was a smell in the air like matches.

I sat down on the chair on the other side of the desk. The skin on his face was stiff and waxy. I felt awkward looking at him; as if I'd disturbed him while he was doing something private.

I recalled the wisteria box, painted with my father's name, that the military affairs clerk had brought to our house the week after his ship had gone down. "The Great Sea Battle of Leyte Gulf," the newspapers had called it. My teacher had given me the honour of sticking the little Japanese flag to the map on the wall. We'd spent the rest of the afternoon drawing lavish pictures of the battle, sketching the smoking funnels of aircraft carriers and whizzing Zero fighters.

My mother and Satsuko and I had sat together in my father's bedroom. The box lay on the floor in front of us. I stared at the whirls and knots in the wood; they looked just like the shapes of the Philippine islands on the map.

The next day, I'd hammered the cedar sign to our front door. *A House of Honour.* "You're the man of the house, now," Mrs. Ota had told me, as she watched. I remembered the sound of the nail, splitting the wood.

I stared at the blood soaking slowly outward in Mr Suzuki's shirt. *The man of the house.*

I closed my eyes.

Finally, I stood up and walked to the door. As I pulled it shut, I caught a final glimpse of Mr. Suzuki in the lamplight. His fedora lay upside down beside him on the floor.

I walked over to Mr. Isamushi's noodle stall and sat down at the counter. He wiped it down, then poured out a big bottle of beer in front of me. "Where's the boss tonight?" he asked.

I shrugged.

"Well you're very welcome anyway, sir," he said. "You've got a new suit."

I nodded and swallowed. "What soup are you using today, then, granddad?"

He ladled steaming broth into a bowl. "Rat and snake today, sir. Delicious." He spooned a pile of noodles on the top.

As I sat there, I held up the noodles on my chopsticks and blew away the steam just like Mr. Suzuki had always done. When I'd finished, I carefully slurped away the soup and lit a cigarette. The smoke twisted in the air in front of me.

I put my hand in my jacket pocket, rubbing the bank notes between my fingers. I glanced around at the covered stalls, wondering if Yotchan was around tonight. I pictured her, lying beneath me, her breasts heaving away.

I left three copper coins on the counter and sauntered away along the market passageways. The food stalls were packed with ex-soldiers now, their faces lit by orange lanterns. At the liquor stand on the corner, I drank a glass of "special" that made my eyes water. One of the ex-students slapped me on the back and poured me out another.

My head was swimming as I crossed the road to the station. The place was swarming with men and women coming back from the demonstrations, their signs all tattered as they crammed through the doors into the ticket hall where the other children and I had once slept beneath the stairs.

Around the back of the station, in the wasteground beneath the railway arches, I saw whores at last. They stood around the big puddles, and my stomach coiled into knots as they called out to me. I glanced at them quickly as I stumbled on through the darkness.

The red brickwork of the wide railway tunnel was brightly lit, and the struts of the ironwork began to tremble and squeak as a train rolled overhead. My heart started to pound. A solitary girl was sitting on a railing in a pool of light in the middle of the tunnel, wreathed in a white cloud of cigarette smoke. I fingered the notes in my pocket and swallowed, my flesh hopelessly tightening as I made my way toward her.

33
MAY DAY
(HAL LYNCH)

For a moment, as I awoke, I couldn't remember where I was. The room seemed naggingly familiar, and the light coming through the window had the distant, luminescent effect of sky seen from beneath the ocean. Slowly, I recognized my desk, the whitewashed wall, the flower print dress draped over the schoolroom chair. A pale ivory body lay beside me, the silken black hair splayed upon the pillow. A ridge of spine beneath the skin rose and fell minutely as Satsuko slept on.

As I dressed, she woke up and slid her arms around my chest. Her head rested on my shoulder as she buttoned my shirt with careful fingers. I kissed her hands, pressing her palms to my lips. In a low voice, she whispered that she would like me to meet her later on that evening by Asakusa Pond. The bench where we'd sat and watched the cherry blossoms on our first date.

I'd tell her everything tonight, I thought. Explain my plan. Ask her to come away with me, to wait for me. To trust me. Our reflections gazed back at us from the mirror against the wall, and I felt suddenly romantic and chivalrous and sure of myself.

I'd promised to meet Ward at the press club before going over to watch the May Day protests. Judy was due to arrive at Yokohama on the USS *New Mexico* tomorrow. Perhaps we could all go out and celebrate together, I thought, somewhere expensive and exquisite, before I embarked upon its long return voyage two days later.

As I walked out into the road, men and women were emerging from the muddy side streets carrying placards and banners. Protesters were packed like sardines into the tram as it curved on its rails toward the Imperial Plaza. I alighted at Yurakucho and walked over to Shimbun Alley. The lobby of the press club was deserted. Everyone was already gone, covering the action.

Upstairs, the ballroom was empty and a dusty haze floated over the tables. There was a stink of old cigarettes and spilled liquor. I glanced at my watch. It was late already.

~

Thick crowds surged beneath the bridge by the Imperial Hotel. A great swathe of the population was represented on the street: students, young women in kimono, men in suits, elderly folk in yukata. When I reached the edge of the park, I was astounded. It was a forest of red flags and hand-painted banners. Some were written in Japanese, but most were in crude English for the benefit of the Occupiers. The bandstand was festooned with flags, and applause came from the crowd as a trio of men emerged onto the stage, holding up their hands. The bull-like man in the jersey whom I'd seen before bellowed into a microphone, his voice overwhelmed by shrieks of static. The crowd erupted, drowning him out with their applause. Wind gusted over the crowd, setting the banners fluttering.

The park darkened perceptibly, as apocalyptic storm clouds began to swallow the sky.

As the man on the podium began his oration, rain began to fall. The gaunt faces of the people remained determined as the drops soaked the banners and dripped down their cheeks. They began to chant, their voices rising up in chorus, their forearms beating the air, and as the rain swept over their heads, the noise swelled and strengthened. Another man stepped onto the rostrum, and his shrill voice was welcomed with a huge surge of applause as he waved an accusing finger toward the high stone wall of the palace beyond.

"The emperor sits behind that moat," he cried, "gorging himself with delicate dishes while outside, the people starve!"

There was a sharp tremor in the air. A bright flash of lightning pierced the grey sky and the crowd jostled forward. Suddenly, a strange, warrior-like cry rose from their throats: "*Washo . . . washo*!" A low rumble of thunder rolled over the park, like some ethereal call to arms, and then I was caught up in the crowd as they began to run, the figures on the rostrum waving them forward. We surged over the soggy grass, the horde clapping and howling as they swarmed over the bridge into the Imperial Plaza, fanning out along the stone banks of the moat. Just for a moment it seemed as though they were going to try to storm the palace, that the emperor would finally come face to face with the wrath of his people, but a solid line of white military jeeps and uniformed American troops stood beside the bridge house with its medieval gates and the turret of a tank swivelled casually to face us. The crowd jittered, the muscles tightening in their faces. From a bullhorn came a bark of an order to retreat as rifles were raised in unison.

Tiny clouds of smoke drifted from the barrels of the guns a split second before the thundering shots cracked open the sky. The crowd writhed backward like a shoal of fish, falling and stumbling onto the sodden yellow gravel. Rifles reported again and panic gripped the crowd, people slipping and screaming as they were trampled underfoot. The rain lashed down and the banners toppled to the ground, the letters smeared and the paper disintegrating. I was carried along by the mob toward the fortress of the Dai-ichi building — General Headquarters. A phalanx of military police and soldiers surrounded the granite columns, their rifles directly levelled at us. A shot erupted above our heads. The crowd swerved away and pounded onward through the driving rain, in the direction of the prime minister's Lloyd-Wright residence further on up the avenue.

It was at moments like this that revolutions could break, I thought, that great tragedies occurred. That the world could slip its bonds of gravity and calamity could come raining down. There were hands at my back. A man fell in front of me. I tripped over his body and flew through the air. My head collided with the road, hard, and I curled up into a stunned ball as boots thudded around me.

The asphalt was wet and cold against my cheek. The air was filled with shrieks and pumping rounds of gunshot. A hand grabbed my throat and pulled me up; I felt the scratch and stink of an overcoat against my face. A tall Japanese man was gripping my shoulders. He was dressed in a long, camel hair overcoat, a black bowler pinned to his head. His round glasses were speckled with raindrops.

"Had enough, Lynch?"

The voice was purest Brooklyn. With unexpected strength, he took hold of my arm, and, striking out with his elbow, pulled me through the crowd. After a moment, we reached the line of troops. He flashed a badge and they parted to let us through. We paused for a moment on the steps of the building. My jacket was ripped all the way down one seam and my pants were smeared with mud. Fresh blood stained my hand, though whether it was my own or someone else's I did not know. The man popped a piece of gum into his mouth as he watched the mob surge past.

"So, Lynch," he said, scratching the side of his face. "How long have you been a commie?"

~

G2, Intelligence Division, was sequestered on the top floor of the GHQ building. The ceilings grew lower, the atmosphere more muffled, as we ascended the echoing stairwell. By the time we had reached the frosted glass door of the office, the tumult outside had softened almost to a rumbling melody, punctuated by the occasional whistle. The spook led me into a small, windowless room, where a short, trim man with a neat blond moustache stood up behind a desk and twisted his hand in salute.

"Afternoon Lynch. Colonel Wanderly. The sumo wrestler is Captain Ohara."

I saluted back. "Harold Lynch."

"We know who you are."

The room was lined with metal drawers, and the entirety of one wall was taken up with a large map of China, Siberia, and the Japanese islands. As the door closed, the office became muffled and silent. I was suddenly put in mind of my sealed cabin in our F-13, right before takeoff.

"Why don't you park yourself down there, Lynch?" Wanderly said, gesturing at a hard metal chair. "Sorry about the mess. They won't let me get a woman in."

He placed a pair of spectacles on the end of his nose as Ohara perched on the edge of the desk.

Wanderly licked his fingers as he flipped through a thick manila file, picking out photos and press clippings. I recognized my photo of the railway men in the hospital at Hiroshima, then saw a clipping of my first piece in the *Stars and Stripes*. I almost smiled. Our rat man report, written way back in September. I felt a strange wave of nostalgia as I saw the old man's wild face again, gazing forlornly up the river. Wanderly chuckled.

"Well, I've got to hand it to you, Hal. You've got a good eye. And a fine way with words."

"What's this about, Corporal?"

"How long have you known Mark Ward, Lynch?" Ohara interrupted. His face was pockmarked. I remembered him now from the lobby of the Imperial Hotel, the night when Ward and I had gone there for drinks. General Willoughby's hawk eye behind the monocle, scrutinizing Mark, as the man pressed upon his tailored uniform arm.

"About six months. We met on a train."

"Never met him at Columbia — your alma mater?"

"Must have been before my time."

"Tell you much about his career during the war?"

"He spent time in China."

"Ever tell you where?"

"All over, I guess. I was stationed in Chengtu for a time myself."

"We know you were. Ward was based mainly in Shaanxi. That ring a bell?"

"Well, sure."

Shaanxi had been the headquarters of Mao's forces, his "Golden Land" up in the hills, where the Red Army had ended their long march and the exiled Japanese communists had holed up during the war. I recalled Ward's distraught face the day after he'd been dragged in by G2, after his return from the Snow Country. *Don't you see, Hal? I'm next on their goddamned list!*

"Where he enjoyed the hospitality of Mao Zedong for several months. As did Wilf Burchett."

"Burchett?"

I frowned, recalling Burchett's gleaming eye, as he pulled tight the straps of his kitbag. *Good luck, mate. You're going to need it.*

"Well," I said, "they were both war correspondents, after all."

Wanderly's eyes softened and his voice took on the tone of a sympathetic teacher. "Look, Hal. I think you're tangled up in something you don't understand. I think people may have taken advantage of you. They sense you're vulnerable. You reek of self-pity. They've used your misplaced guilt to their own advantage."

"We've seen your medical, Lynch," Ohara butted in. "Reads like a horror movie. Still can't sleep?"

Wanderly glanced up at him in apparent distaste. I folded my arms. The room had darkened, but he didn't switch on the lamp. He spread his hands out on the desk, like a priest about to begin a sermon.

"You tell me, Hal. What are we to make of it? You ask for a transfer almost the day the war ends. You turn up in Tokyo and start knocking on the door of every red agent in town. You travel to a prescribed area with what looks like the express intention of embarrassing the Occupation. What are we to make of it, Hal? What are you doing here, anyway?"

I pictured Tokyo from the sky, looking down at the neighbourhoods and parks, the schools and the temples.

"I guess I wanted to see what was left."

I glanced furtively at my watch. Satsuko would be on the tram by now, heading toward Asakusa Pond.

"This Hiroshima piece," Wanderly said, as if embarrassed to mention it. He flipped through the folder and I made out the original carbon of my story.

"'Aftermath of the Atom.' Very portentous, Hal," Wanderly said.

"Did Ward tell you what to write?" asked Ohara.

As Wanderly held up the ink-stained article, I pictured Frayne Baker in his office, flinging the pages into the air. *Radiation disease. Horse — shit!*

"I've already been fired for that, Colonel."

"And a decision regarding your tenure in Japan has been made, Hal."

There was a pulse in my stomach.

"You know I met a Jap last week, Lynch?" Ohara had come around and now stood behind me, resting his hands on the back of my chair. He bent over, and I could feel his hot breath on my neck. "Worked as a doctor at a medical institute up north during the war. A planeload of our boys crash-landed not far away one day. The Japs took them along for treatment. Hell, you might even have known them. Smiling boys, about your own age. Well, I asked the man what they'd done to them, how they'd died. He was as cool as you like. Do you know what he told me?"

Ohara's hands moved to my shoulder blades, his fingers squeezing.

"He said they'd performed live experiments on them, Lynch. Cut out their lungs. Injected them with chemicals. Just to see what would happen. As if they were rats. How do you like that?"

It was grotesque, macabre. I tried to resist the bait. "And what was Hiroshima, gentlemen? Wasn't that an experiment? The live vivisection of an entire city?"

"It was just a bomb, Hal," said Wanderly. "A bomb that saved the lives of thousands of young American men."

"But they're still dying in Hiroshima, Colonel."

"Here's something that might interest you, Hal." Wanderly slid another sheet from the dossier. He held up a glossy photograph of Ward. He raised his eyebrows. "Your friend. Maxim Alexandrovich Warszawski. Born in Minsk, Russia, 1905. Studied at the Soviet Institute for Teachers, Librarians, and Propagandists, 1920 to 23. Moved to New York to study at Columbia University, 1925. Quite a coincidence, wouldn't you say?"

My stomach knotted as his words sank in. I saw Ward coming aboard the train at Kyoto, wheezing as he slung his kitbag onto the luggage rack. At the press club, that first night, exchanging fluent jovialities with the Soviet correspondents. *Don't get them mixed up, Lynch — they'll break your arm!*

"Two summers ago, Hal, the FBI raided Ward's office in Chicago. They discovered documents recently stolen from the Office of Strategic Services, concerning the battle plans of Chiang Kai-shek. Six months later, Ward was in Shaanxi along with Mao, Burchett, and all the other Reds. Six months later, he arrived in Tokyo. What's he doing here, Hal?"

A vein in my temple began to pulse. I remembered the glow of Ward's cigar in the train carriage, his crinkling face as I unburdened myself to him. My fierce, wounded sense of self-pity, my intense desire for forgiveness.

"He help you write that piece, Hal? Or was it just spiritual encouragement?"

Are you still bothered by what you did up there, Lynch? I remembered the look of sympathy in his eyes behind the wide spectacles as I'd bowed my head, like a boy in a confessional box.

The big hand on my shoulder, as I told him about my trip to Hiroshima. *You know I'm proud of you, don't you Hal?* That profound feeling of solace. As if he was a priest, granting me absolution from my sins.

"You've been a sap, Lynch, a first-class fucking sap," Ohara spat. "Radiation disease. They'll give you the Order of fucking Lenin. Thought you were a hotshot, Lynch? Or did you know you were taking pictures for Joe Stalin?"

Wanderly paused, looked at me, then continued.

"I'm going to be frank with you, Hal. You're an intelligent man. Mark Ward is a Stalinist agent. That's a simple statement of fact. Now. There's another war coming soon, Hal. Did you know that? Sad, but true. In fact, it's already begun. There will soon be a time when we will need a strong Japan, Hal, when we will need this country on America's side. This kind of thing could tip the balance. That's why Ward is here. He's no teacher, and he's certainly no librarian. You've been made a fool of, Hal. You can see that now. Bad people have taken advantage of your weaknesses to damage our position. We'd like to give you a chance to show us whose side you're really on."

Ohara moved from my chair and went to the other side of the table. The room was almost entirely dark now, the map on the wall obscured. Wanderly leaned forward.

"Tell us about Ward, Hal. He's your friend isn't he? He trusts you. He confides in you."

"What are you asking me, gentlemen?"

"Hal, he's been using you. Don't you see that? You don't owe him a thing."

"Where are the fucking negatives, Hal?"

Ohara's words reverberated in the darkness. Wanderly smiled thinly, his fingers drumming the manila envelope. I felt a sudden flash of unexpected advantage, like a poker player whose opponents inadvertently reveal the weakness of their hand. I pictured Dutch handing me the envelope. My trumps. Hidden in a cigar box, under the floorboard of the room in a downtown saloon.

"Negatives?"

"Fuck off, Hal!" bellowed Ohara. "You know what we're talking about!"

I leaned slowly back in the chair, holding his gaze.

"What are you asking me, gentlemen?" I repeated.

Wanderly tapped the envelope, the smile lingering on his face. "We're asking you to consider your position, Hal. Your future."

A thrill of incipient victory flashed through me. I slowly shook my head.

After a long pause, Wanderly sighed and shrugged his shoulders. "Oh well."

He replaced the outlying documents in the dossier and closed it carefully.

"The *New Mexico* is leaving for San Francisco in two days, Lieutenant. You'll be on it."

I tried not to smile as I pictured the ticket in my jacket pocket. I imagined the moment, six months from now. Standing on the dock at Oakland. Watching the ship steam beneath the San Francisco Bay Bridge. The passengers coming down the gangplank. Satsuko pausing, her dark eyes searching the crowd.

"You can't take the girl, Lynch."

My heart jolted.

Ohara's face was hidden in the shadows. "Sure," he said. "We know all about her."

Another photograph was placed on the desk. Satsuko and I, squinting in the spring sunshine outside the Senso Temple. *Smile!*

Eugene. Just the kind of bright, callow boy that Intelligence loved to employ. Ambitious. Venal. Naive. *They started it, didn't they, Hal?*

I remembered his sudden stated desire to see something of the world; his unexpected passion for journalism. His nocturnal visit to the newsroom, the night of my return from Hiroshima. The look on his face, as he saw me come into the office the next day, like that of a whipped dog.

"Pretty girl," Ohara said.

I swallowed. "The *Exclusion Act* won't last six months."

Wanderly placed a square sheet on the table. I glanced down. The paper was covered with Japanese writing, unintelligible stamps.

"Going to tell what that is?"

Wanderly picked up the sheet, and drew his finger across the ideograms at the top.

"'Recreation and Amusement Association,'" he read. "How do you like that?"

"You know they register their whores here in Japan, Lynch?" Ohara said. "They're a bureaucratic bunch."

My stomach quivered, my senses suddenly alert. Wanderly stared at me over his spectacles.

"Not the kind of girl we want in America, Hal. Sorry."

"Undesirable is what they call it, Lynch."

"Tend to be crawling with all manner of disease and such. The rules are very clear. She won't make it past immigration. Not now. Not ever."

A hollow pit opened up in my stomach. Just as I had felt every night, as our plane had lurched from the end of the airstrip, pitching just yards above the churning indigo waves. As I stared at the words and stamps, the green ink blotting into the cheap fabric of the paper, I pictured Satsuko, sitting on the bench by Asakusa Pond, pulling her shawl around her. *An undesirable.*

Ohara was gazing steadily at me. "They'll never let her in, Lynch. I will personally make damned sure of that. And you will never come back to Japan, as long as I am here."

"Let's make this easy, Hal," sighed Wanderly. "Give us the negatives. Forget about Hiroshima. Forget about the war. Go back to your nice saloon. Make an honest woman of her. You can take that sheet away with you if you like. Start again from scratch."

I pictured her, helpless in my arms, as we'd stood in the ruins of her house. Clinging onto me, burying her face in my chest. The intensity of that feeling — as if we were the only two people left on earth.

I picked up the sheet and rubbed the rough paper between my fingertips.

"Why don't you start again, Hal. Make a new life from all this ruin."

A soft explosion came from somewhere far away. The men's voices seemed to spiral around me in the darkness.

"What's it going to be, Lynch?"

"There's another war soon coming, Hal. Sad but true. Whose side are you on?"

"You need to make a decision, Lynch. Them or us. What's it going to be?"

34
THE FLOWERS OF EDO
(SATSUKO)

I waited at Asakusa Pond for what seemed like hours as the rain drummed upon my umbrella and dripped into puddles by my feet. The water soaked through my sandals and into my socks until they were quite saturated. Men walked past my bench, their sly faces lit by glowing cigarette ends as they leered at me from the darkness.

The night was cindery and bleak and I remembered a neighbourhood fairy tale my mother had once told me, about the tap-dancing girls from the Casino Folies, whose ghosts still danced upon the roof of the building, long after it had been closed down. It was just the kind of story she had loved.

Time passed, and I looked at the little wristwatch that Hal had bought me. It was getting late. I began to wonder whether I had made our arrangement quite clear, whether I'd told Hal the correct time and place. I remembered the scent of his cedary cologne, the starched cotton and the swell of his back as I'd clumsily buttoned his shirt that morning. I saw his room in my mind's eye; the pigskin suitcase and the locked type-writer case. A stab of panic went through me. Was he planning to leave? What if he'd already gone? Sailed away for America, without so much as a goodbye?

I tried to recall the times that we'd spoken those past weeks. There had been the joke about taking me to America, of course, but nothing had really been said after that; certainly nothing had been decided one way or another. As far as I knew, I could still just be his Japanese plaything, a temporary mistress. I felt a pang of ridiculous jealousy as I imagined a wife back home. She would be beautiful, I thought, charming, like Ingrid Bergman. With a deep sense of humiliation, I remembered the rash letter I had posted to Michiko, blithely declaring that I'd soon be off to California to take up my new life in the sun. My stomach knotted.

What an idiot I'd been.

I hoped fervently that the letter hadn't arrived, that it had been lost in the post before reaching her studio.

What a stupid, ignorant girl.

Why had I thought he was any different to the other Americans? What vanity had let me flatter myself that I was any different myself? I was just one more girl amongst thousands. I clutched my swollen stomach, picturing myself from above, a pregnant, unmarried woman, sitting in the rain in a soaking kimono, waiting...

A thud of footsteps came from the arched wooden bridge. Hal was stumbling toward me in the rain. As he came closer, I almost screamed. His trousers were ripped along the seam, dark and wet, and buttons were torn from his shirt. He looked at me desperately as I reached up to embrace him, pushing my fingers through his soaking hair, pulling his wet body against me.

"Have you been robbed?" I asked him urgently, cringing as I imagined some brutal gang of ex-soldiers, beating him. "Are you hurt?"

He stood motionless as I buried my face in his chest. I held him for a long moment. Then I realized that he wasn't responding. Something was wrong. I stepped back and looked at him. His eyes were downcast, and his arms hung loosely from his sides. Finally, he lifted his head and gazed at me. He placed his hands upon my shoulders, with a gentle, almost tender motion.

"Hal-san," I murmured. "What is it?"

His mouth twisted into a terrible smile. Rain dripped down from his hair onto his cheeks.

I somehow knew that something dreadful had happened, something final and irrevocable. A hard lump rose into my throat as I pictured the hours I'd spent in Mrs. Ishino's parlour room that afternoon, as she brushed my hair and softly spoke to me, as if soothing a jittery horse. I'd imagined Hal and I, sitting on this bench in the last of the evening sunlight, his face crinkling, his deep blue eyes filling with wonder as I told him about our baby that was growing inside me. This wasn't how I'd imagined it. No, this wasn't it at all.

He was shaking his head. Over and over, he was shaking his head.

He took my hand. Barely able to swallow, I let him lead me through the park to the battered arcade where we sheltered beneath the eaves of an overhanging stall.

He swept the water out of his hair with one hand, attempting to wring the rain from his dripping jacket. He patted his pockets for his cigarettes, and finally lit one with his metal lighter. His fingers were trembling. Then he turned to me with a terrible smile.

"Well, Satsuko," he said. "I'm going home."

Rain tapped on the wooden roof as I looked up at him. With my heart in my mouth, I held a hand up to his cheek.

He stared at me.

A sharp image came into my mind. The day of the surrender, as we'd all knelt down in the gravel of the factory yard, the cicadas whirring, the hot sun on our backs, listening to the emperor's speech. I remembered how, just for a second, my heart had leaped when I thought his Imperial Majesty had said that Japan had won the war; before Mr. Ogura's sudden groan, his pounding fist in the dust.

"Take me," I whispered. "Please."

He started to laugh. He took my hand, kneading and squeezing my palm. His laugh became wilder, and suddenly, he dropped my hand and slammed his fist against the wooden shutter of the stall. I leaped with a shriek as it rattled in its frame. He put his head in his hands.

Rain was falling all around us, making patterns in the wide puddles in the gravel path. His clothes were saturated, his face hidden away. A wave of hatred and revulsion suddenly clawed its way through my heart.

Mrs. Ishino had been wrong, after all. I had been right. He was just another American, like all the others.

"I'm so sorry," he was whispering, pitifully.

So sorry. I felt a cold sense of calm. He would go. I would stay. "Okay." I felt a sudden urge to batter his face with my fists. Instead, I leaned down and grasped him under the arm.

"Get up."

He tried to clutch my hand again, but I slapped him away. Slowly he faced me, dripping in the darkness.

"You," I said, pointing. "Come."

I stalked away beneath the scaffold of the Treasure House Gate and into the precincts of Senso Temple. The hem of my kimono was heavy and wet. Stray dogs lurked by the ginkgo stumps and darted around the stacks of timber that lay soaking in the yard.

The rain blew in fine, blustery clouds. At the far side of the shrine, I paused until I heard the American trudging behind me. He was calling out my name. I waited until he was a dozen paces behind me, and then turned sharply down Umamichi Street.

~

The patch of earth was overgrown with tall, wild grasses and littered with saturated lumps of charred wood and broken brick. Ghostly walls seemed to hang around me as I stood and imagined the eel tank, the rows of tables. Up above, the overhanging wooden balcony where we used to sit in the summer as the smell of broiling food floated up in the air. The room where Hiroshi and I used to fall asleep to the sound of the shop sign, creaking like a frog in the summer rain.

The American was standing behind me. I pointed at the black, abandoned earth.

"Here," I said, in Japanese. "My house."

He nodded, a muscle trembling in his forehead. He tried to put his hand on my shoulder, but I jerked away.

I sprinkled my fingers in the air.

"Your planes," I said. "Fire."

A strange look came over his face, and he slowly squatted down. He looked up into the sky, as if he could see them now, roaring in over Tokyo.

I remembered the first vibration on the horizon, the air quivering like the struck string of a shamisen. The American was weeping, crying like a child left alone in the dark, and I hated him then, and I was glad, because I had never wished to hate anything as much before in my life.

The high wind came from the west, batting at the paper lanterns along the alley and rattling the wooden shutters of the shops. The last thing my mother did that night was to feed a few pinches of crumbled rice cracker to the goldfish that she kept in a bowl in the family alcove and which she insisted was a lucky charm against fire.

I woke around midnight to a dull thudding. The roar of the American planes in the sky grew louder and louder until it sounded like a continuous peal of thunder. Then the house was shaking and Hiroshi and I sat up in bed, the room flickering with shadows. Outside the window the sky was as bright as day, filled with whirling orange flame.

Just then, there was a flash and a trail of blue sparks shot across the room. I screamed and leaped out of bed, pulling Hiroshi with me as he struggled to put on his padded air-defence helmet. Together we tumbled down the stairs to go to the underground shelter, but it was already too late. Outside the house, the world was like a glowing orange playground, the wind blowing fiercely hot as incendiary bombs pelted down from the sky. Our screaming neighbours filled the street, dashing wildly to and fro, some with coats over their heads, others trying to throw hopeless buckets of water at the incendiaries as they landed. Mrs. Oka stumbled out of her house carrying her cedar buckets of pickles; the bran was bubbling with heat and smeared along their sides.

I heard my mother's voice calling my name and I looked up: she was leaning over our balcony in her nightclothes, screaming at us to get away.

"Hurry, Mother!" I shouted back at her. "Please hurry!"

I stood there clinging onto Hiroshi's hand as great gusts of hot wind blew around us. A tongue of blue flame was crawling up the eaves to the roof. I screamed at my mother: "Jump, Mother, please jump down!"

She dashed inside, wasting precious seconds, before she finally emerged in a loose blue kimono. The roof of our house suddenly crumpled behind her in a shower of sparks.

Most of the street was on fire now, the flames crackling in great swirls, the heat terribly intense as the fire ate away at the buildings. My mother was in the street now, waving at us. Just then there was a blinding flash behind her. Heat blasted toward us. The store beyond ours that sold cooking oil had exploded. I felt my eyelashes crinkle away and I looked up with streaming eyes. My mother was running toward us, screaming. Her kimono was a sheet of flame and her beautiful hair was a dancing halo of fire. She tottered forward, still holding out her arms, then collapsed onto the ground a short distance in front of us, writhing as the flames devoured her.

People were running past us now screaming, "We're going to die!"

Hiroshi started shouting, refusing to move as I tried to drag him along the street.

"Come on!" I shrieked.

"Father's pot!" he shouted. "I promised him! I need to go back!"

"It's too late!"

Flaming beams crashed around us in showers of blazing sparks. The sky exploded with shells that spurted flame and hissing blue tendrils like blazing morning glory. People were running helplessly toward the Kamiarai Bridge, and we were swept along with them, past the police station and Fuji Elementary School. The shelters at the side of the public market were full of panicked people who pushed away the newcomers, shouting that there was no room left. As we approached the Yoshiwara canal, fireballs began to pelt down from the sky and thick, smoking wind gusted along so strongly that it almost swept me off my feet. We were in hell.

Through the cloud of whirling smoke, I saw that the buildings on the other side of the canal were on fire, red flame belching from inside the windows. The dark water was alive with dashing reflections, bobbing with people who had jumped in, steam rising from its surface. I held Hiroshi's hand, and together we leaped from the concrete bank, splashing down into the scalding water. When we came to the surface, he cried out. His face was yellow as we looked up at the burning buildings on the bank.

"Father!" he started to shriek. "I promised him!"

"Come back!"

I scrabbled for Hiroshi's fingers in the water, but he plunged over and seized hold of the iron ladder that led up to the bank. He clambered up, crouching down as he approached the flames. He turned back to face me, silhouetted by fire.

"Stay there, Satsuko!" he shouted. "I'll come back! I promise!"

It was madness. Overhead, the entire sky was filled with thundering silver planes, so low now that I could see the figures of the pilots behind the glass noses.

"Hiroshi!" I screamed, but he started sprinting along the bank, straight toward the firestorm.

A sharp whistle came from above, and there was a deafening explosion. The water swept up in a great scalding wave. The chemical works along the canal had exploded. The sky turned phosphorus white as I splashed forward and desperately tried to hoist myself up out of the boiling water onto the ladder. The iron rail was scorching and the metal stuck to the skin of my hands. I wrenched them away in agony, the skin tearing away, sticking there like flapping cloth as I rolled onto the bank. People were crawling around me on all fours, their faces black, their clothes all burned away. Blazing timbers crashed into the water behind me and whirling figures screamed in pain as incendiaries pelted the water. I desperately searched for Hiroshi. There was nothing but fire. To the side of the street I saw an irrigation ditch and I crawled blindly toward it. A rushing cloud of black smoke blew toward me, and then the ground disappeared beneath me, and I was tumbling down the steep banks to the bottom.

The American was hunched over on the ground, rocking back and forth. I knelt down and wrenched his hand away from his face. It was wet with tears. I forced him to look at me.

"Why?" I asked. "Why?"

His lip trembled as he raised a hand to my face, but again, I struck it away.

"I'm so sorry —" he whispered.

I stood up. "You go. I stay. Okay."

Leaving him in the wet earth, I strode away, past the ruined houses, along the incinerated alley. I heard a strangled noise behind me, half sob, half shout, but I didn't look back.

Asakusa Market was bustling with people and I walked on until I reached a group of low stalls. There, ignoring the looks brought about by my sodden clothes and tangled hair, I ordered a glass of shochu from the ugly stallholder and drank it down in one before ordering another. The rough liquor burned in my belly, and I drank another glass, and another, before stumbling along the alleys in the direction of Matsugaya, then Inaricho. Without knowing how, I found myself climbing the metal steps of the bridge overlooking the mass of shimmering train tracks that snaked out of Ueno Station.

Trains were shuttling in and out, their carriages lit, their wheels sparking. Speckles of rain flew against my face as I watched the white and red lamps of the carriages worming into the violet black night that covered the distant hills.

Almost without thinking, I took a pot of rouge from my satchel, and with my fingertip, smeared it heavily across my lips and cheeks. I tugged the combs from my hair and hurled them over the railing so that my wet hair dangled loose around my face. I started to walk across the bridge, my sandals slipping on the metal as I crossed over the tracks and walked down toward Ueno Station.

On the other side, I took out my pocket mirror. I grimaced in satisfaction. The reflection was that of the cheapest kind of slut. *This is what I am,* I thought. *This is what I have become.* I laughed out loud, my voice uncanny and shrill in my ears.

I stumbled toward the railway arches, where the pan-pan girls were hunched around the wide puddles, bedraggled from the rain. I gazed at them unsteadily as I walked through the underpass that led beneath the tracks.

I stopped in the middle of the tunnel and perched upon the railing in a pool of streetlight. My fingers trembled as I lit a cigarette, sucking it hard and feeling myself enveloped by white smoke.

Footsteps were coming toward me, and my stomach quivered. With my fingertips, I slowly drew aside the fabric of my kimono to show my white thighs.

The footsteps stopped and I felt a light hand on my shoulder.

"Miss?"

I opened my eyes.

A boy was standing there, holding out a palm full of notes and coins. His face was horribly disfigured and scarred.

His eyes widened.

The lights of the tunnel whirled around me as Hiroshi's clammy fingers reached out to touch my face.

PART FOUR

NIGHT TO NEXT DAY

AUGUST 1946

35
THE YOKOHAMA ROAD
(HAL LYNCH)

There is a stretch of the Hudson Highlands where the cliffs shoot straight up from the river, deep and wide now as it curves around Mount Storm King. Heavy beech and oak line the ridge, an outpost of the green panoply that stretches over the whole northern half of the state. The *Eastern Chief* rides alongside here for a while, cutting through the forest as if through virgin land, before the track curves around and the distant shapes and stabbing spires of New York City appear on the horizon.

I'd ridden trains all the way across America. Along the coast from San Francisco to Los Angeles, then inward over the arroyos and canyons and red earth of the southwestern states. I crossed the Mississippi and the endless, flat wheat plain of Kansas, curved up into the Midwest, and finally arrived in Chicago on a grey, humid day in July. I ate a pizza pie in a red-stone Italian joint, then walked back to the station and took a seat in the waiting room amongst a gang of long-bearded Amish men, dressed in white shirts and black pants, who spoke in singsong voices about the price of grain and chickens. Later, they sat contentedly in the observation carriage as I went to my cabin and sipped whisky, looking out over the vast, lonely expanse of the Great Lakes until I finally fell asleep for the last, long stretch to the Eastern seaboard.

The train paced itself like a steady racehorse as it rode the track high up above the tenements of Harlem, where the first foundations of grand housing projects were being laid. Then came the towering brick apartment buildings of Manhattan, the shining glass of skyscrapers, and then the gargantuan mechanical workings of the city, grimy with oil and dirt, the screeching tunnels and dark galleries drifting away on each side as we pulled into Grand Central Station. I slung my kitbag over my shoulder and clambered out onto the platform. I stood there alone, as the commuters pushed past me, not knowing where the hell I was going next.

I took a room in a boarding house on West 28th Street, not far from Penn Station, where I lay low, sweating in a box room, smoking cigarette after cigarette and taking no other diversion than the occasional slaughter of a cockroach beneath my shoe heel. The Sicilian operetta of the argumentative couple who ran the place drifted endlessly through the floorboards. New York was wilting hot. The sun poured right down from the sky. I prayed in the evenings for the summer storms, for the thunder that would crack open the night and drench the earth for a few sacred minutes before the moisture evaporated and the restless heat rose up to smother the city once more.

~

The Yokohama road had been as bad as I remembered, pitted with holes and craters. Life along the highway had grown more vigorous now — shanties extended far along each side, swarms of people, young and old, eking out an existence amongst the crinkled tin, the chicken wire and tarpaulin. Garden plots lined the perimeter, tended by withered old men and women with babies on their backs. Stray dogs and naked children watched from the side of the road as we passed, no longer curious enough to wave or bark. At the dock, young GIs, fresh off the boat, laughed and joked as they sold off their gear, exchanging dollars with beaming yakuza men in white summer hats and vests.

The press club had been clamouring, alive with talk of the day's events, when I'd rushed back the night before. The prime minister's residence had been stormed; troops were still out on the streets; the government was about to fall. The faces of the newspapermen lit up as they traded rumours and swapped war stories, snapping their fingers for drinks as they boomed and brayed. Chaos was their amphetamine, I thought, as I sifted their ranks urgently for news of Mark Ward. I finally found Sally Harper from *TIME*, comforting a tall, blonde woman who sat sobbing on the piano stool. I remembered a photograph on Ward's kitchen table: Judy.

"Where is he?" I shouted, above the din. Sally stared at me in astonishment.

"I thought you were his friend!"

"His what?"

"Haven't you heard? Where have you been?"

"Heard what?"

"Mark's been arrested. They're saying he's some kind of subversive!"

I pictured the hammering on the screen door, the burly MPs storming in. Seizing him by the arms, dragging him from his wicker chair. The ballroom hung heavy with smoke and the furor of relentless gossip and confusion. I crept away behind the curtain and lay down on the carpet.

When I stumbled over to Mrs. Ishino's the next morning, the place was a wreck. The curtain was gone from the entranceway; chairs scattered about on the floor. Big tin signs were nailed to the wall, and warnings were scrawled in red paint over the front of the building: "Off-Limits to Allied Personnel. VD."

I rushed upstairs. My room had been trashed. Everything was gone. My notes, my cameras, even my typewriter. All that was left were a few ripped paperbacks and the zinc pail on the floor, overturned, saturating the tatami. This, then, was the reason for the untimely visit from the public health inspectors. For my extended interview with Wanderly and Ohara. Just one more thing to add to my conscience. With a prayer on my lips, I knelt down in the corner of the room and prised up the floorboard. My heart flooded with relief.

The cigar box was still there. I picked it up and held it in my hands, my eyes closed, breathing in the cedary tobacco smell. Then I stuffed it into my jacket. Downstairs, I paused by the bar. I scribbled a hopeless note for Satsuko: the name of my ship and the time of its sailing. I took out most of the remaining yen notes from my wallet and left them in a useless stack on the splintered bar.

Over the rail of the USS *New Mexico*, I gazed down as Japanese girls hugged their American boyfriends, as kisses, tears, and fervent promises were exchanged. The ship gave a great, mournful bellow as the massed turbines cranked up. The last of the lovers hugged each other and the men hastened up the gangway as it lifted. On the dock, the girls waved white handkerchiefs, calling out in plaintive, high-pitched chorus as the GIs jostled around me on deck, shouting out wild endearments, pledges of eternal love and return.

The horn gave a deep bellow, and a quickening vibration pulsed through the deck as the chains drew up the anchor. Then, with a great shudder, the ship began to pull unmistakably away from the dock. Another high-pitched wail came from the assembly below; whistles from the men around me; shouts and applause. A sea of handkerchiefs fluttered up and down, and my eyes searched restlessly amongst them for Satsuko. Up and down, up and down the handkerchiefs went, every one a love story, every one a heartbreak.

No part of me wanted to leave. And yet, here I was, on the deck of a vast, ocean-going ship, Japan drifting irrevocably away from me. A yawning gulf opening up, a chasm that grew wider, deeper, and more achingly lonely with every inch that we pulled out to sea.

The island was finally lost beyond the carved sapphire horizon. The lonely screams of seabirds gusted around me in the sky.

I went below deck and climbed onto my bunk. A young, rat-like man in uniform lay on the bed beneath mine, his leg in plaster cast. He was reading the funny pages of the *Stars and Stripes*, chuckling to himself.

"Going home, huh?" he said, without looking up. I grunted forbearingly, but he carried on talking.

"Old Nippon sure is a swell place. No place like home though. Say, where's home for you, fella?"

I wanted him to shut up. I desperately wanted to be left alone in my despair, as if the banality of his conversation might somehow impinge upon the purity of my bitterness.

"New York," I muttered.

"New *York*, huh? You don't say..."

He appeared to contemplate the feasibility of human beings inhabiting New York City, then, apparently satisfied, he began to talk again, his voice brimming with knowing, locker-room insinuation.

"Say. How about those Jap girls, huh? Sure are cute, ain't they?"

I saw Satsuko in my mind's eye. Her harrowing eyes.

"Foxy little geisha girls... You ever meet one of them, huh? You ever have one of them geisha girls?"

The look of distress, of fury.

Take me.

I buried my face in my blanket with an uncertain noise, my hands over my ears.

Throughout those dog days of summer, I walked the New York streets like a hunted animal. It seemed almost overwhelming in its banality. Cabs went up and down Lexington Avenue. Steam rose from the manhole covers. Old women walked their poodles in Central Park and messenger boys sprinted between the office buildings. At five-thirty sharp, men in suits poured out from the skyscrapers into the bars by Grand Central Station, before hurrying off to their air-conditioned lives of domestic bliss.

The city was like an impenetrable fortress. The world might lie in ruins, but it was business as usual in New York, heir to the postwar world, its citizens engrossed in their buying and selling, eating and drinking, their greatest victory this vast, blithe antipathy — an insurmountable wall against which I pounded my head. I stopped in the middle of the streets as the crowds rushed past, clutching onto the walls for support. The cars and the people went by like an endless zoetrope, and it was all moving so fast that I was terrified of stepping into the current, of being swept away entirely.

I was standing outside the 42nd Street subway station when a chubby man asked me for a match to light his cigarette. As I held out my lighter, he made an amiable remark on that evening's performance by the Brooklyn Dodgers. A sudden, liquid fury passed through me. Before I knew it, I was clinging onto his shirt, shaking him furiously.

I saw myself suddenly from above — a madman, gripping onto another like some desperate succubus. I slowly forced myself to release him. He sprinted up Broadway, clinging onto his hat, glancing back at me in terror.

I walked all across Manhattan that night. The next morning, at the boarding house, I settled up with Mrs. Dannunzio and told her I'd be leaving later on that week. Something had to change. Something had to give.

~

At a photography studio in Murray Hill, I methodically worked up my Hiroshima prints. As I stood in the dim, red light, leaning over the enlarger and counting off the seconds, the trip came back to me in vivid bursts. The lonely train guard in the ruined station. Snowflakes, hovering in the air outside the police station. As the images swelled in darkening hues from the developing fluid, I stared once again into the eyes of the aged dance teacher; saw the faint, fragile smile of the railway man, who thought that the wind would come and carry him away like a feather. It occurred to me that they were all now, most likely, dead. As the prints hung dripping on the line, I felt a profound affinity, as if I, like them, were now just a ghost, a restless shadow on the fabric of the world.

I packed sets of the prints into envelopes and over the course of the next few days delivered them personally, with a short typed note and full release, to the offices of *TIME, Atlantic Monthly*, *LIFE,* and *Harper's*. Then I knew that I needed to rest. I went up to Vermont for a couple of weeks and rented a cabin in the White Mountains. I fished and swam in the nearby lake, chopped wood, took long walks in the forest. I retired early and lay in bed, listening to the wind in the pines and thinking of Satsuko.

Gradually, I felt my strength begin to return. The great, perpetual roar that I had lived with for so long was finally starting to fade.

Every other day, I hiked the five miles to the village to pick up groceries at the mom-and-pop store. They had the occasional magazine there, and one morning, I arrived to find that month's edition of the *New Yorker* on the rack. The front showed a typical Manhattan summer scene: cheerful citizens playing games in the park. As I leaned down to pick it up from the stand, I noticed a strip of paper around the cover, printed with an editorial message.

"Hiroshima," it read, in underlined type. "This entire issue is devoted to the story of how an atomic bomb destroyed a city."

A strange, distant sensation coursed through me. I paid the old lady and I walked away up the street, reading. The whole magazine had been given over to a piece by a correspondent whose name I didn't recognize: John Hersey. A writer who'd just returned from Japan. It followed the stories of five survivors of the A-Bomb, from the moment of the blast until now, more than a year later, when the city had finally been opened up again. I sat outside my cabin that morning and read the magazine from cover to cover, over and over again.

It painted a picture of fractured lives, of souls caught outside of time. It depicted citizens, shocked and confused, still struggling to comprehend the thing they had witnessed in those bright, searing seconds that fine August morning. I recognized much of the description: the points of reference, the landmarks and cardinal points. Then, toward the end of the article, I gave a great cry of vindication. To my fierce delight, the story began to talk of radiation disease, of "Disease X." Hersey documented its victims, its symptoms, and its causes. And presented it all as medical fact. Not as propaganda. Not as a bargaining tool. Not as "horseshit."

The story went on until the very last page. There were no pictures. But after the words, they would come, I thought. My pictures.

A tranquility descended upon me as I reread the article in the silence of my cabin. It was done now, I thought. It was over.

That evening, I sat on the bank of the lake and looked up at the moon as it slowly rose above the treetops. The water lapped against the shore and a million stars stretched out against the sky. I thought about Satsuko with a terrible, throbbing ache in my heart. Where would she be tonight? What cramped back room, what urgent back alley? I broke down and shook with tears for a long time; one man, alone in a forest, beneath the starry sky.

Finally, my sobs subsided, and all that was left was the freshness of the night around me. A cool breeze sprang up and the tops of the trees sighed as they waved back and forth in the moonlight. I stood up and brushed myself off, then walked back through the wood to my cabin. I took off my shirt and climbed into my narrow bunk. Within moments, thank God, I fell into a profound and utterly dreamless sleep.

36
ONE WONDERFUL DAY (OSAMU MARUKI)

"Wrap!" Kano cried, as if pronouncing a wonderful blessing over the assembled cast and crew crowded below the edge of the soundstage. Michiko Nozaki stood for a second, her hand frozen in tableaux. Slowly, her face dissolved into her wonderful, trademark smile. She flung out her arms, and rushed down the steps toward Kano, kissing him on both cheeks in the French manner. Kinosuke, her leading man, strode over and spun her about in his arms. Hoots and catcalls came from the crew as she emerged from his embrace, blushing and breathless. Only then did she notice me and hurry over.

"Sensei," she said. "You've come to see us at last!"

She pecked me chastely upon the forehead as Kinosuke strolled over. He slid his brawny arm around her waist and held up his other hand in the air.

"Well," he called, "I propose now that we all offer a heartfelt *banzai* —"

Disconcerted noises came from the crew and he stopped himself with a chuckle.

"Excuse me — perhaps I should instead say that we offer 'three cheers' — to our director, Kano. That we might express our respect and gratitude to him from the bottom of our hearts."

He turned solemnly and touched his hands to his forehead. An appreciative purr came from the rest of the crew as Kinosuke raised his fist in the air: "Hip, hip, hooray!"

Kano smiled, his face half-hidden behind a pair of thick American sunglasses.

"Thank you," he said. "Though it is I who should really be expressing my thanks. To our stars —" He gestured at Kinosuke and Michiko, and everyone applauded enthusiastically. "— the artists —" He turned to the smocked designers, who held up their paint brushes and grinned. "— and to the crew." He waved up at the lighting box, from which bright bulbs flashed in gratitude.

"Thank you, all of you," he said. "But there is one more 'thank you' I would like to add, one that has perhaps, regrettably so far gone unexpressed in the production of this picture. Without saying any more, I would like to dedicate this film to its true creator."

I felt an expectant tingle of pride and bowed my head as Kano raised his hands.

"To Tokyo. To the city, and to its people."

My head jerked back up.

"To a city that will, one day, emerge from the ashes again, as it has so many times in the past."

Heavy applause came from all sides.

"I have expressed the idea before that a city cannot simply rebuild itself like some robotic automata. Its true spirit lies in the hearts and the habits of its people."

The crew nodded earnestly.

"This is what we pay tribute to today. As long as the spirit of Tokyoites lives on — gruff and arrogant as it may be — so will their city survive. Thank you everyone for your hard work!"

We stamped our feet and applauded. We flung our arms around each other. At that moment a deep and quickening sense of dignity came upon me, such as I had never felt before in my entire life. I embraced them all. My colleagues; my friends; my comrades.

I sat at my usual spot at the counter of the Montmartre, drinking Scotch, tapping the stiff toe of my russet Oxford brogue against the stool. I wondered about the reviews that might appear in the cinema magazines the next week. *Dreamy and melodramatic*, they would say. *Innacurate — naive.*

I shook my head. The critics, for once, did not concern me. I only hoped that I might have managed to capture something of the peculiar spirit of the times, the spirit of the burned-out ruins. Of the curious resilience of human hearts in the face of chaos and destruction; of our potential to rise again from tragedy, to cast off the burden of time as a butterfly shrugs off its chrysalis.

We held the gala premier performance, at Kano's insistence, in the ruins of an old theatre in Shinjuku that he had visited regularly as a child. The roof was still mostly open to the sky and battered chairs were lined up in the amphitheatre to face an improvised canvas screen. Michiko Nozaki sat down in the front row, whispering to a friend she had brought along. A matronly lady sat on one side of her, and on the other was a teenage boy, smartly dressed in long shorts and a white shirt. Her friend turned her head.

What a strange and curious thing.

Satsuko Takara wore a flowing cotton summer dress, her hair pinned and fastened with a simple comb. Would she recognize herself up there on the screen? I wondered. In the character who owed so much to my imagination of her?

With a profound sense of humility and providence, I swore that I would go to her after the film had finished. That I would offer the hand of friendship again. That I would, if I were not too ashamed, ask for her forgiveness.

The lights went out and the projector began to whir. A thick beam of smouldering light hit the screen, and the symbol of a torch flickered onto the canvas. The name of the film appeared in stuttering ideograms, followed by the names of Kano, and then of myself. With an excited murmur, the audience settled back in their seats.

It was like nothing I had ever dreamed of. A new world came into being as Michiko Nozaki appeared on the swaying screen, and her bird-like voice emerged from the speakers. Everyone in the audience felt it too, and their breath seemed to emerge in a soft, collective sigh.

Up above, the beautiful face turned this way and that, smiling and nodding, her skin translucent, her eyes glistening. With the blurry backdrop of the ruined city behind her, she began to run down a narrow alley between rows of low, tenement houses . . .

The audience gazed at the screen. With spectacular longing in my heart, I closed my eyes, willing myself to cling tightly to that beautiful image forever.

Wonderful faces, shining with light.

37
THE STAR FESTIVAL
(SATSUKO TAKARA)

Michiko skipped along a street, low wooden houses set to each side, dodging puddles in the path and throwing her hands this way and that like a dancer. Blurry ruins were painted behind her, distant buildings and a smudgy sky. She stopped at the edge of the stage and put her hands on her hips. She flashed her beautiful smile at the cast and crew. With a flouncing curtsy, she skittered off to one side, where handsome Mr. Kinosuke stood holding a lacquer box of powdered mochi cakes. She pinched his nose, giggling, and promptly popped one into her mouth.

Hiroshi stood on a crate, squinting through the viewfinder of the camera, supported by Mr. Mogami, the cinematographer, who was spinning him smoothly around to film the action. The film made a sound like a flittering clock as it whirred through the contraption. The director, Mr. Kano, stepped forward and raised his hand.

"Cut! Cut!" he called.

The rest of the assembled actors and stagehands laughed and clapped as Hiroshi opened his eyes. He blinked in the bright stage lights, a bashful smile growing on his face.

I tried not to think of the excruciating shame that I felt as I came to, lying in the tunnel beneath the railway arch. My kimono was soaked, my crimson nails chipped. Hiroshi's eyes were wide. I could hardly believe how grown up he looked. He wore a collar shirt and smart woollen trousers. I felt a stab in my heart. Coursing across my little brother's face, were thick, swirling welts.

Slowly, I got to my feet. We stood there in the tunnel for a long time, barely able to look at each other.

Finally, he spoke.

"Big sister," he said. His voice was deep, now. "You're alive."

A sob rose in my throat. "And you," I whispered.

He bowed his head, and placed his palms formally together. "Please forgive me," he murmured.

Tears filled my eyes. "Forgive you?"

He knelt on the ground, touching his forehead to the concrete. "Please forgive me, sister. For leaving you alone that night."

I saw him, silhouetted by fire. I desperately shook my head. He finally sat back cross-legged on the ground.

"I needed to fetch the pot, you see," he said, frowning. "Father was counting on me."

"Of course."

He drew his arms around his legs. I gazed down at him, wondering what could possibly be passing through his mind.

"Did you find it, Hiroshi-kun?" I finally asked.

He shook his head.

"Well. Perhaps we might go to look for it together one day."

He glanced up at me.

"Are you still in pain?" I said, gesturing to his face. His cheeks looked angry and shiny in the streetlight.

He shook his head again.

"Hiroshi-kun —" I started. He glanced at me.

"Please, Hiroshi-kun," I said. "Let's not mention anything that has happened."

He stared at me for a moment, then nodded.

I walked over to him, and leaned down, holding out my hand.

"Please, brother," I said. "Will you come with me?"

As we approached Mrs. Ishino's shop, I saw that something was wrong. On the wall outside there were scrawled letters and tin signs just like the Americans had put up outside the Oasis.

Inside, it was as if a typhoon had swept through the place. Chairs had been thrown aside, streamers pulled down, and broken glass littered the floor. I shivered as a memory came to me — of how the Americans had torn away the little curtains that covered the girls' rooms at the International Palace.

Sobbing came from the back of the bar. Mrs. Ishino was slumped over, her thick arm hugging a bottle of shochu. On the table was the photograph of her husband in his flying jacket, the glass shattered in the frame. The gramophone played a mournful fragment of "The Apple Song" over and over again.

Hiroshi's eyes were so wide that I was terrified he would bolt. I wouldn't have blamed him. But instead, he sat down on a stool as I shook Mrs. Ishino and tried to pour water down her throat. There was the sound of a motorcar in the alley outside.

The whole scene had the feel of a dream then, as the rain blustered in through the open doorway. I heard a soft knock. A voice called my name.

Standing there, dressed in a pleated white skirt and wool sweater, was Michiko.

~

The workmen tottered on a ladder in the alley, and I called out in direction as they hoisted up the sign with the name of our new shop painted upon it in large crimson letters: Twilight Bar. Inside, two carpenters were sanding down the new counter. There was a strong smell of paint and sawdust. Hanako and Masuko were sitting with Mrs. Ishino, poring over the shopping list for our opening week. Hiroshi stood with them. He had all kinds of connections at the market now, he said, and could get food especially cheap, though I didn't care to know how.

Several of his photographs were framed on the newly painted walls. Shoeshine boys buffing the boots of American soldiers in Ueno Plaza; a four-car train travelling through the countryside. Above the bar was a photograph he'd hung there specially: a portrait of a tough-looking gangster, dressed in a three-piece suit, scowling away beneath the big sign at the Ueno Sunshine Market.

Michiko had barely asked a single question, that night. She had stepped over the threshold, calmly taking in the wreckage of the bar.

"Aren't you going to introduce me, Satsuko?" she asked, gesturing at Hiroshi.

"This — this is Hiroshi-kun."

"Your brother?" she asked, staring at me in amazement.

I nodded. "Well, well," she said, and she walked over to him and pushed the hair out of his eyes. *She really is a good actress*, I thought.

"Satsuko," she said, taking one last look around. "Why don't you fetch everybody's things and come along with me."

Every afternoon that summer, on her return home from filming, she brought us gifts: slabs of chocolate; summer clothes for Hiroshi; fish, rice, and vegetables for the rest of us. I cooked our meals in the evenings and we all ate together at her Western dining table of her luxurious apartment. It was all hers now, her admiral having been sent back to America following some scandal. Mrs. Ishino, who had fallen quite in love with Michiko by then, told stories of Tokyo theatres of the past, of the glory days when she had danced in the cabarets and operettas. Michiko told us all about the antics of the actors and stagehands, about her famous leading man Kinosuke, and the screenwriter, who she said always looked so tragic.

One evening, the conversation turned to the subject of Hollywood. The film *My Darling Clementine* had just opened, and Hiroshi had come back from the cinema earlier on that day, breathless with excitement.

"Hollywood — well!" Michiko said, a familiar look coming in her eyes. "Wouldn't that be the dream."

My chopsticks hesitated over my dish. "Really, Michiko?" I said. "Doesn't it seem a very lonely place, despite all its glamour?"

Michiko raised a quizzical eyebrow.

"Really, Satsuko?" she said. "I'm surprised. Didn't you once write to me to say that you were intending to go away to America yourself? San Francisco, wasn't it?"

Silence fell. Hiroshi glanced at me. Mrs. Ishino cleared her throat and served herself some more rice.

"What on earth made you think that, Miss Nozaki?" Mrs. Ishino asked pleasantly. "Why would a girl like Satsuko-chan possibly want to go to America?"

We all laughed politely. Michiko's eyes narrowed, and held my own for a second.

"Please excuse me," she said. "I was thinking of someone else entirely."

As I say, she really was a very good actress.

But there was a matter which I couldn't brush over, one that became harder for me to conceal as the summer went on, however much I might try to do so behind loose-fitting cotton dresses. Finally, Mrs. Ishino took me to one side and said that we would have to make preparations for any eventuality.

Certain officials, she said, could be persuaded to draw up certain documents, if the right gifts were slipped up their sleeves. She assured me it was for the best, that it would avoid all sorts of complications later on. She returned later that week with a stamped marriage certificate, with my name upon it. The other name was that of a twenty-five-year-old man, who had apparently been born in Gunma Prefecture. Mrs. Ishino told me that he had died soon after his return to Japan from Manchukuo.

"Your husband, Satsuko. A lightning affair. Poor soul."

My child would have a father, then, on paper at least. But I agonized over what the child would look like. Would the eyes be charcoal black, like mine? Or would they be sky blue?

On the morning before the gala premiere, Mrs. Ishino helped dress me in my green and gold summer kimono and Hiroshi and I took the tram up to Asakusa. We had promised to light some incense for our parents in the ruins of our old shop, and to have one last look for our father's pot. It was as busy as it had ever been, men in shirtsleeves going to and fro on bicycles in the warm afternoon sunshine. The Nakamise Arcade leading up to the Senso Temple was bustling with stalls again. The sound of sawing and hammering came from the temple precincts and little cedar prayer plaques were hanging in bundles from the gates in honour of the Star Festival. We bought our own little plaques, and wrote our secret requests on the back in the hope that they would be answered by the Goddess of Mercy.

We bought the incense and then walked rather solemnly toward Umamichi Street. Flags fluttered, advertising new restaurants, theatres, and vaudeville shows.

"Look!" Hiroshi said suddenly. Up above the shell of a building was a billboard advertising Michiko's new film, her painted face beaming out.

"The old neighbourhood's really coming back to life, isn't it, Hiroshi?" I murmured. He made a noise of assent. I studied him. He was so much taller now, his eyes so alert. I wondered what he could have possibly gone through during those long months when we'd been apart. I wondered if we would ever talk of it. Probably not, I thought. Not at least until we were very old.

We found the square cistern, and stepped into the rubble of our old shop, overgrown now with feverfew and stalks of wild sugar beet. Hiroshi poked about for a while, but found nothing but a few blackened fragments of ceramic. I looked at him in question. He gave a rueful smile and shook his head.

I placed the incense in the centre of the patch and he bent down to light it. We both clasped our hands and bowed our heads as the fragrant smoke twisted up around us.

I felt the child inside me, then, for the first time, kicking gently inside my belly. I gasped, imagining the little feet and toes, the tiny mouth and ears, as it lay curled inside my womb. It would be an autumn child, I thought, just as I had been myself. At that moment, the image of my mother came into my mind. I felt, quite intensely, that she was standing beside me, stroking my hair with her hand. I raised my head. The sunlight fell in my eyes, and I felt my father there too — they were both standing quietly behind me, one hand on each of my shoulders.

Cicadas were whirring loudly as we walked back to the street. I noticed a sign advertising a summer *matsuri* and I wondered out loud how lavish the processions might be this year, whether the men would still heave portable shrines up to the temple.

"It's strange," Hiroshi murmured. "I was just thinking the same thing."

It would be firefly season, soon, I thought. There might be a hunt down by the banks of the Sumida. Bright fireworks would fill the sky above Tokyo throughout those hot, summer nights and we would light fires, offer prayers and food to the spirits of the dead, set lanterns adrift upon the water. There would be so many offerings this year that the river would be like a galaxy of floating stars.

Autumn would draw in, and before long we would prepare to go up to Asakusa together to listen to the ringing of the New Year's bell. The child would be with us by then, I thought — my baby.

Winter would deepen then slowly dissolve. The days would lengthen once more.

Before long, there would be plum blossom.

ACKNOWLEDGEMENTS

This novel was inspired and informed by numerous works of non-fiction and fiction, of which I am particularly indebted to the following:

Embracing Defeat: Japan in the Wake of World War II by John W. Dower

Japan at War: An Oral History by Haruko Taya Cook and Theodore F. Cook

Japan Diary by Mark Gayn

Hiroshima by John Hersey

The Japan Journals: 1947–2004 by Donald Richie

Further reading:

Modern Japanese Literature: From 1868 to the Present Day by Donald Keene

The Scarlet Gang of Asakusa by Yasunari Kawabata

The Setting Sun by Osamu Dazai

Confessions of a Mask and *Runaway Horses* by Yukio Mishima

Confessions of a Yakuza by Junichi Saga

The Sea and Poison by Shusaku Endo

The Children and *The Makioka Sisters* by Junichiro Tanizaki

A Drifting Life by Yoshihiro Tatsumi

The Essential Haiku: Versions of Basho, Buson, & Issa by Robert Hass

The author would like to thank the following people for their help, advice, and support during the writing of this book:
Will Eglington
Pete Harris
Kieran Holland
David, Gordon, and Sally Mitchell
James Parsons
Carrie Plitt and all at Conville & Walsh
Averil & Conor Sinnott
Jo Unwin
Susan Watt
Janie Yoon, Sarah MacLachlan, and all at House of Anansi

AUTHOR PHOTOGRAPH: BEN BYRNE

BEN BYRNE was born in 1977 and studied Drama at the University of Manchester. He later moved to San Francisco, where he worked for several years as an international consultant, ethnographic filmmaker, and musician, and during which time he travelled often to Japan. He returned to England to dedicate himself more fully to writing, and his short fiction has appeared in *Litro* magazine. *Fireflies* is his first novel. He lives in London.